Praise for Mercedes Lackey

"A very enjoyable thriller with a sense of humor."
—*Locus* on *Children of the Night*

"[The heroine has] a wry, practical sense of humor. Further pluses include an almost complete lack of sexual stereotyping or politics. Anyone who likes their supernatural yarns laced with intelligence will find this novel more than satisfying."
—*Dragon* magazine on *Burning Water*

"The characters, love triangles, and action will hook the reader immediately. The plot weaves a magic spell of its own. This is a hard one to put down, and readers will clamor for the rest of the series."
—*Booklist* on *Jinx High*

Mercedes Lackey

CHILDREN
OF THE NIGHT

A Diana Tregarde Investigation

TOR®

A Tom Doherty Associates Book
New York

CHILDREN OF THE NIGHT

Copyright © 1990 by Mercedes Lackey

A Tor Book
Published by Tom Doherty Associates, LLC
175 Fifth Avenue
New York, NY 10010

www.tor.com

Tor® is a registered trademark of Tom Doherty Associates, LLC.

ISBN 0-765-31318-9
EAN 978-0-765-31318-8

First Hardcover Edition: August 1990
First Trade Paperback Edition: August 2005

Printed in the United States of America

0 9 8 7 6 5 4 3 2 1

Dedicated to
Melissa Ann Singer
for more reasons than I can count

CHILDREN
OF THE NIGHT

ONE

Diana Tregarde sighed, propped her chin on her right hand, and leaned on the countertop. *Of all the jobs I could have taken, working in an occult supply store is not one I'd have chosen on my own. I like my profile low, thank you very much. Too many people know I'm into the Craft as it is. This just boosts my visibility.* She stared out the window and tried not to feel like some poor GI in a bunker, waiting for the next scream of "Incoming!"

I hate being exposed like this. But I owe Annie . . . She flexed her shoulders, forced herself to relax. *Your paranoia is showing, Tregarde. There's no reason to be this gun-shy. It's not that bad. This isn't like the Bible Belt, where I'd get crosses burned on my lawn for being a witch. And most people I run into here are either gonna take me for a flake, or a phony. Besides, I've learned my lessons about staying invisible but doing my job. Nobody's going to have to show me again, especially not the hard way.* She finally laughed at herself for being so nervous. *After all, what could possibly happen to me two blocks off Forty-second Street?*

Then again . . .

She sighed again. The noon rush was over at Bell, Book, and Candle; now—afternoon doldrums.

This is ridiculous; I'm letting this gloomy weather get to me. All is well. We made the rent at noon. Come three, it'll be profit. The turn her thoughts had taken reminded her of the morning rush, and she snorted, thinking what the reaction of most of the otherworldly types that frequented this occult emporium would be to the word "profit." *A profit is not without honor, save when it's not in your pocket.*

She yawned; stretched, looked at her watch. *Still got a little time. At least the lull gives me a chance to think about that stupid almost-seduction scene in chapter four.*

She mentally reshuffled palm trees, sand, moonlight, hero and heroine one more time, made some internal notes—then looked out the shop window and stifled another yawn.

I should never have let Morrie set up this category-romance deal. I'm just not the type to turn out marshmallow white-bread story sandwiches. I know I need the money, but—this heroine is such a ninny. The stuff they want me to do with her is bor-ing. And I don't need to be reminded about how awful the Apple is in the winter.

"Just follow the outline," says Morrie. "It'll be easy, no thinking, just writing," says Morrie. "Bubie, you can't lose," says Morrie. "You need the dough, they want the book. You got 'em by the, you should excuse me, short hairs—they need this book and you're the only writer I got or anybody else has got that isn't contracted up right now." Morrie, you shark, I'll get you for this. You owe me. I wanted to do another Regency. I wanted to have something with a little humor in it, and something like a bit of historical accuracy. Not Hollywood's idea of Caribbean pirates. You didn't tell me the editor with his ass on the line was your brother-in-law. You creep, you knew I was a pagan, you knew I wasn't gonna be doing Christmas stuff like everybody else you've got—or even Hanukkah stuff, you snake. You knew I'd have "free time." Gods, I'm gonna get you for this. "Limpid, heavenly-blue waters of the Bahamas, sparkling beneath the full moon, as she gazes adoringly [and mindlessly] into his ebon-dark eyes," phooey.

It all only made the filthy October weather and the drab New York street outside the shop seem bleaker and the possibility of making getting even with Morrie even more appealing.

I'll fix you, Morrie. I'm gonna write that honest-to-gods historical Blood and Roses *and I'm gonna make you sell it. And read it, too. Gods forbid you should learn something from it. Give you something to read on your Las Vegas vacation next year.*

"*I* need a vacation," she muttered, while the wind flung dirty bits of paper past the grimy window. Grimy despite the fact that she'd cleaned it once this week. "Gods above and below, I need a vacation."

After a moment of self-pity, she chuckled and shrugged to herself. "But I also need to pay *my* rent. Morrie was right about that, anyway. I can't *quite* make it on writing yet, and the reserve is getting lower than I like."

I should be thankful I've got an agent as good as Morrie. I should be grateful I've got an agent at all. If it hadn't been for Itzaak tangling with that dybbuk and me bailing him out with fairly light damage, he wouldn't have talked his good old uncle Morrie into taking me. She grinned a little. *I'll never forget Morrie's face when he saw the bite mark on 'Zaak's thigh—and 'Zaak told him where it came from—and then told him where the dybbuk had been aiming in the first place . . .*

. . . like, forget about "be fruitful and multiply."

The glass rattled in a gust, and a listless spatter of rain drooled across the black and gold lettering. Even the storm predicted for this afternoon couldn't get up the enthusiasm to do more than threaten.

She rubbed her eyes, and shifted her weight—and sent a little more energy into the shield around the shop. *Umpty bizillion people in this city, and half of 'em unhappy at any one time. With weather like this, probably most of 'em unhappy. Yuck. Hell being an empath in the Big Apple. Hell being a big shiny target the way I am. Every time I do something arcane I feel like I've sent up a big* neon sign—"GOOD EATS"—with an arrow pointing right down at me. "Hi, I'm the blue plate special." Too damn many things I can't handle. Too damn many things I can take, but only if I get 'em from behind. She shook her head. I've got to snap out of this mood. I'm getting paranoid again. This is ridiculous. It's probably just because I'm tired.

After six hours behind the counter, her feet did hurt. She wasn't used to spending this much time on them.

And the thought of spending some time in someplace remote, isolated—and warm—

"Now if somebody would just give me enough money to pay for a vacation. And the rent. Now what's the odds I could find a sugar daddy . . . ?"

She laughed at herself. "Right, Tregarde. A sugar daddy and you. Sure. Being real bad at taking orders is the reason you don't have a mundane job. Oh well. I guess I'll have to settle for turning the heat up and putting the ocean record on when I get home."

Today had not been a good day to boost the mysterious and otherworldly atmosphere that Annie preferred to cultivate. "Mysterious and otherworldly" tended to be gloomy and chilly.

Not today. Di had turned on every lamp in the place, turned up the heat a little, and chosen cinnamon incense and spice candles and set them burning as soon as she opened. She closed her eyes and took a deep breath; it was as cozy in here as in a kitchen full of baking pies. Could be worse, could be worse. I sure can use the cash Annie's paying me. Gods, I hope the baby comes soon, though. I want to get this damned freebooter romance out of my hair. She tasted the cinnamon in the air, and thought about a hot cup of tea—

And looked up.

Looks like the afternoon rush just started.

Across the street she saw three people she knew so well she'd recognize them a mile away—and they were heading straight for the shop.

And in front of the shop was a young man with a notebook sticking out of his pocket and a peculiar look on his face. Curiosity and distaste.

Oh double hell. A re-port-er. Just in time for the afternoon rush.

The young man pushed the door open, and the string of bells over it jingled in the rush of cold, damp air. They chimed with a cheer Di could not force herself to emulate; the sour expression this lad wore did not bode well.

"May I help you?" she asked, making face and voice as neutral as possible.

He started; *she* could see the whole shop from where she was, but the arrangement and sheer volume of merchandise crowded into the tiny storefront tended to confuse the unwary—

She ran a practiced eye over him, as the bells on the door jingled again and Melani, Jorge, and Nita slipped in, heading straight for the "reserved" shelf and the books Annie ordered for her "regulars" in the back.

It isn't in yet, kids, but I'm glad you showed.

She watched the reporter carefully, keeping all her "feelers" tucked in, reading only body language. No use in advertising— and if he was marginally sensitive she might freak him.

Hmm. Caucasian, brown and brown. Um—twenty-five, tops. Gods. A "cub reporter." Betcha they sent him out to get him out of everyone's hair, after a silly-season fill story; he has visions of coming up with something weird enough that the wire services will pick it up. She gritted her teeth. *Gods, give me patience, and give it to me now. Why can't I get more like that nice chick from the six o'clock news last week?*

The classical station on the radio behind her finished baroque, and began modern, grating and interminable. *Not my day,* she concluded, and turned it down. The reporter looked for a path through the bookcases and standing racks of incense, notecards, and transparent "stained glass" window decals. He clutched his notebook to his chest possessively, and made his way toward the counter, emerging eventually from between two coatracks festooned with rainbow-colored "ritual robes," specifically made for the tourist trade.

Di smothered a grin at his grimace of distaste. The robes weren't real, and Annie was no dummy. Not with B, B, and C being just off Forty-second Street. The tourists and teenyboppers came looking for weird and outré, and she was perfectly happy to separate them from their money. These "magic robes" sold especially briskly just before Halloween and New Year's, and at twenty-five bucks a pop, the polyester horrors would buy a lot of diapers for Baby. And no one who patronized the shop for serious purposes minded—because Annie kept a stock of *real* robes, made by hand (and about as ornate as a monk's habit) in the back.

Di noticed empty hangers as he pushed past the rack, and made another mental note. *Going to have to remind Annie to get Jillian to do another batch of red, black, and purple, we're low.*

She knew before he even opened his mouth that *this* reporter was going to be one of the obnoxious ones.

"Are you Miz Sandstrom?" The very tone of his voice, strident and demanding, set her teeth on edge.

"She's on vacation," Di replied, polishing the counter with a piece of chamois and quietly signaling the trio at the back of the shop to stay out of the way for a minute. "I can probably help you."

She watched him out of the corner of her eye. His face fell, and he actually pouted. "I *expected* to talk to Miz Sandstrom. Give me her home address."

Without even a "please" attached. "I'm sorry," she said insincerely, wondering if he'd go away. "I can't give out that kind of information."

Because if I did, you'd print it, you little creep, and then Annie would have nuts trying to break her door down, to save her soul from the Devil.

He sulked, and glowered at her as if he blamed her personally for keeping him where he was, at the bottom of the journalistic pecking order. "My editor said she'd be here. My editor said to get an interview with a real witch."

As if Annie ran her life by the dictates of his editor. She smiled, a conciliatory, saccharin-dripping simper, and debated doing something to drive him off. *But if I don't give him something to write about, he'll make up a story. Then may the gods help us. He'll be certain we're hiding something, and he'll have us sacrificing chickens and drinking acid-doctored blood cocktails at Friday night sit-down orgies.* So she groveled a little, and batted her eyes, and said, in a confidential tone of voice—"But *I'm* a real witch."

The corner of his mouth twitched. "You are?" he asked, making no secret of his doubt.

"Uh-huh." She nodded vigorously.

"Well." He sulked a moment more, then said ungraciously, "I guess you'll do, then."

She caught Melani's eye and gave her the nod; the three of them swarmed the counter.

"Excuse me a minute—" she said. "Customers—"

Thank the gods for friends.

"What's up?" Jorge asked, making a big show of asking for some of the herb powders behind the counter.

"Reporter," she said sotto voce, and Melani grimaced. Di measured powdered dragon's blood into a plastic bag. *These* three were some of Annie's steadier customers—and if it weren't that they all *had* jobs, Annie would have asked one of them to mind the store for her instead of Di.

"Hey." Nita spoke up—a rarity. She usually let the other two do all the talking. "Tell you what—you bore him, and we'll carry him off, okay?"

"I love you," she said gratefully. "I go, I go—"

Di returned to the visitor and went fully into a character she'd created for moments like this one, the persona of "Gladys Eisendorf" (which was the name she gave him); the *dullest* human being on the face of the planet.

She gushed, she wheedled, she fluttered. She talked through her nose, so her voice was as whiny and grating as possible. She pitched it just on the bearable side of shrill. She giggled like a fool.

And she gave him *nothing* he wanted.

When he asked about Halloween ceremonies, she corrected him primly, like a schoolteacher. "It's Samhain," she said, deliberately mispronouncing it, then spelling it out for him. With a sanctimonious air she described a ceremony that made a Tupperware party seem licentious revelry by comparison. Before he could draw breath to ask another question, she proceeded to a tedious homily on Harmony, Peace and Love, and the Role of the Spirit in the Universe. It was a piece of tripe riddled with the clichés of every "The Universe is a *friendly* place, my child" type she'd ever had to put up with. And it was so boring that even had the young man possessed the temper and patience of Saint Francis he'd have thought longingly on satanic sacrifices before she was finished. With *her* as the starring attraction.

Both of these dissertations were punctuated by flirtatious asides and hungry looks—"I'm *single,* you know"—"If you'd like to come to the ritual, I'd be *happy* to vouch for you"—"We're allowed a guest, and I'm *single,* you know—"

It would have taken a stronger man than he was to shrug *that* blatant attack off.

He took notes—then *pretended* to take notes—and finally stopped even pretending, waiting with growing and visible desperation until she paused for a breath. He flipped the notebook closed, shoved it into his pocket, and spoke before she could get started again.

"Thank you, Miss—" He'd obviously forgotten her name, and hurried on so that she wouldn't notice the lapse. "Thank you very much, you've given me *plenty* of information. I'm sure I can do a *terrific* article from what you've given me. Of course, I can't promise that my editor will *print* it—"

She hid a grin. *Weaseling out of it already, hm?*

"—but you should know, middle-class values, bourgeois materialism, chauvinistic prejudices—"

You rattle that stuff off quite well, laddybuck. Covered the peace movement lately?

"—but of course I'll try, sympathetic exposure, put a word in the right places—"

He was babbling now, and backing away, carefully, as if he were afraid that if he turned his back on her she'd throw a net over him. She encouraged that belief.

"You don't have to go—" she cried faintly, flapping her hands frantically. "I have *plenty* of time. No one *ever* comes in here this time of day!"

"No! I mean—"

The trio, who had been awaiting this moment of retreat, swooped down on him.

And suddenly, with Nita, exotic, dark-eyed Nita, Nita the professional belly dancer, cooing at him, "witchcraft" became a *lot* more interesting. And the shop a lot *less* interesting. And the absent "Miz Sandstrom" a creature of no importance. She watched the transition with veiled amusement. Before thirty seconds had passed, the "terrible trio" had him neatly bedazzled and were luring him out the door; notebook, the shop, Annie, and "Gladys" forgotten.

When they passed out of sight, she leaned against the counter and wheezed, laughing too hard to get a full breath, tears coming to her eyes.

She'd managed to get herself under control when the bells jingled again, and a middle-aged couple who had *tourist* writ across their expressions in letters of flame crept in. By now the classical station, as if in apology for the first two pieces, was playing Dvorak's *New World* Symphony.

That was usually a soothing piece, but—

I don't think they're soothed, Di thought, watching them inch their way into the shop. *I don't think they know what it is they've gotten into. They're actually scared. Poor things. I'd better be gentle, or they may have heart attacks right on the threshold.*

"Hi!" she said brightly, when she was certain they'd spotted her. "What can I do for you?"

Mister Tourist peered at her while Missus Tourist clutched at his arm. "What is this place?" he asked, blinking. "This some kind of hippie store?"

She came out from behind the counter, so that they could see her. Mister was at least six feet tall, so he towered over her by a good foot. The disparity in height seemed to reassure him, as she'd intended. "Well, not really," she admitted. "We're kind of a religious supply house."

"You mean—" Missus Tourist whispered, looking over her shoulder for demons, "—*Satanists?*"

Di laughed, projecting reassurance as hard as she could. "Oh, heavens no! We get a lot of people into Eastern religions in here," she told them, with perfect truth. "Some odd kinds of Buddhists, for instance. And we carry a lot of books on spiritualism and the occult. Fiction, too. In fact, the name of the shop comes from a play—" She beamed, and stuck her hands in the pockets of her jeans. "I bet you saw the movie version by the same name, I think it had Kim Novak in it—"

Both of them perked up and relaxed at the hint that she did anything so mundane as go to movies. And about then, Missus Tourist subconsciously noticed the cinnamon scent in the air, the familiar odor relaxing her still further. In about five minutes they were chattering away like old neighbors—

There was method to her madness. The *next* time someone back in Davenport, Iowa, said something about horrible hippies practicing witchcraft, it would be Di that Fred and Edna remembered. They'd think about the friendly, cheerful girl who looked more like a refugee from American Ballet Theater than anyone's notion of a "witch"—the girl who'd encouraged them to stay and chat until they'd warmed up, in a store that smelled

like apple pies baking. And maybe, just maybe, they'd tell their
neighbor a thing or two—

It turned out that they'd wanted something out of the ordinary in the way of a souvenir, and the hotel clerk, perhaps in a
fit of maliciousness, had suggested Annie's shop.

That annoyed her enough that she went out of her way to be
even nicer to them. Before they left, she'd *found* them their "unusual souvenirs"—a book on the ghosts of New York City, and
another on the purported Viking ruins found up and down the
New England coast—and she had Fred Blaine joking with her,
while his wife, Edna, smiled at her and said she wished now that
she'd had at least *one* daughter instead of all those boys.

"I always used to carry one of these," Fred remarked at last,
while Di rang up his purchases on the store's ancient preelectric
cash register. He had spotted, then insisted on buying, an over-
priced rabbit's-foot key ring. "Dog got my last one, and I
haven't felt lucky since. Of course it wasn't so lucky for the rabbit, now was it?"

Di laughed at the joke—no mean feat, since she'd heard it at
least once a day since she started tending the store. But they
were, at bottom, *good* people, and she felt a bit more cheerful as
she wrapped their purchases and waved them out.

Her good humor lingered, which was just as well, because the
rush was on.

The trio returned from reporter seduction just as the classical station moved on to Praetorius's suite from "Terpsichore."
She was weighing out their purchases when the shop began to
fill. There were a couple of book browsers, who would probably come back for another couple of days before they made up
their minds, a couple of teenage girls, and three young men
of about college age who scanned the store and came straight
for her.

That was so out of the ordinary that for a moment she was
taken completely aback.

"Hi," said the bespectacled blond who seemed to be the leader of the trio. "We need some help—"

She stiffened.

"Just a second—"

The loaded words hit her like a slap in the face with a cold washcloth. Her adrenaline kicked in, and her heart started racing—because those words held special meaning for her. *They need some help? Oh my god—what now?*

She rang up the trio's purchases, hoping they wouldn't notice how her hands were shaking. An innocent phrase like that shouldn't throw a scare into anyone—

Unless you were a Guardian.

"We'd like some books on Druidism and the Norse," said the second, a thin and dreadfully earnest type, while she handed Jorge the brown paper sack. "We war-game, I mean the hobby, and we're just getting into something called 'fantasy role-playing games.' Napoleonics we know, but we need *rules* so we know how to run magic and religions—"

Her knees went weak with relief. *Only a game? Lord and Lady, for a minute I was afraid they were Calling on me—*

"See you later, guys—and thanks." She waved her friends through the door, and turned back to the newcomers (trying to keep a weather eye on the two teenagers). "Is this something like—uh—re-creating battles with toy—I mean miniature—soldiers, only doing it, like, with Tolkien?" she asked, vaguely remembering a couple of her war-gaming friends talking about something like this just before they all graduated from college. *Gods, that was Itzaak and his lot, and the bunch of them were like kids with a new pony. What did he say? "A very new twist on traditional war-gaming. Using maps and miniatures—only you fight dragons instead of dragoons—"*

"Exactly!" The blond beamed at her as if she'd just come up with the unified field theory. "And we need some help, the guys playing clerics are getting away with practically murder—"

"We don't mean anything sacrilegious," the third, tall and

beefy, and altogether looking like a jock, interrupted meekly. "I mean, we're not making fun of anybody or anything—honest!"

That set off the other two, who were nowhere near as shy as the muscle boy.

"Whoa!" She brought the torrent of explanation to a halt. *Lord, the intensity here, and for a game! Was I ever that earnest about anything?* "I know Tolkien and most of the other major fantasy works pretty well; why don't you just tell me what your game is closest to, and I'll tell you what books I think will suit your purposes best."

That pair of giggling girls that *couldn't* be older than fifteen watched her pull books down off the shelves, surrounded by the three boys. She ignored them for the moment; she was doing mental calculations and trying to keep in mind the fact that these young men probably didn't have much spare cash.

Lord knows Itzaak never did. Were we really ever this young? Has it only been two years—less—since I graduated? It feels like I'm a hundred years older than these kids. Itzaak, if I ever catch up with you, I don't know if I'm going to kill you or kiss you for getting me on Uncle Morrie's client list. Though right now "kill" has an edge.

Their finances, when pooled, got them the first four books on her list. "Believe me, that should hold you for some time," she told them, while the two girls whispered and eyed the young men from the shelter of the astrology section with predatory interest. "We're not talking a couple of hours of light reading, here. *The Golden Bough* has been used as a comparative religions text in more than one university." The talkative two looked a little daunted; the jock perked up. "Gimme that one, okay?" he said, reaching for it. "And the Wallis Budge. You two can take the others."

Di raised an eyebrow at him. "You're tougher than I thought."

He actually blushed. "Hell, ol' Budge didn't put me to sleep with the *Book of the Dead* in Egyptology, I don't figure he's gonna do it now."

Di's other eyebrow rose.

Egyptology? Have we got a budding psi here?

But before she could say anything, they'd gathered up their books and headed off into the cold.

The two girls sidled up to the counter, killing her chance to call the boys back, and a tall and saturnine older man slipped in behind the exiting boys. She heaved a mental sigh and turned her attention to the girls.

It didn't take ESP to figure these two out. They were just like the bunch that had come in at noon, all cast from the same mold, so fierce in their nonconformity that they set an entirely original standard of sameness.

Bet if one started a sentence, the other could finish it.

"Hi," she said, when they just stared. "Need something?"

"Um," said the short-haired, aggressively made-up blonde. "Like, we're having a Halloween party, you know? Like, we kinda wanted something different, you know?"

"Like, spells and stuff, you know?" finished her partner in crime, a baby-faced redhead. "Like, it's just girls, and like, we wanta do love spells, you know?" She giggled, trying to hide obvious embarrassment.

Lady bless. Just what I needed. Well, at least they came here. They could have picked up something from that bastard Ulrich, and if there's anybody in that little clique that's got even marginal Talent—gods have mercy.

"Well," she said slowly, "you know the problem with doing stuff like that is that the ingredients are *awfully* expensive."

"They are?" the blonde said, beginning to look doubtful.

"Sure," Di replied cheerfully. "Take your average love spell— to *start* with you'll need a whole mandrake root—" She began naming off ingredients at random, taking care that they were some of the most expensive herbs in the shop. ". . . and you finish up by binding it all together with attar of roses."

At one hundred dollars an ounce. Sheesh. Good thing we seal the bottle with wax every time we have to open it.

Since the prices were all posted openly, she watched with amusement as the girls made some hasty mental totals.

"And *then,* of course, you have to take what you've made and consecrate it. The ritual's in here—" She reached out and snagged a copy of *Sword of Wisdom* off the shelf behind her. She picked it for its size and small print. The redhead turned a couple of pages and put it down, unread.

"How long would it take?" she asked, subdued.

Di shrugged. "Depends on the ritual you choose, and the stars, and the moon phase. Could take all night."

"Oh." This, obviously, was *not* their idea of a good time.

"On the other hand, there's always the folk charms—they're quick, and real easy, and a lot of fun."

"The what?" they chorused, brightening.

"Folk charms. Like the teenaged girls in Salem probably used to do—at least when their Puritan daddies weren't looking." She winked, and the two of them giggled again. "They're mostly geared toward finding out who your lover is going to be, and you'll find most of what you need in your kitchen. Here—" She snagged another book, this one on American folk magic, a book she *knew* was harmless. *No demon-summoning in here, thank the gods. I do not need a repetition of what Mark Valdez did to me.*

She opened the book on the counter, and the two girls put their heads together over it, whispering. She grinned to herself, wondering how many boys were going to get "love apples" the day after Halloween. "The book's three-fifty," she said helpfully. "And what you can't find in your kitchens you can get at the Arboretum if you ask the guys nice, or even in Central Park or the Zoo."

"Like, heavy! Okay," said the blonde. "And we want this, too—"

She put a Ouija board on the counter. Di stifled a groan. *I should have known. I should have known.* While she rang up their purchases—blessing, instead of cursing, the recalcitrant cash register, since it was buying her time—

She needed time. Time to cast a "quick" shield on the board. All it took was one Sensitive kid—one open, the way Mark had been—and one Ouija board—and you had a combination that spelled (in all senses of the word) Trouble in River City.

But with her shield blocking it, the only messages they'd get would be from their own dear little subconscious minds.

She promised her twisting stomach a nice cup of tea, and fought the blurring in her vision caused by the draining of her own power. *I shouldn't be doing this, even inside the shop shield. If one of the browsers is a psychic—if somebody's looking for a Guardian—damn, damn, damn. If I didn't have to work four times as hard to set this stuff so I didn't leave psychic fingerprints all over everything—*

All Di's internal alarms started shrieking at top volume— telling her that Real, *Living* Trouble was already *in* the shop, poised on the threshold.

Christ on a crutch—

Now she got a good look at the guy who'd slipped in when the three boys had left. Six three, if an inch, and dressed with expensive flash in a velvet Edwardian jacket and lace shirt, he was saturnine, brooding, and aquiline—and oozed charisma.

A baited trap if ever I saw one—

And he was a hungry hunter on the prowl. A "chicken hawk," which wasn't unusual, not this close to Forty-second Street— but this particular gentleman might well be hunting with other senses than the normal five. And in any case, in a moment he'd zero in on the girls and do his level best to reel them in—

He'd use them, however they let him, then use them up.

Over my prone corpse. Gods, I hate advertising my presence. He could be stronger, meaner than he looks. But if I don't deal with this—it'll come back on me. And when I'm not ready. Just like that—thing. She suppressed the nausea *that* memory caused, gritted her teeth, and prepared to challenge. *Let's see for certain if he's after more than the physical—*

Di slapped a barrier up right in his face; he started to take a step forward and encountered it, and his expression changed in a split second from bored to enraged, then to cautiously wary.

She flared her shield just enough to catch his attention, knowing that if he could be stopped by her barrier, he was more than good enough to catch a belligerent aural flare.

And if he could be stopped by her barrier, he probably was someone she could handle.

He responded, as she'd expected him to, and she trapped his gaze with her own.

He smiled, very slightly, and nodded.

She did not return the salutation. His eyes narrowed, and she saw his thoughts in his expression and body language as clearly as if she'd read them directly. He'd taken her at first for a fellow Hunter. Now he knew her for a Guardian. He was not amused.

Out, she thought at him, with just a touch of psi bolt backing the word, and saw him wince. She distracted the girls with a comment about the section in the book on love charms using apples, which sent them hunting it. While their attention was on the book, she drew a glyph in the air between him and the girls. It wasn't visible to outer sight, but to Inner it flamed as fiery as the candles behind her.

Out, she repeated. *Out, or I'll call Challenge. This is my Place, and you aren't welcome in it. Find another hunting ground.*

He tried to contest her will, locking eye to eye—

But in the end it was his eyes that dropped, not hers, and he turned and left without a word, though she could see a tenseness in his jaw that probably meant he was grinding his teeth in frustration.

Maybe if he had been on his own turf he would have fought her. But he wasn't—

Oh gods. She went weak-kneed and held on to the counter to keep herself standing; she was just as glad he hadn't tried to force the issue.

Maybe I'm stronger than him—but a Challenge is not the way to find out for certain.

And it wasn't *that* long ago that she'd forced the poltergeist out of Keith's workshop.

Thank the gods I didn't have to push things before I got a chance to recharge.

That incident was more than she wanted to handle this afternoon, and when the girls took their goodies and left, and the browsers—happily oblivious to the whole incident—followed, she headed for the front of the store and the "Open" sign in the window. It was more than time for a nice cup of strong tea—

Actually a nice shot of strong Scotch would be a lot more welcome. Oh well.

She had her hand on the sign and was actually starting to flip the plastic rectangle over when she heard a sound coming from the curtained-off entrance to the storeroom.

She jumped a foot, and came down in "ready" stance, facing the threshold and the intruder, halfway expecting it to be Mr. Trouble back for a rematch, and that he'd somehow gotten in the service entrance.

Facing the front of the shop—and panting a little—was a dusky, exotically handsome young man—

Or boy; after a moment she was no longer certain of his age. Gold glinted in his ears—and for one moment she thought, *Gay?*

Then he moved hesitantly into the light, and there was no doubting his antecedents; if he wasn't Romany she'd eat the scarf around his neck. The universal uniform of jeans, rock T-shirt, and CPO jacket did nothing to disguise his origins, nor his halfhearted attempt to look like "everyone else." He couldn't; even his curly hair didn't match, as it was a little shorter than the current standard.

His chest heaved, and he stared at her blankly, his forehead beaded with sweat in spite of the cold.

Oh my; oh yum. For that, I could be tempted into cradle-robbing. Hey, little boy, want a chocolate-chip cookie, hm?

Then she saw his expression, and her paranoia kicked into

high gear. Her self-amused and slightly lascivious thoughts wafted away like fog in a high wind.

Because beneath his self-imposed calm, he was *terrified.*

"*Drabarni*—" he said, holding out a hand in entreaty, with an air of expecting to be slapped down. "Where—please, where is Annie Sandstrom?"

"*Drabarni*"—*I think that means "sorceress," or something like it. Which means he knows what I am*—

She weighed all the consequences, then dropped into the Sight, and felt her eyes widen as she sucked her breath in with surprise.

Ee-ha, he knows what I am, all right. He's got it, too. Lady bless, he reads Potential Power like a small nuclear reactor. He may be damped down now, but that's because he wills it that way. Talk about different—I thought it was only the women of the Rom that were into the Power. This one must be something really special.

"She's going to be gone for at least another couple of weeks," she said. "But I'm a friend. I'll help you if I can."

Relief made him go limp, those huge black eyes of his turning luminous with gratitude.

"Lady—" he panted, "there is someone—"

"After you? The law?"

He shook his head, and his curls bounced. "After me, yes. No one's law but his own."

Within the safety of the shop shields, she dared expense of power and augmented observation with a delicate probe. There was something of a "feel" of amorality about him—but then there was always that "feel" about gypsies.

Not surprising, given that by their lights God created the rest of us to support them.

She made a snap judgment in his favor. "Do you need sanctuary, help, or just an escape route?"

More gratitude, this time tinged with wry surprise.

"I told you, I'm Annie's friend. Those of us with Powers get hassled, too," she pointed out, letting one corner of her mouth quirk up for a moment. "Probably as often as the Rom get it. And we aren't as good at hiding as the Rom are."

He spread his hands and shrugged, acknowledging the truth of her statement, and admitting her as a kind of kindred, all with the same expressive gesture. She wished briefly that *she* could manage body language that eloquent. "I looked for a hiding place, for now," he replied nervously. "The shop will break my trail. The Hunter is good, not *that* good. I don't think that one will find my trail again, once broken."

Mr. Trouble? Naw, couldn't be. Too much of a coincidence. She pondered him a moment more.

Damn. He's into something deeper than he can manage—and he was hoping Annie could help him with it. Double damn. Granny always told me—"With powers like yours you got no choice. You either use 'em to help the ones that come to you, or the things after them'll come after you." She shivered. *I wish she hadn't been so right.*

She dug into her back pocket and came out with one of her personal cards—the one with her name and home address on it. "Look, it sounds like you've been hunted by this guy before— am I right?"

He tilted his head sideways. "Yes—" he said, a bit warily. "So?"

She inched past the incense rack—for once it didn't snag her—and got close enough to him to hand him the little rectangle of pewter-colored paper. "So if you're in trouble in this neighborhood—" She shrugged, trying to look casual. "Allies are always useful."

He only then looked at the card, and smiled his gratitude at her, a brief flash of white in his dark face. "I—thank you."

"Better get while the getting's good," she said, pointing. He nodded, and moved—

He didn't *run*, not exactly, but he certainly wasn't walking. She saw little more than a flash of sneakers, then heard the alley door scream open and slam shut before the curtain had finished fluttering.

She waited for a moment to see if his pursuer would put in an appearance, but the street seemed oddly deserted. Perhaps it was the sky: dead gunmetal, going to red-lit charcoal; the threatening storm and the grim dusk were not likely to induce anyone out at this late an hour. Besides, with this much overcast it was going to be full dark in a very short time. No one ventured *here* after dark, not without an appointment.

Time for that tea—then, warmed and fortified for the subway ride, she'd be able to shut the shop down and go home.

She put the kettle on the hot plate in the dark, redolent storeroom, and hunted through the clutter of teabags for cinnamon. The incense had put her in the mood for it. She realized as the water started to boil that she hadn't turned the sign to "Closed" after all, or locked the front door.

Oh well. Nobody likely to show now—

The classical station on the radio behind her began something tinkly, precious, and baroque; with a grimace she turned it down a hair. As her hand left the knob, the phone rang; she reached out across the hot plate, and opened the miniature coffin where it lived. "Bell, Book, and Candle," she said, as brightly as she could.

"Hi, sweets," Annie Sandstrom replied, her voice thin and tinny. "How's tricks?"

"We've done a bit better than normal, and dammit, if your back hurts, lie down." Di could tell by the strain in Annie's voice that it had been a far-too-long day. "Drink some chamomile tea. Put Brahms's 'Lullaby' on the stereo and stick the headphones on your tummy."

"You really think that would make Baby settle down?" Annie sounded pathetically hopeful.

"Well, the chamomile should cross the placental barrier," Di replied absently, as she peered out the curtain to the front window and wondered if there was *anybody* out on the street. "It won't hurt her any, and it might calm her down. And What's-her-name swears by stereo headphones in the last month. You know who I mean, the one with the guy with the head shop?"

"Oh yeah, the one that changed her name to Azure Asphodel. Had any flakes today?"

Di snorted, and twined a strand of her hair around her fingers. *Damn mop's getting out of the knot again.* "Makes me glad I'm finally legal to buy hard liquor. I got a *mob* of teenyboppers in here at noon. One of them wanted to know how to throw a curse on somebody, and his girlfriend wanted a copy of the *Satanic Bible.* Just what we all need."

"I trust you threw a good scare into them?"

"Need you ask? You'd better spawn soon, lady. That fifth of Scotch I bought isn't going to last much longer. Why did I *ever* let you talk me into running this joint for you?"

"Because you have a soft heart." Annie chuckled. "You couldn't *bear* the notion of me fighting my way through the subway with a monster under my belt."

Di grinned, in spite of her sore feet, and leaned up against the wall. Three weeks ago Annie had resembled the Goodyear blimp. She hated to think what her old college friend looked like now.

"Besides," Annie continued, as the street beyond the glass grew perceptibly darker, "you're the only one I've ever Worked with that I'd trust to handle the nutcases that show up around Halloween. I mean, can *you* picture Siobhan with a reporter? Or Alicia with a teenybopper who wants to play at the Craft? Or Stazi with those two would-be black-magickers you had this afternoon?"

Di shuddered. "The spirit quails. Stazi would probably have sent them over to You-Know's place. And gods forbid they had any *ability,* guess who'd end up pulling their fat out of the fire."

"You or me, or one of the others. The Terrible Trio, maybe, they're good at—" The words were followed by a stifled gasp.

"Baby rambunctious?"

"She's taking after Auntie Di," Annie said, a little sourly. "She's doing karate katas. Listen, if it seems dead, shut down early, okay? No use in you sticking around for nothing, not with the weather like it is right now."

"Okay," Di agreed readily. "Bye-bye, darlin'. Give Bob a big kiss for me."

"Ciao, Bambi."

Click.

If she calls me Bambi one more time . . . Six days to Halloween. Feels like six weeks. Oh hell, I forgot to ask her about that gypsy boy. And the chicken hawk. Maybe I'd better call her back—

But the back of her neck prickled, and she had the strongest feeling that she really *ought* to check on the front of the store, just in case—

And when your psychic Gifts were as reliable as Diana Tregarde's were, you didn't ignore prickling on the back of your neck.

She sighed, turned the heat down, and stepped to the front of the store—

And saw *him* standing uncertainly in the light of the lamp in the window, peering through the glass, as if trying to make out if the shop was tenanted or not.

He was, without a doubt, the foxiest, *sexiest,* man she had seen in a year.

For a moment, with his eyes dazzled, no doubt, by the contrast between the dark of the street and the lighted shop, he couldn't see her—but she could certainly see him.

He was short—he probably wouldn't top her by more than a couple of inches—and lean; but it was the slightness and leanness of a panther that *he* put her in mind of. His face was that of a medieval angel; fine-boned, with high, prominent cheekbones and the most beautiful dark eyes she'd ever seen in her life. Those eyes—

Oh yes. Eyes that grab you by the throat and won't let go. Centuries. Like he's seen centuries pass, and he's learned from them, but he hasn't let them make him disenchanted or bitter—

His hair, like the gypsy boy's, wasn't long by modern standards, but it was dark as the boy's, and long enough and silky-looking enough to make her itch to run her hands through it.

For a tiny moment she indulged herself in a fantasy of doing just that—she *was* a romance writer, after all.

Then sighed. *Business, my dear.* She squared her shoulders, controlled her expression, and moved forward.

He was quick; she gave him points. She'd scarcely taken a step when he spotted her by her movement, and locked his eyes on her. She nodded; he tightened his lips a bit, and opened the door.

My gods, he should be freezing. No coat, nothing but a pair of jeans and a sweater—

He hesitated on the threshold; she had the oddest feeling that he was *waiting* for something.

She wanted to extend and "read" him, both intrigued and a little suspicious, but decided against it. *Odd. Very odd. I don't ever remember seeing him around here, and Annie would have mentioned a fox like him.*

He was still hesitating, one hand on the doorframe. It was his right hand, and the gleam of metal on his wrist above the cuff of his dark sweater caught her gaze for a moment.

He was wearing a very wide, heavy silver bracelet—and *that* was odd too, since he was wearing no other jewelry at all, and the bracelet itself seemed snugged to his wrist, but had no visible opening or catch. It might almost have been soldered onto his wrist.

And as he continued to hesitate, she remembered the gypsy boy, and became suspicious. What if *this* was what had been hunting the boy? It certainly seemed an odd coincidence that he should show up on *this* foul night right after she'd broken the boy's trail with the shop.

But even if he was after the boy, *she* could take care of herself, *he* couldn't know she'd aided the kid, and she *might* be able to buy the boy a little more time by occupying his attention for a bit. She smiled, and nodded.

"Come on in," she said cheerfully. "I don't bite."

He seemed to find the remark amusing; he chuckled as if to himself, anyway, then smiled back at her, slid his hand down off the doorframe, and glided gracefully across the threshold, closing the door behind him. She found herself envying him: he *moved* like a panther, too; both elegant and powerful.

"I beg to disturb you so late," he said, his words faintly accented. It took her a moment to identify the accent as French. "I am certain that you wish to close and return to your home—but could you tell me if there was a particular man here an hour or so ago? He is tall, taller than six feet, I believe; he is very dark, with narrow eyes and a prominent nose—he tends to favor somewhat flamboyant clothing."

She raised her eyebrow at him. *Mr. Trouble? Now what on earth could this one want with* him? *Unless this is just an excuse—or unless they're working together—*

One way to find out. "He was," she said shortly, admiring the graceful way his hand lay along the counter in the back of her mind—and taking notes on it for possible use in her book. "He left."

The young man sighed; and unless she was *grossly* mistaken, it looked like he was relieved. "Then he must not have bought— or found—what it was that he was looking for," he said, so softly that he might well have been speaking to himself. With his next words he raised his voice. "I do not suppose that you would be able to tell me his direction—would you?" He sounded wistful, as if he really wasn't expecting her to cooperate.

He didn't mention the kid. Maybe he's okay. Maybe he isn't. Still, it can't hurt to tell him. He aroused very ambivalent feelings in her; she was *certainly* attracted to him, yet he made her very uneasy. *I'd just as soon be rid of him,* she decided. *Better safe than up to my neck in kimchee.*

"He headed down toward Forty-second," she told him. "The less savory side."

"Ah." He nodded understanding. "My thanks. I shall not detain you any longer—"

As he turned away, she caught sight of his face, and the expression had changed completely. There was something so implacable about him now that she found herself backing up a step. She could readily believe that he would calmly commit murder if he felt the circumstances demanded it.

"If you're having trouble with him, isn't that a job for the cops?" she said, carefully, frightened by the change from urbane and quiet man to cold killer.

His eyes bored into hers, and she had the unsettling feeling that he not only knew *what* she was, but that he was weighing and calculating her every arcane ability down to the last erg of energy. "Do not," he said levelly, "play the fool with me, mademoiselle."

One moment he was *there,* the next, *gone.* And so quickly the bells above the door scarcely moved.

She stared into the dark for a moment, then moved carefully to the door and peered out at the street. There was no one, no one at all, in either direction.

"That is *enough* for one night," she said out loud. "Come to Mama—"

She held out her arms and gathered the shields *she'd* put on the shop back around her. They settled into place automatically, and she dismissed their presence from her conscious mind.

"Time to blow this popstand." She flipped the sign to "Closed"; in five minutes she had shut everything down, grabbed her coat, and was out the door—before something *else* could happen.

TWO

The wind muttered sullenly around the street lamps, and not even a mugger wanted to be out on a night like this one. Di shoved her hands down into the pockets of her jacket, hunched her shoulders against the bite of the wind, and wished she'd had the sense to hunt out gloves this morning. *It's colder now than it was when I left, it has to be. Gods, I'm freezing my tush off.* The echo of her boot heels on the pavement only made the street seem emptier. There should have been plenty of traffic, but not tonight. Only an occasional car blundered by, windows staring at her blankly. This was one of those night when she would have appreciated owning a car. *Thank heavens the subway station isn't too far from home, or I'd have to thaw my hands before I could type.*

She bit her lip as she got one of those unpredictable surges of homesickness. A night like this in Connecticut could be so shivery and delightful, with the wind twining around the trees, the clouds streaking across the moon, and a fire in the fireplace—

Home isn't there, anymore, kid. Home is here, where people need what you can do. A real, honest-to-gods Home is where people who love you are, anyway, and by that measure you haven't really had a "home" since Granny died.

When she reached her block, she could see the squat bulk of her building just ahead. The apartment building was ablaze with lights—it was *always* ablaze with lights, night or day. Considerably older than the buildings to either side of it, and several stories lower, Di's apartment house huddled in their shadow most of the day—so the tenants never turned their lights off except to sleep. No use putting plants in the window, not even ferns—there wasn't enough direct light available to keep *anything* alive.

Not that the occupants gave a damn about sunlight, direct, or otherwise. They were in hot pursuit of another sort of light. Footlights, limelights—and the dreamed-for, prayed-for spotlights.

With the single exception of Di, the building was tenanted, attic to basement, by dancers. All manner of dancers; jazz, ballet, modern, Broadway. They were crammed four and six to an apartment, and endured the cranky plumbing, the scarcity of electrical outlets, for two reasons. The lesser of the two was the heating—*unlike* the plumbing, it was utterly reliable. No small blessing in a New York winter. *That* was the reason everyone who lived here quoted when asked.

But the second and most important reason they stayed (and the one you never told anyone you couldn't trust) were the Living Rooms (capital L, capital R) in each and every apartment—

Di scampered up the grimy cement staircase, and dove into the entrance; unlocked the outer, then the foyer doors, and walked into a wall of warmth and dim yellow light. Before her was the only way up—no elevator in *this* building; she took the worn wooden stairs beyond the foyer two at a time. The fat, gleaming radiators lining the landing bathed her with heat, and already she felt better.

Cooking smells wafted past her. *Jimmy's on his liver diet again. Good thing he has tolerant roomies. Somebody baked brownies; naughty naughty.* Her apartment was only on the second floor and just off the staircase; a blessing on a night like this, when all she really wanted to do was get back and unwind. She unlocked her door and pushed it open carefully, just in case there was something in the way.

Sure enough, one of the others had picked up her mail for her and shoved it under the door. *A third reason; we're a family here. Mail gets picked up, packages get accepted, brownies get shared. And one noise out of character, much less a scream, and everybody in the building comes running with knives and baseball bats in hand. One "SOS" tapped out on the radiator, and our modern-dance fan, the super, checks every apartment in the building to see if somebody's sick or hurt—wonder how Kay's ankle is doing? Have to make some pea soup over the weekend and take her some.* She bent and scooped the mail up off the floor without breaking stride, and flipped on the living room lights with her free hand.

Before her, lined with mirrors on two of the walls, empty and equipped with a practice barre, was *her* Living Room—

Every one of the apartments in this building boasted a room identical to this one; so big it echoed. She knew people who didn't have *apartments* this size. It had a solid wooden floor, gently worn, smooth, but not polished—and substantial enough that you could teach an elephant to tap-dance in here.

And as if that weren't wonderful enough, it was more than big enough and high-ceilinged enough that you could do full lifts if you were a ballet dancer. It was, point of fact, a small practice studio.

Rare was the dancer in New York who could have a studio at home to practice in. Rarer still was a home studio with a ceiling high enough to do full lifts. The Living Rooms in this building had both size and height; these apartments dated back to a time when people Entertained. The building itself had once stood in isolate splendor amid a carefully tended garden—true *garden* apartments. *That* had been very long ago.

The people that owned this building were unaware of the peculiar amenities of their property—if they ever found it out, they'd undoubtedly raise the rent to an unholy rate. So some time ago—how long ago, she'd never found out for certain—someone had set a certain small spell going here—

A spell of deception.

Maybe I'll collect karma on it, she thought, just a bit guilty. *I didn't set it—but—I don't know. Still, I couldn't survive long anyplace else. . . .*

Her predecessor had explained the workings of the spell to her; a sarcastic, gnarled old man they told her had danced with Ted Shawn. "You pay in personal energy," he'd said. "You maintain the spell out of your own strength, and you live here, and you have a safe harbor. And the landlords never learn what it is they're renting."

Because *this* apartment had always belonged to a Guardian. Guardians needed peace and space; occasionally enough space to conduct minor warfare.

There was no harm in allowing others to share that peace and space; on the contrary, it made excellent camouflage.

That a Guardian had retired just when *she* needed a base of operations—*that* was why she was *here*, and not elsewhere in some other city. Or so she suspected. Things like that happened to those with Guardian-level magic and psi powers. Maybe it was to make up for being such a large and inviting target.

Most people, even those as involved in the occult as Annie was, never even guessed the existence of the Guardians.

There's a good reason for that, if I can just think of it, she mused, pulling off her scarf. *Ah. Self-sufficiency, of course, and responsibility. If they knew about us, they might not be quite so alert about covering their own asses. They might start expecting us to pull their fat out of the fire.*

Di suspected there had been Guardians as long as there had been cities; cities seemed to breed predators like Mr. Trouble. The Guardians could recognize each other—and Teachers, like Di's Granny, could recognize those born to be Guardians, and see that they got the kind of education they needed, the reassurance that they *weren't* going crazy because they saw and sensed things no one else did.

And Guardians become Guardians because they have no choice. Because you either use *what you have, or—or the things the Guardians Guard against come hunting you. Even if you want to be left alone, they'll come hunting you, and come for you when they are most ready. So you deal with them before that can happen.* She sighed. *Maybe I won't get karma from the spell. Maybe this pad is like hazardous-duty bennies. I pay for it in blood.*

She did a quick scan of the apartment, then the building; nothing whatsoever amiss. She hadn't expected there to be— but why take chances? She closed the door behind her and flipped the locks.

I just wish to hell one of the bennies was a salary, she thought wistfully. *Or at least job choice if I* have *to have a job. Or, for the gods' sake, choice of projects.* Then she gave herself a little mental slap. *Now dammit, I've only got myself to blame for that. But I swear I will* never *let Morrie talk me into category work again.*

Guardians and Teachers ran in her family tree—though the rest of the relatives rarely suspected anything. She was only one of a long line of practitioners of magic who protected the innocent from some of the things that could—and did—prey upon them. *Poor Mom; here she was trying to raise me a good Episcopalian, and there's Granny sneaking around behind her back, raising me a good pagan.*

Guess which stuck.

Then that drunk took Mom and Daddy both out, and the potential conflict was moot . . . things like that happen to Guardians, too.

More guilt, guilt that she had not been able to see what was going to happen, somehow—that she had not been able to stop it. As always, she stomped on the guilt with the only answer that made sense. *You do what you can, when you can, with what you're given. No one can be everywhere at once, not even a Guardian. And you weren't even half-trained back then.*

Di's Living Room was a studio, too; but she used it to practice karate katas—and, on certain nights, to hold Circle.

And on other nights, to save lives, and sometimes souls.

But not tonight. She stretched a little, and crossed the empty room to pass into the dining room (which had been set up as office, lounge, and *real* living room). *Not tonight. I've done my share for today.*

As she passed the door, she flipped on the living room lights without even being aware of the motion, and sailed on through into the hallway that led to the bedroom, flinging her coat into a chair on the way past.

Last set of lights, and she was staring at her unmade bed with a wince. *Granny would have a cat.* The bedroom held only her bed, a low bookcase that served as a nightstand, and a single bureau. She had an enormous walk-in closet that took up the entire wall opposite the door, but it was mostly empty. Clothing was of a lower priority than just about anything else. After all, hardly anyone ever saw her.

In a couple of minutes she'd stripped off her "good" pants and sweater, thrown them on the bed, and changed into a karate *gi*, tights, and a leotard.

Sensei would have a fit to see the ballet gear, but sensei isn't here. I like leotards. She stretched; thought about dinner; decided against it for the moment. *Katas first; I'm like a bundle of bridge cables.*

She trotted back out into the living room, centered herself, and listened to the life sounds around her. She didn't so much hear them as *experience* them. Others might find it maddening; she found it soothing: the sound of dozens of feet tapping, sliding, and leaping all around her. It reminded her of what life was all about—

She waited for the moment to be right and her *ki* to be perfectly balanced—

—and began.

It was a good workout; she was warm, and calmed, and all the knots were loose again when she finished and sank down to the floor in full lotus. She closed her eyes and let herself *feel* everything, then dismissed the sensations one by one from her conscious mind. The lingering hint of incense from the last Circle, the smooth, warm wood under her, the sweat cooling on her forehead, the heavy weight of her hair knotted at the nape of her neck; all dissolved and floated away, as she centered her *self* and let her mind still, let whatever was most important float to the surface to be looked at.

In other words, let's rewind the tape and look it over. What happened today that could come back and bite me later?

Not any of the kids—though she had a feeling she'd see that jock sometime in the future. *Good potential there. Good material. Open mind, cautious, but doesn't freak easy. If he's psi, or he's Talented, and he needs someone to teach him, he knows where to look now. Hmm. Might even be me.*

Mr. Trouble though, and the gypsy boy—*Bad juju. That certainly has all the marks of something that may return to haunt me. Oh well, couldn't have done anything else. I'd rather take him on my terms than his. Still.* She shivered, as a cold finger of premonition slid up her spine. *One nasty piece of work, that man, and the more I think about him, the nastier he seems. I wonder why he* didn't *Challenge me?*

That led her thoughts inexorably to the Frenchman, and she felt a pleasurable tingle about him—at least at first. *I don't know what he* is, *and under other circumstances, I wouldn't much care—*that's *one I sure wouldn't toss out of bed for eating crackers.*

Then she thought about the other face he'd shown her. *He* does *bother me. He's dangerous. Lord and Lady, if it was just me, I don't think I'd mind a little more danger in my life . . . but it isn't just me. Analysis. He didn't threaten me. He was going after Trouble, or at least that's what he said. He did* show *me that darker side of him. That alone is interesting. I'd better keep a weather eye out for him. Other than that, I can't see what else I can do. Except that I'd better warn Annie about both of them, and ask her about that kid. The last thing she needs is to find the shop turned into a battle zone.*

She let her thoughts roam for a bit, but nothing else popped to the surface, which meant there was nothing else likely to get in the way of work, at least not tonight. So she refocused on her *outer* self; felt the world come back with a tingle of returning awareness along every nerve—opened her eyes, and stretched, letting the stretch pull her to her feet.

Just in time; there was a knock on the door at that exact moment.

But since nobody'd buzzed to be let in the front—it had to be someone from the building. And since the knock had come at *precisely* the moment she was ready for it, there was only one person *really* likely to be calling on her—

This was home base, and safe to let some things "show." She extended a mental finger just a little and encountered familiar shields. Very familiar, since *she'd* put them on *him* less than six months ago, when he'd moved in upstairs, then homed in on her door with the surety of someone who knew *exactly* what he was looking for.

She strolled over to the massive wooden door, and threw all the locks. "What's kicking, pony?" she teased, pulling the door open. A lithe and light-boned young man who was the very image of Kipling's version of Puck, right down to ears that gave an impression of being pointed, and artistically tousled dark hair, waited indolently on the threshold. "I thought you'd have headed home to ole Virginny at the first drop of sleet this afternoon. Aren't you tired of cattle calls yet?"

"Bite your tongue," Lenny Preston retorted. He lounged decoratively against the doorjamb, posing for her appreciation, a bouquet of chrysanthemums in one hand, a thick bundle of candles in the other. "I *never* get tired of cattle calls. I just get tired of not being called back. I told you, I'm staying in this lousy town until I get somewhere. There's not much call for a dancer in Amaranthus, Virginia—not unless you want to spend the rest of your life teaching little girls to stagger around on pointe shoes."

"And watching the fathers of little boys *waiting* for you to make a move on their kids so they kin whup th' faggot upside th' hayde. A point." She took in the elegant sweater he was wearing, and gave him a raised eyebrow. It *looked* like alpaca. "Where *do* you get your clothes, you fiend? I *know* you don't have any more money than I do—"

Lenny chuckled. "If you're good, maybe someday I'll tell you. Here—" He flicked a lock of long hair out of his eyes with an elegant toss of his head, and handed her the flowers and candles. "These are from Keith."

She took them, rather surprised. She certainly hadn't expected anything from Lenny's friend. *These candles are beautiful—and I bet it's not accident that they're in the cardinal colors—but who told him what I needed? I doubt it was Lenny. Len is far too cautious about letting people know we're Wiccans. Unless—Keith did attract that poltergeist, and he's very psi, even if he doesn't know it—*

"*They're pure beeswax,*" Lenny said archly. "*Virgin* beeswax. Linen wicks. Hand-dipped."

Uh-huh. Nothing artificial, nothing man-made. "Working" *materials. Something is going on here—*

"Did you tell him?" she demanded.

Lenny chuckled, wrinkling his nose at her. "Not me, deary. *He* jumped on *me* the minute you were out the door, but I kept our little secrets to myself. Then yesterday he called me up and told me to come by the studio, he had something for you. The exact message is, quote, Thank you for getting rid of my houseguest, and I'm certain someone like you will get use out of these, endquote."

She laughed, as much in surprise as anything else. "Well. Are you suspecting what I'm suspecting?"

Lenny shrugged. "Could be he's Reading you subconsciously. Could *also* be he knows something about Wicca. I know he reads SF and fantasy, and there's a lot of that sort of thing showing up in the literature these days. I don't see any reason to worry about it."

She bowed to his judgment. "If you say so, I'll trust you on him. How's he doing? No recurrences, I hope? Any clients?"

Lenny made a face. "Business as usual. The candles are selling, the sculpture isn't. But no, he doesn't have things flinging themselves into the vats of melted wax anymore."

"Well, a poltergeist around flames, hot plates, and liquid wax is a Bad Idea; I figured I was just doing my bit to help enforce the fire codes."

Lenny grinned at that. "All *I* have to say is that if I didn't *know* what was going on, I'd be jealous. He's never given *me* candles and flowers!"

She spread her arms and gazed up at the ceiling for a moment. "Give me strength—" she muttered, then looked back down at him. "Play your cards right, and you won't have any reason to be jealous, nit."

Lenny straightened from his slouch, all his feigned laziness gone. "You think so?"

She snorted. "I'm a bloody *empath*, remember? *Some* of that poltergeist was him—and my suspicion is that he did it to get you to come around more often. He didn't get into trouble until he pulled in the real thing and he couldn't control what was going on anymore. *That* was when it stopped being a good excuse to have you come by and started getting dangerous. But I tell you, scared or not, every time he happened to look at *you* it got hot enough in that studio to broil meat. Speaking of food—I've got enough salmon for two—"

He started to shake his head. "Not—well. I have to be out of here *some*time tonight. I've got an extra rehearsal tomorrow. Choreography being made on me, for me."

She raised an eyebrow. "What, a *solo*? Coming up in the world, are we?"

He grinned again. "Not only that, but this show may actually open. Bob Fosse it isn't, but it's got its moments."

"But Off-off-off Broadway, no doubt."

His grin got larger. "Nope. Only Off. All the chasing's beginning to pay off. Not to mention hard work and dedication and kissing the right—"

"Feet," she interrupted him. "Keep it clean, m'lad."

He gave her a mock bow. "Anyway, I've gotta get some *sleep*. And *alone*."

"As if I were your type—get *in* here. I *won't* let you drink too much, and *I* have work to do tonight."

He followed her into the kitchen and draped himself over a chair and watched with acute interest while she broiled fish and steamed vegetables. "You look like a dancer, you *eat* like a dancer—I really don't know why you aren't a dancer."

"Because I don't get into pain," she replied wryly.

He winced. "Set, point, and match. We are masochists, aren't we?"

"You spend sixteen of the first eighteen years of your lives turning your bodies into machines, and your heads into a space where you can dance with injuries that would send a quarterback to the sidelines and do it with a smile on your face." She turned the fish, deftly. "Then you all come to New York and compete for a handful of jobs and starve so you can spend three evenings a week on a stage. And because of what you do to yourselves, you have a likely active dancing life of *maybe* twenty years. Hell yes, you're masochists. Go set the table; we'll eat like civilized human beings tonight."

He meekly obeyed; more than obeyed. When she brought out the food, the wine, and the coffee, she discovered he'd arranged the flowers and twisted the napkins into little—lilies, she thought.

"Nice."

He bowed, then held the chair out for her. "My pleasure."

"You know what made me decide *not* to go into dancing?" she asked, as she served. "Aside from the fact that there were other things I wanted more."

He paused in mid-bite. "What?" he asked, around a mouthful of salmon.

"Agnes de Mille's autobiography. The place where she talks about one of her teachers in London—I think it was Marie Lambert—showing the girls how to tape their toes, so that when their blisters broke and bled *it wouldn't leak through and stain the pointe shoes.* Not *if,* Lenny. *When.* That's when I decided the dance was *not* for me. Pain is *not* my friend. Besides, I like writing better."

"Different kind of masochism, but still masochism," he retorted, pointing his fork at her.

She sighed, thinking about the current project. "I wouldn't argue that point. Eat, eat, eat, you're too thin. How you gonna get a husband, you're so thin?"

He laughed, and speared a carrot strip. "I want to get serious."

"What?" She batted her eyes at him. "Are you proposing?"

"You said yourself you're not my type. *Serious,* Di. I have a question."

She sighed. "Fire away."

"How come I never See you unshielded?"

The non sequitur took her off balance. "What brought that on?" she asked, stalling for time to think of a good answer.

"You told me a year ago that if I was still here you'd tell me what you were doing here," he replied, contemplating a piece of broccoli, then nibbling it. "I've been waiting for a good time to bring the subject up, because you've got me puzzled as hell. You're the only odd one in this building, Di. Everyone else is a dancer. Everyone else has three roommates, or more. *Almost* everyone else is of a traditional religious background. *Nobody* but me is psychic. What's wrong with this picture?"

She waffled for a moment, debating whether or not to tell him—at least something. Like she told the gypsy boy, it's always a good idea to have allies.

"You may not like it."

"There's a lot of things I don't like. I can't imagine you being anything I wouldn't like." He put his fork down, and folded his hands. "I mean that. You and Keith are about the only real friends I have."

"It'll make you a target, if you know," she warned, concentrating on her plate, giving him a last chance to beg off.

"So?"

She checked and double-checked the shields on the room, the apartment, the building. They all seemed secure.

She dropped her personal shields for a moment; less than a minute, but Lenny gasped anyway. When she brought them back up, she deliberately finished the last of her salmon, and *then* looked back up at him.

"That's why," she said quietly. "I *have* to shield; otherwise I might as well strip naked and run through the woods in deer season with antlers tied on my head." She poked him with one finger. "Wake up. It looks more impressive than it is. There's plenty of things out there tougher than I am."

"What do you *do* with all of that?" Lenny whispered, eyes glazed and bedazzled.

"I fix things," she replied, shrugging. "I have to. If I don't use it, the power starts to leak through my shields and radiate. When that happens, I can be seen. And *things* would come after me."

"What kind of things?" Lenny asked, blinking.

"Things. Nasty things. Like that guy that came sniffing around you in high school. Like Keith's poltergeist." She pushed her plate aside and took a long sip of her wine. "Anything, everything. Stuff like Dion Fortune hinted about. Works like this, or so my grandmother told me—*anything* or anyone who 'makes a living' exploiting others psychically—or hurting or killing them—is going to be acutely sensitive to Power. They are *going* to see me. When they see me, they're going to know I'm well trained. When they know that, they're going to assume that I'm just like they are. A higher predator. A jaguar doesn't even allow its own mate in its territory except for mating—same principle holds. So—I have no choice; I either take care of *them*, when I see them and I'm ready, and they're *not*, or I stand around and let 'em come for me on *their* terms."

Lenny nodded and refilled her glass. "I never did believe in Superman," he said with a wink. "I kept wondering why he didn't just compress a ton of coal into diamonds and retire to Buenos Aires. Next question—why are you worried? Because you are, or you wouldn't be so secretive."

She sighed. "Well, I *was* kind of making a virtue of necessity, because I really do want to help people. Having abilities and not using them to help makes me—guilty, I guess. Maybe that's the same thing that makes a *good* cop. Then I broke up with my boyfriend over being involved with the occult and I wanted to quit. I tried."

"Why didn't you?"

"Because I found out that my granny was right the hard way. Right after she died; without her nagging at me to go play hero, I thought I could just lay back in some remote place and not be bothered. Maybe get to be like normal people. Wrong-oh. I got munched."

Something must have penetrated her light tone. "Was it bad?" he asked, just touching her wrist.

"Well—yeah. It was." She shook her head. "I managed to get away; it wasn't easy, and it only happened because I was lucky. It took a long time to—get over it." She shivered away the memory. "And now—I get panic attacks. I *can't* be alone, I *have* to have people around me. And I protect my rump like nobody's business, which means striking first and preventing that ever happening again. But I still want to help people, so there's still that business of making a virtue out of necessity."

But when my gut figures I'm in over my head—I'm helpless because of the attacks. I haven't had one for a while . . . but I'd sure like to have somebody around who knows I'm likely to freak.

"Last question." He raised an eyebrow. "Why are you pecking out ninety-five-cent romance novels? Seems to me with Power like that, you ought to be doing better."

The laugh she replied with was real. "Because, my good friend, playing hero is not lucrative. I *have* to make a living. Things happen if I use my Power—and Things will see the fire-works and come looking for what's smelling so tasty. So—I write romance books. I *like* writing; I'm all right at it, and I think I'm getting better. I like writing romance novels; they're fun, and I think maybe I can do a little something about the prevailing theme in them that 'anything He does to you is all right if He loves you.' Other than that, I *don't* take what I'm writing seriously, and it's a good escape from the feeling of something breathing down my neck."

"Good enough." He drained the last of his wine, and shoved away from the table. "Now I know to keep one eye on you and one on me. And I'm *not* so bad at Seeing danger and yelling 'Look out!' as you well know."

She was touched. She'd *hoped* for this reaction, but—she hadn't expected it.

"Now, I really *have* to get upstairs, get some practice in, and get to sleep."

"I'd like you to stay a while—but I have work to do, too." She let him out. "Break a leg," she said. "And don't forget to bring your robe to Samhain. I keep telling you, I don't do skyclad."

He pouted. "You're no fun."

She shrugged. "Let's just say it's a lot colder in Connecticut than Virginia, and I'm easily distracted. You know, you *might* see if you can talk Keith into coming. If you two do start to get serious, he should *know* about your strange tastes in religion, and not just guess. Besides, it might be a chance to do something to—um—cement the relationship."

Lenny went as big-eyed and innocent as a Woolworth painting. "What, *me*? Cast love spells? What on earth could you be thinking?"

She shoved him out the door, and he skipped off, laughing, doing a two-step up the stairs.

She turned on the classical station; retyped an offending scene and started up again where she'd left off, cursing at the typewriter when she mistyped "the" as "teh" for the third time. And mentally berating her heroine for being such a damned wimp. Such a damned *thoughtless* wimp, sashaying along the beach at midnight, never mind there were supposed to be pirates in the neighborhood. Sashaying along a *deserted* beach. With no dwellings around for a mile. She *deserved* to get ravished. *Oh to be able to afford a computer. Or a typing service. Helluva note; here I am with enough psi to stop Hunters on the threshold, and magical ethics forbid my using it to make my publishers give me bigger advances and more contracts!* She took a swig of Coke, and chuckled at herself. *My strength is as the strength of ten, because my heart is pure. Pure* what, *I don't think I want to know.*

The Halloween party swirled through every room of the luxe Village apartment. In the glitter and glitz and the occasional actual costume, the band members' beaded jeans and appliquéd shirts with "Wanderlust" embroidered across the back didn't look out of place. Dave Kendall leaned back into the corner of the couch he was sharing with his lead singer and Jason's acquisitions, and watched Jason Trevor make his moves—and suppressed a twinge of envy. The sensuous, classically handsome rocker had a girl snuggling up to him on either side, a brunette with a *nice* tush on his left, and a redhead with great kabambas on his right. And chances were the lucky bastard would not only lay *both* of them before the night was over, he'd get a third and go home with a fourth.

Dave felt a drop of sweat run down his back, and tried to ignore the faint headache that the babble of shrill conversation all around him was giving him.

"—so then *she* said—"

"—pure quill, my man, and big as my head—"

"—right there in *Billboard*—"

"—and I told him, 'Look, Morrie, you're a *good* agent, a fine agent, but—'"

They'd come straight over to the party from their gig; invites to parties like this one didn't come along too often. The party was hot, in more ways than one, and at uncertain intervals his grass-blown senses made the room seem too big, too crowded, and much too bright. Still—this was a good party to be seen at. Probably the best Halloween party in the Village; looked like everybody who meant anything was here. And they seemed to recognize the band members, which was a good sign.

So he'd stay. It was worth putting up with. Even if everybody else in the band seemed to be having a much better time than he was.

He looked over at Jason, taking up three quarters of the couch—and *shit,* he'd just collected a *third* chick, curled up at his feet with her back to Dave; a raven-haired chippie in a pair of tight leather pants that made it perfectly clear that nothing got between her and the leather. He took a quick check of the others.

The drummer, Jack Prescott, was off in the corner by the hot buffet, scarfing down egg rolls and schmoozing with the guy from *Rolling Stone* he knew from back when. That was real good; Jack had mentioned the guy before, but Dave had never been able to figure how good the acquaintance was. Looked like it was enough.

That ain't bad. That ain't bad at all. I'll remind Jason tomorrow. Maybe Jack can get somebody to come by and give us a listen, or something.

He looked for Doug in vain for a while; then the bassist strolled in with a disheveled just-past-teenybopper hanging on his arm, and he had that funny grin on his face that he always got after *he'd* been laid. . . .

Dave sighed, and grabbed a hit off someone's doobie as it made the rounds. *What the hell, the food's great, the dope's good, and the wine sure as hell ain't Ripple.* He wedged himself back in the corner a little more as the brunette next to Jason shoved her tight little ass into his thigh.

It was getting awfully crowded on this couch. It fit four—if they were polite. This chick wasn't real polite.

She had her hands all *over* Jason, and Jason didn't look like he planned on stopping her anytime soon. The black-haired chick on the floor seemed oblivious; the redhead looked annoyed.

Dave wondered if the brunette was stoned enough to start something with the lead singer there and then.

Well, maybe she's bored. It's Halloween, and it don't look like anybody's gonna bring in apples for her to bob for.

He watched her for a moment longer—Jay was still dressed, but the clothing didn't seem to be slowing her down any—then his neck started to get hot, and his own pants started feeling way too tight, and he decided it might be a good idea to get up and get a drink or something.

The minute he got up, she curled her legs up on the couch where he'd been, and—

He decided enough was enough, and went looking for the potato chips.

He didn't find chips, but in the first room and near the door he found a marble coffee table holding the remains of some other munchies. In the rubble was an unclaimed bottle of wine and a bowl of cashews, and beside the table, a leather beanbag chair that seemed unoccupied. He took all three.

Just as he got settled, a latecomer arrived, with a fair amount of fanfare. The voice wasn't anybody Dave recognized, but about half the people in this room seemed thrilled to see him, effusing all over him, and calling him "Master" Jeffries. So many people swarmed over to greet the man that until he actually drew opposite Dave, the guitarist couldn't see him. When he did, he wasn't impressed.

The man would have been darkly handsome in a brooding sort of way, if it hadn't been for the two black eyes he sported, and the cast on his left arm. *"Master" Jeffries, huh?* Dave thought to himself, trying to get the man's measure. *Master of what, I wonder. He sure doesn't look like a martial artist.*

"Master Jeffries," asked a guy with an earnest and pained expression and a nose like a ship's bow. "Whatever happened to your arm—"

Jeffries gave the younger man a *look* that could have peeled paint. The offending party withered under it, and slunk away.

Dave became impressed. *Now* that *I wish I could learn.*

He was beginning to get the measure of this gig, but this Jeffries just didn't fit in any category Dave could come up with. The party was just about equally divided between the young and up'n'coming (like the band, a scattering of dancers, and a slew of writers and artists), some teenyboppers with daddy's bucks to blow, and the middle-aged and terminally hip, also with money to blow. One of the latter, a trendy ash-blond woman whose skin had the tight look of one-too-many face lifts, accosted Jeffries in the moment of silence left by the questioner's departure.

Dave couldn't hear exactly what she was saying, just something about a "reading." Whatever it was, Jeffries was all smiles again, and he took her beringed hand and led her over to the couch next to Dave's chair.

Dave was impressed for a second time: he didn't even look at them, much less say anything to them, but the current occupants of the couch abandoned it without so much as a murmur.

For a moment, Dave was afraid that the guy was some kind of writer, or worse, a poet, and that he was about to be involuntarily subjected to a reading of Literature.

But no.

The man held to the socialite's hand as they sat on the leather couch, spread her palm out in the light from the track-spot behind them, and began spinning her some kind of tale about what he was "reading" from her hand.

Dave was both relieved and amused. *Uh-huh. "Master" Jeffries, now I know what you're supposed to be. A guru. Just another phony mystic.* He listened a little, and poured himself another glass of wine. *He sure is good at body language, though. He's reading her like he could read minds.*

Jeffries segued from the woman's recent past to a description of her "past life" as a Roman slave girl. Interested now, Dave eavesdropped without shame—and had to stuff a handful of cashews into his mouth to keep from laughing out loud when he recognized *where* Jeffries was getting the material he was using for the woman's "past life."

Shit, if that isn't The Last Days of Pompeii *I'll eat this chair. I thought every kid had to read that tripe. Guess not. She sure doesn't look like she recognizes it.*

The woman's eyes were moist and glowing, and her attention uncritical and total. She looked like a Moonie having a major religious experience.

After a few more minutes, Dave had to admit to himself that the man was *good.* He didn't miss a trick, and if Dave hadn't had some coaching on how to spot the phonies from that flaky ex-girlfriend of his in college—

Di might have been off in the ozone about half the time, but you couldn't pull one over on her—God, Di, why couldn't you have been fixated on something else, something I could have gotten a handle on?

But the memory hurt too much; their breakup hadn't been easy *or* pretty, and it had left enough scars that he hadn't written anything since. He shoved the recollection back into the corner where it came from, grabbed another jay making the rounds and took a big hit off it to numb the pain.

He looked around for the rest of the band, figuring that it was no bad thing for *somebody* to keep tabs on the others, and it might as well be him. Jason was nowhere in sight. Doug had another groupie, a blonde, and this one couldn't *possibly* be anything but underage. She was leeched onto his arm, rubbing up against his side, and running her hand through his shoulder-length hair, and he wasn't doing anything to discourage her. Jack had lost his friend from *Rolling Stone,* and drifted in just as Dave started looking for him. In a few minutes he was sharing a monster joint with some gay artist and his lover-of-the-week. *Keep that going, Jack-ol'-buddy. I've heard Burton has friends in the music biz.*

The murmur of the woman's voice brought Dave's attention back to Jeffries. She was thanking him, with tears in her voice, for "enlightening" her. There was something odd about her, and for a moment Dave couldn't quite place it. Then he realized, as she drifted off in search of other prey, what it was. When she'd accosted this Jeffries, she'd been lively to the point of manic, and quite vivacious. But *now* she secmed drained and exhausted. She looked depressed, and complained to one of her friends on the way out of the room that she had a terrible headache.

He took a quick look back at Jeffries, to see if the man had been affected in the same way.

He hadn't. In fact, he looked better. His black eyes seemed to have faded visibly—Dave would have been willing to swear that they were real shiners when he came in; now they were just a faded purple, and hardly swollen at all.

Dave shook his head. *I'm stoned, that's all. Too stoned to know what I'm seeing. Maybe it's time to go home—*

But a commotion over at the side of the room drew him and everyone else in the direction of their host, some kind of avant-garde writer, who was enjoying a wave of popularity for his current, terribly relevant novel of life on the streets.

He had something in his hands; from where Dave stood it looked like a bowl. A plastic bowl, with a cover on it.

What is this, a Tupperware party?

"All right, kiddies, it's trick or treat time!" he called over the party noise. That got him silence, and he smiled archly. "It's the witching hour, boys and girls, and you all know how witches used to fly away on Halloween. I've got you something that'll send you to the same place."

He pulled the lid off the bowl, and Dave could see that it was full to the brim with capsules; small ones, a maroon color that was just a shade under black. They bothered Dave for a moment; then he figured out why. They were the color of dried blood.

"Thought we'd all like a little *adult* trick or treat; the trick is that these little darlings are *new*—so new they not only aren't illegal yet, they don't even have a name yet. The treat is what they *do* to you." Their host smirked, and Dave saw that his eyes were so dilated that there was no iris showing. "I promise you, I previewed them yesterday, and they are *dynamite*. So share the wealth, kids—"

The bowl began to make the rounds, and Dave found he was reaching for it with all the others.

"—party left eight dead of unknown causes," the news announcer said. "Meanwhile, more news of Watergate—"

Di tuned him out. She'd only put the news on in the first place to see if there were any after-Halloween incidents that might involve her. But a druggie party in the Village had no consequences to anyone but the ones stupid enough to dope themselves into the next life, and Watergate was out of *her* league.

The news left her feeling very sour. Nixon would get off; you didn't have to be a fortune-teller—a real one—to know that. He knew where too many skeletons were hidden, and he had too many connections who'd be only too happy to make sure certain witnesses never got to testify. About the only *good* thing would be that he would never hold office again.

As for the fools who popped whatever came to hand—*I don't do Presidents, I don't do druggies, and I don't do windows. Eight dead. Damned fools. Some people never get beyond the stage of sticking everything they find into their mouths.*

She had more pressing difficulties; something she could and would have to do something about. How to get the ravished maiden on board the privateer *without* having the rest of the crew find out and demand a piece of the—ahem—action.

Hard to do when the smallest dory takes two men to row, and Sarah ain't bloody likely to help. She's too busy fainting. What a wimp!

She chewed on the end of her pencil and scowled at the typewriter. Inspiration was not forthcoming.

Why didn't they cover this in the outline? Maybe if Nicholas buys off the first mate—

Sound of the feet overhead. Hard little taps, running, and thuds. Ballet. Paul and Jill were rehearsing "Le Jeune Homme et la Mort" again.

Maybe I ought to go up and watch. They shook me loose last time I had a problem. Besides, they're so good on that piece—

She stood up and shoved her chair back—

—and suddenly found her knees giving; grabbed the desk and hung on.

Shield, shield, dummy—this is coming from right outside—

A wave of pure fear battered at her and drove any vestige of real thought from her mind. It took her a breath to fight back; another to get control of herself.

A third to realize that the wave of violent emotion was carrying with it an unmistakable call for help, magician to magician, psi to psi.

By the fourth breath, her keys were in her pocket, her ritual knife and flashlight were in her hands, and her door was gaping wide behind her as she took the stairs at a dead, flat-out run.

A second wave of fear broke over her just as she hit the landing—she stumbled, then recovered—

But when she reached the foyer, there was—nothing. Nothing at all, just a mental emptiness.

And that was more ominous than the fear.

She hit the outer door; there was nothing in either direction on the street. That left the alley. Which she did *not* want to go into—but there was no choice.

She scrambled around the corner and shone the flashlight ahead of her; it was a powerful light, heavy enough to use as a club if she had to. The light wobbled around the alleyway as her hand shook; then there was a flash of something pale off to the side.

She steadied the beam.

A person. The intruder was bending over something in a kind of half-kneeling position. As the light struck him, he turned, and snarled—

And vanished.

"*Oh dear gods!*"

Di nearly dropped the flashlight; she put her back to the cold brick of the alley wall and tried to make sense of what she'd just seen.

Because the "intruder" was the strange Frenchman from the week before. And when he had snarled at the light, she had seen—fangs.

And *then* he had disappeared.

She waited, heart pounding, for him, for *something*, to come after her, but as the moments crawled by, and she got colder and colder, nothing did. Finally she managed to scrape up enough courage to approach whoever was lying in the alley. *Whoever,* because she was dreadfully afraid that she knew who had called her tonight.

The powerful beam of light was pitiless, and cared nothing for her remorse. It showed her what she didn't want to see; that the thing in the alley was a body, that the body was that of the gypsy boy she had given her card to, and that the boy was dead.

She knelt beside him, sick with grief. *I failed him. He came running to me for help, and I was too late to save him. He* thought

I could protect him; I'd promised protection, and I failed that promise. Oh gods.

That was enough to hold her kneeling motionless on the wet, filthy pavement for a long time. It was really only the *other* thing she'd seen that broke her trance of self-accusation and made her take a closer look at the boy to try to discover what had killed him.

And that was the Frenchman; the Frenchman with *fangs*.

Because she had just seen something that didn't, couldn't exist.

A vampire. A real, classical, blood-sucking vampire.

THREE

Patrolman Ron St. Claire stared into the murky brown of his third cup of coffee and hoped that he'd be able to *finish* this one. It hadn't been a good night for finishing much of anything; coffee, conversations, dinner.

"Hey, Ron."

He looked up from the coffee and grinned at the elfin waitress wrinkling her nose at him. "Hey, yourself. What's cookin', honey?"

April Santee, the third-shift waitress of Dunkin' Donuts number five-three-seven mock-glowered at him. "How many times do I have to tell you not to call me honey?"

"Till I stop."

"One of these days," the little brunette told him, pointing a threatening finger at him, "I'm gonna bring my girlfriend the karate champ in here, and you *will* stop." She saw then how tired he was, and dropped the banter. "Babe, you look like somebody's been giving you the short end of the stick all night."

"Something like that," he replied, rubbing his right eye with one knuckle. "It's a big night for indoor crime and craziness, and it isn't even half over. Three breaking-and-enterings, five assaults, two assault-with-deadlies, and seven domestic violence. And before you ask, here's the stats of the ones I think your gang should talk to." He pushed a half-sheet of lined note-book paper across the counter to her.

April frowned down at the list, and shook her head. "There's only three names here," she said, accusation shading her voice with suspicion.

"Two of the seven you already have. One walked out on her old man after clobbering him back with a cast-iron frying pan; I think that was the first time he took a hand to her, and I *know* it's gonna be the last. One was a woman beating up on her old man. That leaves you three. Better talk to number two quick; she had that look in her eyes. She's in a trap she can't break out of, and if she doesn't get some help there's gonna be a homicide."

"Gotcha." April folded the piece of paper and tucked it into her apron pocket. "I'll phone 'em to the hot-line desk on my break. Thanks, big fella." She refreshed his coffee without being asked. "You know, I never asked you: what do *you* get out of this? You could get fired if anybody ever found out you were passing names and addresses out to us. Never mind we're saving women from wife beaters, that's invasion of privacy."

"What do *I* get? Let me tell you what I *don't* get. Corpses. Bodies on my beat I don't need." He'd gotten two just before he met April; some poor, worn-out thing beaten to death by her husband—and a husband hacked to pieces with a cleaver by a wife who couldn't take it anymore. He looked up into April's muddy-brown eyes, the exact color of his coffee, wondering if she had any idea of what he was talking about. He needn't have wondered; the grim set to her mouth told him she'd seen a cou-ple of corpses, too.

"Helluva job, isn't it?" she said rhetorically.

"Could be worse. I could be an MCP and be laughing at you gals, instead of trying to help." He drank half the coffee and smiled, wearily; April made *good* coffee.

About then the box at his belt squawked. "Oh hell," he groaned, pushing off the stool.

"Yo, Ron!" He looked up just in time to catch the plaid thermos April tossed at him. "Full, fresh, black, and sugar. Compliments of the Women's Shelter. Move out, soldier."

He grinned, transferred the thermos to his left, and saluted. "Yes, *ma'am.*" He turned smartly on his heel and trotted to the squad.

"Got a weird one," the dispatcher told him, when he reported in. The interior of the squad car was still warm; he hadn't even been inside long enough for the heat to dissipate. He started the engine, and grunted with relief when it caught.

"Weird how?" he asked, waiting for traffic to clear.

"Runaway bus—well, runaway driver, anyway. We took five calls on it before the captain decided it wasn't a prank, and we just took call number nine a minute ago; he says this looks like something we'd better step in on, especially after the last call."

"What's the deal?" Ron asked, backing out of the parking space and onto the street.

"Bus on route twenty-nine isn't stopping to pick people up. Sticking to the route, but not stopping. It's damn near empty, so that's not why."

"So?" Ron said scornfully. "Let them take care of it. Bus company's got radios and cars. So they got a stoned driver, let them handle it. Maybe he's pissed off at his bosses. Why should we mix into it?"

" 'Cause the last call was a guy the bus *did* stop for. He was all alone, he started to get on—and when he happened to look over at the other passengers—he swears on his life they were wounded or dead."

A finger of cold ran up the back of Ron's neck. "You're sure this isn't a hoax?" He swung the squad onto a route that would bring it to intersect with the bus's in about ten minutes.

"Not hardly," Dispatch said wryly. "Caller number nine was Father Jim O'Donnel from Saint Anthony's."

"Hell." He turned a corner and saw the bus up ahead of him, lights shining harshly through the windows. "Roger. I've got 'em in sight."

He hit the lights, then the siren—

But to no effect; the bus didn't even slow down.

He swore, pulled alongside—

He fought a battle of "chicken" with the thing for ten minutes, sweat popping out all over him, his armpits getting soggy. He asked Dispatch for some help—but there were gangfights all over tonight, and a rash of armed-and-dangerous, and there was nobody to spare. Finally he managed to force the vehicle into a cul-de-sac.

The bus rolled to a gentle halt, stopped. As Ron flung his car in behind it, slewing it sideways with a squeal of tires so that the cul-de-sac was blocked, someone turned the bus engine off, the lights flickered, then went to battery—

And nothing happened.

No one got out; no one moved. Not even the driver.

Sweating, Ron called in what he was about to do, asking for backup. Just in case. Dispatch said they'd try. He waited a few moments; decided he didn't dare wait any longer. Then, before he had a chance to think about it, he pulled his gun, kicked open the squad door, and dove out, like a baseball player diving for home plate, into the meager shelter of a battered old Rabbit.

Silence, except for the ticking sounds of cooling metal.

He waited, while the sweat on him froze, and his chest went numb from contact with the cold pavement, and still nothing happened. He gathered himself, a human spring coiled tighter and tighter—then he lurched to his feet, and dashed to the side of the bus. He didn't slow in the least as he neared it, just ran straight for the side of it, plastering himself there with a thud as he hit the metal.

Still nothing. No sign of movement, and no sound.

This was getting spookier by the second. With sweat pouring down his back, and his piece cocked and ready, he inched along the freezing side of the bus until he came to the rear exit. He tested it, pushing on it. It gave a little, so it wasn't locked up. He took a deep breath, trying not to cough on the diesel fumes, and shoved it open, then flung himself inside, sprawled in the stairwell, elbows braced against the top step.

"*Freeze*," he shouted, targeting the driver's head, thinking *Now it comes*—

But nothing happened.

Except that he smelled the burned-iron tang of blood, and his knee was getting wet where it was jammed against one of the stairs.

He looked down at the floor of the bus. He'd heard the phrase "awash with blood" before, and had laughed at it. He wasn't laughing now, not when blood was running down the aisles, and trickling over the stairs in a thin but steady stream, soaking the knee of his uniform.

He stumbled through the open door to the smog outside, clung to the side of the door and threw up.

They'd given him one of the soundproofed rooms used for questioning suspects so that he could concentrate. There was a pot of coffee on the table next to the stack of forms he had to fill out, also (presumably) to help him concentrate.

What if I don't want to concentrate? What if I just want to forget the whole thing?

The door opened and shut behind him. "St. Claire—"

Ron looked up from the pile of papers in front of him, his eyes dry and aching and foggy with weariness, his stomach sore from heaving. He'd never had a multiple homicide before; he'd had no idea there were so many papers to fill out for each victim. He had just completed Schetzke, Leona (Female, 45, Cauc, brown, brown) and was about to start on Paloma, Marie Annette (Female, 43, Hisp, brown, black).

And it's a good thing I didn't have to fire my piece, or I'd have had about fifty ballistics reports to fill in, too.

"Captain." He nodded as the precinct captain eased himself past the edge of the table and sat down in one of the old wooden chairs on the other side. A stranger in a suit so crisp it looked as if he'd just taken it out of the box gave him a long, measuring look, then took the other chair. Ron suppressed the urge to look at his shoes. Shiny black shoes would have meant he was FBI. If the Feds were mixed in this somehow, Ron didn't want to know about it.

"Ron, can you give it to us one more time? After you got back on the bus." The boss looked unhappy; Ron's hackles went up. There was something severely wrong—

"I got back on the bus," he replied, clenching his hands into fists, and feeling his gut clench, too. "I started taking a body count. First was a pair of females, that's right opposite the rear entrance. Second was an old man in a tailored business suit—"

The stranger took notes. So the FBI *was* involved. As he detailed the body count, working his way up to the front of the bus, he wondered what on earth could have happened to bring Feds into this. Was this a terrorist action of some kind? Something involving the Mob?

"—the last one was the driver, I guess," he finished.

"At least, he was wearing a bus uniform. He was the only one not cut up any, but he was as cold as the rest of them—and they were *cold*." There was a snap and he looked down at his right fist, startled. He'd broken his pencil in half. He put the halves down, carefully, and reached for a new one with the same deliberate care.

"You're sure," the captain persisted. "You're *certain* that the last one was wearing a bus uniform."

"Yeah," he replied, too upset to be angry. "I mean, that's not something I'd make a mistake about."

"Was this him?" The stranger pushed a Polaroid across the table at him, the kind they took when they checked bodies into the morgue. Ron took a cursory look. It was definitely a picture of his corpse.

"Yeah, that's him."

"Thanks, St. Claire." Without any explanation, they pushed their chairs away from the table, legs grating on the linoleum, and started to get up.

"Wait a minute," he said belligerently. "Don't I get to know what's going on? You come in here, make me go over that—slaughterhouse all over again, and then you don't even tell me *why?*"

The captain paused for a moment; the stranger stopped halfway to the door.

"Go ahead," the stranger said, with what might have been a shrug, except that it was too slight a movement to even wrinkle the shoulders of his suit.

"We had some bus dispatchers in here to identify the man," the captain said slowly. "They got here about half an hour ago."

"So?" Ron prompted. "What happened?"

"He wasn't there."

Ron shook his head, thinking he must have misheard. "He wasn't theirs?"

"No—*he wasn't there.* He was gone. Vanished. Poof. Right out of a morgue drawer."

"Gone?" Ron said faintly, feeling very, very cold.

"Gone."

Suddenly the paperwork seemed very attractive indeed, as an alternative to thinking.

Di poured herself a double Scotch and picked up the phone, dialing the emergency number. In a voice that shook, she reported screams and gunshots in the alley beneath her window. No, she hadn't gone out to look. No, she didn't think it was cars backfiring, there hadn't been any cars down there at the time. No, she didn't know if anyone else had heard. The sexless, passionless entity on the other end of the line took down her name and address, and said someone would be around to check the alley shortly. They hung up; so did she.

Thank the gods Lenny isn't home tonight; he'd have been out there with me. She sagged against the desk chair. *He might have beat me there. He couldn't have missed the vibes. And he could have gotten* himself *killed.*

Then she drank half of that double Scotch in one gulp.

Her hand shook so hard that the ice cubes rattled against the side of the glass. She put it down, and stood beside the desk, bracing herself against it. She simply held that position for a long time, staring at the dark reflection of herself in the windowpane.

After a while there were sirens below, and red lights flashing against the bricks of the building opposite her. She took her drink to the kitchen, refilled it, and returned to her living room to curl up on her shabby old brown sofa.

She half expected the cops to come and pound on her door, but no one arrived, and eventually the red flashes went away from the window.

No. No panic attack, she told herself sternly. *Not now. I can't afford one.*

Fight or flight, fight or flight, adrenaline flooded her system, trying to override her ability to think. She *knew* the mechanism, *knew* it right down to the chemicals involved, and it didn't help.

No. Not. Now. It ran from me. I can handle this.

She had won. This time, she had won.

When her hands stopped shaking, she began sipping the Scotch, trying to get everything straight in her head.

There wasn't a mark on him, not one. But he was *drained; drained of psychic and emotional energy until his heart literally stopped. That is* not *"traditional" vampiric attack.*

Vampiric attack? What in hell am I thinking of?

But I saw the fangs, I know I did. *I did* not *imagine them.*

But it wasn't blood he was drained of, it was emotional energy. Like a "psychic vampire." Like the kind of person who walks into a party and leeches onto the liveliest person there, and when he leaves, he's feeling wonderful *and his "victim" feels like the bottom of the biorhythm chart. I've known psychic vampires that could drain you so low that you'd catch every germ that walked by, just because the immune system is so tied into the emotional system. And ones that left you ready to commit suicide but too tired to pick up the knife to do it.*

But that's psychic vampires. "Psivamps." Granny told me that "vampires" were a myth, that the psivamps were the only kind of vampires there were.

What if she didn't know?

That's crazy. That's not what killed the boy—

And psivamps can't kill. Or—can they?

What if there's very rare *psivamps that can? What if those long teeth are an outward sign of a really strong psivamp? What if I really didn't see fangs, what if what I saw was something my subconscious produced, so I'd make the connection between the boy's death and vampirism?*

I can't *have seen a vampire.*

But I did.

Oh gods.

She sipped, and got only ice, and she looked at her empty glass in some surprise.

What if I'm wrong? What if there are *real vampires?*

But if there are—who killed that boy? Why did they kill him? What made it so important that they kill him before he reached me? Did they know he was coming to me? Am I a target now? What did he know—and did he plan to tell me about it—or was this all coincidence, and was he simply running to the nearest safe harbor he knew of?

And if this man is a real vampire, a classical bloodsucker—why did the boy die of emotional drainage?

She wanted badly to have another drink—but if she was a target, she knew she didn't dare. She *had* to stay alert and on guard, and she could not give in to fear. Instead she spent the better part of the next two hours reinforcing every shield on the place, then showered and went to bed—

But not to sleep. She left all the lights on, and stared up at the ceiling, waiting.

Dave woke up—sort of—around five the next night. But his eyes wouldn't focus right, and he felt as if he hadn't gotten any sleep at all. He tried everything to jar himself awake, from a cold shower to downing a whole pot of espresso, black—but when he blanked for "a minute" and came to at midnight, slumped over the kitchen table (with a roach doing the back-stroke in the half-empty cup in his hand), he decided to hang it up and go back to bed.

He was in that kind of half-daze for almost forty-eight hours; half waking, trying to get up, going back to bed again. And God, the dreams—

The dreams he had were real bummers; like no dreams he'd ever had before. Nothing visual, either. Just a blackness and the feeling that millions of people were shouting their most inti-mate thoughts at him. They were really repeats of the stuff those damned red pills had done to him. He felt like he was stuck in-side of peoples' heads, feeling what they felt, eavesdropping on whatever they were doing.

Made him feel like some kind of damned pervert. Some kind of *Twilight Zone* Peeping Tom.

Finally, *finally*, he really woke up, around four on the second day after the party. And looked at the calendar on the wall above his bed, and realized they had a gig at a club they'd contracted to play in before Halloween—in four hours.

Oh hell. Oh goddamn hell. I feel like shit warmed over.

He struggled out of his tangle of sheets and blankets and into clothes—gig clothes; he'd have to hustle his buns like crazy to get to the club as it was. He was a little surprised to see the clothing from the party-night tossed over a chair; he didn't remember doing that. Come to think of it, he didn't even remember getting home.

I must've taken a cab. Thank God I took the axe home before I went over there. Thank God Jack's got the amps in the back of his car—

He didn't have a stomach so much as a hollow, echoing cavern just under his ribs. His throat and mouth were dry as a critic's soul, but the hunger was worse. *God, I'm* starved*—I should be sicker'n a dog, but I'm starved—*

But there was no time—he grabbed what was in the fridge, threw baloney on bread, snatched up his axe, stuffed it in his gigbag, and headed out the door—

And at the door of the building, he hit sunlight, and it felt like hitting a wall.

He backed into the entryway for a second, and fumbled in the pocket of his jacket for his shades. *Is it just me, or did somebody clean out all the pollution while I was out? God, it's like stagelights.*

He got the shades on, walked out of the building again, and looked around—

And nobody else was even squinting, while to *his* eyes the sun was only just bearable with his shades.

Must've been that stuff. Damn if I ever take *anything red again—*

He wolfed the sandwich down as he loped to the bus stop, but it did nothing to ease the gnawing hunger in his belly. When he made his transfer, he stopped long enough at a newsstand to pick up half a dozen candy bars, but a sugar megadose that would have left him feeling bloated a couple of days ago didn't ease his sore throat or even *dent* the raging that was gnawing at his backbone.

Now *that* was even stranger than his sudden sensitivity to light.

Hell, I didn't eat for two days. Probably some kind of deficiency. Potassium, maybe. I'll deal with it when I get home.

Besides, he had a head that felt like a pumpkin—and he sure didn't need to add to his problems by stuffing himself and then turning sick. *That'd be a great way to end the act, barf all over the stage. Real impressive, Dave.*

Once he stopped moving, depression set in. He cradled his axe in his lap and stared out the grimy bus window, wondering if Wanderlust was *ever* going to get anywhere. The night of the party, it had looked like things were coming up, but now? God.

The sun crawled behind the skyscrapers, and he was finally able to stuff his dark glasses back into his pocket.

Three years we've been at this, and we're still basically a bar band. I wish I knew what the hell we're doing wrong. Maybe we should try moving to LA or 'Frisco—naw, that wouldn't do any good. Man, I can't take La-La-Land, even if we could afford the move, and nobody's picked up any new bands out of 'Frisco since I can't think when. Since Graham closed down the Ballroom. He slumped down in the slick plastic seat, and tucked his chin down on his chest, hoping vaguely that his head would stop throbbing. It didn't hurt—but the sensation was uncomfortable and disorienting. *Maybe we oughta pack it in. Maybe I oughta go back to school. Finish out, get my degree. Go be an accountant or something. Shit, I haven't written anything in years, even. All the stuff of mine we're doing is three years old at best. Maybe I just can't cut it as a musician. Maybe I'm a has-been; shit, maybe I'm a never-was.*

He was so sunk in depression that he almost missed his stop; shaken into alertness only by the flash of neon as somebody turned the club's gaudy orange and red sign on just as the bus rolled past. He yanked the cord *just* in time, crawled over a sea of knees, and escaped into the cold of the street.

The club wouldn't open till eight, so he had to take the alley entrance, and for some reason tonight his nose—that he'd *thought* was used to New York—wasn't handling the mix of rotting garbage and urine at all. He gagged, and held his breath until he got inside. The other guys were already there, setting up, though from the looks of things they hadn't been there long. Of all of them, only Jack looked in any shape to *do* anything.

"You look like hell," Doug said, as he hauled himself up onto the tiny carpet-covered stage.

"No shit, Sherlock," he replied sourly. "I *feel* like hell."

"Join the club," Jason muttered, setting up mikes with a clatter of metal. *He* was still wearing *his* shades; Dave didn't think he wanted to know what *his* head felt like.

"Next time Frazier brings out one of his treats, hit me if I take him up on it, okay?" he said to Doug.

"You too, huh?" The bassist pulled his baby out of her bag, and frowned at her—and Doug *never* frowned at his baby.

"Yeah."

"I dunno why that shit got to you guys so bad," Jack commented from somewhere behind his kit. "All it did was give me rainbows around everything for a while, and giggle fits."

"You checked in with the news?" Jason asked suddenly, turning to face them, and raising his shades to reveal eyes like two holes burned into the flesh of his face.

Dave mutely shook his head. Doug did the same.

"Nope," Jack seconded. "Didn't have time. Why?"

" 'Cause we're the lucky ones. They took 'bout eight of Frazier's friends home in body bags."

Jack whistled; the sharp sound passed *through* Dave's head, and he winced.

Doug grimaced, though it was hard to tell if it was in reaction to the news or the noise. "Shee-it. Who?"

Jason paused in his mike placement, and pondered them both for a moment from behind the shelter of his glasses. "Only ones you might know would be that dancer, Tamara, and the two dudes she's been playing threesies with."

Dave started, and covered it by fiddling with the pickup on his amp. Because one of the few clear memories he had of when the drug kicked in was a strange hallucination of *being* Tamara and her two partners in turn, as they screwed each other's brains out. If it hadn't been so weird and embarrassing, it would have been an incredible turn-on—he hadn't considered that Tam's lovers might be bi; and he hadn't *dreamed* that there could be—that anybody could—God, the kind of things three creative and athletic people could do with each other!

That's crazy. It's just a coincidence. Just a real strange coincidence, and my own gutter-imagination.

"Christ on a crutch," Jack said, subdued. "Hey, next time we do one of Frazier's parties, we stick to what we know, okay?"

Dave swallowed, then nodded, considering what *could* have happened. No telling why or how they'd croaked, but that was *too* close. "Dig it. Man, we are just stone lucky we weren't on last night—we'd never have made it."

Jason pushed his glasses back down over his eyes. "Damn straight. And *that* would have spelled 'finito' to *this* band right then and there. So let's get this show on the road, huh? Or we may not make it out of *this* gig alive."

Privately, Dave had this figured for a Bad One. There was *no* electricity, *no* drive when they warmed up; they were just walking through the songs, making the motions, but not much else was going on. It didn't get any better, and when the hired hands showed and started setting the place up, *they* did not look impressed. The owner walked in halfway through, listened, and grimaced a little; the bouncer looked flat bored. Dave's heart sank.

The owner put the floor lights on, and vanished down the corridor behind the stage; a couple of seconds later the canned music started, and a couple of customers filed in.

The four of them wordlessly racked their instruments and jumped down off the stage; give the place half an hour to fill, then they'd be on.

Half an hour—too much time, and not enough.

They edged single file down the icy, cement-block hallway to the break room, each in his own little world. This one was like a little prison cell, painted cement walls, a couple of foggy mirrors, metal folding chairs and a table, a fridge full of soft drinks. Dave grabbed a Coke; his mouth was so dry now that it rivaled his hunger for discomfort level. He chugged it in seconds, then grabbed another—the ache in his gut eased up a little, and his throat didn't seem quite so dry. He chugged a third, beginning to feel better.

Damn if it was something missing—what's in Coke? Vitamin C maybe? Di always used to swear by vitamins, but I can't remember which ones.

Doug caught on, then Jason. Together they must have finished about half a case inside fifteen minutes. Jack looked at them with a funny expression for a minute, then went off into his trance, staring at the floor about five feet in front of him, air-drumming.

Dave actually started to feel like a human being again, and went into *his* preset ritual of pacing in little circles while going over every song, every riff, in his mind. He wasn't sure what Jason thought about, but *his* thing involved dance stretches. Doug just sat, eyes closed, so quiet you couldn't even see him breathing.

The overhead light flickered twice; moment-of-truth time.

If we can pull this gig off, lousy as we feel, then we've got it enough together as a band for us to keep trying, Dave decided suddenly. *Yeah. That's how I'll play it.*

He jumped up onto the stage feeling like a gladiator must have felt in the arena. Make it or break it—

They usually opened with the Stones' "Satisfaction," but Jason had decided they weren't going to do anybody else's work on this gig but their own. So they opened with one of Dave's pieces, the last one he'd written, "Crawlin' the Walls."

It began with a falling scream from the lead guitar, a monotone snarl from the bass, and a screech that rose to meet the lead from Dave's—then Jack's drums came in like thunder from the gods—

Out of the corner of his eye, across the thin haze of smoke, Dave could see every head in the place snap around to face the stage, eyes going wide with surprise.

Well, that sure as hell got their attention, anyway.

Then the lights came up on them, angry and red; Jack began driving the beat like a manic pile driver, Doug pounded the bass line, and the rumble was on—

For the first half of the song it *was* a rumble; his line fighting Jason's for supremacy, the bass muttering threats underneath, and the lights pulsing on them in alternating reds and hot yellows. But the crowd seemed to like it that way; there were heads nodding out there, and feet starting to tap, and a couple of dancers, braver than the rest, out on the floor.

The drumbeats started to get inside Dave's head; to throb in his blood.

Then Jason started his vocal line.

Dave had been dreading this; Jason had a voice as smooth as chamois suede most of the time, but tonight he'd been awful. He'd wandered all over the landscape, pitchwise, and he'd been hoarse and rough—Dave had been real tempted to ask him to sit this one night out and let him and Doug handle the vocals.

But when the first note left Jason's throat, he knew everything was going to be all right.

I'm gonna buy stock in Coke, he thought, with wonder verging on reverent awe. *I don't care if they're capitalist pigs, I'm gonna buy stock in Coke. My God, our ass is saved—*

The song poured from Jason in a flow of molten, red-hot gold, every note round and perfect, every nuance shaped exactly as Dave had heard it in his head.

And Dave could *feel* the crowd responding; feel the energy rising up from the floor and beginning to build. There was a wave building up out there, in the dark, past the reef of light and sound—a throbbing power and a tightwire tension waiting to be released, *begging* to be released, and lacking only the trigger—

Oh God—

It was coming round to *him* now, he was supposed to come in with the harmony, and oh God, *how* was he going to match what Jason was doing? He was going to screw it up, he was, he didn't dare sing, he didn't dare *not* sing, he grabbed his mike like a lifeline and—

"Set me free!"

Oh dear God *in heaven—*

It was beautiful, it was cosmic—their voices rose together, so perfectly matched they even had their vibrato in unison. It was the Holy Grail, it was orgasm, it was everything he'd ever *dreamed* that song could be—everything he'd despaired of it ever becoming—

And the wave of energy from the crowd crested and broke over them.

Suddenly they were *alive*, like they'd never known what it was to *be* alive; and hot, and jamming like they'd never jammed before. He hadn't seen anybody move from the tables, but suddenly there was a sea of faceless bodies out there on the floor; they were packed so tightly in front of the stage there was no room to move, they just jigged in place, a sea of arms waving wildly over their heads, making eddies in the sweet grass smoke that billowed around them like incense around the altar. *They* were on the altar, the band was celebrant and sacrifice in one. *Life;* that's what was pouring from the audience into him. He soaked it up, his hunger ebbed away like it had never been there, and still the energy flowed into him, sweet as sin, more intoxicating than any drug.

He couldn't stop, not now. He threw back his head to toss his hair out of his eyes and segued right into the next piece, "No Time Out." Jason followed him like they'd planned it that way from the start. Doug moved in on his mike and they made the same kind of sweet harmonies *he* and Jason had achieved, and Dave just closed his eyes and let his fingers do the walking.

The flow was incredible—

They jammed on that song for a full ten minutes; it felt like no time at all, and when they brought it round, it *hurt* to have to end it.

Then it didn't end, because *Jason* licked right on into "FreeFall," and when Dave came in on the vocal line, all of a sudden *Doug* was in there too, and it worked, oh dear God in heaven, it *worked*, and Dave's throat ached with the purity of it.

Then from that straight on into "Meltdown," then "Breaking Glass," then "You, Baby, Too." They switched mood, they swapped leads—nothing broke the energy, the flow, it just kept coming and coming—

The next song was Jason's and the last of the set; all Dave had to do on this was lay down his guitar line and go with the flow. He was sweating like a racehorse, and feeling like a god—and when he *finally* really looked at the others to see if *they* were feeling the same way, Jack gave him a thumb's up and the wickedest grin he'd ever seen in his life. He volleyed the grin right back, and turned to Jason and Doug—

—and felt a cold chill walk down his spine.

Jason had lost the glasses somewhere; Doug was in shadow. Their eyes were closed—Jason's *and* Doug's. Doug was backed off right behind the lead, like his bodyguard; head down, and cranking that bass to her limits—Jason, face streaming sweat, hair plastered down to his skull, crooned into the microphone, bathed in a single golden spot.

They both wore exactly the same expression, right down to the quirk at the corners of their mouths—and it was that expression that made Dave's blood chill.

They were feeling that energy, no doubt of it. They wore the same expressions they wore after they'd just been laid. Sated, and no little smug.

But—they still looked hungry. Like they wanted *more*.

A *lot* more.

———

But there was no time to think of it; they were in the break room barely long enough to get drinks and dry off a little, then the crowd *pulled* them back out onto the stage just by sheer force of their collective will.

It can't be that good again, Dave thought, as Jack began to pound the solo intro to the next set. *It was a fluke. We've never done anything like that before—*

Then Doug and Jason hammered down, and the impossible happened.

It *wasn't* that good again. It was better.

The four of them were like pieces of a single machine; they'd toss changes at each other and no one ever missed his catch. They took a little longer rest this time; Jack had to have one, he'd played like he had eight arms up there, and one more song might have sent him into cardiac arrest. And Jason lay right flat down on the concrete floor, trying to dump some of the heat from his body. But within twenty minutes they were back out on the stage again, and it was like they'd never left it.

The manager finally had to get the bouncer to drive people out at closing. Nobody wanted to leave.

Dave tried the same trick with the floor that Jason had, hoping to leech the warmth out of his overheated body before he broiled; God, it was wonderful, feeling that cold concrete suck the heat right out of him. The club manager showed up at the door of the break room and started babbling; Dave groaned, and opened his eyes, and gave him the look that said *Not now—* but the guy wasn't taking that answer, and he started to lever himself up onto his elbow—

"I'll take care of this—"

The tone was commanding, even arrogant, and Jason rose up out of his chair like Apollo rising from the Sun-throne—

And suddenly there was a perceptible shift in balances.

Everybody froze for a moment, even the club manager. Only

Jason moved, and only his eyes, which went to Dave's and locked with them.

Dave had seen that look before; from one gang member challenging for supremacy, from the beta wolf going for the alpha, from a stallion claiming another's herd.

Are you going to fight me for this?

Up until now, Dave had been the de facto leader of the band, mostly because nobody else wanted to be the one to make the bookings and give the orders. But suddenly there was a new set of priorities, and the world skewed about 90 degrees.

Do I want to fight him on this? Dave asked himself, and met those hard gray eyes—

Then looked away.

No. No, it's not worth it. Jason wants the hat, Jason can have it.

He lay back down on the concrete, but not before he had seen Jason's eyes narrow and then glint in satisfaction.

Dave closed his eyes and heard two pairs of feet walking away toward the manager's office. About ten minutes later, one pair came back. He opened his eyes, and saw Jason standing over him, with a dark bottle in one hand, offering the hand that wasn't holding a bottle.

"Lay there too long and you'll stiffen up," the blond said.

He took the hand and Jason hauled him to his feet without any effort at all, which surprised the hell out of Dave. He'd never suspected that much strength in that lanky body.

"So what's up?" Doug asked, as Jason grabbed a Coke, drank half of it, and poured dark amber liquid back into the bottle. Dave sniffed, caught the heavy scent of rum.

Not a bad idea. He swigged down half his Coke, snagged the bottle of rum, and followed Jason's example. He cast a glance sideways at both Doug and Jack as he did so; they seemed to have adjusted smoothly to "Jason as leader" instead of "Dave as leader." He wasn't sure whether to be annoyed or relieved.

"Needless to say," Jason said with heavy irony, "Clemson is

pleased. I made money noises; he caved in. I made extension noises; he'd have given us till 2092 if I'd asked for it. I didn't, but I *did* let him talk me into staying on until after New Year's—"

Dave frowned. "Is that a good idea?" he said. "If we jam even *half* as good as we did tonight—"

"We will," Jason cut in, with a smile of complete satisfaction on his lips. "This is just the beginning."

"All right, then—we could fill a place *twice* the size of this, once word gets around"

"That," Jason replied, reaching across the space between them and tapping the table with his forefinger for emphasis, "is *just* the point, bro. We *could*—yeah, and we'd be competing with uptown names. But if we *stay* here—those people out there are gonna talk, and they'll bring their friends, and their friends will do the same—before long, there's gonna be a *line* to get into this joint, and that line is gonna get longer—and *that* is gonna bring in the media, and the high rollers—and who else?"

"Producers—" Dave breathed.

"Dig it. Scouts, execs, managers—all wanting to see what in hell is making people stand in line in *November* for God's sake. So they get in here—and we're on *our* turf, right? Not some pricey uptown gig, but this dive where our flash don't look like trash. You readin' me?"

"Loud and clear." *Jason, baby, you want it, you got it. No way am I gonna fight you when your brain just got up and kicked into warp drive.*

Jason leaned back in his flimsy chair and swigged rum and Coke with a grin, then threw his head back and shook all his hair out of his eyes.

"Gentlemen," he announced to the ceiling, "this band is on the move."

FOUR

Morning finally crawled across the city; a gray, grim morning that was just about gloomy enough to match Di's depression. She didn't want to get up—but she didn't have much choice.

And lying here isn't going to accomplish anything, either.

Fighting off a panic attack always left her emotionally, mentally drained. She'd had to fight off attacks three times last night. Now she didn't have much left to run on except nervous energy.

The alarm had jarred her out of enervated paralysis; her heart raced, pounding in her ears. It finally calmed enough that she could breathe freely after a few minutes. Showering was a matter of fatigue-fog and constantly looking over her "shoulder." She brushed out her waist-length hair; tied it into a tail, then bundled herself into a gray sweater and bleached-out gray pants that had once been black. Breakfast was a disaster. She didn't pay much attention to what she was doing, and set the toaster too high. As a result she burned the toast, but it didn't matter, she didn't taste it anyway.

I'd like to be invisible. She tasted fear again when her gut realized she was going to go *out there.* Where whatever had killed the boy waited still.

After several minutes of screwing up her courage, she left the dubious haven of her apartment for the uncertainty of the streets.

She paused at the stop of the steps for a quick scan of the neighborhood, but there was nothing out of the ordinary. Cold drizzle—a scant degree from being snow—wept greasily on her, penetrating her coat and chilling her until the bones of her wrists and ankles ached.

Physical aches came as a welcome distraction.

Guess I'd better get a move on.

She trotted most of the way to the subway station; she was sweating when she got there, but it wasn't enough to warm her, not *inside*, not where it counted.

The subway ride was a test of endurance, spent in a wash of sullen misery from the passengers around her. Shields that were normally adequate to keep her well insulated from empathic miasma had been thinned by the stresses of last night; they were barely good enough to keep the psychic muttering down to background noise. She hung to the overhead bar and made herself as small as possible. Tried to be inconspicuous. Tried to feel less afraid.

And tried not to breathe too much.

Her stomach churned with unease, and almost anything could set nausea off. Inside the swaying subway car, the odor of wet wool battled with perspiration, stale urine, and beer for ascendancy. Twice somebody stepped on her foot; once somebody tried to pick her pocket. Since she'd long ago learned to carry her purse inside her coat, all he got was a Salvation Army wallet full of pieces of newspaper and cardboard. This morning it certainly didn't seem worth the effort to try and stop him.

The street was quiet, with only other shopkeepers fighting the miserable weather. She opened the shop with her mind only half on the tricky lock; the rest of her stayed alert for possible danger until she was safely within the shelter of the shop's shielding. But nothing happened, not then—and not for the rest of the day.

She spent the hours that dragged by in self-recrimination and entirely alone. Not one customer, not even a teenybopper, and not one telephone call.

It happened that way, sometimes. With a store that sold things so esoteric, customers came at uncertain intervals. You couldn't close it, because you never knew when the stranger, the out-of-towner, would come in and buy something that would make the rent for the rest of the week.

Not a good situation when what she needed was company. And that idleness gave her plenty of leisure to examine last night in rerun, and find a hundred new things she had done wrong. Finally, mental and physical exhaustion drove her into a dull lethargy in which nothing seemed to matter. She was too depressed to be hungry, so the lunch hour came and went without her noticing. Even the weird radio story about a dead bus driver ferrying around a load of even deader passengers couldn't claim more than a few moments of her attention.

Until the phone interrupted the thin voice of the afternoon radio concert with its shrilling.

She started, her heart sent into overdrive. It shrilled again, and she caught it before the second ring was over. "Bell, Book, and—"

"Di? Di, is that you?"

She blinked. *Is it—it's Lenny—I think—*

"Di, it's Len—" He confirmed her guess, and he sounded panicked, hysterical. "It *is* you, isn't it? Di?"

"Len?" she replied, her brain still responding in slow motion. "Yeah, it's me. What—"

"Di, Di, you've gotta help me, please, I don't care what you do, you've gotta get over here and—"

Oh gods; the magic words, "you've gotta help me." I have one disaster on my hands already. I have one enemy—maybe after me—now. Unless this is related—

But the goad of Lenny's fear, of those words, was clearing her brain of fatigue-poison and fear-clouds. "Whoa, slow down a minute, Len—" She broke into his babbling. "What's happened? Where are you?"

"The morgue. Downtown."

"The *what?*" She nearly lost the handset in surprise. "You're *where?* Why? What's happened?"

"That bus, you know, the one last night, Keith's ex was on it, and he still had a card with Keith's name on it as emergency number—"

She concentrated as hard as she could; when Lenny got either drunk or freaked he tended to slur his words together and his accent got a lot thicker. When that happened, she couldn't always make out what he was saying through that Southern twang.

"The police called Keith and Keith called me, he said he couldn't face it alone, and I said okay and I understood and we went over here together and they pulled out the—and gods, Di, you've *gotta* get over here—the—I Saw something, I mean I used Sight and I *didn't* See and—"

His voice was rising with every word, and started to crack on the high notes; it was pretty obvious that *he* was teetering on the ragged edge. And that very loss of control on his part, oddly enough, gave her control back, and energy.

"Lenny—" she said, trying to get his attention; then, when he kept babbling, added the force of command-voice and will. "*Lenny.* Ground, boy. Slow down. One word at a time. What did you See?"

There was an audible gulp on the other end of the line. "*Didn't* See," he corrected, speaking slowly. "The soul—it wasn't there—oh gods—"

"Of course it wasn't there—" she began, reasonably.

"Gods, no, that's *not what I mean!*" He was getting increasingly shrill again, and she judged that she wasn't going to get any sense out of him over a phone line.

"Look, *stay* where you are," she told him. "I'll be there as fast as I can. Okay? Don't freak out on me. Okay?"

He took a long, shuddering breath. "Okay," he replied, voice trembling. "Okay."

"Don't leave."

"Okay."

She hung up; glanced at her watch and shrugged. Three-thirty.

No customers all day, not likely to be any now.

Besides, it gave her an excuse to think about someone else's problem.

And maybe—maybe the two were linked.

She grabbed her damp coat, shut everything down, flipped the sign over to "Closed," and headed out.

They weren't actually in the morgue itself, but in the waiting room; a place of worn linoleum, plastic chairs, and too-bright fluorescent lights. A room that tried to be impersonal but smelled of formaldehyde and grief.

The two young men sat side by side in cheap, hard, vacuum-formed plastic chairs. They weren't in physical contact with each other, although Di could see in the way he held himself Lenny's longing to touch Keith, to hold him and comfort him. And some of it leaked past her shielding; a longing so intense it carried over even the mingled swirls of fear and shock that she felt coming from him.

She had to reinforce her shield against him immediately. He was too close to her, his emotion was too strong; he was just too raw to handle. Keith was easier to deal with; purely and simply mourning. He slumped in his scarred gray chair with his elbows on his knees, hands dangling, head hanging, staring at the scratched and gouged floor.

Lenny looked up the moment she entered, and revived a little, his eyes taking on the pathetic brightness of a lost child sighting his parent.

And she could tell that was *all* he was thinking about.

Uh-oh. He's not going to watch his mouth.

She took a quick look around for possible eavesdroppers. The swarthy attendant was talking quietly to a cop; he glanced up at her curiously as she passed his desk.

"I'm with them," she said, pausing a moment, and indicating the pair at the end of the waiting room with a wave of her hand. "Lenny called me; he sounded a little unhinged so I said I'd get them home."

The attendant nodded in a preoccupied manner and returned his attention to the cop, dismissing her into the category of "not part of my job."

Lenny jumped to his feet and started stuttering something as soon as she got within speaking distance; she hushed him and took a seat between him and Keith. The artist's long, dark hair and black sweater would have made him look pale under the best of conditions, and the fluorescent lights washed color out of everything—but he was *white,* and when Di touched his hand, she got a distinct impression of "nobody home."

"Keith—"

He didn't respond, so she risked an exercise of Power and sent a little tingle, like an empathic spark, through the point where she touched his hand. He jumped, jarred back into reality, and looked at her sharply in surprise.

"Keith, are you going to be all right?" She pitched her voice in such a way that the question balanced equally between sounding concerned and sounding a little impatient. He blinked, and chewed on his lip—but then he looked over her shoulder and must have seen the strange expression Lenny was still wearing, and his eyes widened.

"Yeah, I—yeah. It's just—hard—"

She softened her tone and squeezed his hand. "That's okay, kiddo—I just don't need both of you falling apart in public on me. Wait until I get you home—"

She didn't wait for his reply, but turned back to Lenny; he was perched on the edge of his chair, hands clasped, face even whiter than Keith's. "Now, tell me slowly. One word at a time. What's wrong? What happened?"

He took a long, long breath, a breath that trembled and ended in a choked-off whimper. "You know I've got Sight," he whispered.

She nodded; the fluorescent fixture above her head flickered and buzzed annoyingly.

"Something didn't seem right so I, so I invoked Sight. I thought maybe Tom was hanging around, trying to tell me something. Like when Jo-Bob keeled over at rehearsal with a coronary. You remember—"

She frowned at him, thinking only that invoking Sight in a morgue full of bodies, mostly dead by violence, was probably one of the most outstandingly stupid things Lenny had ever done. He winced when he saw the frown, and said defensively, "I shielded! I'm not an idiot!"

She kept the reply she wanted to make—about not being so sure of *that*—purely mental. "Go on."

He closed his eyes and began to shake. "I, I Saw something. A hole. A hole where there shouldn't have been one. A—I don't *know*, but it wasn't like Jo-Bob, or my gramps, or the guy in the drugstore when I was a kid—not like somebody who properly died and the soul left—it was like the soul was torn out when the body died! And, and there's no *trace* of Tom anywhere—"

"Whoa—" She cut him off so that he couldn't spiral off into hysteria again. "Let me go have a Look for a minute. There's probably a good explanation."

Five minutes with the attendant convinced him to let her into the morgue. She managed to spin a realistic enough story that he didn't bother to check on her claim of being Tom's sister. Thirty seconds with the body, and she was as white as Lenny and just as close to hysteria.

Because he had been right. Something had killed Tom, but torn his soul out of him before he had properly "died"—and there were none of the traces that would have shown where the soul had gone.

Which meant it had been destroyed.

She managed to maintain an outward, completely false shell of calm all the way out to the waiting room; managed to call a cab and get both young men into it. Managed even to get them all into her apartment.

Then *she* had hysterics, but only when she had locked herself into the bathroom. And only after she had turned on the water in the sink to cover the sound of her own moaning.

This *was* a panic attack, and one she couldn't hold off; she knew the symptoms only too well.

She couldn't control herself, no more than she could have when that *thing* came hunting her and caught her alone, and offguard.

Nightflyer; that's what she'd found out it was called later. Much later. After it had almost killed her. After she'd found out the hard way that there were things too tough for her.

It had been a long time before she'd learned to sleep with the lights off again.

Once again her subconscious had decided she'd met another creature as bad as the Nightflyer.

Once again her body wanted to grovel and give up, held her prisoner in a sea of fear.

She hadn't had an attack for a long time, not since before she'd come to New York—

She'd managed to keep from having one yesterday.

That wasn't stopping her from having one now.

I can't do it. I can't do it. I can't handle this and it's going to come after me—

She huddled on the bathroom rug, hugging herself, rocking back and forth, and whimpering, tears streaming down her face. She was shivering so hard she couldn't stand, her heart was racing. Her mouth was dry, but her hands were sweating.

All the—the classic signs. Oh gods. Oh gods. I can't face this thing.

The bathroom was *the* most heavily warded room in the apartment; it was tiled floor to ceiling in sea-green porcelain, and all clay products held a charge as readily as anything man-made could. But the heavy wardings could not guard her against her own mind—

Only she could do that. And she *had* to. She was a Guardian. There was something out there that only a Guardian could handle. It would come for her if it got the chance—and she had been asked for help against it.

Time to pay the rent.

If she could just keep from falling apart.

She knelt on the tiny braided rag rug, bent over her knees, with her head hidden in her arms.

Breathe. Slow. Center. Oh gods.

Gradually the trembling stopped, and the tears; slowly her control began to return.

Think. You're not helpless. Whatever did that, it has to have enemies, vulnerability. You'll find its weak spot. Whatever it is, it's mortal. There was no trace of the Otherworld there. If it's mortal and vulnerable, it can be dealt with, destroyed if necessary. And you're not the only Guardian in the city. If you have to have help, you can get it. There's that guy in Queens, and Rhona in Jersey and Karl in Harlem—

Just the bare thought that there were other Guardians was comforting. No matter that Karl was in the hospital with a broken ankle, Rhona was seventy-odd, and the guy in Queens wouldn't leave his house if he could help it. For something that could destroy a soul, if it proved out that Di alone couldn't handle it, he'd find the courage to leave his house, Karl would grab crutches, ignore his pain and rise up out of his bed, and Rhona would have the strength of a teenager. Because if they had to, like Di, they would deal with it.

They won't have to. I'll handle it.

She had no choice, really, because Di *was* the youngest and the least handicapped of them all—and the best at troubleshooting. That meant she had *damned* well better do what she could on her own, first—

But that's all it means. If I really need them, they'll come—

Even if they kill themselves doing so. No. I can control myself. I can, and I will. I can handle this thing. It's been handed to me, and I can handle it.

She took three deep, slow breaths, and straightened from her crouch, tossing her hair back over her shoulder. *I won't have them on my conscience.*

She grabbed the cold, slick edge of the sink and hauled herself to her feet, biting her lip—her feet had been asleep and now they tingled and burned as life came back into them. She averted her eyes from the mirror.

No sleep last night, no makeup this morning, and now a crying jag. I probably look like I was buried two days ago.

She reached for the faucet and turned the water off; dipped a washcloth in the icy water still in the basin, and swabbed the tearstreaks off her face. She looked carefully into the mirror. Bags under the eyes, and white as a sheet, but not looking likely to break again.

I've looked worse, she decided. *Besides, they're so shook they won't notice.*

When her feet stopped tingling, she unlocked the bathroom door, pulled it open, and went from there straight into the kitchen.

The minute she opened the door to the bathroom, she could feel the two young men in the living room; Lenny like a sea urchin with sharp spikes of distress all over him, Keith a dull, gray blob of sorrow. She walled them out as best she could—

But there was something oddly comforting about them being there, despite their own troubles.

I'm not sure I could have faced an empty apartment . . .

I haven't had any food but that toast, and I'll bet neither have they. And there's something I need to be able to think this out— something I need a lot more than just food.

After a couple of false starts, moments that had her clinging to the counter and shaking, she managed to find three reasonably sized tumblers—and the bottle of vodka. And the frozen orange juice.

Damned if I'm going to think about this sober.

While the blender whirred, she cut up some cheese and half a loaf of French bread that was supposed to have gone up to the spaghetti party and hadn't. The orange juice went into a plastic pitcher that had seen much better days; the tumblers each acquired a few ice cubes. She brought it all out on a tray and plumped it down on the table in front of the couch. The two faces turned toward her wore such identical expressions of puzzlement that she would have laughed if she'd had the energy after her own bout with hysteria.

"Di—what—" Lenny stammered, looking from her to the glasses and back again.

"Gentlemen," she replied solemnly. "I have a proposition."

"W-what is it?"

She poured herself a *very* stiff screwdriver, took the armchair, and seated herself in it with care. "I propose," she said, after pausing for a long swallow, grimacing at the bitter undertaste, "that we get very, very drunk. Because at the moment there is nothing we can do. And because if we get very, very drunk, we might be able to come up with some kind of an answer—or at least a place to start asking questions."

Yuki pulled her coat collar up a little higher, shivering as the frigid wind curled around the back of her neck. She'd only had the Sassoon cut for a week and already she was sorry—her hip-length hair might have been a stone bitch to take care of, but at least it had kept the back of her neck warm!

And it was a *long* walk to the bus stop. Especially in the winter. *Most* especially in this micromini. There was nothing between her legs and the cold wind but her tights and boots. There were times—

But you couldn't work the kickiest boutique in the Apple wearing a *pantsuit* for God's sake. Not looking like some old lady from the Bronx. And jeans wouldn't do either. Not when Greg was such a leg man.

There *was* a stop right in front of the boutique, but taking that route meant a long ride in the wrong direction and a transfer, and a total of almost an hour and a half on buses. Whereas a fifteen-minute walk—if she hustled her buns—took her to the bus she *wanted*.

Just—it was dark, and cold, and at this hour, mostly deserted. You could probably shoot an M-16 down this street and not kill anybody right now.

She winced away from *that* unbidden thought. The war was over. Tricky Dicky had made one bold, bad move too many. There wouldn't be any more M-16's. No more Nams.

The wind moaned through the man-made cavern between the buildings and wrapped around her legs, and the streetlight just ahead of her flickered and went out. She shivered again, and this time not from cold.

They hadn't had but a handful of customers all day, and Greg evidently hadn't had enough Halloween. He'd started in on some real spooky stories that he swore had happened to people he knew—and when *he* ran out, he started teasing the others into telling ghostly tales. When Yuki's turn came, she'd tried to get out of it—but Greg had been insistent, and he was *so* foxy—it was impossible to resist him for long.

"You know Japanese ghost stories, don't you?" he'd asked coaxingly. "Things your grandma used to scare you with so you'd be a good little girl?" He'd winked at her over the shirts he was putting up.

"Well—"

She hadn't fought much, truth to tell. The stories had seemed so impossible in the well-lit boutique, with black-light Peter Max posters everywhere and rock music going as a background. And it had been a way to keep Greg's attention on her, and a way to keep from dying of boredom with nothing to do but put out new stock. But now—now she was beginning to be sorry she'd given in to him.

"I always did have too much imagination," she muttered, trying to bury her chin in her collar.

There was *no one* on the street, and still she could have sworn somebody was following her. Twice she whipped around to look behind her; in both cases the street behind her was just as empty as the street in front of her, which made her feel *really* stupid. Nothing in sight but blowing papers and the occasional headlights of cars at the intersections.

"Halloween jitters," she told herself aloud.

But the emptiness of the half-lit street, full of shadows and hundreds of places to hide, only contributed to her nervousness. It *should* have been reassuring and utterly normal; she knew every crack in the sidewalk, after all, she walked this way every night. But it wasn't; the echoes that were coming off the alleys were distorted tonight, and the way the streetlights kept flickering made those shadows look as if they were going to solidify and take on life. It didn't seem like the street she knew, but like something out of *Night Gallery*.

She kept glancing up, she couldn't help herself; she didn't really *expect* to see Flying Heads lurking on the windowsills above her—but she wouldn't have been surprised to find them up there.

"Bad drugs. God, I've *got* to stop letting Sasha talk me into going to parties with him."

She was speaking aloud just to hear something besides the warped echoes of her own footsteps on the pavement. Her spine was crawling, for once again she could *feel* something behind her—and she was afraid, even as she scoffed at her fear, that if she turned around this time, she'd see a black cloud rolling down the street toward her, against the wind.

It wouldn't *be* a cloud, though; it would be the hunting form of a *gaki*.

She swallowed, and picked up her pace, the chunky heels of her boots making her feel a little unbalanced. *Gakis* were myths, no more real than Dracula. By day she could laugh at them. But in the deserted street—she couldn't laugh at them now. She had taken Greg a little too literally. *Those* were the stories that had kept her huddled in her bed at night, afraid even to go to the bathroom. The stories about *gakis,* the demons who could take the form of anyone they had slain—

"Dammit, those are just bogeyman stories!" she said, trying to talk some sense into herself. "There's *nothing* in them!"

—and when feeding took the form of a cloud of dense black smoke with eyes—a cloud that violated the rules of nature blithely, which was the only way you could tell what it was. The hunter who saw the smoke from his campfire acting oddly, the monk who noticed that the incense was not drifting away on the wind, the traveler encountering an unexpected patch of fog that refused to disperse—all those had been the heroes—or victims—of her grandmother's stories.

And a city the size of this one, with all the hiding places it contained, would make such a perfect hunting ground for a demon—especially one that could look like a cloud of smog.

She started at the sound of footsteps behind her; but she didn't turn around this time. That wasn't an echo of her own tread back there, keeping pace with her. There *was* someone following her, now.

And there wasn't a cop in sight.

Fear suddenly leapt out of her gut and into her throat. It had a life of its own, and she couldn't control it. It took over her body, and made her legs slow, and she found she *could not* get them to move any faster.

She glanced behind her; yes, there *was* a man back there, muffled in a dark overcoat with his face in shadow. Just seeing him back there gave the fear a little more control over her, made her knees go to water, slowed her pace further, until she felt as if she were forcing her way through glue. Even more frightening, she got the distinct impression that the man was matching his speed to hers, that he was toying with her.

The third time she looked back, she wanted to scream—but it only came out a strangled sob. She had been wrong. There wasn't *one* man tailing her—there were *two*.

And they *weren't* together.

She faltered—and broke; the fear took over her thinking, and she lurched into a wobbling run. With the high heels of her boots catching on the cracks in the sidewalk, she stumbled and caught herself before she fell into the wall. She paid no attention to where she was going; she couldn't really see, in any case. Fear skewed everything, made it all as surreal as a nightmare and she couldn't recognize her own surroundings anymore. She made a quick right turn, thinking she was finally on a street that had a regular cop on the beat—

And wound up staring stupidly at a blank brick wall. This wasn't a street at all, it was a cul-de-sac, and she was trapped.

She whirled and put her back against the brick, as footsteps told her that her first pursuer was rounding the corner.

Now she could see him; tall, swarthy, his complexion sallow in the yellowish light of the street lamp above her. A gust of wind blew paper past his legs. He smiled, but it was not a friendly smile, it was the smile of a hunter who had finally cornered his prey after an invigorating run. His eyes were dark, and so deeply sunk into their sockets that they looked like the eyeless holes in a skull; his mouth was cruel, with full, sensuous lips.

She was so terrified that she could hardly breathe. Her heart raced, and she fought against a faint—he smiled again, and licked his lips with the tip of his tongue, a gesture that was somehow repellent and voluptuous.

Then the sound of a second set of feet on the pavement behind him turned the smile into a feral snarl, and he pivoted to face the newcomer in a crouch.

She could still see the face of her hunter in profile—and that of the man who had interrupted whatever it was the first had intended to do to her. And as the second man stepped fully into the light, she began to hope.

Though he wore the studded black leather of a street-gang member, he was Japanese.

She started to speak; to stammer out something about being glad to see him, to try to pull an "us against the WASPs" number on him—but the words stuck in her throat.

Because he was watching her with a faint smile of amusement; a superior sort of smile that told her he had *no* interest in helping her. The smile broadened as he saw her read him correctly, and turned into one identical to the smile the man had worn—the look of the hunter, with the prey trapped in a corner and in easy striking distance.

He ignored the other man, whose snarl had turned to a frown of perplexity.

Then the first man straightened, and stood aside with a mocking bow—and she saw with dumb surprise that his perplexity had given way to a look of extreme amusement. The young man gave him a wary, sidelong glance—

And slowly began dissolving, becoming a dense cloud of dark smoke.

She choked, her hands scrabbling at the bricks behind her as she tried to press herself into them. This was, literally, her worst nightmare come true. She was face-to-face with a *gaki,* and one who, by his actions, could only be one of the three kinds of *gakis* that killed—those who devoured the blood, those who devoured only living flesh—or, worst of all—those who devoured the soul.

She had paid no attention to the other man, who had moved toward her as the *gaki* had begun to change. Now, as her knees finally gave out on her and she began to slip to the pavement, his hand shot out and grabbed her shoulder, crushing down on it with a cruel, hard grip that kept her from moving.

The cloud drifted closer; it still had eyes, and a kind of sketched-in caricature of a human face. The lips stretched in a suggestion of a grin. Only the eyes were clear, the sulfur-yellow eyes. The demon-eyes. The *gaki's* yellow eyes switched from her to the man and back again, and she wondered if the thing was going to take *both* of them.

If it went for the first man, would she have a chance to escape?

The man spoke, practically in her ear. "A moment—"

She yelped, started, and the man's hand held her in her place, shoving her against the rough brick of the wall, with the bricks prickling the backs of her thighs. His voice was deep and harsh, and it had the tone of someone who was accustomed to being obeyed.

"I think," he said, as the cloud paused, and the face in the cloud seemed to take on an expression of surprise, "that we seek something similar, but not identical, you and I. I think that if it were to come to a conflict, we would both lose."

The face vanished for a moment in a billow of the smoke, then returned. The face seemed less a sketch and more solid, and it was definitely frowning thoughtfully.

"I think," the man continued, as her shoulder grated beneath his hand, "that perhaps we might come to an accommodation. Could we not be—allies?"

The face vanished again, and the clouds billowed and churned. Silent tears poured down Yuki's face, blurring her vision; tears of complete hopelessness. She was doomed, and knew it. There was no trace of humanity in either of these—creatures. Unlike the heroes of the stories, there would be no Shinto priest or ronin versed in magic to rescue her.

Finally the cloud condensed—

And once again the young man stood a few yards away, just within the cone of light cast by the street lamp. He pondered them both, his face as impassive as a stone Buddha, with his head held slightly to one side.

"Perhaps," he said, after a silence that stretched on for years. Yuki moaned—which brought his attention back to her.

And he *smiled* at her.

This was an entirely different kind of smile than the first; it was *horrible*, it was like being eaten alive and hearing your devourer make little noises of appreciation while he ate you, and it made her fear leap up and take control over everything—

And it froze her in place so completely that she couldn't have moved to run even if the way had been clear and a cop car in sight.

The *gaki* looked back at her captor, and blinked twice, his eyes glowing a sullen sulfur. "Perhaps," he repeated, and nodded. "Would you care to discuss the possibility . . . over dinner?"

It's A Beautiful Day sang something that was probably deeply meaningful if you were stoned instead of drunk. Overhead someone was practicing piqué turns, and falling off pointe every so often. Just out of reach, Lenny and Keith were still in full possession of Di's couch. The couch tended to sag in the middle, and the more they drank, the more they leaned toward each other. They probably didn't even realize they were doing it.

Di cleared her throat. "I've got an idea—"

Both sets of bleary male eyes turned toward her.

"Let's have another drink. I can still tell which foot is mine."

"Oh, Di—" Lenny groaned. "We're *supposed* to be—"

"Drinking." She held up her glass and studied it for a moment. The ice was holding up all right. "I told you I *wasn't* going to think about this sober."

"Why not?" he retorted. "*You* always told me that you have to have a clear head to do occult work."

She'd had just enough to be honest, and too much to keep her mouth shut. "Because I'm too scared to think about this sober. I'm on the edge, Len. On the ragged edge. I've already had one panic attack, and I'm trying to hold off another one. Okay?"

Lenny's eyes widened, and he moved a little closer to Keith. Keith gave her a look that showed no understanding of what she'd said. She ignored both reactions and poured herself another stiff one. She'd stopped tasting the vodka two drinks ago, which meant she was *almost* drunk enough to analyze the situation without triggering another panic attack.

Someday maybe I won't have to do this. But right now—She tossed it down.

Keith had demolished two to every one of Lenny's, matching Di drink for drink, and with as much reason, given the level of his grief and self-accusation. *He* was now numb enough that Di no longer had to wall him out so completely.

When this is over I have to talk him through all the guilt he's feeling about Tom—

Gods. I hope I'm around and in one piece.

He leaned forward a little, and fixed Di with an unfocused stare. "Diana?" he said, hesitation making his voice soft, vodka blurring it. "Diana, I don't understand—"

"You don't understand what?" She ate an ice cube, taking out some of her frustration by crunching angrily down on it.

"Why you're so upset. *You* didn't know Tom, so that's not it. And Len didn't know him well enough to get so—so hissy-fit—" He licked his lips, and looked at her with anxiety overcoming the alcohol. "So it has to be something else. That *other* stuff. Like the thing in my studio?"

"Yeah, sort of." She slumped a bit farther down in her chair.

"Is that why you're afraid?"

She pointed an armed finger at him, and fired it. "Bingo. I don't know what it was, or how to deal with it—and I *have* to."

Fortunately he didn't ask why. He studied *his* glass. "There was something wrong. It didn't feel right. I knew it when they brought me in there. Then Len"—his right hand reached for Lenny's left, and found and held it, without his seeming to be aware of the fact—"acted like somebody'd just dropped a box of spiders on him. Then *you* freaked out." He looked up at her with a hint of defiance. "Are you going to tell *me* what pulled your chain?"

"You won't believe it," she replied, without thinking.

"I believed in the thing in my studio. I *know* that you got rid of it. Why shouldn't I believe you now?"

"Because—because I'm not sure I believe it."

"Try me," he said. Lenny shivered.

She decided she was drunk enough now. "Something—something destroyed his soul."

He looked at her with his eyes getting bigger and bigger, his face getting paler and paler—and abruptly he reached for the bottle and poured himself a double-strength drink, gulping it down as fast as he had poured it.

Beautiful Day gave way to Buffalo Springfield. Di sighed, and tilted her head to look straight at Lenny. "What do *you* think?" she asked.

He shook his head. "I don't *want* to think. I don't want to know anything about something that could destroy a soul."

"Neither do I," she confessed gloomily, staring at the empty glass in her hand. Not even a panic attack was going to get through that much vodka. "Not really."

"I mean, think of the *power* it had to have."

"Yeah. And *how?* How did it *do* that?"

Lenny squeezed his eyes closed, solemnly clicked the heels of his sneakers together, and just as solemnly intoned, "There's no place like home. There's no place like home. There's—"

"How could something eat a soul?" Keith interrupted, utterly bewildered, in his blurred state not making a distinction between being "destroyed" and being "eaten." "Why would anything want to?"

Lenny began to giggle, still too near hysteria. "Fillet of soul, anyone?"

Di squelched the threatening hysterics with a glance. "I didn't say 'eaten,' I—" She sat straight up in her chair; not an easy feat, since she had been sitting in it sideways with her legs draped over the arms. In faithful counterpoint, Lenny had echoed her movement a fraction of a second behind her.

"Soul-eaters!" he exclaimed, before she could say anything. "Ye gods. *Those* I know about!"

"The library—" She scrambled out of her chair, and wobbled to the workroom; he stopped only long enough to pull a very bewildered Keith to his feet, and followed on her heels.

"Egyptian—" she heard him call out as she snapped on the light. "Dibs on Egyptian."

"Grab the easy one. All right; I'll check the Celts."

She began pulling books down, scanning the indices, and putting aside those that mentioned soul-eaters. Lenny, who had secretly yearned to be an archaeologist, got the *Egyptian Book of the Dead* down and launched into a detailed explication of the Eater of Souls to Keith. Lenny tended to pontificate when drunk.

Di put up with it for ten minutes, then interrupted. "Lenny," she called sharply. "Can it."

"But—"

"I said, can it. I've got a lot of books, and I've checked ten while you've been blathering."

"I wasn't—" he replied.

"You were. Ten minutes' worth."

He shut up and got back to work.

Five A.M. and they had a list—a very *short* list, but Di's library was nowhere near as extensive as the one in the shop—and they had come to the end of the books. Di put the last of them back on the shelf.

She turned back to the other two.

Keith was sitting on a stool they'd brought in from the kitchen; he knew shorthand, so he'd been made secretary once he was sober enough to take notes. Lenny was looking over his shoulder and making a face at the scrawls on his notepad.

Di felt her nervous energy beginning to fade. After all that frenzied activity—

"Now what?" she asked aloud. Lenny looked up; Keith frowned at his notes.

"What do you mean?" Lenny replied, after sneezing, and rubbing his nose with a dusty finger.

"Okay, we've got a list—but a list of *what?* Of all the mythical and semimythical things on it, which one is *real?* And—what are we going to do with what we've got?"

Lenny bristled. "Are you thinking of giving this up? Leaving something like *that* loose in the city? How many of our friends is it gonna eat before you're willing to do something? Or are you afraid to try?"

She shook her head. "No. No, of course not. But if we don't go at this logically, we're going to get nowhere."

"This list isn't that long," Lenny pointed out. "And since our killer isn't likely to be a god or a demigod, like the Egyptian Eater of Souls, well—I think we ought to go hunting. We ought to look for other kills like this one; we ought to look for psychic traces—"

She was about to interrupt him, to object that "looking for psychic traces" wasn't that easy, when Keith cleared his throat.

She looked at him in surprise; she'd forgotten he was still there.

"Even if Tommy and I broke up," he said, carefully, "we broke up still being friends." He glared at Di, as if he defied her to contradict him. "I want you to count me in on this."

Di raised one eyebrow. Her head was starting to ache, and she was glad that today was her day off. "You're drunk," she replied mildly.

Keith shrugged. "Sure. So are you. So's Len. Drunk or sober, count me in."

Di rubbed her head and sighed. "All right. You're in. We can use all the help we can get. I just hope you don't live to regret this."

FIVE

The bedside clock said five, and it sure as hell wasn't A.M. Dave opened his eyes a little farther, and winced away from the last red rays of the sun, light that was somehow leaking past the slats of his dusty venetian blinds, and groped on the nightstand for his sunglasses. The blankets were all in a knot; he must have been fighting them in his sleep again. He threw them off, sat up, and squinted at sunlight filtering past the blinds. Even with his shades on, it still seemed too bright; funny, only sunlight affected him that way. After the initial discomfort of the first gig after the party, stagelights gave him no trouble at all.

There was a hollow in the mattress beside where he'd been lying, but the little groupie he'd brought home was long gone; he'd made sure of that before he went to sleep. She hadn't liked it much, being hustled out the door like that; she'd wanted to snuggle and maybe go for another round—

But he kept seeing Tam in his mind's eye—

It has to have been a coincidence, he told himself again; it was getting to be a kind of litany, but he still hadn't quite managed to convince himself of its truth.

So out she went, and no amount of pouting made him change his mind.

He was still afraid—of what, he couldn't quite say, only that he was afraid he might *do something* to anyone who might be near him when he was asleep. Something awful.

Heebie jeebies. He ran his dry tongue over his dry teeth, shook his head a little, and caught his breath. As always, his head began pounding as soon as he moved, and his stomach was an aching void. He planted his feet on the cold floor, and sagged over his knees, willing both aches to stop.

His body wasn't cooperating.

His stomach growled; hunger so sharp it made him a little sick and light-headed—not a good combination on top of the pounding in his temples. He'd learned over the past week that nothing he ate would have any effect on his raging hunger. The only things that could keep him going were liquids; Coke, coffee as strong as he could brew it, coffee milkshakes. Sugar and milk and caffeine. Anything else just sat there, making him nauseous on top of hungry, like having a lump of frozen rock in his stomach.

So he reached out without looking up for the second thing he *always* grabbed when he came to; the can of Coke he'd left on the nightstand beside his sunglasses.

It was warm and acidic; that didn't matter. He poured the whole can down his dry throat in three long gulps, saving one last sip to wash down the bennies he kept beside the Coke.

In about twenty minutes, the sun was down and the bennies were doing their thing, making his blood dance and sparkle. His headache was fading, and he felt like he was going to live.

He tossed the glasses back onto the nightstand, then picked up his jeans off the floor beside the bed where he'd dropped them, and pulled them on, frowning at how they'd stretched. He belted them to keep them on, and began rummaging through his closet for a clean stage shirt. *Got to drop my laundry off,* he thought, wrinkling his nose at the stale smell of sweat rising from the hamper. Funny, how smells seemed so much stronger lately—bennies normally dulled your sense of smell, but—

Come to think of it, everything seemed sharper, more in focus this last week. The bells on his clothes seemed louder; the colors of the embroidery brighter.

There were vests, a lot of empty hangers, a couple sweats, but nothing he wanted to use on stage. Then in the back, *way* in the back, he found a fringed shirt he used to wear before he'd started putting on that weight. He pulled it out and frowned at it—it had been one of his favorites, with beads and Indian symbols all over it, and it had been made to fit skintight. Chicks had really gone for him when he wore it—and he didn't like to be reminded how much he'd let himself go.

Then again—he shrugged. *What the hell. Since I haven't been stuffing my face with junk food, maybe it fits me again. Even if it doesn't, maybe I can figure out something—*

He pulled it on, started to button it—and froze, with his hands on the third button.

It was loose.

Christ on a crutch—

He closed the closet door, slowly, and for the first time since Halloween, he had a good long look at himself in the mirror.

Christ on a crutch—

A near stranger stared back at him.

It wasn't just the shirt—and the jeans hadn't stretched. He must have lost twenty pounds the past week. He didn't look *bad*—not yet, anyway. But he sure looked different. Not quite strungout—he wasn't sure what to call the way he looked now. Wasted? No. Gaunt.

He turned away from the mirror and headed blindly into the kitchen; coffee was the first order of business. He made himself a pot, plopped himself into the metal folding chair next to the card table, and nursed his first cup—black as sin, with five spoons of sugar in it.

What in hell is happening to me?

He stared at the fluorescent light from the fixture overhead rippling across the surface of the coffee, and realized something else. *It isn't just me. It's all of us except Jack. I hadn't really thought about it, but Doug's lost as much weight as I have; Jason's lost more. None of us are showing at the club before the sun sets— except Jack. We're all wearing shades when we do show. From the way I've been seeing Jason and Doug chug drinks—*

He clenched his hands around the cup, then forced himself to relax; finally downed the last of the cup, and poured himself another. *God, I'm hungry enough to eat a—*

But the idea of solid food was revolting.

I might as well eat mud. Bennies help, a little; booze and drinks; and Coke—but the only time it ever really lets up is when the music's rolling and I'm grooving on the vibes.

Just thinking about the vibes—and the way the gigs had been going—warmed the coldness inside him a bit, and coaxed a little smile onto his face, and he began feeling a little more cheerful. *God. We're doing it. It's working. I thought there was no way we'd be able to repeat what we did the first night—but every night it gets better, tighter. Just gettin' higher every time we play.*

He thought about that for a moment. *It started right after Halloween, about the time I started feeling weirded out. Huh. Okay. Maybe it's not a coincidence. Maybe it's all tied together.* He nodded a little. *Okay. If this is what it took, this business of being strung out, to get the band to work—okay. That's okay. I can pay that. Oh yeah.*

He reached for the coffee, and found to his surprise that he'd drunk the last of the pot.

Oh well. I need to get on the road, anyway.

He bundled himself into his torn leather jacket, grabbed his gigbag, and headed out. His footsteps echoed up and down the empty staircase—and there was no doubt of it; his hearing *was* more sensitive than before. Down on the street, the streetlight rocked in the wind above him as he hailed a cab; no more buses for him, not now—

Besides, he thought wryly, as he slung himself into the patched seat and gave the cabby the direction to the club, *I'm savin' enough cash on what I'm not eating to pay for all the cabs I feel like taking!*

He sat back in the darkness, surrounded by the odor of old leather and cigarette and reefer smoke, and watched the back of the cabby's head. Sweet-sour smoke drifted around and through the driver's thatch of long hair. It crept into the back of the cab with Dave and when the cabby turned his head, Dave could see the red coal of his jay. *We've never been so hot. It's like a dream. Weeknights we're filling the place the minute they open the doors—weekends there's the line outside Jason was swearing we'd get. I never could pick up chicks before, not the way Jason and Doug could—now, if I go home alone, it's 'cause I'm the one that wants it that way.* He closed his eyes and sank a little deeper into the seat cushion, cradling his axe against his chest. *And when everything comes together up there and the vibes come up, and I'm grooving—damn. It's better than anything; sex, drugs, booze—it's like being a god.*

"Hey, man—you wanta wake up back there?"

He started up out of his reverie. The neon of the club sign flashed just outside the cab window. He popped the door, overtipped the cabby, and scrambled out into the freezing wind.

And no going around the back anymore, he thought, smiling to himself as the bouncer held the front door open for him, and two chicks giggled and wiggled their hips at him just inside. No time for that right now, though. There was barely enough time to get into the back and get warmed up.

Because they didn't warm up out front anymore, and they weren't suffering the cold concrete break room. *Now* they took their breaks and warmed up in the manager's paneled, carpeted office, and the manager had moved his desk into the break room.

Jack raised an eyebrow as he cruised in the door. "Took your time," he said sardonically, not missing a beat in his silent practice.

The drummer was alone in the sound-baffled room. "Looks like I'm the only one," Dave replied, unzipping the black nylon bag, taking his axe out, and uncoiling the electric cord lying neatly inside. "Unless—"

Jack shrugged; he didn't look worried, but then he never worried about anything much. "They ain't here, man. Dunno where they are. They'll show when they show."

Dave grimaced. "Probably stuck in traffic somewhere—Doug's got the van, right?" One of the first things they'd done with their newfound prosperity was to buy a used van for the heavier equipment.

"Yeah, that's—"

The door swung open, then knocked into the wall, interrupting him. Jason edged in, looking like nothing so much as a pile of flimsy white cardboard boxes with legs. He was followed by Doug, similarly laden. Doug kicked the door shut behind them.

Dave stared at the incongruous sight, and started to laugh. "What the hell is this?" he demanded. "You guys raid Bloomies, or something?"

Jason put his load down carefully on one of the cocktail chairs they'd "borrowed" from out front, and straightened up. His eyes had the gleam of excitement that Dave usually associated with a good set or a foxy chick.

"Better than that, man," Jason replied, his expression smug, gloating.

He picked up the first couple of boxes, checked something on the end, and tossed one to Dave.

"We're changing our image," the lead said, shaking his hair back over his shoulder, and nodding at the boxes. "This is the new gear."

"What image?"

Jason laughed. "That's it, man, we ain't *got* an image. Last night we looked like every other bar band in town. After tonight, they'll not only remember how we sound, they'll remember how we look. Go on, man, open it."

He did; broke the tape holding it together, pulled the lid off, and nearly dropped the box, contents and all.

"Shit."

Jason grinned.

He put the box down carefully and took out a pair of pants. He'd known from the aroma that hit him when the lid came off what they were, but the supple and unmistakable feel of the material in his hands still came as a shock. Leather. Black leather. *Expensive* black leather, soft as a kiss, and from the look of it, tailored to be just short of pornographically tight. He put them down *very* carefully. Those pants cost more than his entire wardrobe—

And how in hell had Jason managed to figure out what was going to fit him—especially given that he'd just lost twenty pounds?

Jason smirked at his expression. "This week's lady is a theatrical costumer," he gloated. "She designed this shit, and she doesn't *need* a tape measure."

Dave couldn't think of any way to respond to that, and waited for Jason's next trick.

Jason tossed him a second box; this one had soft shirts in it, also black, and the label said something about them being one hundred percent silk, dry-clean only.

Doug got up out of his chair with a smirk, and dropped a heavier box on top of the shirts. This one held black leather boots—and the label on the box was from an uptown shop that *only* did custom work. No mystery there—he and Doug wore the same size, and these babies were straight-leg. The mystery was how they paid for all this.

He put the boots on the floor and picked up one of the shirts; it had huge sleeves, some very subtle designs in black beads and sequins on the shoulders and back, and it was open to the waist. Sex on the hoof.

He put it all carefully back in its boxes. The van was one thing—

"Jason—" he began hesitantly.

"What the hell does this mean?" Jack interrupted, looking at the pants and boots with a frown of puzzlement on his face. "Are we moving to a biker bar or something?"

He doesn't get it—Dave realized. *He doesn't have a clue how much this stuff costs.*

Jason shook his head. "Nope, we're staying here. Just like I said, we need an image. This is a helluva lot better image than jeans and fringe—I promise you, chicks are gonna go wild for this gear."

There was something about his expression that made Dave very uncomfortable when he said that. This wasn't Jason's usual casual, cheerful carnality—there was something cruel, and yet overwhelmingly sensual, in his half-closed eyes—

"We're changing our name, too," the lead continued. "I had somebody come over from the store and got the drums redone this afternoon. Picked it all up on the way here."

Dave shrugged; he hadn't been in love with Wanderlust, anyway. From the quirk of Jack's mouth, neither had the drummer. "What to?" Dave asked.

Jason turned slightly to face him, and his stance took a faint hint of challenge. "Children of the Night."

A whisper of cold touched the back of Dave's neck, and he bit his lip to keep from giving away his unease.

This is getting real spooky. That name—the gear—hell. Man, it's like that mind-trip stuff Di was in; that occult crap. I hate that stuff; dammit, that's why I broke up with her in the first place. All that freaky weird-out stuff, mind reading and that other shit—she ended up spending more time chasing ghosts than she did with me, out half the night sometimes, then too tired to do anything when she did show. That's why I told her it was Ouija boards or me—

He shied away from the memory; it *still* wrenched his gut to think about that last scene he'd had with her. It hadn't been a fight, exactly. In a way, it was too bad; a fight would have been easier to take than the stricken look in those dark eyes, the silence in which she walked out.

He waffled for a minute, trying to come up with a good reason *why* he felt uneasy about the rigs, the name—and couldn't think of one. So instead he launched the only objection to the "new image" that seemed sane. "Look, Jason—I know we're startin' t' do all right, but man, this stuff, this's *money,* man, *I* can't afford this kind of rig."

Instead of replying immediately, Jason looked over at Jack, who just shrugged. "I don't much care what's on the front of the kit," the drummer opined, "and I don't much care what you put me in—just as long as it ain't comin' outa *my* wallet."

Jason grinned in triumph; Doug's smile an echo of the lead's. "Stay cool, man," he advised Dave. "There's not penny one of *ours* tied up in this."

He didn't follow; it didn't make sense. "Huh?" he said. "What do you mean, we've got no cash in this?"

Jason's grin widened. "We have a patron," he gloated. "We got ourselves a patron. And this is just the beginning of what he's gonna do for us. Just wait and see."

Di stared resolutely at her coffee, or her hands, or the faces of whichever of the two guys she was talking to, and *not* at her surroundings. Keith was into superrealism, and his studio looked like Doctor Frankenstein's workshop. Body parts in fiberglass were everywhere—and they were frighteningly lifelike.

Panic was behind her—for now. Whatever it was, it hadn't come for her yet. Those realistic body parts were only realistic *looking.*

Too bad Keith couldn't be a little more realistic in what he expected of her.

"Dammit, Keith, it's a *big* city," she protested, trying to get past his barricades of ignorance and emotion. "This *isn't* a TV show! I can't just wiggle my nose and make things happen!

Magic doesn't *work* that way. Magic isn't *easy* in the first place; it takes more energy to do something magically than it does to just *do* it, always assuming you *can* do it mundanely. And this— it's worse than trying to find a grain of rice in a warehouse of wheat—"

Not like Five Corners, Connecticut, population 2,500 and ten cats. And two psychics. And no empathic interference. Hell, even New Haven was better than this—a much smaller area to scan, and it still took me months to pinpoint Emily.

"—the thing could be anywhere," she continued, worrying at a hangnail on her thumb with her fingernail, "and if it knows how to hide itself, I'd never find it unless it slipped up at the same time I was scanning right where it was."

And where does that gypsy boy fit into this? I can't believe it's coincidence. Maybe that—that vampire—if that's what he was—maybe if he can eat emotional energy, he can eat souls, too. I wish I'd paid more attention to him when I saw him the first time—

If he isn't involved somehow, I've got no clues. Everything on our list is either a god—and I can't believe there's a god running around out there, sucking the souls out of scuzzy bus passengers— or something vampiric. Like the Greek vampires—people they latched onto never showed up in the afterworld, so the implication is they got eaten. That Egyptian demon, the "Eater of Souls." Those African whatsis-things—

There's vampiric swords too, but—no, I can't buy that one. Besides, I haven't seen a single instance of one in the occult literature that predates Michael Moorcock, which leads me to think the notion got "borrowed," lock, stock, and copyright.

Does it know it's being hunted? Does it know me? Is it only lying low until it can choose the time and place to meet me?

Keith frowned, and fiddled with a snag on the sleeve of his sweater. "It's been five days—and we still haven't gotten anywhere. You didn't have any trouble with that thing that was in here," he protested. "Maybe I'm being dense—but it looked to me like you just sort of zeroed right in on it, trapped it, and threw it out. Why can't you find the thing that way?"

Lord and lady, she groaned to herself. *The man wants me to turn myself into a soul-eater detector. Just flick a switch, set a dial—*

"I can't, because I don't know what I'm looking for," she tried to tell him. "I knew *exactly* what I was going after in here; I knew what it 'felt' like, what it 'looked' like. I'm—I don't know how to describe this, exactly—I guess the closest thing would be like a bloodhound. I need a scent. I need to know what this thing 'feels' like, or I can't track it."

"That's what's called a signature, babe," Lenny said, trying to be helpful. "It'd be like you setting up to do a portrait bust on a verbal description; without the signature, Di's moving blind."

She sipped her coffee; Keith was into herbal teas with cosmic names, and the coffee he kept around for guests was awful. And Keith still didn't look convinced. Water was dripping somewhere back behind her; it was beginning to get on her nerves.

"Can't you just look for something that doesn't look like a regular person?" Keith persisted.

She sighed. "I could do that, yes. It'd be just like going out into the street and *looking,* physically, for someone who didn't quite look human. How many people are in the Apple? New York is just *too damned big* for me to go sifting through it, looking at people's auras. I'd die of old age before I found anything. And that assumes that whatever we're looking for *doesn't* know how to shield itself from detection, which is probably a real bad assumption."

"But—" Keith began again.

Lenny touched his shoulder, interrupting him, and gave her a look of understanding and patience. "Di," he said, "why don't you go on home. You look tired to death. I'll explain it to him."

I hope you can, she thought pessimistically, *but I'm not going to bet on it—*

But Keith finally seemed to *see* her—and she knew damned well she looked like hell. She was just as glad Annie wasn't

around to mother-hen her. Too little sleep, too much going—
it was taking its toll. She wasn't sure how long she was going
to be able to keep burning her candle at both ends *and* the
middle.

*Just please, no more panic attacks. Not now. Not when I'm so
low already.*

"Take a rest, Di," Lenny said quietly; Keith nodded, and he
looked just a shade guilty. "You aren't going to get anywhere if
you burn out on us."

She nodded. "I know, I know. I should know better, and
somehow I never learn." She wanted to smile, or something, and
just couldn't manage it."

"Out—" Lenny ordered sternly. "This is an order. Go home.
Get some rest." He pointed across the glaringly lit studio to the
black mouth of the door.

"I'm going, I'm going—" She grabbed her beat-up wool CPO
jacket and obeyed, but only to the extent of leaving the building.

She was too restless to go home; too much nervous energy,
and she couldn't face the thought of the empty apartment. Being alone could trigger another attack.

Besides, she thought, hunching her shoulders and burying
her chin in her coat collar, *if it is looking for me, a moving target
is a lot harder to hit.*

The wind was cold, though; there'd probably be snow soon.
Not tonight, but soon. Would snow drive this thing into a lair
for the winter? Somehow she didn't think so.

Keith's studio was just outside the Village proper; after a
prowl of two blocks, she turned a corner and reached streets
that were populated. There were clubs here, and restaurants that
were popular enough to have customers despite the cold wind
and the late hour, and the fact that it was a weeknight.

And it's harder to see a moving target around other targets ...

She had no particular destination in mind; she just wanted to
walk, and maybe shake something coherent out of her thought
processes. And despite being among people, despite having just

left about the best friend she had in the city next to Annie, she was feeling very alone right now.

And sorry for yourself. Snap out of it. Depression isn't going to get you anywhere but into a rut. Meep, meep, meep, you sound like Sweet Sarah, Soppy Sobber of the Spanish Main. Or a Guinea Pig.

She crossed a street against the light—not enough traffic to worry about—and suddenly her shields went up and her internal "bad" detectors went red.

Whoa! That wasn't unusual. The last time it had happened— had been just before the Nightflyer—

But that had been when she was alone, not with people all around her.

It occurred to her that she was feeling more alert by the moment; as if fear was spurring her now, instead of enervating her.

Oh please, let that be true.

She stopped cold, saw she was just outside a rock club. It had a flashy neon sign that buzzed annoyingly; in the few moments she stood there, she watched several people going in, opening the door just enough to slip inside, but not enough to let her see or hear what was going on in there.

Just another club. What in hell could have—

The door opened again, this time as wide as it could get, and a blast of hot air heavy with pot smoke and music hit her. And it was the music that sent the "wrong" feeling a little more into the red. There was something she couldn't put her finger on—it was like the smile of someone who's secretly into sadism and bondage. A nasty sort of knowledge lay behind the lyrics and the heavy backbeat—

Maybe it didn't have anything to do with the soul-eater; but that bus's route *had* gone through the Village. And there was something predatory about this music. It was something that needed looking into.

She pulled the door open slightly, and slipped into the club, moving as quietly as she could—

Which is "very," thank the gods.

A massive bouncer in the entryway nodded at her driver's license without ever taking his eyes off something at the back of the club.

You could get a stark-naked fourteen-year-old hermaphrodite past him and he'd never notice—Ye gods. This is beyond weird. The cops have been coming down on the clubs in the Village lately; he should be really watching IDs. What in hell is going on here?

The club was jammed to the walls; she had to inch her way through the elbow-to-elbow mob inside, it was literally standing-room only. The very faint spots over the bar and the stage lights were all the illumination provided, but that didn't matter to the audience; their focus, like the bouncer's, was *all* on the tiny stage at the rear of the club.

Di regretted—for once—being as tiny as she was. She couldn't *see* the stage over all the heads. She wormed her way between people, putting out a "don't notice me" aura with all her concentration. There was something in here—and she didn't want it to have any notion that she had walked into *its* territory.

As she got to the bar, she was *very* glad she was shielding and hiding.

Speak of the devil and he shall appear—

Enthroned on a stool at the far end of the bar was Mr. Trouble himself; he looked very elegant—and Di would far rather have been swimming in a tank with a tiger shark than be in this room with him. He was in full "hunter" mode; other than that, she couldn't tell anything without probing him, which she did *not* intend to do. This was no place for a confrontation. And it was all too likely, from the relaxed way he was sitting, that this was *his* territory.

Not tonight, thank you.

He was trolling for something a bit older than chicken tonight—but his intent was undoubtedly the same, and his plans. There were more than enough "the universe is a friendly place" types to serve as fodder for someone like him, and a club was a good place to find them. There was a hint of movement just beyond his shoulder; she waited a moment for her eyes to adjust to the light over the bar before trying to pierce the shadows beyond him.

Well; he's hunting in tandem tonight. I can't say as I like that—

Beside him was a young Oriental woman with a short, stylish haircut that shrieked "in"; she was dressed sleekly in a black leather jumpsuit and a heavy gold metallic belt.

Japanese, I think. And about the trendiest chick in this bar.

The woman's eyes were hard, but opaque, giving nothing away. She swept the crowd with her gaze for a moment, and Di ducked behind a tall blonde student-type. When she looked again, the woman had gone back to watching the band.

Definitely not chicken. Definitely shark. Sharks don't usually run in pairs; I wonder why this one's teamed herself with Lover Boy? I wish I dared scan them—

But there was something about the music that seemed to be damping her ability to think and to read even the surface of those around her, as if it were setting up some kind of jamming or interference patterns that were scrambling anything psi outside her shields.

Another good reason not to pry just now. The trouble is, it's also making it damned hard to think.

She withdrew from the area around the bar and let the crowd pull her deeper into itself. Too late she realized that she'd gotten caught up in an eddy that was heading for the dance floor, and there was no way to get free of it without drawing attention to herself.

Crap.

She gave up, and danced with the rest of them, letting the dance take her nearer to the stage.

I ought to get a look at these guys anyway. I don't like the music or the feelings they're putting out. They're hot—and they're damned good—but there's something wrong *with them. It's all "take" and no "give." And—damn, but I could swear I've heard the guitar work on this song before somewhere—*

She was concentrating so hard on the song's arrangement, that she didn't realize how close she'd gotten to the stage—not until a wild guitar lick screamed out of the second in answer to a growl from the base—a solo riff that was *paralyzingly* familiar.

I know that style!

Her head snapped up, her mouth open in shock, her body frozen in place.

At first she couldn't see him; the tangle-haired lead was in the way; she noticed then that the entire band was done up in black leather and silk in costumes that were meant to evoke absolute raw sexual attraction.

There were patterns in black beads or sequins on their shirts—patterns that stirred vague memories that wouldn't quite come to the surface, but which made her shiver. They *were* occult; no doubt of that. Some of the animal magnetism the group was putting out was being generated by those patterns. But there was something else there that went deeper—

The name on the drum kit—Children of the Night—that bordered on the occult, too.

The lead stared off into the crowd over her head, his eyes focused somewhere other than the interior of the club. He seemed to absorb the stage lights, and the strange, *hungry* smile he wore actually frightened her. Then he lunged for his mike as the second guitar screamed again in that hauntingly familiar way—and she saw who was behind him.

Oh my god—

Dave Kendall.

Her heart stopped as he smiled, and closed his eyes—a smile she knew better than her own—a smile that took her back to—before. If he'd smiled like that, instead of getting angry and *demanding* that she choose him or magic—

Oh god. I'd have given it up. I'd have given it all up to keep him. Oh god—

But he hadn't; he'd forced her to make the choice before she was ready—more than that, he'd *forced* her to make the choice. Then before she could begin to explain, he'd gotten mad, called her crazy—then walked out on her.

It hurt then. It *still* hurt. *Davey, Davey, if you'd just waited, waited till I was finished—I was almost at a nexus point. I had a replacement online. I think—I think I could have taken a break, given it a little rest and been patient until you understood—but you wouldn't wait—*

She could hardly breathe, her chest was so tight; the club was stiflingly hot, but she hugged her arms to her chest and shivered, and couldn't move—

Then he looked down, and saw her.

He froze for a heartbeat, staring down into her eyes—and from the dumbfounded look in *his* eyes, she had no doubt that he'd recognized her.

Oh god—

She broke the contact; forgot all about trying to be unobtrusive, forgot why she'd come in the first place, forgot even the hunters at the bar. All she wanted was to get away, away from him, away from the pain.

She bolted for the exit, shoving her way across the dance floor and into the crowd, elbowing aside anyone who stood in the way too long. The door loomed in front of her; she didn't wait for the bouncer to open it; just hit it with her breath sobbing and her chest on fire, and burst out into the cold and the wind and the dark—

But even that wasn't far enough for her. She *kept* running; ran all the way back to her apartment—slammed and locked the door behind her—

And dropped to the floor right beside the door. She was so exhausted she could go no further, could not even get as far as a chair or the couch. And she cried like a child until her eyes were sore.

And *then* she went to the kitchen, found the Scotch, and got drunk for the second time in a week.

Dave's world stopped.

Di? My god—

All he could see were those eyes, those huge eyes, deep brown and haunting—

When the world stopped, so did he; it wasn't long, no more than the first half of a heartbeat before she wrenched her eyes away from his, and tore off into the crowd. No more than a single downbeat.

But that was enough; he *felt* Jason's glare as the lead looked over his shoulder. It was the kind of look he'd expect to get for infanticide and it jarred him back into reality like a slap in the face. He picked up where he'd dropped his line, still smarting under the hot lash of that snarl—

Shee-it, it's just a damned song—

Yeah, but it was *Jason's* song, one of the very few he'd written. As Dave tried to make up for his screw-up by *really* getting down, the sting faded.

It's Jason's baby. I know how I feel when somebody drops the line on one of my babies. And I almost "killed" his baby there. I guess it was infanticide.

His fingers were flying, and Jason seemed happy again—at least his shoulders weren't angry-tight, and he looked in profile about the way he always looked, lately. Waiting and hungry.

Wonder if his sex drive's gone up the way mine has? Given what he was like before—hell if I wouldn't look hungry too, I guess. And sex does seem to take the edge off, like getting stoned does. Just—ah, the hell with it.

His concentration was gone, and he knew from experience that nothing was going to bring it back for a bit.

The last person I ever expected to see in the Apple was Di. Christ on a crutch.

Shit, she looked so good—

And I look like hell. Bet she took one look and figured me for wasted.

Anger flared, and he let it run out his fingertips into the guitar. Jason turned around again, but this time the look he threw back over his shoulder was one of approval.

Hell with her. Hell with what she thinks. We're doin it, we're hot an' gettin' hotter. I'll be doin' champagne an' up t' my neck in groupies while she's still playin' those stupid mind games—

The anger didn't last. It couldn't last, not when she hadn't really been at fault. Maybe he should have been a little more tolerant. She'd never really gotten on his case about his drugs—

He hadn't had a steady girl after her. Lots of chicks, but no girl.

He settled the second part back in behind the lead, and just followed what Jason was laying down. His thoughts were definitely not on the music.

Seemed like nobody else could touch him inside, down deep, since he'd broken up with her. Not the way she could—had—anyway.

His best stuff had all been written while they were together. It was like she'd been able to do things to the way he was thinking that just turned on the creative juice and let it flow like there was no tomorrow.

Except there had been a tomorrow, and when she was gone, the stuff he wrote just sounded like The Elevator Version of the Greatest Hits of the Dentist's Office. No juice, no excitement.

Like part of him went into deep freeze when he'd walked out on her.

Jason gave him another *look;* and he realized he'd been doing noodles instead of riffs.

Shit; this is getting me nowhere. She's gone, and that's all there is to it. And from the way she tore out of here, she ain't likely to want me back. Screw her. I don't need her back.

Jason had his eye on him, for sure, and Dave felt his anger coming back; fire in his gut and coals in his soul.

Who the hell does she think she is, anyway? What the hell did she think she was doing? Worthless bitch, off in the ozone and wanting me out there too, because she couldn't handle the real world! Christ on a crutch, I didn't need that! I never knew where she was going to be, never knew when she was going to be home— never knew when I was going to find the living room barricaded by some jerk that wouldn't even let me talk to her 'cause she was off communing with the spirits or something. I don't need that kind of shit!

The anger rose, and his face set in a frown; he attacked the guitar line, attacked it like it had offended him, and Jason stopped watching him.

After that, it was a clean run to the end of the set.

SIX

L ookin' good, man."

Pausing on his way into the back to count up the night's receipts, the club owner gloated at Jason, while the four of them broke things down and packed up their instruments and the precious—and expensive—new mikes.

More largesse from this "patron," whoever he is.

"I *like* the new look. So did the crowd. Many more nights like this one and I'm gonna have t' start chargin' a cover on weeknights, too. You guys on some kind of diet or something? I wouldn't mind losing a couple of pounds."

Jack raised a sardonic eyebrow. "Been wondering myself," he commented.

Jason chuckled. "No diets, just fast living. You go right ahead and charge that weekday cover, so long as we get the percentage, just like we agreed."

Dave stowed the last of the mike stands away at the back of the stage, and chanced at that moment to look up, and caught Jason's veiled smirk. No doubt about it, Jason was very pleased with himself.

"You make us happy, we'll make you happy," the lead continued, his voice shadowed with irony. "Otherwise we can go someplace else—"

"Yeah, sure, no problem," the man said hastily. "Just like we agreed. No reason I should rip you off."

"Exactly." Jason stood up and stretched, his posture deceptively lazy. Dave blinked his eyes; for a moment there it had seemed like the lead was glowing darkly in the smoky backlit tunnel of the club; sleek as a full-fed panther, and no less dangerous. Dave could feel the danger, a hot radiation of thinly veiled threat, and the back of his neck prickled.

But the club owner was gone, and the air of controlled threat faded.

Then a pair of shadows detached themselves from the end of the bar, and approached the stage, moving silently, sinuously.

Dave blinked at them in amazement, because he *knew* the bouncer had run everybody out. He couldn't imagine how he'd missed these two.

Then again—he caught the gleam of gold at hand, waist, neck. The bouncer wouldn't have missed them—unless they were too important to be booted out with the rest of the rabble—

The dark and shadowed strangers entered a cone of light thrown by one of the dance-floor spots, and shadows resolved themselves into a man and a young woman, both in black. The man wore an elegant variation on their own costume, sans beads and sequins, the young Oriental woman at his side a black leather jumpsuit that *was* pornographically tight. The man looked naggingly familiar. In another moment, Dave knew why. He'd been the guru at that ill-fated Halloween party, the guy who'd been sporting a cast on his arm.

The one all those people had fawned over, calling him "Master."

And Jason dropped what he was doing to greet them like a pair of old friends.

"Master Jeffries!" The lead jumped down from the stage and approached the strangers—but oddly, did not touch either of them. "I was hoping you'd be here tonight!"

Dave caught movement out of the corner of his eye, and turned enough to see that Doug was standing quietly—nodding a silent but respectful greeting to the two.

Doug—respectful?

The idea was unbelievable, but Jason drove that wisp of a thought out of his head with his next statement. "Dave, Jack— this is the patron I told you about. Right, Master Jeffries?"

The man smiled urbanely enough, though Dave thought he detected just a hint of irony behind the smile. "Nothing so important as a *patron,* Jason. You know I can't do anything about getting you contracts. All I can do is get you contacts with the right people, and help you showcase yourselves."

"Which is more than we were able to do for ourselves," Jason replies, his smile as broad and bright—and ironic—as their "patron's." "Let's face it, you can't get anywhere these days by just bein' good, you gotta look good too, and you gotta know the right people an' the right things."

"A sad commentary on our times," Jeffries said, while the girl beside him remained as quiet and still as an icon of ebony and ivory.

Except for her eyes, which never stopped moving. Flick, flick, flick—she covered the whole room within a minute, then began over—as if she were watching for something.

"I think we ought to celebrate the successful debut of the new image, don't you, Jason, Doug?"

Dave was so fascinated by the girl's ever-moving eyes that he didn't realize he'd agreed to go with Doug and Jason to the man's apartment until the words were out of his mouth. Then he was suddenly, inexplicably, afraid. He racked his brain savagely for an excuse to beg off, but couldn't think of anything that didn't sound lame. He turned toward Jack and hoped for a refusal from the drummer—but he only shrugged. "Sounds good to me," he said. "I never turned down somebody else's booze or grass in my life, an' I don't plan on starting now."

The man smiled sardonically, as if he found Jack naïve and amusing. "It's all settled, then," he said, turning away with the aplomb of a king who has just completed an audience. "I'll see you there."

Not in this lifetime—Dave thought.

How do I get myself into things like this? Ten minutes later, Dave found himself sandwiched on the front bench of the van between Jason and Doug, and very grateful the van didn't have a stickshift, or he might have lost a kneecap somewhere along the trip. Doug was driving, which was enough of a thrill for twenty lifetimes. Not even cabbies would challenge Doug's kamikaze attacks on the traffic patterns.

And he had a foot like lead. They were always either accelerating, or being thrown against the dashboard as he slammed on the brakes. Good thing Jack was in the back, keeping the guitars from getting smashed. Dave didn't envy him back there.

Jason was paying no attention to the suicidal maneuvers Doug was pulling. He kept up a calm but steady colloquy on the subject of "Master Jeffries," all praise. Doug chimed in from time to time with grunts of agreement.

"—lucky," Jason was saying, as Dave pulled his terrified gaze off the cab Doug was running up onto the sidewalk.

"Huh?" he said, when Jason paused, expecting a response.

"I said we're lucky. To have gotten his attention."

"Uh, right. Lucky."

Jason heaved an exaggerated sigh. "Just wait. Wait till you see his place. *Then* you'll understand."

I'd just as soon pass—Dave thought—then Doug wrenched the van around, brakes screaming in an abrupt right-angle turn. He flung the van down a ramp that opened up in front of them, leading into the bowels of a dark parking garage. The ramp bottomed out—and so did the van—and Doug hurled it at the back wall, where Dave could see written in huge red letters the words "Visitor Parking Only."

Sweet Jesus Christ—he's not gonna make it—

He squeezed his eyes shut as Doug applied the brakes and the brakes howled in protest—and the wall came at him at fifty per.

The van shuddered to a stop—without Dave eating the windshield. He cracked his right eye open, slowly, and saw the beam of the headlights bouncing off concrete *one inch* away from the front bumper.

He sagged with relief. *Christ.*

"Come on," Jason said, bailing out of the passenger's side of the van, and grabbing Dave's arm to haul him along. "Master Jeffries doesn't like to be kept waiting."

"I'm coming, I'm coming."

If I can walk.

His knees were not exactly what he'd call "steady." In point of fact, he wasn't sure they were going to hold him for a minute when he climbed down out of the front seat. Jack clambered out of the back, and Doug could see he wasn't in much better shape—which made Dave feel a little less like a wimp.

On the other side of the van, Doug was holding an elevator open for them; white fluorescent light glared out into the half-empty garage, and the door kept trying to cut him in half. Jason hustled them inside, and Doug let the door do its thing.

If this is supposed to give me an idea of how well heeled our patron is, I'm not impressed.

The elevator was an industrial, bare-bones model; gray linoleum floor, gray enamel walls, two cheap, buzzing fluorescent tubes behind a plastic panel in the ceiling.

This isn't exactly your Fifth Avenue address, either. I dunno exactly where we are, but we're someplace west of the Village.

Jason punched 2, and the elevator cage rose, a bit jerkily.

Jack shoved his hands into his jeans pockets and looked around with a slight frown. "I thought you said this dude lived in pretty good digs." The frown deepened. "I hate to tell you, guys, but I'm pretty underwhelmed."

Dave definitely saw Doug and Jason exchange a strange look. Secretive? There was something of that in it. Also a hint of something more, both shadowed and knowing.

It was very peculiar—and it vanished from their faces before Dave had a chance to be certain he'd really seen it, and not misinterpreted a frown of puzzlement or the crease of a headache.

The door slid open; they escaped the metal box before it could snap its jaws shut again and trap them. The hallway was as utilitarian as the elevator had been, gray plaster and dark gray carpet, and Dave began to wonder if his idea and Jason's of opulent surroundings were *that* far apart.

Jason paused outside a plain brown doorway and knocked; it swung open soundlessly to admit them before he'd knocked more than twice.

As the door swung shut behind them, Dave immediately revised his earlier impression. If this wasn't opulence, it was a damned fine substitute.

The place *was* heavy-duty weird, no doubt about it; it was done up like some kind of ashram. There was very little furniture in the living room; mostly low tables and piles of pillows everywhere; one long table against the far wall with an incense burner and a couple of dishes on it. Four low-wattage lamps, one on each wall, supplied a dim and amber-tinged light.

But the lamps were heavy bronze and hand-leaded glass; custom-built, and no doubt of it. Dave had never quite believed in the "carpet so thick your feet sank into it"—until now, now that his feet were sinking into one that was so thick he literally couldn't feel the floor. The walls shone, papered in an expensive mottled metallic, and the pillows gleamed a rich ebony, like the same kind of heavy silk their stage shirts had been made of.

Incense hung in the air, making the dim light a bit dimmer—and it had an odd smell to it. It wasn't like anything he was familiar with, it was sweet with an undertone of sour; and—was it making him high? He seemed to be getting light-headed—

"What's that stuff?" he whispered to Doug, who had moved in close behind him. He waved at the dish on the table, which was sending up a thin streamer of bluish smoke.

"Belladonna," Doug said shortly. "Don't worry about it."

The name tickled a memory at the back of his mind, but it eluded him before he could bring it up to the surface. Something-something about some friend who'd—smoked it? OD'd on it? It worried him for a moment—but the worry slipped away, and in a few moments he couldn't remember why he'd been concerned.

Jack was looking around, his uneasiness now plain for any-one to read. "Listen," he said to Jason, ignoring Master Jeffries. "All of a sudden I'm hungry. Why don't we go grab a burger or something?"

There was a whisper of sound behind them—no more warn-ing than that.

The Japanese girl materialized from the shadows behind Jack—except that she had inexplicably turned into a Japanese *boy*—and before Dave could move or even say anything to warn him, he (she?) had pinioned Jack's arms behind his back.

Christ—what in hell?

Dave *tried* to move, his *mind* wanted to spring to Jack's aid, but his body would *not* obey him. He struggled against a dark something holding his mind and his body, like a fly trapped in glue. His body wasn't *his* anymore, it was obeying someone else, and that someone wanted him frozen where he was.

No one spoke—not even Jack. Dave could see Jack's eyes, though, and they were terrified.

Like maybe he can't even wriggle, either?

Suddenly Jeffries, Doug, and Jason were moving in on Jack like sharks circling in on a tasty baby seal.

Dave started shaking—at least inside—because he could *feel* Jack's fear, exactly the way he could *feel* the vibes in the club when they played.

His hunger was fading.

The way it did when he made love to a chick, or even more, in the club when they played—

His stomach heaved as he realized what that meant. He'd been feeding on the vibes, oh Christ, he'd been *living* off the vibes at the club—no wonder he'd been losing weight. No wonder he hadn't needed to eat.

And now his hunger was being appeased by a different, darker sort of vibe.

I think I'm gonna throw up—

Jason turned to him, and smiled. It was the same kind of smile that he had exchanged with Doug in the elevator; sly, knowing. "You can feel it, can't you?" he said softly, with just a hint of seduction in his voice. "It's better than the vibes in the club, isn't it? Like the difference between stale bread and steak—"

He walked over to one of the low tables, and when he returned, there was a knife in his hand, black of hilt, silver of blade. The blade reflected amber from the wall lights all along its length, the light flickering and moving as Jason turned it in his hand. Dave stared at it in horror and fascination.

Doug smiled and nodded, and Master Jeffries wore an expression of proprietary approval.

Jason ran his finger down the back of the blade in a measured caress. "I can make it even better, can't I, Master? Better than steak. Better than anything you can imagine." He reached for the front of Jack's shirt, and tore it open in a savage parody of some TV melodrama. "Oh, I can make it *much* better."

He extended the knife blade like an artist's paintbrush, and used it to draw a thin line down Jack's chest, leaving behind a thin thread of blood. "I can make it ambrosia."

Jack's pain and terror surged.

Dave felt a vile wave of satisfaction.

Oh God—he's right—I'm gonna be sick—

Dave's hunger was almost gone now—it was being rapidly replaced by a warm glow of pleasure and a satiation that was better than the afterglow of sex.

Jason extended the knife again, and drew a second line parallel to the first. Jack whimpered.

"Poor Jack," Jason said conversationally, his head cocked idly to one side, his tone as ordinary as if they were all sitting around the break room. "The rest of us woke up supermen—but *he* just woke up hung over. And we *can't* have a Child of Day jamming with the Children of the Night, now can we?"

Then Jason laughed, and touched Jack's throat with his free hand.

Jack threw back his head and screamed, a lost howl of pure, animal terror.

The sound gave Dave his body back.

He found he could move—and he did. He turned his back on the awful tableau, and ran.

He didn't remember hitting the door; he didn't remember taking the elevator—all he could hear was Jason's laugh, and the rest joining in; all he could feel was wanting to vomit and being unable to. This couldn't be happening—his friends had turned into something out of a horror movie. He didn't know them—

He didn't know himself.

He ran down dark streets until he couldn't breathe and his side was in agony. How long he ran, he didn't know, there was no time, only terror, shadow, and cold; a cold in his gut that nothing would ever warm again. He finally stumbled into the better-lit streets of the Village, aware only of blurs of light and dark and nothing else—until he caught the yellow haze of a cab light out of the corner of his eye and stumbled into the street, frantically waving it down. Miraculously, it stopped. Somehow he got into it, fell into the back seat, gave the cabby directions to his apartment—and tried, without success, to forget that horrible laughter that had followed him out into the street.

They slipped me something. Windowpane, yellow sunshine. It's all a trip. Tomorrow I'll go back to the club, and we'll all have a good laugh.

He huddled on the back seat of the cab, disoriented and sick, wincing away from the moving shadows outside the cab windows, but watching longingly for the signs that he was back on his own turf. He saw them, but they gave him no comfort. His heart pounded so hard he could scarcely hear the cabby; he didn't understand what the man was saying until he realized that the cab had stopped in front of his own building. He paid the man, crawled out of the cab and up the stairs to his apartment.

Only when he reached his own door did he begin to feel safe. Only when he had opened it did he feel as if this had *really* all been some kind of mad nightmare; he turned and closed the door behind him with a shudder of relief.

And then stepped into the living room—

And saw Jason and the Japanese standing there, waiting for him.

He started to scream—only started, for Jason reached out and seized him by the throat, choking off his cry.

Dave went limp with fear, and whimpered. Jason's hand on his throat was *terribly* strong. He could scarcely breathe, and he couldn't even imagine trying to fight.

"Now," Jason said, softly, fiercely. "You just keep quiet, and you listen to what I'm gonna tell you, bro. You're gonna keep your mouth shut about what happened tonight, and you're gonna go with the flow. You're *one of us* now. You've had a taste of the good stuff—and *believe* me, friend, that taste made you *ours*. The vibes from the club won't keep you going anymore. Once you've fed on fear, *you have no choice.*" He shook Dave the way a man would shake a rag doll. "You hear me, man?"

Dave swallowed; the crushing grip on his throat relaxed just enough so that he could nod. *I'm not like him. I can't be like him. I won't—I can't believe that—but I'm sure as hell not going to tell him that.*

Jason let him go, and he stood as passively as he could, rubbing his bruised throat. "Too bad about Jack," Jason said with a faint smile. "But—well, we haven't *really* lost him, have we, Hidoro?"

The Japanese boy nodded—then *blurred,* as if he were melting, or Dave was watching him through a mist. Dave's gut did a kind of backflip in revulsion as the boy briefly dissolved into a cloud of smoke, then faded back in again.

Only it wasn't the boy standing there now.

It was Jack.

Dave staggered back as the familiar face grinned, and familiar hands flexed long, bony fingers. "Beats the hell out of getting somebody new to learn the sets," Jack's voice said pleasantly.

Darkness came down over Dave as the ground came up to meet his face. The darkness beat the ground by a fraction of a second.

He came to in his bed—with the rays of the late afternoon sun streaking through the cracks in the blinds.

He blinked—and chuckled.

"Shit, nightmares at my age," he said out loud, grabbing his shades off the nightstand, and reaching for the Coke he left there the night before—

Only his hand met nothing. No Coke.

Fear clenched his gut, and he scrambled out of bed.

"I forgot it, that's all," he told himself. "I was stoned, and I forgot it—"

And he almost had himself convinced—until he turned on the bathroom light.

Scrawled across the bathroom mirror, written in what looked like dried blood, was a single word.

"Remember."

The hunger rose, clawing at him, like a weasel trying to tear its way out of his stomach. He clutched the bathroom sink to hold himself up—and cried.

———

Di paced the space behind the counter, too restless to stand, too unhappy to really want to think.

But the "activity" of pacing was doing nothing to stop her brain from working.

She'd just hung up on Annie's husband, Bob; he'd been babbling, truth to tell. *But then, you kind of expect the new daddy to babble. Little Heather Rhiannon is going to be spoiled rotten if he gets his way. I'm kind of glad he was so wrapped up in being New Daddy; if he had been his usual sharp self, he'd have picked up on bad vibes from my tone of voice before I'd gotten three words out. Then he'd have wanted to know what was wrong. I don't want any of them in the line of fire. It's bad enough having Lenny there.* She turned, and stared out the window for a moment. *Thank the gods Annie's going to be able to take over again soon. I can't take much more of this, maintaining protection on two places, dividing my attention like this.* Her lips twitched. *Two weeks at most. Bob at least remembered to tell me that.*

She registered a twinge, and her lips shaped an ironic grimace. *I think I'm jealous.*

Because Bob was *so* supportive of Annie, and *so* happy about everything—and he'd been just as terminally mundane as Dave when he and Annie met.

Her spirits sank another inch. *That whole conversation just made me more depressed than I had been, if that's possible. If it were Annie in this mess—Bob would be right in there slugging away beside her. He adjusted—then he accepted—and now he joins in.*

Oh hell. The situation isn't *the same.*

She leaned against the counter and buried her face in her hands. It was one thing to know intellectually that her peculiarly strong psychic talents put her into a class by herself, that she was *always* going to be forced into the front lines by the very strength of those gifts. *Along with the rest of the fortunate souls who have the dubious pleasure of being Guardians.* But to know it viscerally—that had to come very hard. *Oh, very few fortunate souls, we are. I couldn't tell you if we're cursed, or blessed. All I know is that we're different. Annie's not in my league; why should she have had to make the same choices? I'm an F-15, a Sherman tank; Annie's a Piper Cub, a VW bug.*

But seeing Dave again—

I thought I'd gotten over him. The wounds weren't healed, they were only scabbed over. Now they're bleeding again.

All the little demons of loneliness she'd thought she'd been ignoring successfully were coming back for their revenge. And it sure didn't help that Dave had looked *incredibly* sexy. Leaner, his eyes dream-haunted and soulful, like the poet *she* had always known he was, even if he didn't believe it.

It's probably drugs, she told herself savagely. *I'm probably seeing only what I want to see. He's probably burned-out, not soulful. That's not the spirit of a poet looking out of those eyes, it's the fact that there's nobody home in his skull.*

She squared her shoulders and raised her head, staring at the tumble of books on the shelf opposite her, but not really seeing them. *I've got to snap out of this. I've got more important things to do than moon about my lack of a love life. I still don't know who—or what—killed that gypsy boy. I still don't know what killed Keith's ex, or where it is. I don't know if the two deaths are related. I don't even know if it knows about me.*

She went back to pacing again, her mind going in circles, fruitlessly, until it was time for closing.

As she began locking up, her eye fell on the display case of jewelry, and because of the way the light fell on some of the silver pieces, she suddenly *noticed* them, gleaming softly in the shadows. Bell, Book, and Candle catered to folk of a multiplicity of esoteric religions—and some of them were nominally Christian.

There were at least three heavy silver crucifixes in that case. And legend swore to the efficacy of a crucifix against vampires.

The gods knew she hadn't anything else to go on but legend.

Before she could change her mind, she opened the display
case and took the largest and heaviest of them, shoving it into
her coat pocket.

Gods, I feel like a fool—

But that didn't stop her from walking out the door with it
tucked into her pocket.

Di slunk her way along the route between the subway station
and her apartment building. Every nerve was alive to changes,
movement. She felt like a sentient burglar alarm.

*If something doesn't break soon, I'm going to look like a Brillo
pad made of nerve endings.*

It had been another overcast day; the sun had set about the
time she closed the shop, and this was one of those nights when
the air seemed to devour all available light, leaving the eyes confused by shadows that wouldn't resolve into substance.

Shadows that could hide anything. Hunter, or hunted . . .

For the first time in weeks, that line of thought did not bring
a crippling surge of panic.

She had been expecting one; braced for it. When it didn't
come—the confusion made her stop dead about ten feet from
the steps of the apartment building.

The street lamp on the other side of the steps cast long,
murky shadows, shadows that hid the side of the building and
part of the sidewalk. Before she could shake herself out of her
stupefaction, a man-shaped shadow solidified out of the murk
and blocked her path to the steps.

She didn't think—just acted. Street-smart instincts and a
karate sensei far more interested in keeping his pupils alive than
in perfect form had gotten her to the point that under a given
set of conditions, her body took over, no matter what state her
mind was in.

In fact, she could *hear* her sensei even as she struck.

"You don't ever warn, you don't re-act. You act.

She knew that—but more importantly, her *body* knew it.

She was analyzing his stance without having to tell herself to do so; doing it as fast as her eyes could react to him being there; her *ki* was balanced and she was ready to strike as soon as he took that critical step that brought him within range.

He did.

She struck for the throat, not the (expected, and consequently, often guarded against) groin shot; she already knew as she was moving that she would follow that up with a kick to the knee, and once he was down she'd get past him and into the building—

Except that it didn't happen that way.

He didn't move out of the way; didn't pull a weapon. He just reached out and caught her wrist before she connected. And held it.

She'd never seen anyone but her sensei move that fast. And even her sensei couldn't have caught her wrist and absorbed all the energy of the strike without showing *something*.

But that wasn't the last of the shocks she was going to get; the man turned slightly so that his face was no longer backlit by the street lamp, and she saw *who* it was that had her prisoner.

The Frenchman.

He smiled grimly; a smile that showed, without a doubt, the ends of very elongated and *very* sharp canine teeth.

"You are Miss—Tregarde, I presume?" The voice was soft, faintly accented. Neither it, nor the man's expression, gave her any clue to what he wanted, or what she could expect. But the moment he spoke, she had no doubt that this was the same man who had stopped briefly at the shop; the same one she'd seen bending over the gypsy boy's body in the alley.

Cold wind making her knuckles ache penetrated the fog of fear. One hand was still free—

It might be stupid—but it might be her only chance. She thrust her free hand into her jacket pocket, yanked the silver crucifix out so fast that she heard the sound of ripping cloth, and shoved it into his face.

He stared at it for a moment, still holding her wrist captive; stared at it with his smile fading and puzzlement creeping into his expression. He looked from it, to her, and back again—and she actually saw his eyes widen with sudden understanding.

With a real smile, one tinged with sadness, he took the crucifix from her shaking hand. He took it gently, unwinding her fingers from the base; kissed it in the old manner, and just as gently replaced it in her untorn pocket.

"I have nothing to fear from the Son of God, mademoiselle," he said, patting the pocket. "Only from the sun that rises at dawn. I did not intend to frighten you, but I see that you are very frightened indeed. If I release you now, will you consent to remain and speak with me?"

I don't exactly have a choice, she thought. *If he can move like that—he can get me before I run two steps.*

"Mademoiselle," he said softly, "I have no means to reassure you, I can swear by nothing you would trust. But I mean you no harm. I only wish to ask you questions. No more."

I'm toast if he wants it that way. What have I got to lose? Besides, I'm getting tired of having my arm hanging in the air. She nodded assent, and he released his manaclegrip on her wrist.

She let her arm drop and rubbed it surreptitiously, as he fished in his jeans pocket and came up with a business card.

What is this, he's handing out cards? Have hemoglobin, will travel? She was close to hysteria; so close that she felt wired, and inconsequentials kept getting in the way. *Cripes, he's still not wearing anything more than a sweater—don't vampires get cold?*

"This is yours?" he asked, showing her the card.

She successfully throttled the hysteria down and squinted at the card. She didn't have to give it more than a cursory glance; it was creased and smudged, but hers. She nodded, and shift her weight to her left foot.

"You gave it to Janfri—the young man who—perished here?"

She nodded again, and tried not to shiver as a cold gust of wind went down her collar.

He turned the card over; written on the back was some kind of sign or glyph in red felt-tip. "Have you any idea what this means?"

She shook her head. "I don't know much about the Rom," she replied, her voice little better than a whisper. "That's A—"

She bit off what she was going to say. *If I tell him about Annie, she could be a target—*

"I know of Lady Annie," he told her, as if he had read her thoughts. "She is in no danger from me or mine. This sign—it is a Romany sign for—oh, I think the concept of 'sanctuary' or 'safehouse' is the closest. Did you say or do something that might have implied an offer of such sanctuary to Janfri?"

Another cold breeze cut right through her jacket, and she shivered, nape to knees. She nodded again; swallowed, and dared a bit more. "Look," she said, trying to keep the shaking out of her voice. "Is this all you wanted to know? If it is, I'm freezing; if it isn't, I'm *still* freezing."

He gave her another one of those measuring looks, the kind he'd given her the night she'd first seen him, as the icy breeze ruffled his silky hair. "Is there somewhere nearby where we may go to talk?" he asked finally. "I—it is only fair to tell you that there is truth in some of the legends. Truth in the one concerning thresholds, for example. Until you *invite* me to cross yours, I cannot. Once you do, I can enter at my will. Public places, however, are no problem. If you would prefer it, choose some place neutral to both of us. A bar, perhaps."

She narrowed her eyes, thinking. *He's giving me information. He hasn't done anything to me except stop me from hitting him. And he could; strong as he is, he could have had me around that corner and into the alley in seconds, and have been breaking my arms until I told him what he wanted to know.*

"Is that legend about wooden stakes true, too?" she asked finally.

He nodded, and flicked his hair out of his eyes with a long, graceful hand. "It is. I shall give you this freely—any weapon of wood can harm my kind, and it will take long to heal of the damage. Days; sometimes weeks. Metal will harm us not at all. The sun—as I said—can kill."

A snowflake fluttered down and landed on her nose. She shivered again in the wind, and a second flake landed on her arm. She sneezed. That decided her.

"Come on," she said, taking her keys out of her purse, and heading for the steps.

"You—wish me to follow you? Into your home?" He sounded more than surprised, he sounded flabbergasted.

"Yeah, you might as well." To her own amazement, she could feel herself smiling as she turned back toward him. "I've had everything else in my apartment, I might as well have a vampire, too."

Out of the corner of her eye she could see him watching everything with suspicion. *I think he's more paranoid than I am,* she thought in surprise, and for some reason the thought was comforting. Nevertheless, before they entered the (small) living room, she took a wooden knife from Africa down from the display of weaponry on the wall of the hall, and when she sat down in her favorite chair, she put the knife on the table beside her.

He gave it a cursory glance; made an ironic little bow in her direction, and seated himself on the couch, pointedly ignoring it.

He didn't just *sit*—he *took* his seat; made it his own, for the moment. *Gods, if I live to be a hundred I'll never be that graceful—what am I thinking? He probably* is *a hundred.*

"So—" she said, pretending to a bravado she didn't feel. "I have a vampire in my living room. It would be nice to know the vampire's name, and if he'd like anything to drink besides the usual. *I* wanted some hot tea."

"The vampire's name," he replied, with a ghost of a smile, "is André LeBrel. And the vampire would very much enjoy tea. It is a most civilizing custom, tea. I regret, however, that I cannot enjoy any hospitality other than liquid."

"Let's just stick to tea, shall we?" she replied hastily.

Unless she was dreadfully mistaken, the smile grew—just a hair—and there wasn't so much as a *hint* of anything other than playful amusement in it.

This is weirder than snake shoes.

He maintained his silence through the first half-cup, as she slowly thawed and slowly grew used to his presence across from her. He was just as foxy as she'd remembered him; maybe a little more, now that he had a reason to be charming to her. Completely composed; completely confident.

He should be. This oversized splinter isn't going to do me any real good against him unless I happen to hit a vital spot. She watched him out of half-closed eyes; his very calm was calming her. *I don't want to hit a vital spot. I've never seen a more attractive man in my life. If I didn't have to worry about unauthorized nibbles on the neck . . .*

But he's not pushing; he's doing his best to put me at ease. He's succeeding. He's trying to convince me I can trust him.

And it didn't ring false.

It was he who first broke the silence, speaking in a voice of brown velvet that she'd have paid to hear on the stage. "Can you tell me, Miss Tregarde, what you know about Janfri, and why it is that you gave him your card? I can tell you that he already was great friends with Lady Annie—" He smiled again, this time ironically. His wide brown eyes held a hint of amusement. "Well, as great as any Rom can be with *gadjo.*"

She put the cup down, carefully. "I don't know much of anything; Annie's never said anything about him, and I haven't had the chance to ask her. He came in that afternoon by the service entrance. I think he was expecting Annie; I think he was startled and maybe frightened to see me instead. But he probably figured if Annie'd left me in charge I was okay, so he stayed back there until the customers had all gone, and then came out."

"Yes?" André prompted patiently. "What did he tell you?"

"That he was hunted. He didn't tell me who by; I didn't ask.

But he looked to *me* like somebody who'd gotten himself into unexpectedly deep kimchee, and I didn't want to leave it at that."

"So you gave him your card?"

She nodded, and sipped at the cooling tea. "I told him if he was ever in trouble in my area he could come to me for help."

André raised his eyebrows. "Are you often so impulsive, mademoiselle?"

She flashed a look of anger at him, and he grimaced. "Pardon. I tell you not to toy with me—now I play the word games with you. You are one of those who guards, yes?"

She didn't reply. *Does he know about the Guardians? Who told him?* She looked at him with a new wariness. He waited for her answer; coiled strength, dark grace. She truly wanted to tell him—

She couldn't. Couldn't expose herself and the others.

He shrugged. "Janfri was hunted, as he claimed. I was attempting to find him so that I could deal with the hunter. He did not, or could not, return to his people, so that I was following the rumor of him only. I was—too late in finding him."

She realized suddenly that she had let down her personal shields in his presence so that his emotions—if a vampire *had* emotions—could get through. And that only happened when her subconscious had analyzed a situation and deemed it safe.

And there are times when my subconscious is smarter than I am. It's usually more paranoid than I am. So why has it taken my shields down? She analyzed what was coming from him, and found herself assessing him in an entirely new light. There was guilt there; and mourning, and a deeply felt depression that seemed a great deal like her own. His eyes held shadows within shadows; shadows of pain, and a loneliness that had endured longer than anything *she'd* ever known.

He had emotions all right; as real and as unfeigned as her own. This was an amazingly patient and gentle man, under most circumstances, but there was a steel-hard core to him. Like the dancers she knew, he would smile and do what he had to, and you'd never know he was bleeding.

"So *you* didn't kill him—" she blurted.

"*Le Bon Dieu* forbid!" He looked angry now—and she sensed he was profoundly unhappy. She felt the claws under the velvet, but felt also that they would in no way be turned against her. "*Mais non.* It was as I told you. I was hoping to protect him, as I have pledged to protect all of his clan."

"Protect him from what?"

"In this case—one who wished to use him. That one found him, I think. But how he was killed—"

"Who did it? Who was chasing him?" The words tumbled out, and she leaned forward in her eagerness to hear the answer to one of the mysteries plaguing her.

"The man I asked you of, the one I described to you." His jaw clenched, and his anger smoldered just under the surface of his words. She winced a little at the heat of it. "I feel sure of this. The man is called Jeffries. 'Master' Jeffries by some. Master. *Merde.*" He brooded for a moment, eyes fixed on his mug. "He wanted something of Janfri, of which revenge for a plan I thwarted was a small part. Janfri's death was that revenge. But I do not know *how* he murdered the boy. You say that he never actually reached you?"

"No—do you know what an empath is?" He nodded, and she continued. "That's—one of the things I do. I 'felt' him calling for help before he died. I think you saw me; I reached the alley after you did, so I don't know who murdered him, or why—but I *do* know how he died."

"How?" Her words galvanized him; he raised his head and stared directly into her eyes as if he could pull the knowledge directly from her mind into his. She couldn't look away; didn't want to.

She described psychic vampirism in detail, as André sat tensely on the couch and clenched his mug tightly in both hands, as if he wished he could lock those hands around one particular neck.

". . . so it looked to *me* as though this time the psivamp drained his victim so completely that he killed him," she concluded. "The boy was a burned-out husk, psychically speaking."

Now André shook his head, doubt beginning to creep into his troubled eyes. "Not possible—" he objected. "This thing—it cannot be possible."

"Huh." She snorted. "This afternoon I would have said *you* were impossible. Not possible? Tell that to Janfri. It happened, guy."

She was interrupted by a scratching at the door—and cool, collected André LeBrel jumped a foot, and pivoted as though expecting an enemy to burst through the door at any second.

Di was secretly pleased to see him shaken up a little. "I'll take care of that," she said, before he could object, and rose to let in the building cat—because 'Tilly was her final test of character. If this supernatural creature sitting nervously on the end of her couch could pass 'Tilly's judgment, then he could be believed, and trusted.

"Attila the Nun" was the cat's full name; a registered Maine Coon, she weighed in at nineteen pounds, all muscle (hence "Attila") and was a neutered female (hence, "the Nun"). They hadn't had a bit of trouble with rats since Jerry the super had brought her home, and she was allowed the run of the entire building.

Theoretically she "belonged" to Jerry, but she was fed by everybody and spent at least half her sleeping hours in Di's apartment. She was also the surest judge of character, occult or otherwise, that Di knew.

Tilly greeted Di with a single rub of the head, and strolled immediately into the living room as if she knew exactly what she was wanted for.

And for all I know, Di thought wryly, *she does.*

She headed straight for André. He extended his hand, palm up, toward her. She leaned forward a little to sniff his fingertips.

Now she's either going to take off two of his fingers, or—She rubbed her head on his hand, and leapt into his lap, where she promptly made herself at home.

He relaxed as the cat began to purr, then looked up at Di with a shrug, one hand busy scratching the cat's chin. "Well, mademoiselle—if I do not mistake you, this was something of a test. Do I pass?"

Di nodded, and smiled and realized that it was the first time she'd really smiled in days. "You pass."

He put the other hand to work on the cat's ears. 'Tilly increased her volume. "Then tell me again of this 'psychic vampirism.' If it happened—it must be true."

She went back over the phenomena in more detail—and as she did so, she found herself silently agreeing with her guest that "Mr. Trouble" (aka Jeffries) *was* the most likely candidate. He *had been* a psychic vampire when she first saw him. And if something had happened to make him even more powerful than he was already . . .

She said as much.

"But what?" he asked. "What could do such a thing?"

She sighed, and contemplated the clean line of his jaw. "I don't know," she said, finally. "But I know it's possible. A couple of occultists have hinted about things like that in their works. And—" *I want to trust him. I want to trust him. I want this man for a friend.* She mentally shook herself. *Gods, what am I thinking? He's a vampire*— "—let's just say I've heard of things that could amplify a psivamp." *Like certain magics only the Guardians are supposed to have access to.*

Finally André nodded in reluctant agreement. He removed the cat (who protested sleepily), set her down on the couch, and rose. "I must go," he said, his expression a sober one. "It seems that I have a great deal to do before dawn."

Di stood too, and moved toward the door. As he followed, she half turned so that she could say something to him. "I could help—" she offered hesitantly, then paused, her thoughts a welter of confusion.

He's a vampire—*I'm not sure I really want to help him, I'm not sure I should—but there's already been one death. It was a death I could have prevented if I'd been a little quicker. I've got an obligation—*

"No, thank you," he replied curtly. "This will be difficult enough for one who knows what to do."

She drew back, a bit nettled by his assumption that she was some kind of clumsy amateur. And that bothered her, too.

Now I am really *confused. I like him; I want his respect. And he's a* vampire, *for gods' sake! But he did pass the 'Tilly test—As* she opened the door, she admired the lithe way he moved, the graceful curve of his back. *And he sure is sexy. A lot more attractive than anybody I've ever met—except maybe Dave—*

Hell, I'll never see him again.

That thought actually caused a twinge. She wanted to see him again—

Yeah, and I want other things that aren't good for me. But at least one of my mysteries is solved . . .

"Thank you, mademoiselle," he said at the door. "For your time—for your help. *Au revoir.*"

And he turned and slipped down the stairs, obviously eager to get *on* with it.

She closed the door behind him; locked it, and leaned on it for a moment.

One mystery solved. But not the big one. I have my real vampire; I have my psivamp—but neither of those is the soul-eater.

She shuddered.

And I still have no notion where it's going to strike next.

SEVEN

While the other three headed for the break room, Dave slipped behind the bar and passed the barkeep another ten. The gaunt, sad-eyed scarecrow of a man gave him a dubious look, but poured him a six-ounce tumbler of straight vodka; no ice, no mixer. Dave tossed it off in a couple of swallows, and waited, eyes closed, elbows planted on the bar, for the shaking, the hurting to stop.

It didn't stop, but it became bearable. He waited a moment longer, while the canned music rolled over him and pounded his brain cells, but there was no further improvement. So he pushed away from the spotlighted bar and wove his way back through the crowd to the break room.

He could *feel* every body in the place; their excitement when he brushed past them, the life in them. The white-heat of them; vibes that had fed him up until last night.

No more. No more.

Jason was right; it wasn't enough anymore. The vibes only whetted his appetite, and he had felt something inside him reaching out for those warm, glowing sources of food.

He'd pulled back every time, before he did anything. But. *But.* It was harder every time to pull back.

And the gnawing, devouring hunger kept rasping away at his self-control. He'd sought, with limited success, for something to hold it off. Booze helped; so did drugs. Snow worked the best, but he only had one hit in his stash and he'd used it this afternoon to get to the club without—consequences. Booze and drugs *numbed* the edge of the clawing hunger in his gut. *Nothing* made it go away.

This was his third drink tonight, and the gig was only half over. Three shots of straight vodka, six ounces each, and he was just *barely* able to keep from grabbing one of the little teenys trying to cling to him, and take her out into the back, and—

He shoved open the door to the break room, and three pairs of cynical eyes met his. He flushed, and ducked his head, wondering if they'd guessed how he was trying to fight this— thing—he'd become.

"Poor Davey," Jason said silkily. "Poor Davey. I don't think he's happy, Hidoro."

"He has a conscience," the thing that wore Jack's face said, complacently cleaning his fingernails with a knife. "Inconvenient things, consciences. Expensive to maintain."

"Maybe he needs another lesson," Jason lounged further back in his chair, and half closed his eyes. "I think maybe he ought to be assigned to get you your dinner, Hidoro."

"Aw, come on, Jason," Dave said weakly. "I'd really—give me a break—"

The blond lunged up out of his chair and had Dave by the throat before the other could blink. "There *are* no breaks, Davey," Jason whispered, pulling Dave's face to within an inch of his own. "It's us, and the sheep. Sheep were made to be slaughtered. Get used to it."

Dave cringed, hardly believing the power in Jason's grip, the speed with which he'd struck. *Oh God, oh* God—*he's so strong*—

"I'm stronger than you are, Davey," Jason continued, as if reading Dave's thoughts. "Mind and body, I've got the jump on you now, and I'll always have the edge on you. That's because I'm *not* pretending to be a sheep. Now you'd better start acting like a wolf, Davey-boy—or one of these days we might mistake you for one of *them*." Jason grinned. "And that'd be too damn bad, wouldn't it?"

He let go of Dave and shoved him at the same time; Dave staggered back into the door, his heart pounding, his mouth dry with fear. He tried to say something; found that he couldn't. Jason resumed his chair, and surveyed him with a little smile, crossing his arms over his chest and narrowing his eyes.

"Go out there and help Hidoro," the lead ordered, after a long, excruciatingly uncomfortable moment. "Go cut him out a nice little lamb. Hidoro will wait for you at the van; just find some chippy and get her to follow you out there." He waved one hand carelessly. "Pick up a runaway. You're good at that."

Dave's face flamed at the reminder that the last two girls he'd picked up here had been underaged teenyboppers with forged IDs. *I seem to attract the kids in women's bodies. Oh God. Kids. I can't—*

He's not going to take any excuses—

"Please, Jason—I—I don't think that's too good an idea," he stammered. "We shouldn't be doing this where we hang out. What if somebody notices? What if somebody comes looking for—"

He couldn't finish. But Jason just shrugged. "A hundred runaways vanish a day in this town. Nobody's gonna notice one or two more dropping out of sight. Who's gonna remember 'em, or tell anybody they were here? 'Sides, Hidoro doesn't leave anything to find. Ain't that so, Hidoro?"

The thing just gave Dave a cynical look, and half smiled.

"Go on," Jason ordered, ice suddenly coating his words. "Get out there and do what you were told."

He found himself outside the door and in the hallway— pushed out by the uncompromising command in the lead's voice.

He leaned against the wall, and shook; shook with the effort of holding back sobs, shook with the terrible hunger that was beginning to take over his very thoughts.

I should just walk. Get the hell out of here. Get out of their reach—

And do what? Oh God in heaven—and do what? *I'm trapped. This thing inside me, this* appetite—*it's a monkey on my back, and I'll never be free of it, no matter how far I run—*

Jason was right. He pounded his fist white on the concrete blocks of the wall. *Oh God, he was right. I'm one of them.*

Pain finally made him look at his hand, at the damage he'd done to himself, in dazed bewilderment. He watched in fascination as blood seeped to the surface and collected in tiny beads on the scraped skin of his knuckles.

Then the hunger cut through his daze, and he stumbled back into the club, onto the mobbed dance floor, into the blacklight and the flashing spots.

He saw her at once, knew *this* was going to be the one, this hard-faced old-young chick with frightened eyes, sensuous mouth, and a calculatedly bored, jaded expression. He moved in on her as she writhed in her own little space on the dance floor; watched her watching him, hoping he was heading for her, not believing he was.

Out of the corner of his eye he could see Jason, leaning against the doorway, keeping him under his eye.

He synched his moves with hers, and the old sex drive went into high gear; now he had two hungers goading him on, and his brain wasn't in the driver's seat anymore. He felt himself smile, saw her eyes widen; slipped his arms around her waist and ground his hips into her leather mini, and watched her melt.

And hated himself.

"Hi," he said, just loud enough to be heard over the pounding drums and screaming guitar of Iron Butterfly. "Tired of dancing yet?"

"Sure." Her mouth shaped the word, though he couldn't hear it.

"How 'bout we go outside—" He jerked his head in the direction of the back exit, and let her go; began parting the squirming dancers and moving out, *knowing* she'd follow him.

Jason was gone by the time he reached the door into the hall; *she* was right behind him. He reached back and took her hand, and it trembled a little in his.

"What's your name, sweet thing?" he said, giving her an arch look and a slow, sexy, ultramacho half-smile.

"Sherrie. You're Dave, aren't you? With"—a worshipful pause—"the band?"

"Uh-huh." He squeezed her hand. "Glad I saw you out there; I thought the evening was gonna be a total loss." She glowed, and he squeezed her hand again. "You want a toke? I got some good stuff in the van."

"Sure—"

He interrupted her, saying what he *knew* she wanted to hear. "You doing anything tonight? After the gig?" His thumb caressed her palm knowingly, and she shivered, her eyes got soft, and her lips parted a little.

"N-no," she stammered, moistening her lips with the tip of her little pink tongue.

"You're pretty new to the Apple, aren't you?"

She looked dismayed. "Does it show that much?"

He stopped just inside the entrance, under the glaring "Exit" sign. "Yeah, just a little. You on your own, honey? You got friends, a guy, anyplace to stay?"

She shook her head, avoiding his eyes.

"Hey." He caught her chin in his right hand, tilted her face up to his. "It's no big deal—just—I got this place, and nobody but me in it—"

He bent and kissed her; she parted her lips readily enough when he tongued them, and he probed her mouth, slipped his hands behind her buttocks and crushed her hips against his—

—and could see everything in her head—

She was fifteen and a runaway from Pennsylvania. She thought in New York she'd make it big, maybe as a model. But looks that had been outstanding at home were nothing here. Then she thought she could make it as a dancer, but the only offers she got were from strip joints. She wasn't shacking up with guys for money, yet, but in a way she was even more desperate, she was doing it for food and a place to crash.

Dave's conscience cringed. *Either she's found out that most of the crash pads are just recruiting stations for pimps, or else she hasn't made a crash-pad connection yet.*

That *he* should be going for her was more than she dared dream now—though when she'd come running out here it had been in the hopes of finding someone like him—somebody to match her daydreams and the lyrics of all those songs.

His body kept putting the screws to hers; his mind writhed and grew more nauseated by the moment.

He broke the clinch when she was hot and gasping, and more than ready. "Hey," he said, smiling falsely into her eyes. "You're okay, Sherrie."

Her lips were wet, her eyes dazed and soft, her cheeks flushed. "So're you—" she breathed.

"Let's go out to the van, huh?"

"Okay—"

She shivered in the blast of cold air that met them when he opened the door; but she didn't complain, and she snuggled against him when he put his arm around her.

His conscience was giving him no mercy. *You traitor, you goddamn Judas—*

He was still inside her head. *The alley was dark; just the one, dim light over the back entrance.*

Yeah. To Sherrie's eyes it was dark—not to his. To his, the alley was in clear twilight, and he could see Hidoro waiting for them beside the van.

The van loomed up on their right, a dark blot against the painted brick of the alley. It cast a long, deep shadow—and Sherrie gasped when Hidoro materialized out of the shadow.

He was still in the band costume, but wearing what Dave presumed was his own face, that of the young Japanese boy he'd seen in his apartment. He smiled, cruelly, and Sherrie shivered.

"Dave?" she said, bewilderment plain in her voice. "Dave? What—"

He let go of her shoulders and stepped away from her. She turned to look at him with her face set in a mask of confusion.

"Sorry, Sherrie," he said, choking on the words. "You shoulda stayed home in Pennsylvania."

Her confusion turned to fear as Hidoro approached her; she was trapped between the Oriental and Dave, with nowhere to run that wasn't straight at one or the other of them.

Dave could taste her fear—and so could the need inside him. Before he could stop himself he was drinking that fear in, holding her paralyzed and weakening as he fed, and the hunger finally stopped gnawing at his spine—

No!

He cut himself off from it, from her; doubled over as a cramp hit his gut.

Freed from what he was doing to her, the girl screamed.

None of them, not Hidoro, nor Dave, nor (from the despair in her mind) Sherrie expected a response to that scream. But one came.

"Hey!"

The voice from the street startled all three of them. Sherrie reacted first, screaming again, louder this time.

"Hey! Y'all leave that gal alone!"

Heavy running footsteps echoed in the alley, preceding Sherrie's would-be rescuer. He was a big man, dressed like a construction worker; with Amerind features and long, straight black hair in a ponytail that waved behind him like a battle banner. He was carrying something—a length of pipe, it looked like, and he was holding it like someone who knew how to use it. With a snarl, Hidoro launched himself at the girl, shoving her into Dave's arms, then he whirled toward the attacker, and dissolved into a cloud of evil, black smoke.

The man ran right into the cloud, seeing only Dave under the light, and probably taking him to be the only threat.

He didn't come out on the other side.

A choked-off cry of agony came from inside the cloud, oddly muffled and distant—then the thud of something heavy hitting the pavement.

Sherrie was shaking in Dave's grip; she whimpered, and the fear flooded from her, and it was so *good*—

Half of him wanted to throw up; but the operable, unparalyzed other half of him was sucking it in as fast as she put it out.

The cloud condensed, slowly, revealing the man sprawled facedown on the pavement as it coiled in on itself. The cloud took on man-shape, then color—then became recognizably Hidoro. The Oriental was frowning.

He shoved the body aside with a booted foot; it rolled, arms flapping limply. "*Most* unsatisfactory," Hidoro said, glaring at Dave as if he were somehow to blame. "I only got the kill. I had no time to feed before he escaped me."

He transferred his frown to the girl, who wilted with fear, shrank in on herself, and cried silently.

The frown turned to a smile, and he reached toward her with one long, pale hand. She whimpered, and his smile deepened. The whimper choked off as Hidoro touched her face, and the fear coming from her was so strong Dave couldn't even feel the hunger gnawing at him anymore.

"Still—" Hidoro said caressingly, "there is this one. Young, and vital. I think she will do."

He made a peremptory gesture, and Dave shoved the girl at him, turning quickly away before he could see the creature transform again.

He stumbled blindly toward the rear door of the club as Hidoro chuckled behind him.

Bile rose in his throat, and he flung himself into the shelter of the shadowed hallway.

And straight into Jason. The iron of the lead's hands catching his shoulders shocked him into cold silence.

"Greedy, greedy," Jason chided, as his stomach roiled. "Jumping the gun on us, huh?" He laughed out loud as Dave tried unsuccessfully to control the revulsion on his face and the turmoil in his gut.

"You should be in *good* shape now, huh? Ready for action?"

Only Jason's hands gripping his shoulders kept him on his feet.

"Good. But action is gonna have to wait." Between one moment and the next, he was shoved down the hall toward the dance floor. Jason stayed on his heels, and gave him no chance to falter.

"It's show time, baby."

"Davey-boy got a little greedy and had some appetizers," Jason told Doug as they herded Dave back into the break room at the end of the last set.

"Well, good," the dark bassist snickered. "Then he won't mind helping you and me get ours, will you, Davey?"

Dave shook their hands off him and headed for "his" corner of the room, refusing to answer their baiting. He mopped his sweating face and neck with a towel, then put his gear away with slow, precise care, hoping that they wouldn't see how much his hands were shaking, or guess how close he was to tears.

God, god, kid, I'm sorry, I really am, I couldn't help it, I didn't have a choice—

He caught Jason raising his head and staring toward the closed door, for all the world like a hunting animal sniffing the air.

"Nothing tasty out there," he said to Doug, who grimaced and nodded. "What do *you* think?"

The bassist frowned, and shook his sweat-damp hair out of his face. "Wall Street?" he ventured. "Some pretty high rollers work out of those brokerage houses. They run just as strung and uptight as coke and uppers can get 'em. On the wire, for sure. A lot of 'em work late. We did Mad Ave last night."

Jason nodded, a tight little smile on his lips. Dave turned

away—but felt a hand grab his elbow and turn him around. Doug was holding out his jacket.

Jason pushed him at the bassist, then released him. "Move it, man," he said coolly. "You're driver tonight."

He shrugged into the jacket, the familiar weight of the leather across his shoulders giving him no sense of comfort. "Where's Hidoro?" he asked, stalling.

"Out." Jason pulled on his own jacket.

"But what about the stuff—"

"That's what Master Jeffries hired us roadies for," Doug interrupted, not *quite* sneering.

Right on cue, a silent and painful anonymous figure in a Led Zeppelin T-shirt came in carrying Dave's axe. He was followed by a second, as like to him as a twin, carrying the mike boxes.

"They'll be picking up the mikes and the instruments and stashing 'em for us every night from now on," Doug elaborated. "If you'd been listening instead of wallowing in self-pity, you'd have heard him tell us that before the first show. Come on, get a move on. I'm hungry."

He laughed at the look on Dave's face, and shoved open the door to the hallway.

It seemed strange to be in the driver's seat for a change; he headed in the direction of Wall Street while Jason and Dave watched the streets and buildings intently, eyes narrowed in concentration, as if they were listening for something. He entertained a brief fantasy of flooring the gas, whipping the wheel around, and smashing the van with all three of them in it against the wall of some apartment or factory—

I can't. I can't. I haven't—

"You haven't got the guts," Jason said coolly in his ear. "So don't even play with the idea."

He jumped a foot, fear cramping his gut, along with the hunger that was growing again.

"You shouldn't've cut yourself off from the flow, shithead." Jason laughed as the lights from cars in the other lane made a moving, changing mask of brightness and shadow out of his face. "Well—maybe we'll leave you a little something."

"Stop here," Doug said suddenly, as they moved into the business district and cars all but disappeared.

"Pull over," Jason ordered.

He longed to disobey, prayed for a reason to be able to keep the car moving, but a parking place loomed up like an unpaid debt, and he was forced to pull into it.

He waited in cowed silence for the other two to leave the confines of the van, but instead of opening the door, Doug looked over at Jason with a nasty grin on his face. "Want to try what we were talking about?" he asked. "I think we got two candidates coming down the elevator now."

Jason nodded; echoed the other's grin, then closed his eyes, a line of concentration appearing between his eyebrows.

Dave—*almost* heard something.

Something in the back of his skull, like a radio with the volume turned too low to make out anything but a vague murmur of voices. Except the voices were in his head.

Oh God, now what?

He gripped the steering wheel and tried to concentrate on the streetlights reflecting off the bumper of the car parked in front of him, but the voices were still there, and they were making the hunger worse.

Footsteps on concrete made him look up; he saw two people, a man and a woman, emerge from the building, talking. They were both dressed conservatively, but expensively; both carried briefcases. The man had an umbrella, one of the expensive oversized English imports with a sturdy steel shaft, meant to last a lifetime. That was all he got to see before the fireworks started.

They paused on the curb right in front of the van; they didn't seem to notice that there was anyone *in* the van. Jason's frown of concentration deepened and the hand that had been resting on his knee tightened into a fist.

And what had been a quiet conversation burst into a violent argument. Within seconds the man and woman were shouting at each other, screaming at the tops of their lungs, oblivious to their surroundings.

Dave could feel the flow of anger pouring out of them—anger that flowed at him and around him, anger that the hunger inside him leapt up joyfully to devour.

And there was something else—

Only *that* "something" was flowing from *Jason and Doug* to *them,* not the other way around. Something wild, bestial. Something that was throwing what should have been a mild disagreement out of any contact with reality, and turning it into something deadly.

Jason and Doug opened their eyes and exchanged a smug little smile; then, as Dave stared stupidly, they got out of the van and bracketed the couple.

Who never even noticed they were there.

Unthinking anger flowered into pure, killing rage—and as Dave watched without understanding, the man dropped his briefcase and took his umbrella in both hands.

Fury roared in Dave's ears and sang in his blood, and unnatural, irrational wrath gave the man unnatural strength. He took a step backward, then shoved the umbrella like a sword—

—right through the woman's body.

She made a little mew of pain—her hands scrabbled at the man's face, then her mouth gaped in a silent scream.

Pain, pain, pain. Rage and lust and hate—

Dave just sat there, too shocked to move, as the man pulled his umbrella loose, and the woman doubled over and fell to the pavement. She lay curled around her wound, on her side, a dark, spreading stain pooling around her, black against the white of the concrete. He stabbed down at her, again and again, until the umbrella collapsed and he trampled the body in a dance of insanity and triumph.

And beside him stood Jason and Doug, pulling it all in, their faces as transfigured as saints in rapture, shining with unholy joy and perverse beauty.

With a little cry, Dave cut himself off, and buried his head in his arms, sheltering behind the steering wheel—

Then, suddenly, there was nothing. He looked up in surprise, and Jason and Doug came back to the van and climbed up beside him. For one wildly hopeful moment he thought maybe this *thing* inside him was gone—

No. He could still *feel* the other two, radiating satiation. It was only that the man had gone psychically, emotionally dead. Burned out. Nothing but a husk.

His hands lost their grip on what was left of his umbrella, and he dropped it beside the body. He stared dully at his own feet, plainly feeling *nothing*.

"There's nothing left for him to feel with," Jason said smugly. "*We* got it all. Pull out and go around the corner. I want to see what happens."

Shock set in, and Dave obeyed, too numb to think about doing otherwise. The man continued to stare at the ground, and didn't even look up when the van engine started beside him.

He pulled up to the corner, and hung a U-turn. With no traffic on the street they could wait as long as Jason wanted.

"Worth putting a little out," Doug said, with a sleepy, satisfied smile on his face. "Just like the Master said." The headlights of an approaching car appeared up the street, and Doug's smile grew sly. "Give the zombie a shove, bro. Wouldn't want to leave too many loose ends."

Jason nodded; Dave *felt* something again, and the man shambled out into the middle of the street—

Right into the path of the oncoming cab.

Dave cried out, flung his arms up, and hid his eyes in the crook of his arm as tires shrieked and there was a distant thump from the direction of the headlights.

Doug laughed, and Jason grabbed his elbow and pulled his arm away from his face. He shuddered, and didn't bother trying to hide it.

Jason slapped him, sharply.

"Get used to it," he said roughly. "Sheep and wolves. If you won't be a wolf—"

He let the sentence hand unfinished. Dave clutched at the steering wheel and got his shudders under control.

"Better." Jason leaned back, ignoring the commotion in the street ahead of them, and put his hands behind his head.

"Now what?" Dave managed to croak.

"Home, James," Jason replied. "Home." Then he grinned. "And we'll see if the Master has anything for you to do."

"Home" meant Jeffries's place now, at least for everyone but Dave. As Dave pulled the van into Jeffries's parking place, he wondered how long it would be before he was coerced into giving up his apartment and moving in, too.

He climbed out of the van and tossed the keys to Doug; turned, and started to head for the outside again. But Jason blocked his exit.

His gut went cold.

"Not this time," the blond said, reaching for his shoulder. "You and Master Jeffries need to have a little talk."

Dave backed up a step, avoiding Jason's hand. "What about?"

The lead shrugged. "What do *you* think? Your attitude Davey-boy. You're just not coming along the way the rest of us are. You better start shaping up fast."

Dave took another step backward.

"Indeed," said a cynical baritone voice behind him. "I would say you lack—ah—enthusiasm."

Dave stumbled, trying to pivot too fast for his sense of balance to cope with. Jeffries stood less than a foot away, and he'd come up behind Dave too quietly to be heard.

Dave was trapped now, between Jason and Jeffries. Nowhere to run. His head spun, he caught himself with one hand on the garage wall and licked dry lips.

Jeffries held out his hand without taking his eyes off Dave, and Doug dropped the keys into it. He was as pale and unfeeling as a granite statue in the cold, flickering fluorescent light of the parking garage. "I would say you are less than committed to us," he continued, his voice echoing slightly, his eyes slitted, his mouth a hard line slashed in his face. "I think perhaps you need to truly learn where your loyalties and self-interest lie."

Then Dave went blank for a minute—

No longer than that—he thought.

But one moment he was standing there, facing off Jeffries. The next, he was driving the van out of the garage, with Jeffries lounging tigerlike on the passenger's side of the bench. And he had no memory of anything in between.

He waited for Jeffries to give him instructions. The man remained silent—yet Dave found himself making turns as if the man had directed him explicitly—until he found himself parking the van outside a quiet, obviously private, club.

A mote of surprise penetrated his misery. *Gentility, antique leather, and old school ties. What in hell are we doing here?*

"Hobbyists," Jeffries said, answering his unspoken question. "These men are all numismatists and philatelists." He sneered silently at Dave's look of incomprehension. "Coin and stamp collectors," he explained, as though to a particularly stupid child. "Wealthy ones."

Stamp collectors? After the atrocities of this evening—

Stamp collectors? What's he gonna do? Stroll in, introduce himself, and—and—show 'em a naked penny?

Dave giggled hysterically, and Jeffries glared at him. "You—you're kidding!" he gasped. "A bunch of dried-up old men like *that?* What in hell good are *they* going to do you?"

Jeffries pointed a finger at him—and his throat closed. He

couldn't breathe. And ice ran down his spine when he saw the man's eyes.

"They have passion," Jeffries said coldly. "These 'dried-up old men' are *full* of tortured passion, passion they never gave to a living creature. If you get your mind out of your crotch sometime, you might learn something."

He made a gesture of dismissal, and Dave fell against the steering wheel, gasping for breath. Jeffries slid smoothly out of the van, and stalked into the bar.

Dave huddled in the van, shivering with cold and emotion and not daring to move.

I hope to hell Jeffries takes his own sweet time. I hope he falls flat on his face in there. I hope—

Realization began to sink in of how entirely helpless and without real hope he was. *Oh God. There's no way out of this. No way at all.*

He pillowed his forehead on his arms and shook. He never even saw Jeffries emerging from the bar with a second man. Didn't realize he was standing beside the van until another surge of fear/lust/greed washed over him from 'outside,' and he looked up, startled, to see Jeffries holding out his empty hand, and a stranger staring into it as though it held the Hope Diamond.

And the thing inside him reached out to feed—

The wave of emotion built, fully as high as the rage and blood-lust shared by the couple Jason and Doug had devoured. Dave clutched at the steering wheel, unable to pull himself away this time, as it built higher still, like a scream that went on and on, and showed no signs of stopping.

But it did. Something *snapped*—

Jeffries shoved the man aside and climbed into the cab of the van. There was *nothing* inside the victim now; he was a dead and blackened hulk, emotionally. There was not even so much as a single spark left. It turned empty, unseeing eyes on the occupants of the van, then shambled slowly, aimlessly away.

"Start the van, David."

Feeling benumbed, overwhelmed, he did so; then pulled out into the street.

"The boys are so crude," Jeffries said smoothly. "It isn't necessary for us to kill to get what we need. That fool will go wander off somewhere, get himself killed or join the winos in some alley. It doesn't matter; he can't betray us, and he's as good as dead. Killing is—a waste of energy. Except for Hidoro, of course—but he cleans up after himself."

Dave began shaking again. The bodies—the girl, Sherrie, and the guy—they *had* disappeared. He wasn't sure he wanted to know *how.*

At least they aren't in the van . . .

"I think you should stay with us from now on, David," Jeffries said, as Dave pulled the van into his parking space. "It's too dangerous for you to be staying on your own."

The tone behind the words left no doubt in Dave's mind that this was no request—it was an order.

He wanted to weep; wanted to tell Jeffries where he could put the whole idea—

He found himself nodding meekly and handing over the keys to the van.

He'd thought his spirits couldn't sink any lower. He now discovered there were further hells below the one where he'd been.

—trapped—

He followed in Jeffries's wake, obedient as a child, his mind cursing and railing at a body that would no longer obey him. The hall was miles long, a throat that swallowed his soul by inches.

At the end of the seemingly endless journey, Jeffries turned to his door and put his key in the lock—but the door opened before he could turn it.

"Master—we had a visitor."

It was Jason. Light glinted off Jason's hair. Jeffries pushed Dave in ahead of him, but Dave froze at the sight of the lead guitarist's condition.

Jason—disheveled, clothing torn, and with a bruise purpling under his left eye—unceremoniously grabbed Dave's arm and hauled him in, allowing Jeffries clear passage of the door. Jeffries stared at the blond with the first hint of surprise Dave had ever seen him show.

"Jason—what on earth—"

Doug emerged from the living room. "Like he said, we had a visitor, Master," the bassist said carefully, touching his own cut and swollen lip. "He just about took us apart. He'd have gotten away if Hidoro hadn't shown up when he did."

Jeffries got a strange look on his face, and strode into the living room; Jason moved around behind Dave, and double-locked the door. "Don't even think it, Davey-boy," he said quietly, though without his earlier sneer. "You just go on inside."

Dave hunched his shoulders and obeyed.

Jeffries was already there, standing beside the prone, unconscious body of a young, dark-haired man. His face was again registering surprise, but that was fading into something like intense satisfaction.

Dave took a closer look at the intruder; he was slim, his apparent age about twenty-five. He didn't *look* all that formidable—which made it *very* odd that he was tied hand and foot with airplane cable, cable that had once been used to secure a bicycle from theft.

"Well," Jeffries said, his voice rich with pleasure, nudging the prone man with one toe. "Well, well. The young man who— threatened me in the matter of that gypsy trash. But—Jason, why the wire cable?"

"That's all that'll hold him," Jason replied sullenly, emerging from the entry hall behind Dave. "He got away from us twice. We tried everything, and he went through us like the Front Four of the Green Bay Packers."

The lead was rubbing his arm, and Dave guessed at other injuries besides the black eye.

"Hidoro had to put him out," the blond continued. "We couldn't. He threw *me* clear across the room."

"He did?" Jeffries looked startled. "I knew he was strong but—where *is* Hidoro? Why didn't he *kill* this man?"

There was something under Jeffries's startlement; after a moment, Dave recognized what it was, and nearly lost his teeth. Because it was *fear* that stood in the Master's eyes, and colored his words.

"He went out hunting again," Jason supplied. "He told me to tell you that he used up a lot of strength subduing this guy. I swear to you, Master, if Hidoro hadn't been here, this— whatever he is—*would* have gotten away. Hidoro said he *can't* kill him. Said you can't kill the dead—whatever *that* means."

Jeffries puzzled over that statement for a long moment— then suddenly grinned. "Well. Well, well, well. If that means what I *think* it does, I know what will take care of him for us."

He cast a look around the living room, then shook his head regretfully.

"No wood," he said, and sighed. "Not a stick of wood in the place. I never thought I'd come to regret my Eastern tastes in furnishings. Ah well. I think there are other ways, things that won't leave any bodies to explain."

What in hell is he on about? Dave thought; he saw Doug and Jason exchange puzzled looks and shrugs.

Jeffries pondered the young man at his feet a moment more.

"Never mind," he said finally. "I don't need a stake; the sun will serve my purposes quite handily."

"The sun?" Doug asked hesitantly.

"Exactly. Jason, Doug, take our importunate young vampire up to the sun porch and chain him there." Jeffries raised his head and stared at the closely curtained windows—and smiled. "It can't be more than a few hours till dawn, and that porch faces due east. I *hope* he's aware by then." He smiled; a shark's smile. "I want him to savor his experience."

"Vampire?" Doug squeaked—and Dave began to giggle hysterically again at the look on his face.

"Of course." Jeffries raised one eyebrow. "What did you *think* he was? For that matter, what did you think *you* were?"

Dave's giggles died, and his heart chilled. He stared down at the young man's slack face with horror as Jason and Doug began to drag him out to the French doors leading to the porch. Jeffries took in the stricken expression on his face, and smiled.

"Indeed, David," he repeated. "What *did* you think you were?"

EIGHT

Di opened the useless little corner cabinet above the sink and contemplated her brand new bottle of Scotch for a moment with her fingers resting on the handle. Bought just this afternoon, it stood in splendid isolation on the otherwise empty middle shelf, replacing the one she'd finished in two bouts of—

Self-pitying indulgence. There's no other term for it. And both inside of a week.

She quietly closed the cabinet, leaving the bottle where it was.

I don't need it, and I've been hitting on it far too often. It doesn't solve the problems, it doesn't make them go away—all it does is make me forget about them. Temporarily. And when I'm drunk on my butt, I'm not doing anything productive about problems or mundania. It isn't helping, and it might be hurting.

She filled the kettle, put on hot water for tea, and gave thought to what she should do with the rest of the evening. When the water was boiling, she picked out some bags of Red Zinger, put them to steep in the hand-thrown pot Lenny had given her, and carried the pot out to her desk. She looked at the pitifully small pile of manuscript pages, then sat herself down at her desk, and resolutely turned back to the tribulations of the lovely, languishing, and thrice-ravished Sarah.

Tomorrow is Sunday, which means I can sleep late. Dave—the wound is raw. I know that. I'm going to have to figure out why and what to do about it. I can't do anything about the soul-eater tonight. I don't know anything more about it now than I did before, I only know what it isn't. I'm not going to go play bait out on the street for it. The only thing I can think of doing is something involving group magic—and I'm not sure about trying that. I want to think hard about running a group-magic Circle on it and weigh all the factors, pro and con, before I even broach the idea to Len. So—let's do something about paying the rent.

Besides, work is supposed to be the best cure for the jitters. That's what Granny always told me, anyway.

All right, Sarah. Let's see if we can get you out of the Captain's cabin and into a little more trouble . . .

Di bent over the typewriter, cup of hot tea at hand, pot of tea on the warming plate beside her. Sarah was disposed to cooperate. Within an hour, Di was humming while she typed. Within two, she knew she was on a roll. By midnight the tea was gone, and Sarah was showing sign of a backbone. By three A.M. the Captain had a sense of humor. Not *precisely* within the outline, but if Di tweaked it gently, she doubted anyone would notice. And it sure made working with those two characters a lot easier.

By five she could hardly keep her eyes open, but the first mate had just begun his mutiny plans and she wanted to get *that* set up properly before she called it a night.

Six A.M. and she was at a point where things would be easy to pick up and run with when she started again.

She stretched, and her shoulders popped; she was a little amazed at all she'd done. *Tomorrow—no, today—I'll have plenty to deal with.* She regarded the pile of typed paper with a bit of weary satisfaction. *The hardest part is going to be keeping this monster inside their specs. I'd just as soon that Sarah challenged the whole lot of them to duels, ran the first mate through herself, took over the ship, and left Tall Dark and Macho to stew on that island.*

She yawned hugely, and rubbed her gritty eyes. *Time to pack it in.*

She was too tired to worry about anything past finding the bed without falling over her own feet and breaking her neck, much less that she had been hostess to a creature of myth the night before. There could have been twenty vampires hanging upside down from her window ledge, and as long as the apartment wardings held, she wouldn't have cared.

She peeled off her clothes, pulled on the oversized T-shirt that served her for a nightgown, and fell into bed without even tying up her hair.

I'm gonna regret this when I have to comb it out—

That was her last thought.

A feeble rattling at the kitchen door, the door that let onto the fire escape, woke her up. She listened to it a moment, confused, before she was able to identify *what* was making the noise and *where* it was coming from.

The wind? No—if it was blowing that hard, my windows would be rattling, too. The cat? Not bloody likely! Attila hates the fire escape.

In defiance of reason, the rattling continued. She rubbed her eyes and peered at the clock beside the bed.

Noon. Not likely to be a burglar either, not in broad daylight. What in hell is out there? Some stray? When Attila finds it, it'll be cole slaw.

Without probing beyond the wardings she couldn't tell for certain—but if "it" was alive, it was at too low an ebb to "feel" from inside the apartment.

So that lets out just about everything, including a stray on Attila's turf. It must *be the wind. Maybe something just coming in from an odd angle.*

The bed was *so* soft and warm; she was just about ready to ignore the noise and drift back into sleep, when the rattling stopped—and she heard the door swing open, creaking, followed by a soft thud, as something large and heavy hit the kitchen floor.

There was a baseball bat under her bed, and a knife in the bookshelf in her headboard; both were in her hands a millisecond after the creaking stopped.

She slipped into the hall without a sound, avoiding the floorboards that creaked without having to think about it—having run this drill at least once a week since she'd moved into the place.

Sometimes paranoia pays off.

She kept herself plastered to the kitchen-side wall of the hallway, eased up on the open door noiselessly, her feet growing cold and numb in the chill air that was blowing in the open door. She peeked carefully around the edge of the doorframe, exposing as little of herself as she could.

There was a dark-haired, slender man sprawled facedown on the worn yellow linoleum of her kitchen floor.

He was half-naked; at least it looked that way to *her.* So far as she could see, he was clothed in nothing more than a pair of mangled blue jeans, more rips than whole cloth; barefoot, and battered, but he wasn't a street bum. Those jeans had been clean and not too worn before whatever it was that got him had hit him.

And he looked like hell. Where cloth didn't protect, he was *covered* with livid burns; she hadn't seen anything that bad since the accident in chem lab back in college with the overcharged gas line. Already parts of his back were blistering.

She stared in horrified astonishment, and the sun came out from behind the clouds, framing the stranger in a square of yellow-gold light. The man moaned then, then scrabbled feebly at the cracks in the floor, as if the light *hurt* him. He succeeded only in getting himself turned onto his back—

But now she could see his face, twisted with pain. Her uninvited visitor was the vampire, André LeBrel.

She dropped the bat, and jammed the knife into the crack between the wall and the doorframe beside the kitchen door. She ran into the kitchen; when her feet hit the icy air from the open door they ached with cold. She just barely registered the pain; she vaulted André's body to get the kitchen door shut, locked, and the curtains over the window closed.

The moment the light was no longer falling on him, the young man stopped moving. He moaned as she knelt beside him, but she could see that he was no longer truly conscious.

She hated to do anything to him; winced at the thought of how her lightest touch would send waves of agony through his body. His chest and arms were worse than his back; terrible burns that had blistered and broken open.

And beneath the burns—a set of ugly slash marks and brutal bruises, clear signs of some kind of fight. His face was battered, one eye blackened, his lower lip cut and swollen, his throat mottled with bruising.

"Gods—" She spoke aloud without thinking.

He stirred, movement making his hair fall limply across his forehead; opened his eyes, and there was sense in them.

His lips moved a little, as if he were trying to speak; his right hand curled in a painful attempt to gesture, but he couldn't raise it more than an inch.

"Don't talk," she said urgently. "Don't even try. You'll only hurt yourself more. I'll get you to a doctor—"

His eyes widened, and he gurgled in a frantic attempt to convey something to her—it was a futile attempt, but the fear in him penetrated even past her shielding.

"Wrong idea, huh? Okay, okay, I understand. I won't take you anywhere." She chewed at her thumbnail in frustration as he relaxed, closed his eyes again, and lapsed back into unconsciousness.

She was frustrated and frightened. Helplessness churned down in her stomach. She didn't know what to do for him, and she didn't know what had *done* that to him. The sun of course— but how had he been caught out by day? Those burns—they were second-, maybe third-degree burns, *not* within the scope of her rough first-aid training. And the other injuries were just as daunting; the slashes looked as though they needed stitches, and she couldn't tell if the bruises were indicative of internal damage. Someone, something, had attacked and beaten him, mauled him, then left him out in the sun to die. Who? Mr. Trouble? But André had been strong enough to take the man down before. *She* had been strong enough to daunt him. If it *was* Mr. Trouble, and he had gotten backing—who could it have been? The Oriental she'd seen him with in the club?

She sat back on her heels, chilled, and shivering with more than cold, twisting a strand of hair in both hands. *What do they do for burns in hospitals? Gods,* think, *Tregarde. Burns—the skin is so damaged already you have to prevent more injury. You've got to cushion them. Aren't they using water beds now? What do I have that I could use? Maybe that air mattress. I've got to get him out of the kitchen, anyway. If nothing else, I can use the air mattress to move him. I sure's hell can't carry him.*

She dove into her bedroom and dug the thing out of the back of the closet and sat down on the floor beside him with it spread out in a scarlet splash on the yellow linoleum. She blew into the valve to inflate it until she was dizzy. It *always* seemed to take forever to fill, but this time was worse than all the others combined.

It was plastic, not canvas. *At least he isn't going to stick to it,* she thought, surveying it and him dubiously. *Provided he survives the next few moments.*

She steeled her nerves, and rolled him onto the mattress, her own flesh wincing at what she was doing to him. He whimpered a little, but did not wake again, even when she dragged the whole mess into the living room.

She was tired and sweating by the time she got him into the warmth and darkness of the living room. She sagged down next to him, and stared at his pain-ravaged face. *Now what?*

He was still unconscious, and it seemed to her that he was weakening. His breathing was shallower; the whimpers and moans of pain he made were fainter, though his face was set in a grimace that told her he *wasn't* lapsing into relaxation, but into further agony.

Dammit!

She pounded her fist against the wooden floor in frustration, striking again and again at the unyeilding surface until she managed to scrape her knuckle.

"Crap!"

She stuffed the injured finger into her mouth reflexively; sucked at it and tasted blood—

And froze.

Blood. What if they drained him of resources to where he can't *heal himself?*

If I stop long enough to think about this—I'll panic.

She got to her feet, and ran out into the enormous empty room beside her living room, headed straight for the tiny altar on the eastern wall of the Living Room.

Living alone as she did, she no longer had to hide her ritual implements as she had when she was in college. Arranged carefully on the plain wooden table were a cup, a dish of salt, an incense burner, a small oil lamp, and her atheme. Made by her own hands—and used more than once in mundane *and* arcane self-defense, it was a black-hilted, perfectly balanced throwing knife.

Good thing I always keep my atheme sharp. The ritual knife was honed to a razor edge and she maintained it in surgical cleanliness. It should be safe enough—no need to worry about blood poisoning the way she would if she used the knife she'd left stuck in the wall.

Think about blood poisoning, and not about what you're going to do—

She shivered anyway as she fought back the early symptoms of another panic attack. *I've got this situation under control. I think. Mostly.* She picked up the blade and returned to the living room.

He was still there, and there was no doubt in her mind as to the gravity of his condition. He was fading by the second.

She knelt at the young man's side and made a careful nick in her wrist.

Now, before I chicken out.

She leaned over, her hair falling across her arm and his chest, and held the bleeding cut to his lips.

There was no warning; one minute she was fine—

The next, she was graying out; her eyes unfocused, and she was overwhelmed by a wave of pleasurable weakness that washed over her and made her sag limply over him—

Then the weakness became *all* pleasure. She closed her eyes and shuddered uncontrollably, caught in overwhelmingly sexual bliss that was like *nothing* she had ever experienced before, and which had no room in it for rational thought.

It ended as suddenly as it had begun. One moment she was all animalistic pleasure, the next, herself.

She opened her eyes, and blinked.

André was conscious, holding her wrist in both hands, keeping pressure on the wound she had made there. It had stopped bleeding, and the edges were sealing together.

He already looked better. His burns were red and painful to look at, but they weren't blistered, broken open, or seeping fluid. The wounds were closed; and his bruises were fading even as she watched.

There was intelligence in his warm, brown eyes—and shame or guilt, or both.

He released her wrist and looked away, past her shoulder, unable to meet her eyes. "I beg your pardon," he whispered softly. "I never intended—that."

She snatched her hand back, and her cheeks burned; she felt embarrassed and confused. *Like I'd been caught writing a porn novel,* she thought. *I don't understand—*She was acutely conscious that she was wearing nothing more than the thin cotton T-shirt; she, who hadn't been body-conscious since before college.

"What—happened?" she asked, getting the words out with some difficulty. She didn't want to know—and yet she did.

"It—what you felt—that is our protection, and the coin with which we pay for that which we must have to live." He whispered still, and there was an equal amount of embarrassment in his voice. That made it easier for her to look back at him.

"If I had known," he continued. "If I had known what you would venture—I would have forbid you—"

That killed any shame.

Oh you would, would you? she thought, anger sparking and burning away the last of her reticence. "You and who else, laddy-buck?" she snapped. "You weren't in any damned shape to do anything to stop me! And I've got a hot news flash for you; *no one* tells me what I will or won't do!"

She tossed her tangled hair back over her shoulder, picked up her atheme, and lurched to her feet, doing her best *not* to show the dizziness that was making the room do a little waltz around her.

"I'm going to put a bandage on this," she said, holding the cut, which her abrupt surge of movement had reopened. "I'll be right back. *Don't you move.*"

The room was still showing an alarming tendency to rotate, and her vision kept fogging, but she managed to flounce indignantly off to the bathroom despite these handicaps. She ignored some strange sounds behind her that might have been anything from gasps of pain to muffled chuckles.

She took advantage of the opportunity to change into something a little more dignified than an oversized T-shirt.

When she returned, wrist neatly bandaged, she felt a bit more in control; sweater and jeans and hair neatly knotted at the nape of her neck made her feel at less of a disadvantage.

Less exposed.

Already André's burns had faded to no worse than a bad sunburn—but he did *not* look good. He was lying flat on his back with one arm over his eyes; his mouth had a pinched look about it, and under the red of burn, he seemed terribly bleached.

She studied him for a moment with her head tilted to one side, trying to assess what she saw with the little she knew—or thought she knew—about vampires. "Are you *supposed* to look that white?" she asked, finally. "I think you look pretty wretched right now, and I don't remember you being *this* pale, but the only vampires I've ever seen were in the movies."

"I—attempted to disobey you, mademoiselle, Diana," he replied, his voice thin with strain. "I met with great lack of success. And to answer your question: no, since I confess to you that I feel quite horrible, I suspect that I do not look as I should. Or if you will, I suspect I look as miserable as I feel. It would be difficult for me to make a comparison, however—the mirror legend is also true."

"Oh," she said, remembering Christopher Lee movies and not much else. "Um—so you, uh, need to get back to your coffin or something?"

He began shaking silently, and she was alarmed. She started to ask what was wrong, when her alarm turned to annoyance.

He's laughing *at me, the little creep!*

He took his arm away from his eyes and caught her expression, and his laughter died in chagrin. "I beg your pardon," he said contritely. "I seem to have offended you yet again. I—am a fool. There is no way you could know what is truth and what is silliness. We do not require the props of bad theater, Diana. Only a bit of one's native soil, and that is safely *here*."

He tapped the wide metal bracelet he was still wearing.

"This is hollow, and contains what I require. My enemies would need to remove my hand to remove this. *If* they had known it for what it is. Now *that*, I suspect, would have killed me. As it was, the sun only hurt me, as did the injuries they dealt me when I was bound and at their mercy. I was stronger than they were, even then; I managed to release myself from the bonds when the sun became too much for *them* to bear."

"You came here," she said, sinking down onto the floor beside him, cross-legged. "Why?"

"I dared not go to my usual shelters," he replied unhappily, his mouth tightening. "I remembered you; and that you had invited me to cross your threshold. I had nowhere else to turn; I hoped that you would help me, or at least not cast me out."

That much talking seemed to have exhausted him. He was still plainly in pain, and every word seemed to take a little more energy out of him. She was alive with curiosity—but it could all wait.

"So," she surmised, "you won't have any problem staying here as long as I keep you out of the sun?"

He nodded, and closed his eyes wearily.

"What do you need besides rest?" she continued. "More—uh, nourishment—"

Now she blushed again.

"Animal will suffice," he said faintly.

"Huh. But not as well, right?"

He cleared his throat uncomfortably. "I cannot lie to you— no. Not as well. But—"

"But nothing. Just leave a little for me—and tone down that 'protection' bit next time, okay? It's a little hard on your donor." She found that she was smiling.

He's too gorgeous for words. And—if he didn't do anything to me when I nearly passed out, I can't see where I'm in any danger from him at all. That—experience—wasn't exactly bad. Just so I don't make a fool out of myself. Lawsy, it would be easy to make a fool out of myself.

He opened his eyes and saw her smile, and returned it, shyly. "Okay," he ventured. "I *can*, if I am aware."

"Which you weren't—not even conscious. Or whatever it is you call 'awake.'" He blinked at a strand of hair in his eyes; she reached out absently and flicked it to one side for him. "Probably last-ditch defense mechanism," she hazarded. "Make sure your energy supply doesn't get away from you before you get what you need. Hm?"

"Probably," he agreed, softly, looking away. A faint flush crept across the tips of his ears.

She chuckled to herself. *Made you blush, did I? Serves you right.* "Look, stay awake for a bit longer, and stay *put.* I'm not going to leave you all night—I mean, day—on a cold plastic air mattress."

She got the spare blankets from the hall closet and made up the couch into a fairly comfortable bed, while he watched with fuzzy interest. She could tell from the glaze over his eyes that he was hanging on to his wakefulness with teeth and toenails. When she had finished, she helped him onto it—and was acutely aware, with his warm body so closely in contact with her own, that he was wearing next to nothing. The shredded jeans hardly counted.

But if *he* was as aware, he was too worn and hurting to show it, or for it to affect him much. His eyes were closing and his breathing growing shallow even as she tucked him in.

She straightened, sighed, and looked down at him. He was already out for the count. His breathing was *very* slow, *very* shallow. Imperceptible; only knowing what she was looking for enabled her to see it at all.

I can see why the legends say they're "dead" by day.

She touched his forehead lightly; his skin was cool to the touch, and she remembered how he had been wearing nothing more than sweater and jeans both times she'd seen him before. *Maybe he didn't need the blankets—well, he didn't object. Do vampires get cold?* She wondered about that for a moment, then drifted over to her desk, and Sarah—who now seemed utterly unreal. From another world altogether.

There's a vampire in my living room. There's a vampire *in my* living room. *I feel like I'm living in Stephen King's head.*

His left eye was still a bit purple, but now that most of the bruises and burns had faded, she could see the dark rings of fatigue beneath both eyes. That only made him look more vulnerable.

Gods, is he ever a fox. Captain Sommers, eat your heart out.

There is no way I can concentrate on Sarah while I've got the vampiric hunk of the century lying on my couch.

She busied herself with domestic chores; her stomach finally woke up from shock and complained to her, demandingly. The cravings that arose were—not surprisingly—for red meat, spinach—

Iron, of course. I wonder how much he got? I feel worse after I've donated blood to the Red Cross, so it probably was less than half a pint. Still.

Physical activity allowed her to get used to his presence; by early afternoon—particularly since she had her back to the couch—she was able to get back to Sarah.

The mutiny was engrossing enough—*action at last!*—to get her involved. Once again, she was on a roll, totally held by what was in her head and going onto the paper, until her stomach growled.

She looked up in surprise, saw that she'd turned on her light without even realizing she'd done so. It was after sundown. *Well* after sundown.

Huh. Best I've done since I started this monster.

Her stomach complained again; she wrinkled her nose and headed for the kitchen, with a brief glance at the couch. No movement, no signs of life.

Or is it signs of undeath? Who knows.

She turned the classical station up enough so that she could hear it in the kitchen as she worked. It was obviously getting on toward Christmas, because they were doing selections from the *Messiah*. She sang happily along with "Unto Us a Child Is Born" until the couch creaked—

Well, the undead hunk is back among the land of the conscious.

"Welcome back," she called, waiting for her soup to heat. "I'll be out in a minute."

"Do you realize how fortunate you are?" a soft, melodious voice replied from the depths of the couch.

He must sing like an angel. "Non sequitur?" she answered.

"The music. I have been listening while you worked. You turn a knob, flip a switch, and *voilà*. Beethoven, Berlioz, Verdi. Accessible to any with the price of a radio, and at all hours."

Bet it's the "at all hours" part that he likes. "Not to mention Pink Floyd, Led Zeppelin, and Crosby, Stills, Nash, and whoever they dragged in this week," she countered. "And I hate to think what the price of *their* concert tickets are. Classical at least you can get the cheap seats."

"*Mais oui,*" he replied agreeably. "Also those. And records, by which a memorable performance may be held for all time. Who would believe Woodstock without recordings, *n'est-ce pas?*"

She left her soup to poke her head around the kitchen door and stare at him. "You mean to tell me that a thousand-year-old vampire is a closet rock fan?"

The top of his head and his eyes appeared over the back of the couch. "Not a thousand years," he said, a chuckle in his voice, and a smile in his eyes. "And not a 'closet' fan."

"Oh, really?" She smelled the soup beginning to scorch, and yelped, pulling back into the kitchen to rescue it.

She emerged a few moments later with a mug of soup in one hand, and two mugs of tea in the other. "Here," she said, handing him one of the tea mugs. "You said yesterday you could drink things. Besides the usual."

He accepted it with what looked like gratitude, cupping his hands around the mug as if drawing warmth from it. "Yes, I did. You remember things well, mademoiselle."

"Comes with the territory. Do you get anything out of this besides the taste?"

"Sadly, no." He half smiled. "It seems that to be nourishing, my drink must be from the living."

"Too bad." She settled herself in the chair beside the couch and sipped her soup. "Now, about your taste in music—"

He brightened, and launched into the subject with cheerful

abandon. This young man was very different from the aloof, otherwordly creature she'd sat across from just the previous evening. There was no doubt that love of music was one of his ruling passions.

And no doubt that his tastes were as catholic as hers. And remarkably similar.

Both loved rock; both abhorred country and western ("Unless they keep their mouths shut—" Di amended, and André bobbed his head emphatically. "Indeed. So long as they do not—attempt to sing—" He shuddered.) and both loved orchestral and ethnic music.

The only place their tastes did not coincide was within the classics. *He* loved opera—which *she* could well do without.

"You mean you loved the little opera-ballet girls," she said accusingly, remembering that at the turn of the century the Paris Opera Ballet had been little better than a recruitment center for expensive mistresses.

He flushed, slowly, beginning with the tips of his ears. "Well," he admitted, under her unflinching gaze. "Uh—yes. But—"

She chuckled heartlessly, and his flush deepened.

She, on the other hand, adored medieval and renaissance music, which he dismissed with a flip of his hand as "mere caterwauling." They argued about that for a good half hour before she decided to change the subject.

"You look better," she observed, finishing off the last of her soup, and relaxing into the arms of the chair.

He held out his hand. It shook, despite his obvious effort to control it. "I do not think I should be much of a challenge to M'sieur Jeffries," he replied wryly. "Not that I was before."

She toyed with a wisp of hair that had escaped from the knot. "Are you going to tell me what happened?" she asked, after a moment of silence.

He looked at her dubiously.

"That's *my* couch you're lying on," she pointed out remorselessly. "You're under *my* roof, sheltering under *my* sanctuary, with *my* blood running around in your system. If you get tracked here . . ."

She pointedly did *not* finish the sentence. He sighed, and inclined his head.

"Very well," he acquiesced. "But—first, a bath? Perhaps clothing?"

She raised her eyebrows, but smiled faintly. "Well, I don't think that's too much to ask. The bath I can manage, at least. I don't know about the clothing—though I think we aren't *too* dissimilar in size. If you don't fit mine, you're out of luck. *I* don't keep men's clothing in my closet for chance visitors."

"The bath would be enough." He pointedly ignored that last sally, held out his hand—which still shook—and she climbed out of her chair and pulled him to his feet with it.

"I thought vampires didn't like running water—" she said, draping one of his arms over her shoulders so that he could lean on her to steady his uncertain steps. No doubt of it, he was weak as a boiled noodle.

"A foul calumny," he replied. "Having only to do with the fact that we are territorial, and tend to mark our ranges by landmarks. They might as well have said we do not cross mountains, or lakes, or major highways."

"Oh, okay." Once again she was acutely conscious of him, and concentrated on getting him into the bathroom with the door safely closed between them.

Not at the moment. If Dave and I couldn't make a thing work how in hell *could I have a good relationship with a vampire?* A dozen answers to that question occurred to her, but she pushed them all aside, hastily, and returned to her bedroom. *He's awfully lean, and not that much taller than I am. Those jeans Annie gave me that turned out to be too big might fit him fine. I've got a couple of baggy sweaters that ought to fit about anybody. He's going to have to do without underwear, though.*

Boy, I can think of a lot of things I'd like to do to him without underwear . . . Jeez, what am I thinking? She blushed, and dug into the back of her closet where she kept clothing that didn't fit but was too good to throw out.

"Are you still alive in there?" she called through the closed bathroom door.

"A reasonable facsimile, mademoiselle," came the muffled reply.

"I'm leaving some clothes outside the door," she told him. "If they don't fit, you're on your own. And it's chilly in the living room."

She didn't wait to hear his answer, but went back to the typewriter and Sarah, before she lost her momentum.

I'm a lot better at this than I used to be, she thought, rereading the last few pages, and chewing the end of her pencil. *I didn't used to be able to immerse myself like this, no matter what. Sure never thought I'd be writing category romances; I used to think it would be historical mainstream, occult thriller, or nothing. On the other hand, if I wrote what I* know—*people could get hurt. Either that, or it'd get rejected as being too unreal. I seem to have a knack for this, anyway, enough so that Morrie thinks it'll pay all the bills by next year. Thank the gods for Granny's nest egg, though. Paid for college* and *my last year and a half in the Apple.*

She flung herself back into Sarah's tribulations, and didn't come out again until André touched the back of her neck with a leaf-brush of a caress.

She shrieked and jumped, and whirled in her chair to meet the imagined threat.

He stared back, equally surprised, and tripped and landed on his rump when his shaky knees wouldn't hold him.

"Don't *do* that," they cried in chorus. Then they stared at each other for several minutes—

—and dissolved into helpless laughter.

She got herself out of her chair, still shaking with laughter, and offered him a hand up. He accepted it without any evidence of shame, and she helped him back to the couch.

"Now," she said, settling into her chair again. "About what happened to you last night—"

He made an expressive and completely Gallic shrug. "I followed this M'sieur Jeffries to where he lives. He left, but knowing now where he laired, I decided to confront him while I still had the advantage of surprise, to ambush him as it were, before he could arrive again. He was, however, no longer living alone. In fact, there were *three* young men in the apartment, one of them Oriental. I saw them first, and attempted to conceal myself, but they somehow detected me. That should *not* have been possible. The two attempted to detain me. They were amazingly strong. *Too* strong, Diana. It is not natural, their strength, it is uncannily like my own. Nevertheless, I nearly managed to evade them. Then the Oriental appeared."

He tilted his head, and his eyes darkened. "What happened then is not clear to me. Something disturbed my mind for a moment. The Oriental—did *something* to me. I think I recall a cloud, or smoke, but my memory is not clear. My head was turned all about, and I was within the smoke, and *it* was within *me,* and it seemed alive."

"A drug?" she hazarded.

He shook his head negatively. "No. No, it was not a drug; drugs do not affect us. Certainly they would not affect me like this. It was terribly cold, terribly painful—it was like a blow to the soul, like—like the closest thing I can remember . . ."

His voice trailed off, and his expression became strange, a little fearful, and very distant.

"*Like?*" she prompted, sharply.

"It was very—like—dying. Only not dying. *Mon Dieu. Very* like dying."

His voice faded again, but she did not prompt him. His eyes looked lost, haunted, and she let him sort out his thoughts himself.

Finally he recollected himself and his surroundings. "Whatever it was," he continued, "it injured me, deeply, who—very

little can harm. The touch of the sun, hurts inflicted by wood—
and not much else. I was not altogether unconscious, but I was
not aware of a great deal when Jeffries returned. He recognized
me for what I am, and determined to have his vengeance. Fortunately, he could find no wood to—"

He shivered, looked off beyond her shoulder, and rubbed his
long, slender hands over his forearms.

I don't think stake jokes would go over very well right now, she
thought.

He looked back at her. "Luck was with me in that. His minions chained me upon an east-facing porch and took revenge
upon my body for what I had done to them in the struggle.
When the sun rose, I could see that they began suffering nearly
as much as I was. When I feigned unconsciousness, they de-
parted, and I freed myself."

He shrugged again. "The rest, you know already."

"You called them 'minions,'" she said thoughtfully. "How
sensitive are you to—uh—nonnatural phenomena?"

"The psychic?" he supplied.

She raised her eyebrow, and he smiled faintly.

"I am rather well read, mademoiselle. There are two places in
these modern times that are safe for my kind to spend the daylight hours—those of us who have not the means to purchase a
secure sanctuary, that is. Can you guess them? Two places safe
from sunlight, and from the curiosity of men."

*Funny, it never occurred to me that a vampire might not be in-
dependently wealthy.* She shook her head.

He chuckled, and held up a slender, strong finger. "Public libraries," he told her, and held up the second finger. "Movie
houses. I can recite the plays of Shakespeare, Euripides, and
Voltaire in two languages. I can also recite the dialogue of every
B movie ever made. *And* I am an excellent picker of locks."

He grinned, a kind of lopsided, quirky grin, and she giggled.

"On the other hand, I believe I have read every book on psychic phenomena ever to enter the New York Public Library sys-

tem. So: to answer your question of 'am I sensitive to these things,' I can answer you, very. I read these books because I needed to understand what I was, and I did not always have teachers when I needed them."

She licked her lips thoughtfully and nodded a little. He continued. "To answer your *next* question, the one you have upon the tip of your tongue, the other young men, or at least the two who first attacked me, they 'felt' as Jeffries now 'feels'—and I can pledge to you that he did *not* 'feel' that way before All Hallows' Eve. Halloween."

He sobered again. "I was able to deliver a clear warning to Jeffries on the hazard of threatening those I protect before that night, with no difficulty. I do not know that I could take him now."

"Not a pleasant thought," she ventured.

"No. And now I believe in your 'psychic vampires.' I did not wish to, before. Jeffries has become one, as, somehow, have those young men."

"What do you mean, 'those you protect'?"

"Ah. There is a particular tribe of the Lowara Romany with whom I have had a—partnership. An arrangement that is beneficial to us all. This has gone on for many years." He quirked one corner of his mouth at her little snort. "Truly, it is of benefit. They are noted for producing *drabarni* of great power. *I* protect them from those outside the Rom who may be attracted to this power, and seek to exploit them. I also protect them in these latter days from others who would—ah—I believe the term is 'hustle' them."

"And what do you get out of all this?"

"They protect me during the daylight. Not always, it is not altogether wise for one of my sort to spend every day in the same place, but—three days out of the seven, yes. Janfri was one of their tribe, and would have been one of the most powerful if he had chosen to flout custom and exercise the power. Usually it is only the women who so choose. But Jeffries—"

She grimaced. "Jeffries saw a nice little thermonuclear power plant and couldn't resist trying to take over the control room. All right, I can understand what happened to Janfri now. And I can see why Jeffries might band together with the two others. I think I could even suggest how to handle them. But what about the third one?"

"The Oriental?" He shuddered, and closed his dark eyes briefly in a grimace of pain. "I do not know what he is. But he *can* harm me. Harm me so that I ache even now."

He *was* in pain; that much was certain, from the faint sheen of sweat on his brow and the pinched look about his mouth. Equally certain was the fact that he was trying to conceal from her how *much* pain he was in.

I could—no. Let him keep his dignity. I bet he isn't used to feeling vulnerable.

He opened his eyes at that moment, and caught and held her gaze. "Mademoiselle Tregarde," he said soberly, "I have never asked help from another creature, living or otherwise, since I became what I am. But I am not a fool, or not so much of a fool as I was before last night. I am asking now, what you offered before. Will you help me?"

She trembled in that dark gaze; something about him was touching her profoundly, in ways she didn't understand, and wasn't certain she wanted to think about.

But he said the magic words. And I am a Guardian. I don't think he'd have asked unless he knew he was at the end of his own resources.

"Yes," she replied simply. "But not now."

"No." He sighed, and sagged back against the couch cushions. "I am scarce able to walk across this room. And I asked you to *help*, not to do it all yourself."

The exhaustion he had been trying to conceal was all too plain when he relaxed. "Do you need—"

"I—should not ask it," he interrupted, a pinched look about the way he held his mouth. "I should not. Not so soon—"

"So much for my scribbling. You need to feed again, right?"

Something flickered in the back of his eyes—first a raging hunger—then determination. "I—will not—demand. I will not take. I will have only what you offer freely. I have, at least, self-control enough for that—"

"Self-control be damned. You *need* it, and you asked for my help. I *give* that help with no strings attached. Except for one condition." She stood up, and he opened his eyes and looked up at her.

"And that is?" he asked.

"That you call me Di. Partner."

He smiled; a smile sweet enough to bring her heart right up into her throat, and leave it pounding there. "*That* will be my pleasure—Di. But—"

"But?" She stopped on her way to the couch.

"The Oriental—bothers me. Me, he can hurt, but he could not destroy me. I fear his power over the living. My memory returns, bit by bit—Di, I believe he was trying to devour my soul when he—"

—I believe he was trying to devour my soul—

The icy hand of a panic attack seized her throat, and the room blackened.

NINE

Panic had her heart in its bony fist; it squeezed her and toyed with her, and would not let her go.

She huddled, kneeling, on the floor beside the couch. She was clutching her knees so hard her fingernails were leaving little bloody half-moons in her skin even through the thick fabric of her jeans, and she was bent over and squeezing herself into a tight little ball, with no memory of the past few moments. There was room only for the fear and the memory of the Nightflyer that had triggered it. She sobbed and shivered, reduced to near mindlessness by the uncontrollable emotion that crushed her. She barely recognized her own living room. There was *nothing* in the world but fear.

Nothing to hold on to, nothing to protect her, nothing she could do to save herself.

This was the worst panic attack she'd had in years. She buried her face in her hands, sobbed and moaned. Completely paralyzed, mind and body.

The memory dominated the dark of her mind. *Like a grotesque mockery of a humanoid bat made of tattered black plastic. It had stood tall against the moon for a moment, then it had her wrapped in its folds as it sucked away at all that* was *her, trying to absorb her into itself—*

The Nightflyer; it wasn't wounded anymore, and there was no way to trick it this time. It was coming back. It was coming for her. This time there would be no escape.

A frightened voice. "Diana—Diana—"

She cringed away from a touch on her arm—

But those weren't the Nightflyer's talons on her shoulders, they were hands. Human hands.

"*Chérie, petite,* come to yourself. These are shadows that you fear. You are safe, in your own home."

Someone was holding her against his shoulder; someone was stroking her hair, gently. The panic ebbed a little, gave her a moment of respite.

Then returned, shaking her like a dog with a rag. She whimpered, and tried to pull away, huddled back into herself, but the hands would not let her go.

It took an age, an eon, before the panic finally faded, leaving her sobbing, limp, and wrung out.

And cradled in André's arms.

She was too exhausted to feel any embarrassment; too drained to do anything except to continue to allow him to hold her. She was shaking too much even to speak, her mind so fogged she couldn't have mustered words even if she *had* been able to speak.

—gods. If he hadn't been here—don't want to move.

Even her thoughts were coming slowly, fighting their way up to the surface of her mind through the sludge of exhaustion.

Finally her trembling eased; her hysterical tears dried. She opened her burning eyes, made as if to sit up, and the arms about her shoulders loosed.

But he took her shoulders in his hands as she pulled away from him, and looked searchingly into her face.

"Are you yourself?" he asked softly.

Her hair had come undone, and it fell into her eyes when she nodded. "I think so," she replied, her voice hoarse and thick with weeping.

He brushed the hair away from her face with a touch so light she hardly felt it, and tucked it behind her ear. "Will you tell me?"

"Panic attack," she said shortly. "It—happens, sometimes."

"Sometimes? When? What is the cause? Was it something that I said?" His eyes were bright and his brow furrowed with concern.

"I—" She began trembling again. "I—can't talk about it. I can't! If I do—"

"Diana, *chérie*—forgive me, I think you must. Does a soldier go into battle with a weapon that may fail him at any moment?" He shook her a little. "You cannot continue like this. *Tell* me."

"I *can't*—" she wailed, pushing feebly away from him, unable to face the possibility of triggering a second attack so soon after this one.

"You *must*." His voice took on urgency. "Listen to me. I depend on your strength, your mind, your abilities. Many others must also. If you permit this fear to rule you, you will *fail* them, and at the worst possible moment."

He was right. She *knew* he was right. It didn't help. She squeezed her eyes shut, and tears leaked out from beneath her tightly closed lids.

"Diana—" She felt a gentle hand lift her chin. "Open your eyes. Look at me."

She did, though her vision blurred with tears. He cupped his hand against her cheek, and spoke slowly and carefully, in a voice tremulous with compassion. "Listen; you *can* overcome this. I can help you. I *wish* to help you, as you have helped me. I know how to help you defeat this fear."

"You do?" She blinked at him doubtfully.

"*Oui.*" His voice admitted no possibility of failure; he seemed utterly sure of himself, and of her. "It will be very hard for you, but it is not impossible. And we shall do nothing for the next several moments. I wish you to hear what I have to say and decide for yourself if you are willing to carry this through."

He rose carefully to his feet, pulling himself up with the help of the couch; she looked at him standing beside her, trembling with weakness, and yet willing to lend her the little he had left—

Oh gods. He's braver than I am—

I have no choice. He's right.

She pushed away from the floor and staggered to her own feet. He backed up to the couch and let himself collapse on it. She joined him. The tendency of the couch to sag in the middle had a predictable effect on their positions—she found herself leaning against his shoulder again.

She made a halfhearted attempt to move away from him, then gave it up. He waited for a moment, then slowly, hesitantly, put his arm around her shoulder.

"Now," he said, after giving her a chance—which she did not take—to object to the presence of his arm about her. "You have these attacks of panic. I hazard it is because of something that happened to you in the past, *non?* Something—something that nearly killed you."

She nodded, unable to trust her own voice, and stared at a spot on the lampshade across the room.

"So now, when something else occurs that brings this into your mind, the fear overcomes you again."

Put that away, the attacks seemed reasonable, inevitable. "Yes," she whispered, fixing her gaze on that spot.

"We—my kind—our passing into this state is often traumatic. It is not uncommon for my kind to have such spells of fear."

Surprised, she twisted so that she could look at him. He smiled a little and nodded at her expression. "Indeed, I speak the truth. Nor can we, who must keep all our wits about us to survive, allow ourselves to be so debilitated. So—we learned how to cure this."

She sniffed, and rubbed at her eyes, frowning in disbelief. "You're—you're kidding, right? I mean—" She thought about it for a moment. "I guess you'd have to, wouldn't you."

He nodded. "And as it happens, these doctors of the mind that have sprung up of late have chanced upon the same remedy we use. Truly. But it is not a pleasant one."

"So—what is it?" she asked, pretty certain she was not going to like the answer.

"We—you and I—will invoke the fear. Deliberately. We will do so until it no longer controls you. We will wear it down, as treading upon a rough place in a path wears the roughness away. But that is not entirely all, Diana—" He held up his free hand to forestall her objections. "Your fear has been creating considerable energy. That will still *be* there. We must find a way to use it, to channel it into something useful, else it will continue to paralyze you."

"Oh gods—" she moaned. "I—André, it—"

He waited, patient, silent—understanding, but as implacable as her granny had been.

"There are no excuses, child."

She could hear the voice in her mind even now.

"There are reasons, but no excuses. And when there are reasons, there are usually causes that cancel out those reasons."

"What happens on the day you meet an enemy, and then are paralyzed, Diana?" he asked softly.

I have no choice. One of these days I will get caught outside a safe shelter by one of these attacks—and then what? I can't be like Josey, hardly able to leave his house.

She shivered, she started crying again—but she nodded.

Taking that as her assent, he prodded her with a question.

"This thing that you encountered—where and what was it?"

She held her arms tightly to her chest. "It—it was after my grandmother died, right after I graduated from college. Just before I moved here. Things had happened in college—I—I'd broken up with this guy over my doing magic. I wanted to quit it. I couldn't see why I couldn't. Shouldn't. I was tired of pulling other people's fat out of the fire. So I decided I was going to say to hell with it; that I was going to take care of me and nobody else."

"So—" he said, satisfaction in his voice. "You *are* one of those they call Guardians. I thought perhaps you were. I thought perhaps that might have been why you offered Janfri shelter."

She swallowed, and hung her head a little. "I am. I was," she said, feeling an echo of the old bitterness even now. "I was *sick* of it, André; it had cost me the only guy I'd ever been happy with. I wanted out. I didn't believe my grandmother, who'd told me that if I wouldn't act to protect others, I'd find *myself* a target. I thought I could go into hiding, you know? And when I found out about this guy who was planning to conjure up some nasty stuff—I didn't stop him. I didn't even try. I just ignored him, and figured he'd ignore me."

She closed her eyes and spoke around clenched teeth. "It wasn't my business. That's what I told myself. So when what he called up aced him and came after me, I not only wasn't expecting it, I wasn't ready, and most of my defenses were down."

The panic was starting to rise, trying to choke off her words.

"They—they called it—a—Nightflyer—"

That was all she managed to get out, before the panic hit her again, and she broke.

Dimly she heard André talking to her; she tried to answer, tried to fight it. She heard something about channeling—

Useless. She rode the attack through, and came out again on the other side spent and drained.

But—*but*—this attack had not been *quite* as bad as the last. He was right. So she gave herself no respite, and no chance for second thoughts.

"Let's—do this again," she said, when she could speak again.

He nodded. "This Nightflyer—describe how you came to encounter it—"

She had been reading. She'd heard something outside, and had thought it nothing more than a stray cat. The Nightflyer had been very apt at cloaking its presence.

The sound repeated, and she decided to investigate, because it hadn't felt quite right. If she'd stayed inside, the house wards would have kept it out, especially in its weakened condition. Perhaps the Nightflyer had sensed this. Surely it had been driven nearly wild by the proximity of a relatively unprotected Guardian

*with all the energy potential a Guardian always possessed. She
would never know, exactly.*

*She only had a glimpse of it, the black that absorbed everything
and gave nothing up, moonlight showing through the places where
its gliding members had been torn. Then it was on her, wrapping
her in its substance.*

*It began to devour her, just as a Venus'-flytrap devours a living
insect.*

*But it was weak; the struggle with the fool that had summoned
it had damaged it. It was desperate, and therefore a little careless
in its hunger. It gave her a tiny opening, and in desperation, she
took it, accepting again her Guardianship and opening herself to
the energies and knowledge only a Guardian could tap.*

*There had been an instant of light and terrible agony—and
when she woke again, she was lying on the ground; exhausted,
wracked with pain, but alone. And still alive.*

*Had she banished it, or destroyed it? She didn't know. All that
she did know was that she could never feel safe again.*

This time, as she cried and shuddered, she was able to *remember* where she was. She was able to bring up the full memory, though she still couldn't *tell* André about it.

"Again—" she said, while she still shook, and her eyes dripped
tears.

The strange "therapy" was working. Through it all André
held her, soothed her, spoke coaxingly to her when she needed
it—and shook her, scolded her, when *that* was what she needed.

There finally came a point where she could see what André
meant—about the amount of hysterical energy she was producing, and how it was holding her in chains of her own forging.

That time through she couldn't do anything about it—but
the next—

The safest way seemed to be to direct the hysteric energy into
her shielding. And as André talked her through attack after attack, and she found she *could* stay in control, she started trying
to do just that.

She had been keeping her eyes tightly shut so as to be able to concentrate, and she didn't truly notice anything out of the ordinary until André gasped and she realized that she no longer felt the light pressure of his arm on her shoulders.

She opened her eyes, and found herself alone on the couch—surrounded by a brightly glowing aura about an inch above her skin.

Glowing brightly enough that she was making the furnishings around her cast shadows.

"*Chérie—*" came a strangled voice from the other room. "If you would be so kind—that is painfully similar to sunlight."

She bit off a curse and dismissed the shield, and André poked his head cautiously around the doorframe. "I think," he said, carefully, "that we can count you as cured."

She licked lips that were salty with tears and sweat. "The patient," she replied hoarsely, "survived the treatment, at least."

He made his unsteady way back into the living room and sagged down onto the couch beside her. "Do you think that you will be able to handle your fear from this moment on?"

She made a careful internal assessment. "I—think so," she said, a little surprised.

"*Bien.* Because I think so also."

She managed a weak and trembling smile. "Now about your overdue—uh—meal . . ."

He shrugged, and put his arm around her shoulders again. "Let it wait for a little."

"He *what?*"

With Jeffries's anger filling the room, the apartment living room seemed far too small to hold them all, even with Dave sitting on one of the cushions over in the corner. Jason stood in front of Jeffries, with Doug slightly behind him. Master Jeffries wasn't shouting, but there was something deadly in the tone of his voice that made Dave shrink back into the shadows of his corner of the living room, glad that he wasn't delivering the bad news, even gladder that *he* hadn't been entrusted with handling the intruder.

That had been Jason's job. And Dave watched as Jason paled at the menace in Jeffries's voice.

"He's not there," the blond said faintly. "He's gone. Just the airplane cable and the locks. No body, no bones, no nothing."

"So. He escaped, despite your assurances that he was going nowhere." Jeffries radiated controlled violence, and Hidoro at his side could have been a statue.

Jason didn't actually move, but he seemed to shrink, somehow.

Dave was amazed: he'd never seen Jason back down from *anyone*, not even the time they'd played a biker bar and one of the locals had taken exception to the way Jason was singing at the biker's old lady. And now that Jason was—whatever they all were—he was twice as cocky-tough.

Jason had been deferential enough with Jeffries, but Dave had wondered how long *that* was going to last. Jason didn't much care to play second to anybody, and he'd let Dave handle the business end of the group only because *he* didn't want to be bothered. For as long as Dave had known him, if Jason saw a lead position he wanted, he'd challenge for it. Dave had expected that to happen here, too. But Jason was backing down from Jeffries.

It looked like the leader of the pack had just found somebody bigger, meaner, and tougher.

That surely was sticking in Jason's craw—but he wasn't showing any signs of it.

"Yeah," Jason ventured, looking away from Jeffries's angry eyes. "It kind of looks like he escaped. I dunno how. I *can't* see how—we worked him over some, so he'd be out of it when the sun came up, but we couldn't stay out there in the sun long enough to see him finished off—"

Jeffries remained silent, and the lead's words trailed off into uneasy silence. Suddenly the man rounded on Doug. "How big is your apartment?" he demanded.

"Not very," Doug stammered, backing up a pace. "It's an efficiency. Jason's got a loft."

Jeffries smiled at them both, and although it hadn't been directed at him, Dave shrank back even farther from the malice in that smile.

"Appropriate," Jeffries said softly, "since *he* allowed the creature to escape. Get your things and mine into the van; we're moving. If my enemy survives, he'll be back here. That young man is not so young, nor is he a fool. When he returns, he won't be alone."

Hidoro, who had been silent throughout this conversation, nodded gravely. It was plain that he agreed entirely with Jeffries on both Jason's culpability and Jeffries's assessment of the situation.

"That is what I would do," the creature said, his voice betraying only a hint of accent, and no emotion whatsoever. "But is there anything we can do *besides* flee? Could we also not move to neutralize him?"

"You mean, take the offensive?" Jeffries raised an eyebrow in skeptical surprise. "Against a true vampire powerful enough to escape in full daylight? How could we, and what could we do?"

Hidoro shrugged. "If we cannot deal with him directly, perhaps we can control him through others. Is there nothing that *he* cherishes, that *he* would protect?"

Jeffries thought a moment—then smiled again.

"Oh yes." He chuckled. "Oh yes, I think so. Jason?"

"Sir?" the lead said promptly, while Dave lost his jaw. He'd never heard Jason call *anyone* "sir" in all the years he'd known him.

We have definitely just become beta wolf, haven't we, Jas?

"Leave the packing to the others. You're coming with me, and we're taking the van."

Jeffries was unmistakably grinning now, and Dave did *not* want to know what the man was thinking of.

"We're going to see about taking a bit of a counteroffensive," he heard the Master say to Jason, as they headed out the apartment door.

Di rested her head back against André's shoulder, and he tightened his arm about her.

"What time is it?" she asked quietly.

"Nearly four, I think."

"I am *too* damned tired to open the shop—"

"Then do not," he interrupted. "Will your friend grudge you one day? If she does, I cannot think she is much of a friend."

"Good point." She sighed, thought about moving, decided not to. "I could sure use an afternoon on the book."

"So. I should get you to your bed, I think." So he said, but he made no move to rise, and neither did she.

She closed her eyes, and felt his free hand smoothing her sweat- and tear-soaked hair.

"Thank you, André," she said, putting as much sincerity into her voice as she could produce around her exhaustion.

"For what?"

"For being something I don't have many of. A friend."

"A friend." His tone was wistful. "I have few enough of those, my own self. The Rom respect me, but they do not offer their friendship. I am still *gadjo*. And my kind are few. None in this city that I am aware of, though it does not necessarily follow that there actually are none. Have you friends beside your lady Annie?"

"Lenny. He's a dancer that lives upstairs. A couple of people in Annie's Circle. No one else."

"Circle?" He sounded surprised. "Are you then a practicing witch?"

"Of course I'm practicing, how could I get to Carnegie Hall if I didn't practice?" She was tired enough that the feeble joke made her burst into giggles. She doubled over her knees, and wheezed. Every time she looked back up at him, his nonplussed expression only made her start laughing again.

He was tired enough that after a few moments of staring at her he joined her in laughter. They leaned against each other, keeping each other propped up, chortling like a pair of fools.

"What—what I meant was—" He gasped for breath. "What I meant was that—how can you be a witch and a Guardian, too?"

"When they handed me my enrollment form I checked 'other' under 'religion,' and they passed me on through," she replied, then burst into laughter again.

He snatched up a throw pillow and hit her lightly with it, unable now to *stop* laughing.

She retaliated by scooting over to the corner of the couch, leaving him to topple over, helpless with mirth.

"*Mon Dieu,*" he said, finally catching his breath. "I have not laughed so in—I cannot think how long."

"Me, either." She let gravity take her back to his side, and laid her head and arm along the back of the sofa. "I should let vampires across my threshold more often. Even if they go and trigger a—"

The sudden recollection of *why* the first panic attack had occurred made her sit up. "Ohmigod. That Oriental. The one that *wasn't* a psivamp. You said what he did to you felt like *what?*"

"As though he were trying to pull my soul away," André replied, his face gone still and sober.

She was putting two and two together, and coming up with a figure that she did not in the least like. "Listen—I haven't *just* been trying to track down the creep that murdered Janfri. I've been after bigger game—"

She detailed the story of Keith's ex-lover and the bus full of dead bodies.

"And you think that this soul-eater may be the one they called Hidoro?" André finished, his eyes focusing somewhere within him.

"What do *you* think?" she countered.

"I think—I think that we need more information. I think also that neither of us is capable of going beyond these walls until tomorrow at the best."

She eyed him speculatively, then held out her hand. It shook and she couldn't get it to stop. He gave her a wry look and held out his own. It did the same.

"We *are* in sad shape, are we not?" he said.

She sighed. "Very sad. I don't like this, but I'm afraid you're right. And I should get to bed."

His hand rested over hers on the couch between them. He seemed to be thinking very hard. "Diana—if this is no business of mine, say so. Have you a—a young man?"

"Me?" She coughed. "Not hardly. Not after the last one. Our breakup was pretty painful, and I swore after the Nightflyer that I was never going to get involved with someone who didn't believe again. Now the only men I *might* be able to tell what I'm into are mostly already paired up, and the rest are yo-yos."

"But what of this Lenny?"

She choked on a laugh. "Len? Good gods, André, he's *gay*. He and Keith are on the verge of becoming a very tight item. I am *not* his type!"

"So. Am I a—'yo-yo' would you say?"

"No. You're not exactly normal, but I've known vegetarians with weirder diets." She began giggling again, until the look on his face sobered her. "Why are you asking me these things?"

"Because—because I follow a kind of code, myself," he said softly. "I do not accept—what I need—from the same person more than twice, unless it is given with—affection." He coughed a little, and looked down at their joined hands. "There is a reason for this. It is the reason I did not wish to believe in your psychic vampires. My kind are something of psychic vampires also. It is not only the blood we need, it is the emotions."

"You mean you people are psivamps, too?" she whispered.

"Of a sort. We who follow the code do not *take*. We only accept what is given. That protection—that is what triggers what we need. It is so for all of us who follow the code. Those who do not—are the origin of the legends, I suspect."

"So not all of you are good guys; yeah, I'd figured that. But the stories claim going vamp *makes* you evil."

He shrugged. "A person who was good before the change generally remains a good person. One who was evil—him, we hunt down and destroy ourselves, for his excesses will put us all in danger."

She nodded. "So what are you asking of me?"

"More than I should," he said quietly. "More than blood. Liking. And if you feel you cannot offer that—I shall regain strength more slowly, then seek what I need elsewhere. From those among the Rom who are willing, probably." He took her hand in his. "I will not demand what I have no right to, Diana. You have already given me more than I can repay. I will understand if you tell me no."

When she didn't reply immediately, his face fell a little. With a resigned sigh, he lifted her hand to his lips.

"Go to your rest, mademoi—"

She turned her hand in his so that his kiss fell upon her palm and not on the back, and she cupped her hand around his cheek to raise his face to meet her eyes just as he had done with her, earlier this evening.

"As easily as that?" she asked, wonderingly. "You go back to loneliness as easily as that?"

"I have," he said, fixing his dark eyes on hers, and covering the hand on his cheek with his, "had a great deal of practice."

"You make me ashamed of myself."

"Why?" he asked simply. "What is there to be ashamed of?"

"I've been doing a great deal of feeling sorry for myself," she pointed out. She freed her hand from his, and took it into both of hers, marveling at the long, graceful fingers, the strength that was in it.

"You have had reason."

"Maybe." She bent her head a bit, and her hair fell into her eyes again. "Gods. I must look like a three-day-old corpse."

"You look—"

The tremulous tone of his voice made her glance sharply up at him, and she held her breath. She hadn't seen a man look at her like that since—since Dave. No, not even Dave. There had always been desire in Dave's eyes—but never the warmth of humor, and never, never, the respect and admiration she saw in André's.

"You are—very attractive to me. Will you consider me as a friend, Diana?"

She felt herself smiling. "I thought you already were a friend, André."

He reached out and traced the line of her cheekbone with one gentle fingertip. "Do you have any fears of me?"

She shook her head, and let the couch take her into his arms. "No. Not anymore. Just two questions."

"Ask."

"The first—I was under the impression that getting bitten too many times makes you a vampire."

He nodded. "A good question. The answer is, not. M'sieur Stoker was correct in that, at least. I *could* kill you, but I could not make you one of us by feeding. For that, there must be the blood bond—the exchange of blood. Which we have not, and could not, without your consent and cooperation."

She sighed. "Okay, I'll accept that. Now the second. Can a friend offer you a—drink? Maybe a little more than a drink?"

He laughed, and kissed her eyes.

It was six when she went to her own bed. Since she knew Bob would be awake already, she called him and told him that she had spent a hell of a night—the truth, after all—and that she wouldn't be opening the shop.

"That's okay, Di," he said. "I got some vacation days coming—I'll tell you what, make tomorrow your last day, take your pay out of the safe, and go back to book writing. If Annie isn't ready for work, I'll take it for a week. Annie said she thought you were sounding stretched a bit thin."

She sighed. "Annie was right." Some of her mental, physical, and emotional exhaustion must have leaked over in her voice; he queried her sharply, recommended a dozen vitamins, and told her in no uncertain terms to get herself into her bed.

She did; and woke about two. She had expected to feel depleted; instead, she felt relatively alert, and a great deal easier in her mind and heart than she had in years.

Certainly easy enough to get back to the perils of her heroine, and let the problem of the man called Hidoro stew in the back of her mind.

She noted with a half-smile that André had repaired the mess that the two of them had made of the couch last night. That little nip of his had quickly led to other things.

A neat fellow, not a slob like Dave was. If I have to have a vampire in my living room, it's nice to have one willing to pick up after both of us.

I wish I could figure out what to do about The Problem. Gods; killer psivamps and a soul-eater—it's like the worst nightmare I ever had.

Jeans and a leotard were the order of the day, seeing as she had no intentions of going anywhere but her living room. While she showered, she mulled things over.

If what André says is true, the psivamps are at least as vulnerable to sunlight as he is. Did he say anything about them getting burned, though? I don't think so—that means it must be visual sensitivity. Okay, that gives us a weapon. If my shield-glow gets him, it'll keep them blinded, too. They can't jump me if they can't look at me. Hmm.

She thought about that for a moment. *I would bet that my shields will keep them off my head, too. So all I have to worry about is that enhanced physical strength. I'm martial-arts trained. They aren't. That may work against them, if they're counting on simple strength. I won't make the mistake of attacking first the way I did with André.*

She was ravenous—not surprisingly. That was twice in twenty-four hours she'd "donated," and though André hadn't taken much, it was enough for her to feel *some* aftereffect. After an enormous sandwich, she felt much more inclined to deal with work.

She took her place behind her typewriter, turned on the radio, and resolutely turned off the rest of the world for a few hours.

It was time for Captain Sommers to rescue himself from his exile on a desert island. When the telephone shrilled at her, just past four, it broke a concentration that was so intense that she jumped and squeaked, her heart pounding.

Who on earth—

She picked up the receiver.

The voice on the other end was very familiar.

"Hi, Morrie," she said wearily.

She listened with half her concentration while Morrie danced around the question he wanted to ask.

"No, Morrie. I really *can't* give you a firm turn-in date right now."

She stared out the window at the darkening sky until he slowed down again.

"Well, my life just got a lot more complicated. Like with your nephew and the dybbuk. Only more so."

Silence. Then, as she had *known* was inevitable, Morrie got excited. When Morrie became excited, half of his words were Yiddish and the other half mostly unintelligible. Only working with him as long as she had enabled her to understand him. He produced a choked-off phrase that only experience enabled her to interpret.

She bit back a smile. *I can't resist this.* "Well, for one thing, there's a vampire on my living-room couch."

A squawk.

Poor Morrie. He wasn't ready for that one. "Calm down, Morrie, this one is on the side of—you should excuse the phrase—the angels. A good guy."

Another squawk.

Well, what do you expect? You knew *about me when you took me as a client.* "How did I get tied up with Itzaak? These things just *happen* to me, Morrie."

A whisper, in which she caught one word.

She softened. *Morrie, I never knew you cared.* "Morrie, you're a sweet man, but I don't think your rabbi could help. This one's a Catholic. I think. As Catholic as a vampire can get, anyway."

A gurgle.

Now we come to it. She sighed. "Look, Morrie, I *promise* I will do my very best not to die and leave you with a half-finished novel on your hands."

Morrie did not sound mollified.

Di made a few more soothing noises, and finally got him to hang up, She went back to work, only to be interrupted a half hour later by someone buzzing her apartment from the foyer.

Now what?

She went down to the foyer herself, not trusting *anything* at the moment. If Jeffries had tracked André here—

But it was only a messenger from Morrie's office. She half expected some kind of written remonstrance from Morrie—but the boy had brought only a large white paper sack from the deli on the first floor of Morrie's office building.

Now what on earth? she thought, thoroughly puzzled now.

The mystery was not to be solved until she got the sack and opened it.

There was a note inside. *You sounded like shit, kid. To hell with the damned book; take care of yourself. If I can do anything, tell me. Itzaak is in Seattle, or I'd send him over with his special stuff, which I don't want to know anything about. You should only eat. And keep that guy on your couch away from your neck.*

And inside the sack, under the note—garlic-laced chicken soup, garlic bagels, garlic-and-chives cream cheese, and a half loaf of garlic bread.

She had to put the sack down, she was laughing so hard. If she hadn't, she'd have dropped it.

"It doesn't work, you know," said a soft voice from the living room.

"What doesn't work?" she called back, conveying the sack into the kitchen with care. The chicken soup was making her stomach remind her that she'd been skipping far too many meals lately.

"The garlic. It does not work the way the legend says. Before you inquire, I can smell it from here."

"I should think they can smell it all over the building. Bernie's Deli makes one *powerful* chicken soup." She couldn't stand it. Her mouth was watering so much she was about ready to take a hunk out of the sack and scarf it down. "Are you *sure* it doesn't bother you?"

"Not at all." André sounded positively cheerful. "Only—I would like some company. If you would be able to spare the time."

"I can't eat and type. Hang in there a mo."

Food in hands she returned to the living room. André looked *much* better, and he accepted the mug of tea she brought with her with a sweet smile that she found herself returning.

"Diana, I hope that you will excuse the impoliteness, but I also made use of your telephone. I needed to tell my Lowara where I was, where I could be reached—"

"No problem. I'm in the phone book," she said, settling herself in her favorite chair. "Better the Rom than a carpet salesman."

"Thank you," he replied simply.

"You know, you're very quiet," she said. "I know you were listening to the radio before dawn, and you picked up the living room, for which I thank you, and you just told me you used the phone—and I didn't hear you out here at all."

"I have had practice," he pointed out. "Many years of it."

That was an opening if ever she'd seen one. "How many years? I'm nosy."

He chuckled, and a lock of hair fell charmingly over one eye. "You have the right, Diana. A bit under two hundred. I was *almost* a victim of Madame Guillotine."

She sipped her soup, then cocked her head to one side. "Almost?"

He sighed. "I came under suspicion as a Royalist sympathizer, and with no one to speak for me, and no gold with which to bribe the proper officials, I was destined to be an example to the New Republic. Except that a certain young lady with unusual appetites had a habit of bribing her way into the prisons—"

She laughed. "Aha! The woman in the case! It's those big brown eyes of yours."

He blushed. "Perhaps. It may just have been that I was young and cleanly, and to tell the truth, very frightened. She was in the habit of offering only a painless death—to me, she offered the blood bond."

"And that's the exchange of blood that makes—"

"The change, yes." He nodded. "So, to shorten the tale, the jailers found one more poor fool dead of fear in the morning, and buried me with the rest in a shallow common grave. Except that I did not remain there long."

She finished her soup. "When did you end up over here?"

"I came over with my tribe of Lowara—they adopted me after I engineered their release from a provincial gaol. That was—let me think—shortly after Napoleon crowned himself Emperor. I have been here since."

He smiled at her; his eyes had softened, and there was nothing of the ice-knife killer about him at the moment. His long hands were laced around one knee, and he seemed completely relaxed and at ease.

Which pose lasted about thirty seconds more.

There as a knock at the door—and his expression underwent a change to alert, wary, and cold as sharpened steel.

"There is someone out there—" he breathed, "—and it is someone I cannot read. There is a wall I cannot pass—"

TEN

A chill of fear crept down her back. *Could it be one of them? But how—and how did they get in the building? How—* She saw out of the corner of her eye that she was beginning to glow a little, as fear translated into shields—

Then she realized what an idiot she was being, and the glow vanished as she laughed at herself. André gave her a curious and bewildered look.

"Diana? What is it that is so amusing?"

"Andre, why would an enemy *knock?* Why would he come in the front door? I think I know who this must be. Hang on a minute." She extended and *touched,* and chuckled again.

"It's more than not an enemy, it's a friend," she said, and put her mug down as she headed for the door to let Lenny in. "You couldn't read him because *I* put shields on—"

She flipped the locks, and the door swung open. Lenny stood framed in the doorway, white with fear; every muscle tensed, a baseball bat in one hand, a sharpened piece of wood in the other. *Good God—I'd better defuse this, fast—*She raised an eyebrow at him. "That's a strange way to come visiting. I know you promised me a steak dinner for Christmas, but that wasn't what I thought you had in mind."

He hadn't been expecting *that* kind of reception, that was certain. He looked at her with his mouth dropping open for a moment, then deflated, and shuffled his feet sheepishly. "I thought—Morrie called me. He seemed to think you might be in trouble."

She cast her eyes upward. "Good old Morrie. I should *never* have given him your number. Come on in. I'm in trouble, but not with my visitor. André is likely to be part of the solutio—"

She caught a hint of movement out of the corner of her eye and realized that André was *there*, beside her, pressed up against the wall where he would be hidden from anyone in the doorway.

Enough already! Her nerves were worn down enough that this was beginning to make her angry. "Will you two *stop* trying to save me from each other?" she snapped—and both Lenny and the vampire jumped, startled.

She grabbed Lenny's wrist and dragged him inside; shut the door and turned him so that he faced André. "Lenny, this is André. André, Lenny. Shake hands and be nice."

Lenny swallowed, and reluctantly extended the hand holding the stake; then realized what he'd just done, blushed, and fumbled awkwardly with it. André recovered first, and saved the moment by taking the piece of sharpened wood from him, clasping his hand with a chagrined smile. "I think we are both fools, *non*? I am pleased to meet you."

Di waited, hoping Lenny would see the man, and not the mythic monster.

"Funny," said Lenny, after a long pause, plainly responding to that smile. "You don't look Transylvanian."

"... So that's what we know so far," Di concluded. "And I would bet any amount of money that by the time we get back to this Jeffries's place, he'll be long gone. I would be if I was him."

"I agree," André seconded. He was curled up next to Di on the couch, but on the end. There was a space of a couple of feet between them, and he was all business. Not even Lenny, who was highly sensitive to body language, would be likely to read anything into his behavior.

All of his other masks were off, though.

He's allowing Lenny to see that he's not all-powerful, that he's vulnerable, and I bet it's because he's figured Lenny will be receptive to vulnerability.

Lenny digested all this, his eyes fixed on the coffee table. "So you figure this 'Hidoro' creep is the soul-eater."

"He certainly fits the profile." Di edged back into her own corner of the couch, and tucked her feet under her.

"Okay. You gonna let me and Keith in on this one?" He looked up at her, belligerently.

She started to say no, then caught André's eye. The vampire was nodding ever so slightly, and she did a quick rethinking of her answer.

"It's bound to be dangerous—" she began.

Lenny interrupted her. "We've already *been* in danger," he told her. "We've been busy. We thought about what you told us, about how you weren't likely to be able to pick the thing out of all the people in New York, and we decided to see if we couldn't stack the deck some. We've been out every night, cruising some part of the bus route; one of us in Keith's car, one on the street playing bait. Trolling for soul-eaters."

It took a minute for the meaning of his words to hit her; then she bit back a curse. "You *idiots!* You're crazy! You could have been killed—no, *worse* than killed!"

He shrugged. "We talked; Keith figured if just thinking about the thing sent you into a panic attack, you weren't in any shape to do anything about it."

Her anger ran out like water from a broken pot. "I deserved that, I guess," she replied, biting her lip. "I guess I wasn't being very effective. But I *was* trying—"

"Di, if you'd found the thing, could you have done anything about it?" Lenny countered. "At least we weren't likely to freeze like scared rabbits."

"That isn't going to happen again," she told him firmly. "I've worked things out. You've got my word on it."

He gave her a doubtful look, but didn't say anything.

André shrugged. "I cannot see where that makes any great difference at this moment. We may know *who* they are, but we do not know *where* they are, nor do we at this moment know *what* Hidoro is."

"I've got a start on that," Di said, grateful to finally be able to bring something useful into the nebulous plans. "Annie has the most extensive occult library in this city, and she keeps it in the back of the shop. I'm going in for my last day tomorrow, and I'll have plenty of opportunity to research the subject. She's got a lot of Oriental stuff, and I'd bet if the soul-eater isn't in some book in there, he's something so rare we'll *never* find anything on him."

"In the meantime—"

"In the meantime—believe me, friend Lenny, you do *not* wish to encounter this man—or whatever he is." André leaned forward, his hands clasped, his mouth a thin, tight line. "You would stand no chance with him. I am stronger than even the finest athlete by virtue of what I am, and *he* was stronger than I am. In his other form, I do not know if anything could harm him. I would not send a squad of armed soldiers against him at the moment—not without knowing his strengths and his weaknesses."

Lenny sat back a little. "Oh," he said, reluctantly.

"I don't believe in coincidences anymore," Di said into the unhappy silence. "Especially the kind of 'coincidences' we've been getting here and now. There has to be a reason why the four of us have met on this. *I* sure couldn't have dealt with it alone. I *still* can't. I think all the signs point to the fact that we need to work on this together, as a team. Len, can you get Keith over here as soon as I come back from work tomorrow?"

"No problem." He lost some of his obvious unhappiness with the situation.

Her head ached, and she was suddenly very tired. "Then let's see what we can do about this tomorrow. I hate to let it go another day, but I don't think we have a choice, frankly. We need information we don't have, André isn't fit to travel, Len, you don't know where the shop *is,* and I'm not prepared to hit the subway at night. It isn't going to do us any good for me to get myself killed by a mugger."

Lenny sighed, but nodded. André gave her a wry smile.

"All right, it's agreed. We meet here tomorrow night." She got to her feet, and tossed her hair over her shoulder, gazing at Lenny. "Out, you. I have a lot of sleep to catch up on. I haven't gotten much the past couple of days."

When the doors were all safely locked behind him, she headed back into the living room. André was still curled up on the couch, staring at the reflections in the darkened window, a frown of concentration on his face.

"I'm ready to crash," she said, quietly. "I can't keep my eyes open anymore."

He looked up, his face haunted for a moment, as if he saw someone other than herself standing beside the couch. "That is a common—complaint," he said softly. "It will pass, if you get a full night of sleep."

She was reluctant to leave him. "Will you be all right out here alone?"

He nodded, slowly, and touched her hand. "*I* will be fine. I think your protections will be enough, even should anything come at us—and I think that is most unlikely at the moment. Tomorrow? I cannot say." He interlaced his long fingers around his knee and favored her with a little grimace. "We have many problems, and I would like to think about them."

"Then I'll crash—if you don't need anything?"

For a moment his expression clouded, and Di sensed that he was struggling with himself. His eyes went cold, and unreadable, and she forced herself to remain where she was, despite the little chill of fear that masklike expression gave her.

Finally he shook his head, and that one unruly lock fell over his eye. "No, Diana. And so soon—that would not be wise for you."

She sighed mentally with relief, then shrugged. "All right then, I'll see you in the morning. You should still be conscious when my alarm goes off."

This time he did smile. "Oh-dark-hundred, is the phrase, I believe. Yes, I shall still be aware. *Bonsoir, chére amie.*"

Good friend. She sighed again as she headed for her bed. *If only—*

But she did not allow herself to finish that thought.

I'm in hell, Dave thought bleakly, staring out the windshield of the van. The dark streets were no longer dark—for him, or for any of the others. The glare of light on ice patches bothered him a little, that was all. He was truly a child of the night now.

I'm in hell, and I'm not even dead yet.

They were keeping a tight eye on him, all of them, from Hidoro on down to Doug. He wasn't allowed out of their sight for more than a few hours—and no matter where he took himself, they always seemed to be able to find him when they wanted him.

Like tonight; he'd been sitting on a bus-stop bench when the van pulled up beside him, and Jason stuck his head out of the window.

"Time's up, Davey-boy," he'd said with gleeful cruelty. "You've had your little wallow in guilt. That's all you're allowed for tonight. Get your tail in the driver's seat. It's time to go hunting, and we don't feel like driving."

This time they were cruising a lower-middle-class, ethnic neighborhood. Rows of little brownstones, dim streetlights, lace curtains in the windows; Archie Bunker territory. Dave went where they told him, and stopped when they told him, and tried not to think about what he was doing.

The hunger was getting past all the grass and booze he'd been doing, and he hadn't been able to make any connections to get anything stronger. It was gnawing away at the base of his spine; beyond an ache, it was so pervasive and invasive it was hard to think of anything else. And all the audience vibes did anymore were to increase his appetite; the scent of cooking food to a starving man.

"Pull over," Jason ordered. Dave obeyed numbly, sliding the van into a spot beside a fireplug.

The only possible target in view was a couple walking down the street; he had noticed them out of the corner of his eye as he'd passed them. He watched them in the rearview mirror as they approached the back of the van. The woman, who kept a careful two paces behind the man, was so self-effacing as to be invisible. The man, a great, stocky bull of Middle-European peasant stock, radiated hostility that Dave picked up with no effort at all.

"What d'you think?" Jason asked in an undertone to Doug, ignoring Dave. "Let 'em pass, or take 'em?"

"Huh. The woman's hopeless. But the man's got enough for both of them." Doug scratched his chin thoughtfully, and peered into the rearview mirror on his side. "We could work him, but not her."

Jason frowned. "But if we don't work the stockbroker scenario on them—"

Doug laughed maliciously. "I know what will work. My old man was just like that old fart. You see the wife? Take a close look at her; she's a good twenty years younger than he is. He wants her barefoot, pregnant, and one hundred percent *his*. You want him keyed up, we just stroll on up and make him think one of us has been poaching. That'll get his blood boiling in no time. Once we get him started, it'll be a breeze to crank him up."

Jason grinned. "The Don Juan'd be me, right? I think I'm gonna *like* this."

Doug closed his eyes for a moment, and a sly smile crept across his face. "This's foolproof, Jason. You won't have to lay a finger on him. He's got a shaky heart. We'll get what we need out of him, and cut out. Heart attack will take care of the rest."

"Good deal. What's the woman's name?"

Doug frowned, his eyes still closed. "Hmm. Hannah, I think."

"Close enough." Doug climbed out first, then Jason slid out of the van just in time to block the sidewalk in front of the man. He was radiating sensuality, and he greeted the woman effusively by name, ignoring the man entirely.

In a maneuver Dave had seen too many times of late, Doug slipped around behind the van to intercept the woman in case she ran. Jason moved toward her, brushing the man aside and touching her arm. She shrank away, bewildered and frightened, and the man's temper exploded in violence, with a roar like a wounded bear's.

Dave closed his eyes and huddled behind the steering wheel.

He could shut out the sight and sound of what was happening, but not the rest. He knew the moment the man tried to grab his wife's arm, and Doug stepped between them. He knew when the man rounded on Jason, and Jason eluded his blows, laughing at him, taunting him with innuendo.

And he knew the moment that the two of them began exerting their wills on the man, building his anger into a red rage that blocked out all attempts at rationality, that sent his blood pressure soaring—

Pain, constricting his chest. Terrible pain, getting past the anger that had been blackening his vision.

The hunger inside Dave sucked at the pain, chortling to itself.

Anger was gone. There was only pain, disbelief, and more pain. Pain that choked off his breath, that made him clutch his chest in a futile attempt to ease it.

Dave shuddered, and wept silently, but made no attempt to keep the hunger from feeding. It controlled him, now. He could no more stop it than stop a hurricane.

Falling. Impact on cold concrete. Clawing at the icy concrete, trying to rise, unable to move for the pain.

Fear. Fear that enveloped him as the anger had. Fear that

choked his breath in his throat, that constricted a chest already tight with agony.

The hunger eased a little, reaching for this richer, stronger mix.

Jason and Doug stood, one on either side of the writhing man, laughing at his struggles to breathe, to live.

Laughter of devils, mocking at him.

Then the abyss. Then—

Nothing.

The hunger, now satiated, curled up in the pit of his stomach, humming contentedly to itself. Jason and Doug climbed back into the van as the woman stared at the body of her husband, mind so numb Dave couldn't even feel surprise in her.

"Get us out of here before she thinks of getting our license number," Doug ordered. And when Dave pulled out too slowly, growled, "*Move* it, dammit!"

Dave started, cold sweat suddenly springing out on his brow, and in his armpits, and floored the gas pedal. The screech of tires on the pavement echoed the woman's scream as they roared away.

Ten minutes later, Jason directed him to pull over again. Since there was no one within sight or sensing in this rundown business district, Dave was momentarily puzzled and no little relieved—until Hidoro materialized out of the shadows between two buildings, wearing his girl form.

"Trolling for rapists?" Jason asked genially, rolling down the window of the van. Hidoro nodded, a Mona Lisa expression of smug satisfaction on his face.

"Have *you* fed full, brothers?" the Oriental asked, in a breathless soprano.

Say yes, Dave prayed silently, staring at the crumbling facade of a building farther down the street. *Oh God, say yes!*

Jason looked back over his shoulder at Dave as if he could hear what the other was thinking. The movement made Dave glance at him out of the corner of his eye. Jason smirked, and winked at him.

"Not yet," he replied, as Dave writhed inside. "There's three of us, after all. We need more than one kill."

"Then I shall be pleased to assist you." Hidoro chuckled. "Shall we try the Village?"

"Good idea." Jason opened the side door, and Hidoro climbed in, draping himself over the back of the bench seat. He retained his girl form, which somehow made him all the more uncanny.

"You heard the man," Jason said to Dave, addressing him directly for the first time since they'd pulled away from the first kill. "Head for the Village."

"Ours is a good alliance," Hidoro said conversationally, while Dave tried to concentrate on his driving and keep his thoughts blank. He feared the Oriental more than all the others combined.

"I'm inclined to agree," Jason replied. "Makes it easier to work if you know you've got somebody watching your tail."

"True—but that is not all that I meant." Hidoro leaned closely over the back of the seat, his black eyes glittering in the streetlight, shiny, cruel chips of onyx. "In time past those with powers such as yours and mine could become something more than mere hunters."

"Oh? And what did you have in mind?"

The Oriental laughed, a laugh like the bark of a fox. "Say that there is a powerful man, a politician, or a powerful criminal. Say that he has an enemy. What would it be worth to such to have a means of eliminating such an enemy without suspicion?"

"Plenty," Doug supplied thoughtfully.

"And again, with your gift at enhancing violent emotion— say that the man does not wish his enemy eliminated, only disgraced. So—he debates his opponent in public, and the opponent becomes incoherent with anger. Who would elect such a man? Say that the opponent is a churchman—who one day is incited to rape. Who would put further trust in such a man? The possibilities are many."

"Fascinating," Jason said dryly. "Have you told the Master about these notions of yours?"

"I have indeed, and he is cautiously in favor. However, he felt that in this case, since the stakes are so much higher, you should hear and think of these things yourselves. He would have no one involved who is not willing."

Jason laughed, throwing his head back, showing his teeth in a bloodthirsty grin. "Oh, even Davey-boy would be in favor if we put it to him the right way. Wouldn't you, Davey? You used to be a real wheel in the peace movement—think about it. Wouldn't it have been a rip to take Tricky Dicky down? How about that jerk that's mayor of Philly? Just think of all the *good* you could do, Davey."

Dave stared unhappily at the traffic and the street ahead, trying *not* to think about it. *How many innocents would we take down in the meantime, just to—feed? How could anything justify that?*

Jason laughed again. "Poor Davey. He's thinking about the sheep again. Think of us as wolves playing sheepdog, Davey. Isn't it worth a few sheep to keep the whole herd safe?"

His head swam with confusion. *I—God, I don't know. I just don't know.*

"Never mind." Jason's voice sharpened. "We'll worry about that later. I've got a target dead ahead. Pull over. *Now*, Davey."

As he pulled in, he saw what must be the "target" Jason mentioned. Two women on the otherwise deserted side street, one fair, one dark. Bundled up against the cold, but their voices sounded cheerful and lively.

Dave could see what made them a choice quarry in Jason's mind. There was so much energy in them that they glowed, and a powerful bond of affection flowed between them—

Christ. Torture one and make the other hurt worse for not being able to help her. Two for the price of one. Jason, you're a bastard—

Last of all, from the scraps of thought Dave was picking up, they were tourists who probably wouldn't be missed for a while.

Canadians, which would muddy the trail back to them even further.

Oh God—not again. Dear God, not again!

"Oh, yes," Jason said caressingly. "I think they'll do *very* nicely. Hidoro?"

I can't let them do this.

"Suitable," the Oriental agreed. "I cannot feed, however. I can only kill while I am full-fed."

"Could you—*hurt* them a little?" Doug asked.

Maybe if I throw the door open—yell at them to run.

Hidoro laughed, and it echoed ghoulishly in the empty van. "My good colleague, I can hurt them a great deal."

The hunger that Dave had thought quiescent rose up and growled in anticipation, and he realized in despair that it had him in thrall again. He couldn't move.

All three of the others slid out of the van, Hidoro coming around the rear to cut them off as the other two closed in from behind.

The one closest to the van, the fair one, threw herself at Hidoro in a doomed attempt to clear the way for her companion to escape, shouting something at her. Something about running for it. And a name, or a nickname. "Fi—"

But Hidoro changed into his cloud shape just as she reached him—and she vanished into the dark smoke.

She shrieked, her cry coming muffled and dim from inside the cloud, as the other two caught and held the other woman trapped between them, helpless even to move.

Dave closed his eyes, and cried, as the pain rolled over him and his hunger fed.

The shop had been blessedly quiet; customers few, and not inclined to gossip. When Di got back from the shop, André was still asleep—or something. She stood beside the couch, looking down at him, little tag ends of thoughts going around in her head.

He looked so young—not much more than twenty-five, if that. And so—vulnerable. It was strange, thinking of him as vulnerable. It wasn't a word she would have thought to apply to a man like him, and yet she'd used it twice in thinking about him in the last two days.

On the other hand, I've seen him at his most helpless, so maybe that isn't surprising.

A knock at the door interrupted her reverie, and by the time she had answered it and brought Lenny and Keith into the living room, André was awake and in the armchair that stood opposite the one she usually took.

Huh. Tactful of him.

She got everyone settled and brought in tea; then got down to business.

"All right," she said, waiting for her tea to cool enough to sip. "We've been dealing with two kinds of victims and multiple killers. We'd just about decided that for ourselves—and what André told us seems to indicate not only that there are psivamps *and* something else, but that they've all linked up. Not that improbable a coincidence, actually. Predators can be pack animals as well as solitary, and pack animals hunt more efficiently. Provided there was no quarrel of leadership rights, it actually make a certain amount of sense for them to have met and for them to decide to band together."

Keith nodded. "I wondered about that. It just seemed like too big a coincidence."

She took a sip of tea, carefully. It still was hot enough it nearly burned her, but she was chilled to the bone. The long walk from the subway station seemed longer in the dark of winter.

"It may not *be* a coincidence, as such," André said quietly. "If you think of the areas both must hunt—relatively deserted, yet with *some* people upon the street—it was inevitable that their paths must cross, soon or late. There are not that many places which qualify as hunting grounds."

He turned his attention to Di. "I take it you did find something that fits the soul-eater, then?"

She nodded. "When I looked up Oriental vampirism in Annie's library, I didn't have a lot of luck, until I acted on a hunch and cross-checked in Japanese folktales. That's when I ran across something called a *gaki*."

Andre considered the word for a moment, then shook his head and shrugged. "I do not recognize the referent."

She rubbed the handle of her mug with her thumb, thoughtfully. "They're—well, we don't *have* an equivalent," she said. "It was hard to make out exactly what they are, and since I don't know Japanese, I couldn't cross-check in the original texts. The word is translated as 'spirit,' 'vampire,' *and* 'demon'; take your pick. They are *not physical*—that is, they didn't start out as human beings, like the *real* Japanese vampires do. Most of them seem to be harmless, and they feed on other things that are not considered 'physical'—like perfume, music, incense, the smoke from cooking, even the emanations of a monk's meditations."

"So far, nothing like our killer," André observed, tracing a little design on the arm of his chair with a long finger.

"I said *most* of them. There are three kinds that aren't harmless—the 'flesh,' 'blood,' and 'soul' *gakis*. The flesh *gakis*—those make Jack the Ripper sound tame." She shivered. "They have to devour the flesh of the victim while the victim is still living."

She swallowed to moisten a throat gone dry with fear. Knowing what she had known—reading those folk tales had been very unpleasant. Annie's books had not been written or translated for kids. She wondered what conventional scholars made of them.

And what would they do if they knew the stories were something more than stories? That the bogeymen were real, a real as the scholars themselves? She felt a little finger of cold touch her back, as she had when first reading the stories, but ignored it as best she could.

"The blood *gakis* are just like the Western notion of Count Dracula; absolutely evil, seeing humans as no more than his rightful prey. Then there are the soul *gakis*. The tales were very clear on two points. First, they *do* devour the spirit after killing the chosen victim, and they seem to delight in making the death as frightening, violent, and painful as possible."

"Which would account for the mangled victims in the bus," Lenny said, after a moment. "I couldn't figure out why this thing would want to do that if it just wanted to—" He gestured helplessly, unable to complete the sentence. Keith just went a little pale, and clutched his mug.

She nodded. "The second thing is, they're able to take on the physical appearance and attributes of anyone they've killed by absorbing the body when the soul has been devoured. Remember the missing bus driver?"

Keith nodded, holding tightly to Lenny's hand. Lenny patted his arm absently, all his attention fixed on Di.

"Let's assume that the bus driver was the first one killed, and that the *gaki* took his form by absorbing him."

"He'd have a rolling deli if he did," Lenny said bluntly, as Keith winced. "The temptation must have been too much to resist."

"Exactly. The *gaki*'s so-called normal or feeding form is like a cloud of fog or smoke, and it supposedly takes time and concentration to switch from that to human and back. When the cop forced him to pull the bus over, he might have figured it was safer to 'play dead'—and once they put him in the morgue, he just went into his other form and got out the ventilation system."

"The cloud!" André exclaimed. "The cloud of smoke that struck me!"

"That's it. That's the only thing that makes sense, and fits in with what you told me. That's why the Oriental boy vanished before the cloud showed up. The only reason you're here now is because you can't 'die' twice—I actually have some theories, but now isn't the time. Now, our problem in going after them is that since the *gaki* has hooked up with the psivamps that killed André's gypsy friend, we're at a bad disadvantage—because they're covering each other's weaknesses. The *gaki* can only be hurt or killed when it's in its human form. The psivamps can drain you down to heart-failure level, probably without even touching you."

"Concentrate on the psivamps, and the *gaki* will go into cloud form and get you. Go for the *gaki*, trying to get him before he becomes a cloud, and the psivamps could drain you." Lenny nodded, frowning. "I don't much like this."

"Do you suppose they are sharing victims?" André asked.

"I would be surprised if they weren't. The psivamps don't give a fat damn about the soul. It's like two kinds of lions, one that only wants the hindquarters, and one that only wants the fore. They complement each other; it makes sense for them to work together."

"How have we got *anything* going for us?" Keith asked unhappily. "This looks hopeless!"

She reached over and patted his hand encouragingly. "Not yet, it isn't—for one thing, there's four of us now. For another, they only know for certain that André is on their tail."

Lenny was thinking; Di could tell by the way he was chewing his lip. "Could we get them to split up or something?" he asked. "Like maybe we could do something to exhaust one of them, so it has to go hunting before the rest of them are ready. Then we could get him."

"Might work. I had some other ideas," Di replied, rubbing the back of her neck. "Most of them *did* involve catching at least the *gaki* away from the psivamps."

"First we must learn where they are," André pointed out. "Did you—"

"Yeah, I checked the address you gave me. Not so much as a mouse; even the cockroaches bailed out."

"So. They have moved, as we both expected. And they will be on their guard. Jeffries will no doubt be waiting for me to return."

She nodded, and put the cold mug of tea down beside her; she hadn't taken more than a few sips and neither had anyone else, so far as she had noticed. She sighed, then a memory she had been *trying* to bring up all day drifted into the front of her mind.

"Well, *hell!*"

"What?" the three others chorused.

"I don't know where they are now, but I bet I know a good place to pick up their trail. I saw Jeffries there just the other night, and he was acting like he owned the place. Not only that, but there was a girl with him, a Japanese girl, and I'd be very surprised if she wasn't your *gaki,* André."

"Where was this?" André asked, looking a bit more lively.

"A club, a rock club down near the Village. It's called HeartBeat."

The phone shrilled.

Jeffries was hiding something. Dave had no doubt of it.

When he and the others returned—they had, thank God, been satisfied at last, and Dave had managed to get himself under control before they returned to the van—Jeffries took Doug aside to tell him something that none of them wanted Dave to hear. Well, that wasn't that unusual, but—

The back half of Jason's loft was one big room; it had been an artist's studio, Jason said. They'd used it for rehearsals for a while—until they got the steady gig at HeartBeat; now they used the club itself. It had always been open, though empty of everything but odd bits of gear.

But now the door was closed and locked.

He discovered the locked door when he got up the next afternoon, and stared at it without doing more than touching it to confirm it had been locked.

There was unhappiness and fear on the other side of the door. And something that filtered that unhappiness and fear so that very little of it could be detected on the other side of the door.

Like they're trying to keep it hidden. And I'm the only one they'd want to hide it from.

He backed away, then returned to the dubious shelter of the room Jason had assigned him, a little cubby barely big enough to hold a cot.

He was recalling the talk of a "counteroffensive" against the intruder—and it frightened him.

He paced the narrow confines of his room, thinking furiously. *They've got people back there. More than one. Oh God, this is wrong, it's wrong—and I don't know what to do about it. Everything I've done is wrong. The booze isn't helping enough, neither is the grass. I—I haven't done anything but drive the van—*

His lips twitched. *Right. And feed off their leavings.* He flung himself down on his cot, and covered his eyes with his arm. *I haven't hurt anyone—but I haven't stopped them. Get real, Dave. Standing by and watching while they kill is just as bad as doing the killing yourself. Oh God.*

He groaned, turned on his side, and curled into a fetal position. *I can't get away—they always know where I am, and they'll come after me. If they think I've blown the whistle on them, they'll kill me. If I go to the cops, anyway, they'll lock me in the loony bin—they'll track me, and then* they'll send Hidoro after me.

"Hey, Davey-boy." Jason interrupted his misery with a sharp rap on his door. "Up and at 'em. Gig time."

He dragged himself to his feet, pulled his door open, and joined the others in the living room, his throat swollen with misery. *And through it all I have to make music—or they'll kill me.*

His guilt gnawed at him all through the gig. Even the wild vibes from the floor couldn't penetrate his misery. As Jason turned on the heat and they screamed through "Why Oh Why," he sang the chorus with real feeling.

If only there was someone he could turn to for help—

That thought—and the coincidence of *that* song, and a girl dancing on the edge of the floor, a dancer with hair down to her ass—all combined to trigger the first hopeful thought he'd had in weeks.

Di.

My God—she *knows all about this stuff, and she was* here, *I saw her*—which *means she's living in the Apple.*

He finished the set in a rush of impatience, and headed straight out the back door afterward, mumbling something to Doug about going for cigarettes. The bassist didn't care; all through the last set he'd had his eye on an aggressively made-up dolly with the look of someone who'd trip a guy and beat him to the ground. Now he was headed for the dance floor. As Dave passed him, Doug made a dismissing motion, and moved out, intent on his own game.

And Jason was nowhere to be seen.

Hidoro and Jeffries, Dave knew, would be holding up one end of the bar. The coast was clear.

He ran the three blocks to the nearest phone booth, closed the door behind him. The cold wind cut off, he fumbled out a dime with numb fingers, praying that she hadn't gotten an un-listed number.

Well, there's a D. A. Tregarde listed. The only one. If it isn't her—

He didn't want to even consider that notion.

He dialed, his fingers feeling fat and clumsy, and waited while the phone trilled. Once. Twice.

On the third ring, someone picked it up.

"Tregarde residence," said the voice he'd been hoping to hear.

"Di?" he said, suddenly uncertain. "It's Dave. Dave Kendall."

Yeah, kid. The guy you used to be in love with. The one who dropped you like a hot rock 'cause he didn't understand what you were into. That it was important—maybe more important than him. The guy who needs *you right now, like he's never needed anybody before.*

"Oh. Dave. Nice to hear from you." Her voice sounded cold, preoccupied, and a little strained. "Look, I'm afraid you caught me at a bad time right now."

"Di—wait, please, don't hang up on me. I—I need to talk to you."

He stared at the stainless steel of the tray under the phone, and willed her not to hang up."

"We're talking now," she said.

Not going well. "Please, Di, it's important, and I don't want to talk about it over the phone. I need to talk to you in person."

There was a long pause, during which he could hear, faintly, something on a crossed line—some other conversation between two women with strident voices. "It's late," she said, finally.

He forced himself to stay calm; told himself that screaming wouldn't do any good. "I know—please. Di—it's not about us, it's about—about something I've gotten into. The kind of thing you—you know. I'm in over my head. I *need help*, Di. I wouldn't lie to you, not about this." More silence. "We could meet someplace if you don't want me around your pad, okay? Someplace neutral?" He swallowed. "I—I was a lousy macho bastard. If you don't want me to come around, I wouldn't blame you. But I don't know where else to go."

"Someplace neutral?" She sounded a little less cold. "Well, I don't know. I—suppose so. As long as I can bring friends."

He leaned against the cold glass of the booth, weak-kneed with relief. "Sure, sure thing, anybody you want. Tonight?" Desperation sharpened his voice. "Please, can we make it tonight?"

There was another long pause, during which he could hear her talking to someone with her hand over the mouthpiece of the phone. "All right," she said at last. "I guess it can't hurt." There was another pause, and he clutched the receiver to his ear to catch every word. "There's a bar over in the club district where a lot of folk musicians hang out. It's called Logres. You know it?"

"Yeah, yeah, I know it."

Oh there is a God. It's only ten blocks from here.

"When do I meet you there?"

"In—" He checked his watch. There was one more set left, then they packed it in for the night. Doug he *knew* had a target in mind, Hidoro would be good for a couple of days yet, and Jason took somebody out in the alley after the first set. If he went off on

his own, quickly, they might think he was running off to feed—
or to brood. In either case, they'd give him at least two hours before coming for him, and they wouldn't go into a crowded bar
after him, they'd wait until he came out. "In two hours. Is that
okay?"

She made a little sound of speculation. "This had better be
good, Dave. Two hours from now is damned late to be dragging
somebody out in this weather. If this is some kind of a gag, my
friends aren't gonna be real happy."

"Yeah, I—"

"You played enough head games with me, Dave. I'm not as
forgiving as I used to be. If you're pulling some cute trick, I
might let my friends have you when I get done with you." Another pause. "I'm a brown in karate now, Dave. I can wipe the
floor with you if I want to, and I'm not kidding."

"Oh God, I swear it, Di, I need your help and it's not some
kind of stupid frat joke." He looked at his watch again. Ten minutes left in the break. "I gotta go. I'll see you in two hours."

He hung up the phone without waiting to hear her say good-
bye, and ran all the way back to the club.

ELEVEN

Di hung up the phone, all too aware that her palms were sweating.

"What was *that* all about?" Lenny asked, very bewildered. "I've never heard you threaten to beat somebody up before."

"That's because my ex-lover never called me up before," she said, flushing, and wiped her hands on her jeans before she sat down again.

"Oh." Lenny looked embarrassed. "Uh—I—"

"The one," she continued, allowing herself no wallow in self-pity, "that dumped me in college. I told you about him when we both got drunk that one time you really screwed up an audition."

"Yeah, you did." Lenny grimaced. "I know this's supposed to be the era of peace and harmony and all that, but—let's just say I don't blame you."

She managed a wan smile. "Thanks. Well, it sounds like he got his, anyway. I was just bringing it home to him that I'm not the same girl he dumped. He *says* he's in trouble, *my* kind of trouble. He was practically crying, and I don't think he was faking it."

"What goes around, comes around," Keith put in. "Thing is, can you afford to mess around with his problems when we've got this other stuff on our hands?"

She frowned, thinking. "That's the odd thing. The last time I saw him was just about a week ago, maybe two—his band was *playing* at HeartBeat. That was the same night I saw Jeffries and what I *think* is the *gaki*. I told you that I was beginning to think that there isn't *anything* connected with this business that's a co-incidence. Seems to me that if Dave's in occult trouble it would be damned odd if it's *not* connected to those two." She rubbed her hands together, trying to massage cramps out of her fingers. "Anyway I said I'd meet him—with some friends—at Logres." She tilted her head sideways a little, and looked pointedly at Lenny and Keith. "You don't have to go if you don't want to."

"I said I was in," Lenny replied firmly. Keith nodded. "I go along with your take on this," the dancer continued. "I can't see how your ex's problem could be occult and not be tied in with something as nasty as those two, not when you've *seen* them lurking in the same club. You know, maybe they own it."

"*That* is an interesting thought, friend Lenny," André said, drumming his fingers on the arm of the sofa. "An excellently baited trap for the catching of unwary mice, *non?* One could pick and choose, and not need to prowl the streets at all—"

"Only part of the time," Di interrupted, sure of her ground here. She'd hunted too many predators not to have learned how they thought. "You don't want to draw too much attention to a particular area by taking all your victims from there. But it *would* be a good place to mark people out for later."

"A lot of runaways hang out down there," Keith put in, face very quiet and thoughtful. "Anytime one of the clubs gets lax about checking IDs, it's all over the street. If you're looking for nameless, faceless victims—"

"Yeah. With a vested interest in *not* going to the cops." Di gri-maced. "I think we've got a lead. Now all we have to do is keep from spooking him."

Di saw to it that the four of them arrived early for the meeting at Logres; early enough to set Lenny and Keith up in a booth at the front, and to have a few words of warning with Jim, the bartender and part owner.

She felt sick to her stomach. *I don't want to do this. I don't want to see him, or talk to him, or any damn thing. And I don't have a choice.*

"You have storm warnings up," the swarthy bartender observed sotto voce, when she leaned over the bar and gave him their orders.

Yeah, no kidding. But I didn't think it showed that badly. So much for the Great Unflappable Tregarde. Another illusion shattered. "You're very perceptive, as usual."

I wish I wasn't involving Logres, but there's no place else that's this well protected. And I don't *want Dave in my home. Sorry about this, Jimbo.* She stuffed her change back in her purse but did not touch the four glasses of Harp on the counter in front of her. "I'm meeting somebody," she told him, in a voice that would not carry beyond the two of them. "There could be trouble."

"Physical, or 'other'?" Jim flexed his enormous biceps unconsciously as he gave a quick glance toward the door. She smiled a little. *Oh Jim, you never stop hoping for the day you can ride to the rescue on your white steed, do you? No medieval brawls tonight, Sir Severale. Sorry about that, too.* He was a Medieval Society knight, a well-trained fighter with rattan blade and shield, and big and brawny enough to take care of most troublemakers without resorting to anything worse than intimidation—which occasionally disappointed him.

"Other. Who's in that might catch fallout?" *I've got to get the innocents out or shielded, just in case—a Guardian does not leave innocents undefended.*

Logres wasn't *just* a place where a lot of folk musicians hung out—or Medieval Society members, though there were plenty of both that spent their time here. It was the watering hole of a fair number of occultists and sensitives—psis like Di, who had mundane jobs and mundane lives, and extramundane interests.

They *had* to have mundane jobs—the bill of drink at Logres was mostly imported, and not cheap.

"Nobody, at least not tonight. Anybody like *that* cleared out an hour ago. You'd think they were psychic." His broad grin invited her to answer it, and she did. "We have the Baron and the Count playing chess in the last booth, and four folkies drinking Guinness like they know what they're drinking right behind you. That's all."

The Baron and the Count are so headblind I could let off a psionic nuke in here and they'd never look up from the game. The folkies—She put a quick shield on them, and sighed. *One more erg of energy I'm out in case I need it—one more time, no other option.* "Bad news for your cash register, but good for me—"

He shook his shaggy, dark head. "Nope; guess again. We had a big crowd in here until about an hour ago. For some reason they all cleared out just before you got here. Not to worry, m'lady. Just try and keep the fireworks contained, hmm?"

"Good enough." Now she took the four glasses, sides slick and cool against her palms, two in each hand. "Jimbo, I'm sorry about visiting possible havoc on your place—"

"Forget it. Logres can take care of itself."

She thought about that; thought about how *she'd* been drawn in here, her very first day in New York, drawn by the warm and friendly atomosphere (psychic *and* mundane); how the place seemed to hold people in protective arms—and how anyone that was *really* trouble had always been dealt with. Summarily. By Jim—or by fellow customers—and a time or two, *she* had helped with the "dealing." And she wondered if the other owner— the one she never saw—might not also be a Guardian . . .

"Listen—" she said, shaking herself out of ruminations. "This guy, when he comes in, get a good look at him. He *might* be bad news, and not just because he's my ex. He told me on the phone that he's in deep kimchee, and I *think* it might be real heavy. You might want to find reasons to bounce him on out of here if he ever comes in on his own."

Jim raised his eyebrow—he only *had* one, a solid bar that stretched across his forehead—and wet his lips. "I've never known you to say that about anybody, m'lady, even people I know you don't much care for. I'll *take* that advice."

His trust of her word warmed her. "It could be mistaken advice—" she felt moved to warn. "I'm sure's hell not infallible."

"And I could be Elizabeth Taylor. Right." He snorted. "I'll have my eye on him, so figure your back's covered. Oh—don't forget; another hour and all I can serve you is juice. Okay?"

"Yeah. And thanks." She bestowed a grateful smile on him, and took the drinks to her friends, Lenny and Keith at the front booth, André parked at a table two booths away from the folk musicians, who were waving their hands in the air and talking taxes.

Gods, my throat is dry. Nerves, nerves, nerves. Maybe I should have taken something. No. I can't be less than sharp.

André turned the glass in his hand and held it up to the light. "Ale?" he asked, sniffing it interestedly. Di was in the middle of a drink and couldn't immediately answer him. He sipped. "Harp!" he exclaimed with delight.

"You have an educated tongue," she said, amused in spite of her worry.

"Practice."

He was sitting with his back to the door; an odd position, but he had assured Di that nothing would be able to take him by surprise—

Of course, the fact that the back wall was one long mirror made that statement something less of a boast.

The door opened and closed silently, and someone was standing uncertainly in the dim light.

He moved, and the light fell on his head and face.

Dave.

Her heart began pounding, and it hurt to breathe. *Gods. I am not ready for this. Oh gods—he looks like hell. He wasn't kidding. He needs me. And I just want to go away.* Her stomach knotted, and her palms began sweating again.

André caught the change in her expression immediately, and his smile faded.

There was a pull from Dave that had nothing to do with sex or her old feelings for him. *I knew it the minute he opened the door,* she thought, angry at herself for allowing her emotions to blind her to what had been in front of her. *And I should have known it when I saw him on stage. Psivamp. He's trying to drain right now, only there's nothing here that isn't protected.*

Dave gave Lenny and Keith a cursory glance, then headed toward the next occupied booth—theirs.

He doesn't have an aura—he's a whirlpool, a vacuum, feeding on whatever he can grab. Gods, he's strong! He always was a little in that way—why didn't I see it before? He couldn't always *have been this strong, could he? And if wasn't—*She felt fear chill her and knot her stomach further. *If he wasn't, what in the name of all that's holy did he do to get like this?*

"Hi," Dave said weakly, stopping beside their table. "I—uh—"

"You!" André exclaimed coldly. "I *know* you—"

Dave started, then turned a little to look at André, as if he hadn't really known he was there until the Frenchman spoke. He started again when he saw André clearly—then stared, his face displaying an odd expression compounded equally of guilt and relief.

"You got away—" he said, in a whisper. "They said—I wasn't sure you had—they lie a lot." He flushed. "I—I'm sorry. God, I'm sorry. I wish I could undo that whole night."

André's expression lost a little of its chill. "Why?" he asked, rubbing his wrist absently. "You did nothing. At least, not to me."

That's it, she thought, clenching her hands. *He's with them. Oh gods, Dave, how could you be so* stupid *about this?*

Dave flushed again, and stood looking at the surface of the table, hands shoved into his pockets. "That's just it. I didn't do anything. I should have stopped them. I should have at least tried to stop them."

André made a sound of contempt. "Oh, *bon*. With *what* would you have stopped them? You are not a match for the weakest of them."

"I take it," Di interrupted ironically, hoping her voice wasn't shaking too much, "that you've met." Dave looked briefly at her, but could not meet her eyes. He mumbled something she couldn't hear.

"Well." She clasped her hands on the table in front of her, and looked him up and down. *He looks like he's been through more than anybody should have to take. What am I going to do about him? Dave, Dave, why couldn't you have just gone off to L.A. or 'Frisco like you wanted to?* "Just what is it you want *me* to do for you?"

He managed to meet her eyes once, then looked quickly away. "Can I sit down?" he asked unhappily. "It's a long story."

André slid out of his side of the booth, and indicated Dave should take his place with an ironic half-bow. When Dave was seated, he slid in beside Diana, carefully positioning himself so that there was neither too much nor too little space between them.

And enough room for me to go for him over the table, if it comes to that, she realized. *Bless you, André. Now somehow help me stay together for this little interview.*

"All right," she said to Dave, pleased to hear that her voice sounded calm. "Let's hear it."

Jim brought a third glass of Harp, unasked. Dave looked at him in surprise, then paid for it. He turned the glass around and around in his hands, while they waited patiently for him to make up his mind to say something.

She tried not to look at him; tried to think of him as a stranger. It didn't work. *Why did I say yes on the phone? Why didn't I just have one of the boys talk to him? Stupid. Because it has to be you, Tregarde, There's no coincidences here. You ended up nearly screwing up your life over him. Now it's come back around, hasn't it? You have to prove your life is back on track.*

"I guess it happened Halloween," he said softly. "I was at this party—the guy holding it had some stuff, new stuff, you know? So we all did it."

You never could keep from taking anything somebody offered you, could you, Davey? I told you that was going to get you into trouble someday. Her heart seemed to have lodged somewhere south of her larynx. *I never thought the trouble would come like this. Gods, if I'd stayed with you—would this have happened?*

"It did some real strange shit to my head," he continued. "Like I thought I was seeing what people were thinking, and when I went home, I didn't wake up for a couple of days. When I finally did—nothing I ate did me any good. Just sat in my stomach like a rock. I couldn't figure it, thought maybe I had the flu or something. We had a gig that night, and I thought it was gonna be a disaster for sure—"

He continued with frequent pauses that stretched over several minutes.

Those pauses twisted her up inside until she thought she couldn't take any more without screaming for the exit. It was all just too raw—

Then André put one hand unobtrusively over hers, and she began to feel calmer. She wasn't alone; she had friends she could trust—one she could trust with her real secrets. And Dave wasn't the same person who'd dumped her. *He'd* gotten more feckless, judging by the story he was telling.

She hadn't gotten over him—not by a long shot, judging by the gyrations her insides were doing—but she'd gotten at least a little more responsibility. She gave André's fingers a little squeeze, and began to pay attention to what Dave was saying.

He began to stammer under Di's scrutiny, and spent more and more time staring at the glass in his hands.

But he told them enough.

Enough to know that the drugs combined with the fact that he was already marginally psychic had somehow made him into a psychic vampire—and that André had been right. That there were three more of them, plus the *gaki.*

Enough for her to know that the psychic vampires weren't killing too many—at least not yet, and not directly.

But what they're doing is worse than killing, she thought unhappily, watching him turn his glass around and around, like the mindless pacing of a caged animal. *He doesn't realize that the people they drain that way are burned out for life, not just temporarily exhausted. He hasn't figured out that once they shuffle out of his life, they probably end up street bums, unable even to care about living anymore. If they ever told him, he doesn't want to believe it. Gods, this has got to stop. I have to stop it.*

Dave, how could you have gotten yourself tangled up in this? Why didn't you come to me earlier? And—if I'd run after you, really tried to make the effort to make you see what I was into— would you be here now?

Am I to blame for you?

"Di?" he said in a small voice, after one of those long pauses.

"I haven't run off," she replied thickly. It was hard to get words out. *Dammit, he's responsible for him, and I'm responsible for me. He's sitting there because of things he did, not things I did.*

He grimaced. "Please, you've gotta get me free of this. You've gotta help me. Please. I can't live like this. Jason an' Doug *like* it—I—I just wanta be sick every time I—you know." He put the glass to his lips and gulped, the first time he'd drunk anything since he came in. When he put the glass down, it was half empty. "I'd rather be dead," he finished flatly, concentrating on his own hands. "I can't keep doing things like this."

Oh gods, Dave—"I thought you were used to using people," she said, as coldly as she could. *I have to know if there's anything left of you to save. If I can save it.*

He winced. "I had that coming, didn't I?" he replied, his deep-set eyes shadowed with emotions she couldn't read through the chaos that surrounded him. "I dumped you when you wouldn't be my little cheerleader, when you told me that there was something out there besides music. And here all along you were right." He laughed hollowly. "Talk about your instant karma. Dump you, get dumped on. And the only place I can go for help is you. Di, this stuff is *wrong*. I'm doing things that are horrible. If I don't stop now, I'm gonna do things that are worse. I can't take this anymore."

There are times I wish I'd never taken up Guardianship, she thought, aching inside so much that she wanted to cry. *And most of them seem to be tied up with Dave.*

"If I had any choice—" she began.

"You should not aid him," André interrupted coldly. She looked at him in surprise, and read true hate in his eyes. "He caused you pain, and doubt, and indirectly threatened your very self. He has participated in the deaths of many. He does not deserve your concern."

"André, he hasn't gone over completely; he's salvageable, and he asked me for help." *That's true. All of it's true. I just wish it wasn't me that has to give the help.* She touched André's hand, then looked back at Dave, trying not to show how much she hurt.

"Your boyfriend's right," Dave said, head down, voice muffled. "You should throw me out. Out of your life, out of here."

She stiffened. *It's my job; it's my life. And I won't let a thing like what you did to me mess that up a second time. That's not the way a Guardian does things, dammit.* "I don't have a choice, Dave. There are pledges I made a long time ago that I have to fulfill. You *asked* for my help, I *have* to give it. And André isn't my boyfriend."

André frowned, but made a little gesture, as if to say, "It's your decision."

I might as well get this over now. Either I can do something for him, or I can't. I'd rather know. I'd rather not have to go through this again.

Forgive me, Lord and Lady. I don't know which *I want. I still can't forgive* him, *even now. I know I wanted him to get hurt enough someday to see how right I was—but I truly don't think I wanted anything like this. Did I?*

She swallowed hard as he stared at his glass. "So—let's see what I can do," she said, flexing her hands, then digging into her purse for some of her "equipment."

"Here?" Dave looked up, eyes startled. "Now?"

"Here's as good a place as any," she replied. "We won't be disturbed—" *—and I don't want you in my home. There's nothing to remind me of you there now, and I don't want anything of you there, ever.*

She glanced over at the bar, and hand-signed "Do not disturb" when she caught the bartender's eye. Jim, who among other things, was a fluent "signer," nodded. "Okay," he signed back. "Keep it quiet."

She half smiled. "Will try," she signed.

She turned her attention back to Dave, and throttled down tears at the haunted look in his eyes. "Now—let's see what you're made of these days—"

It was a good thing Logres never seemed to close.

Di tried every trick in the book—and plenty that had never *been* in any book. Jim ignored the aural flares, the shield probes, the spectacular attempt—which failed—to reverse the complete unconscious drainage. He could most assuredly See all of it; Di had ascertained a long time ago that he had Sight. But he ignored it all, trusting her to keep it within the confines of the booth.

Which she did, though not without cost.

I'm not getting anywhere. Oh gods, I can't do anything with him—

She even considered trying to invoke Guardianship—but *that* came when it wanted to, and tonight it didn't feel like it wanted to. *I guess Dave doesn't rate. He got himself into this—maybe he's supposed to deal with it by himself.*

Finally, when her hands were shaking and her vision blurred,

André put his hands over hers, and said, in a quiet voice, "No more."

She sighed, and closed her eyes for a moment.

It's no good. I can't block him without starving him. And I can't reverse what's been done. Oh God, Dave—no matter what you ever did, you don't *deserve this!*

It hurt; not her pride, there was little enough left of that after defeating her panic attacks. It hurt *inside,* it hurt to know that there was nothing she could do for him.

I'm a Guardian and Guardians are supposed to be able to help people. And I can't help him.

Maybe when I started this it was because I didn't have a choice, but now—there's a hunger. I need to *be able to help. And this time I can't. Oh gods, it hurts!*

"I'm sorry," she said, propping her elbows up on the table and bowing her head into her hands to hide her tears of frustration. "Dave, I'm sorry. I've tried everything."

Silence. "You can't help me," he said, voice dull.

She couldn't look at him. "I can't help you. At least, not now. Maybe before—I don't know. That stuff, that drug you did, it changed your metabolism, so that you were living on bioenergy. You were all right as long as you were feeding off the high frequencies, the positive emotions—but the minute you started taking in the lower frequencies—you changed *again.* Your receiver's been retuned, if you will. I can't change you back. It's like—like weaning a young animal. Once you get them off milk, they can't digest it anymore; their body's changed. Yours has changed, and I can't reverse it. I'm sorry."

"I'm sorry" sounds so damned pathetic.

He laughed, bitterly, and her throat tightened with tears. " 'Once they get the taste for blood,' " he quoted, and laughed again. "God."

She looked up, over her entwined fingers, and his face was bleak and utterly without hope. Her eyes stung and blurred, and she blinked the tears away, silently.

He didn't seem to notice she was crying. "So you can't fix me. Can anybody?"

She shook her head, sniffed, and rubbed the back of her hand across her eyes and cheeks. "I don't know."

He slumped a little farther, huddled in on himself. "So— what do I do now?"

"I don't know that, either," she confessed.

"You were supposed to *help* me," he said bitterly.

Then, suddenly, she was angry. Angry at him, angry at the attitudes that had gotten him into this mess in the first place. If he'd *once* been willing to take charge of his life instead of letting other people make his decisions for him—

"You always wait for somebody else to do your thinking for you, and to bail you out when you get in too deep," she snarled. "And that's why you're *in* this mess in the first place! Why don't you try thinking for yourself for a change?"

Oh gods—now what have I done? She bit her knuckle, wishing she could unsay those last words. *I didn't mean—oh shit. Tregarde, you and your big fat mouth—*

Silence engulfed the booth, silence in which he stared at her as if she were some creature from another world entirely. As if he and she were the only people at the table, in the room, in the world.

"Maybe—" he said, slowly, something stirring in the back of his eyes. "Maybe that's exactly what I ought to do."

She sat frozen in her seat, as he rose slowly from his. As he rose, his face changed; from bleak and hopeless, to thoughtful and determined.

He leaned over the table and kissed her, lightly brushed her lips with his. It felt like a promise.

"I never could hide anything from you, could I?" he said, smiling, in a falsely frivolous tone that broke her heart. "I couldn't even hide where I was. Used to make me so damned mad at you—remember?"

He eased out of the booth, as Di stayed rooted to her seat.

"Ciao, baby," he said, saluting her with two fingers. He looked over at André, and his smile faded. "Take care of her," he said.

Then he turned, and before anyone could make a move to stop him, he was gone.

Lenny was the first to recover—he squirmed out of his booth and dashed out the door at a dead run.

He returned in a few minutes, face like a thundercloud, and slouched over to their booth.

"Gone?" André asked, his voice sympathetic.

"Shit yes." Lenny looked so disgusted at himself she didn't have the heart to say anything. "I don't suppose he told you where he's holing up, did he?"

André shook his head. "Regrettably, no."

Di's mind was slowly coming unfrozen.

"*I never could hide anything from you. I couldn't even hide where I was. Used to make me so damned mad at you—remember?*"

She *did* remember. Now that he'd reminded her. Deliberately reminded her—

"He didn't have to tell me," she said slowly, her heart aching so much for him that she held back tears only because she knew tears would do him no good. "He didn't have to tell me. No matter where he is, I can find him. Even if I didn't already know where the band is playing, now that I know he's in the city, I can find him wherever he goes. I could from the minute we'd been lovers. *And he knows that.* He went out of his way to remind me. Maybe it was so I could find him if I figure out a way to help him—but it doesn't much matter, does it? I can find where they're *all* hiding. All I have to do is stay within range of him. And—"

André nodded, sudden understanding lighting his eyes. Lenny's eyes widened, and his mouth formed a soundless O.

André touched her arm and slid out of the booth. She followed. He looked in the direction of the street door. "It is perhaps three in the morning," he said conversationally. "Perhaps four. Is that time in which to accomplish anything?"

She took a deep breath and steadied herself. "No," she said slowly. "No, I don't think so."

Lenny took a good look at her face, and wordlessly put his arm around her shoulders. She leaned against him, so grateful for his support that she couldn't possibly have put her feelings into words.

Evidently she didn't have to. He gave her shoulders a squeeze, dropped a gentle kiss on the top of her head, then let her go.

Keith spoke up for the first time since they'd arrived. "Should we head on back, maybe get some rest, and see what we can do tomorrow?"

"I—" Suddenly she was tired; tired enough to drop. Certainly tired enough to break down on the spot and cry. "Yeah," she said wearily. "I'm not even up to magicking my way out of a wet paper bag."

"The car's just around the corner," he offered.

She shook her head. "No—no, I'd rather walk. I've got a lot of things to think about."

"Tomorrow night, then." Keith slipped out the door, Lenny beside him. André hesitated.

Before he could say anything, Jim spoke up from the darkness behind the bar, where he'd been standing without her noticing him.

"I'd feel better, m'lady, if you didn't take that walk alone. Lots of nasty things out this late; some of 'em don't take to being exorcised." He grinned, and his teeth shone whitely. "Hard to exorcise a switchblade."

She made a halfhearted attempt to laugh. "Too true, Sir Knight. Well, André—feel up to a walk with a—"

"Yes," he said, before she could call herself any of the uncomplimentary terms she was considering. "I do not think you really want to be alone, *non?*"

"True," she said, sighing.

It was snowing, little flurries that sifted down and melted when they hit the salted sidewalk. He waited until they had gone at least a block, and the cold wind that cut through her coat had at least restored a little clarity to her mind, if not her heart.

"You knew him very well, once," he ventured, hesitation in his voice. "One assumes, that is. Lovers do not always know one another."

She sighed, and studied the deserted street ahead of them. There didn't seem to be any traffic at all out tonight. The sky was still heavily overcast, given the falling snow; in New York it was sometimes hard to tell, since you almost never saw the stars even on a clear night. There was a hint of damp in the air. "Well, I thought I did," she replied after a while. "I sure thought I was in love with him."

He reached for her hand and took it; he held it tentatively, at first, then, when she didn't pull away, he interlaced his fingers with hers. His hand felt warm and comforting, even through her glove. "Something happened to change that?"

She sternly told the ache in her throat to go away, and concentrated on putting one foot in front of the other until she thought she could respond without choking on her words. "Until tonight I thought I was still in love with him. Now—I don't know." She sighed, and her breath made a cloud that wisped away on the light breeze. "I feel sorry for him—*gods,* I feel sorry for him—but there's nothing *there* anymore but pity."

They passed beneath a streetlight, and she squinted against the brightness for a moment. "Perhaps you grew up," André suggested quietly, after they had walked a few more paces, footsteps echoing together on the concrete. "Perhaps he did not."

A car passed; a cop car. The cop inside gave them a brief glance, saw only what looked like a couple out for a little walk, and didn't even slow down. "I—I don't know, André," she answered absently. "I'm not sure of much of anything right now. You know about the way we broke up."

"Hmm." His fingers tightened a bit on hers. "As they say, messy, *non?*"

"Yeah. Messy. Very messy. He wanted me to give up what I was. Am. Magic, being a Guardian, all that. He didn't understand any of it, and didn't want to, because it took me away from him. And he didn't want to share that with me. I guess, anyway."

They reached another streetlight, passed beneath it, and turned the corner. She stared at the sidewalk a few feet ahead of them, at the way their shadows lengthened as they moved away from the streetlight. The flurries were turning into a real snowfall.

"Allow a stranger to correct?" he said tentatively.

A siren howled somewhere in the distance, moving away from them. She hunched her chin down into her coat collar, feeling a chill of the spirit as well as the body. "I'm supposed to 'know myself.' I mean, that's one of the rules of being a Guardian, so I don't get stuck in head games. Sure, go ahead."

The wind picked up strands of her hair and played with them. She thought about freeing her hand from his long enough to tuck them into her collar, and decided she didn't want to.

"He wished, I think, not for a partner nor an equal." He paused for a moment, as if searching for the right words. "I think that what he wished for—at that time—was for you to give up your identity, and become a mirror that reflected him. I think, however, that tonight—perhaps tonight he saw *Diana* for the first time, and not the thing that he wished you to be. I think perhaps that you forced him to truly *see* you for the first time. It was something of a shock to him. It was—an experience for him."

She turned that thought over in her mind, examining it from every angle she could think of. *It feels right. It feels like he's got it pegged.*

They crossed the street, and she stumbled a bit on the curb when they reached the other side. He caught her elbow, steadied her, then let her go when she had her balance.

"How did you know?" she asked. "You don't know him at all,

you hardly know me—how did you manage to get all that figured out?"

She looked at him out of the corner of her eye, and saw him shrug. "I have been about for no few years," he said wryly. He looked at *her* sideways; their eyes met, and he raised his eyebrow ironically. "I have seen his kind, the young and popular male musician, many, many times. It seems that they are either supremely sensitive, or supremely *insensitive.* Sometimes both. There seems to be little or no middle ground with them." He chuckled. "One could do worse than be or choose a shopkeeper, *n'est-ce pas?*"

"Right now I wish I *was* a shopkeeper," she replied sadly. "I wish I was ordinary. Ordinary people don't seem to come in for as much pain."

They walked on in silence, as a steady fall of snow drifted down from the sky, becoming visible only as they entered the cones of light from the street lamps. Her nose was getting numb in the cold, and she sniffed. The snow was beginning to "stick," and as the ground whitened, light reflected both from the ground and the low-hanging clouds. It began to grow noticeably brighter.

"Does it hurt you so much, the past?" he asked softly.

"Not as much as it did, I guess." She took internal inventory, and came up a bit surprised. "Not as much as I thought it should. The present hurts more. Being helpless. Being unable to *do* anything for him."

He raised his free hand, and rubbed the back of his head with it. "As with an injury," he mused, "you have feared to look at it, to test it, until it has mostly healed—and *voilà,* it does not pain so much as you had feared."

"I suppose so."

The apartment building loomed at the end of the block, as always, brightly lit. "You intend to follow through with this—to eliminate the killers."

She swallowed hard, and tightened her fingers on his. "I don't have a choice, André."

"If it means eliminating him, as well?"

"I—yes. I hope it won't. But if I have to—"

The thought of that—*oh gods. Oh dear gods. Please don't make it come to that*—A sob forced its way out of her throat, and she bowed her head. *But—it may. It may, and I have to face that.*

"*Chérie*—" He stopped, and tugged on her hand to make her pause beside him. "Diana, look at me."

She did; she hadn't expected to read what she saw in his face. Pity, sadness, understanding—compassion.

"He knows this, Diana. I do not think he is deluding himself. And I do not think he meant the words in jest when he said that he would rather die than continue as he is." His lips curved in a faint, and infinitely sad, smile. "I did not care for him, not at all, nor did I pity him—until the very last. Until he said good-bye, and told you what you had forgotten. Then something extraordinary—he began changing at that moment, I will swear to it. He is becoming something worthy of admiration, *chérie*. I do not know *what* he will become, but it will not be either petty or evil, whatever end he goes to."

She stared at him a moment longer, and then the tears began in earnest. He took her in his arms, and she sagged against his shoulder and cried while her tears froze on her cheeks.

"I have lost those I cared for, *chérie*," he murmured into her hair. "It is not an easy thing, and becomes no easier with time. Do not be ashamed to care, or to weep."

So she wept. And he held her, carefully, patiently, until she had cried herself out.

They entered the front door in silence. She shrugged out of her coat and threw it at a chair; it missed, and slid down to the floor, and she was too exhausted, mentally and physically, to care.

She didn't bother to turn on the lights; the steady snowfall outside had built up to at least an inch on the ground, and all the reflected city light made it nearly bright enough to read inside the apartment. When they had climbed the building steps, she had looked back over her shoulder at the street, peaceful beneath the frosting of white. It was beautiful, serene, and somehow pure.

And filled with soft light.

She hoped it was an omen.

They both stopped in the hallway, halfway between her room and the living room, and the silence became awkward.

"André—" she began, and flushed. *I don't know how to say this. I'm not used to asking for things. I—I'm not used to a lot of things.*

He waited, saying nothing, merely waiting.

"André, I—I'd rather not sleep alone tonight," she whispered, looking at her feet.

"I think," he said, quietly, but with a hint of humor, "that I am about to make a great fool of myself."

She looked up at him, startled. "What?"

"Ah, come—"

He took her hand, and led her to the couch. When she had taken her seat, he sat beside her, still holding her hand. "I told you, did I not, that my kind—are something of 'psychic vampires' ourselves?"

She nodded, and chewed at her lip, wondering what was coming next.

"I told you that we take only what is given freely and no more? And that I, I have made it a pledge that I take nothing without some feeling between myself and the other, after the first few times?"

She nodded again.

He sighed, and shook his head. "Diana, Diana, I have done so *very* well for so very long with casual encounters—until now."

She blushed. "Until now?"

He reached out, and just barely touched the back of the hand that was resting on her knee. "You have made casual encounters somewhat—distasteful. Am I a very great fool, or have you been something other than indifferent?"

His lips smiled, but his eyes begged for her to tell him that she had *not* been "indifferent."

She shivered. "I'm not sure what to say. I—you're very special to me, André. More than I ever thought anyone could ever be. But—"

His eyes had brightened with her first words—now they looked wary. "But?"

"André—I can't stop being a Guardian. I might not make it through this next one—or the one after that—or the one after that. I don't want to ask you to get involved with me when you could end up hurt. And I don't just mean physically."

He smiled, then his smile broadened until it turned into that lovely silent laugh of his.

Gods, he could stop my heart when he laughs like that—she thought longingly.

"How very odd." He chuckled, reaching out and cupping his free hand around her cheek, without letting go of the hand that he held. "How very odd. That was *precisely* what I was going to say to you!"

She threw caution, bitter memories, and a fear-darkened future to the wind. "Would you consider sticking around—if we make it through this one?"

His laughter faltered and died. "Oh, *chérie*—" He searched her face, looking for something—she wasn't sure what it was, but he must have found it, because he smiled again, and moved his hand around to the back of her neck, burying it in her hair and tugging her closer. "Diana, dear, sweet lady—*chérie, mon amour,* I will stay for as long as you wish me to stay—"

Whatever else he might have said was lost as their lips met.

There was too much tangled up in that kiss for her to sort it out; so she didn't even try, she just gave herself to it, and to him. And when he let her go, whispered, "I still don't want to sleep alone."

He looked deeply into her eyes, and smiled—and before she realized what he was up to, he'd scooped her up in his arms as effortlessly as if she were no heavier than one of the throw pillows.

She gasped, and clutched his shoulders. He chuckled. "This is another legend that is true," he said to her widened eyes. "The strength. *Chérie,* if you do not wish to sleep alone—"

He glanced at the clock on her desk. "It lacks an hour to dawn," he told her, impishly, and began making his way toward the door leading to the hallway and her room. "You shall not *sleep* at all, for a bit—hmm?"

TWELVE

"Ciao, baby," Dave said, trying to keep his tone light, trying to keep his despair from showing on his face.

If I look into her eyes again, I'll fall apart. I don't want to do that, not in front of her. It'll only make her feel worse than she does now.

So he focused on the dark guy, the one with the French accent, instead. *The vampire. Christ.* The man's eyes bored into his; sable, solemn eyes, measuring eyes. Thoughtful eyes.

I've lost her for good—but then, I threw her away, didn't I? I had my chance, and I blew it. You—feel like a good guy, even if you are a bloodsucker. I think you'll back her. I know you understand her better than I ever did. I'm glad she's got you. Before this is over, she's gonna need you.

"Take care of her," he said to the vampire, knowing the man would read more than just that in his tone. Then, before any of them could stop him, he turned on his heel and headed out of the door.

I've got to get out of sight, he thought, shivering in the cold wind, and shoving the door closed behind him, *or one of them is likely to chase after me.* He gave a quick look around; the street in front of Logres was deserted. *I can't let them follow me. If any of the others got hold of them, they'd be cole slaw. Maybe if I duck around the cor—*

He blinked in surprise.

My God, it's a miracle.

At precisely that moment, a cab pulled up to the curb, right at the front door of Logres. A single man got out, muffled to the ears in an overcoat. He paused for a moment, handing money to the driver; then turned and looked directly into Dave's eyes.

He smiled. For one moment, Dave felt all of his problems fall away before the warmth and understanding implicit in that smile—

Then the man was hurrying past, not into the bar, but opening an unobtrusive door at the side of the main entrance.

Dave shook his head—and dived for the cab, ducking inside before the cabby could pull away.

He slammed the door shut, and the cabby pulled out just as the door to the bar began to open.

"Where to, mack?" A cloud of pungent cigar smoke filled the front of the cab. The cabby didn't seem the least interested in anything except the nonexistent traffic on the street.

"Central Park—" He blurted out the first destination that came to mind.

He could feel the cabby's eyes on him; looked up at the rearview mirror and saw that he was, indeed, being stared at. Not surprising—Central Park at four A.M. was hardly a common destination. He slumped down into the back seat, ignoring the stare.

The cabby's massive shoulders shrugged when he didn't respond to the stare. "Okay. You're payin' th' fare."

Dave closed his eyes, tried to steady his mind down, and slouched a little lower. Getting under control—oddly enough— seemed a bit easier now than it had been when he'd first walked out of the bar.

Okay, he thought, deciding to take his problems apart and analyze them. *Di can't help you.* Now. *That's not to say she might not be able to find someone else who can. Wasn't that why you reminded her that she knows how to find you, no matter where you are? So maybe—*

He suddenly flashed on Di, walking, say, into the club. *This time knowing what Jason and the rest really were.*

Oh shit. Oh holy shit.

She knows about the others. What they've been doing. She's not likely to sit around and let them keep eating people alive. She's gonna use that line to you to get at them, shithead. She's gonna come after them.

And then they're gonna kill her.

He bit back a moan of anguish. *God, there is no way she can take any of them out! They're gonna have her for* lunch—

—*if she's lucky. If she's not—*

—*Hidoro's gonna get her.*

Oh God, what have I done?

His gut knotted with anguish. Bad enough watching them take on strangers, but *Di?* He couldn't even bear thinking about it. *She's gonna die—or worse—and it's gonna be my fault.*

Oh God, what can I do? What—

He suddenly froze, as he realized what he was thinking. *What can I do—*

I've got to think for myself. There has to be something I can do.

He opened his eyes and stared out the window of the cab at the street passing by, not really focusing on what lay behind the glass. Light—dark—light—streetlights and shadows made an abstract patterns that he scarcely noted. Except that there was so much darkness. So little light. So much cold, so little warmth.

So little hope.

He was hardly more than Jason's shadow. If Di couldn't do anything about *him,* how could he expect her to stand up to the others? Even Doug was stronger than he was—

Because Doug hasn't been trying to hold back, he thought bitterly at the dark city. *Doug hasn't been trying to stay a good guy. They all think I'm a fool for fighting this. Shit, I could be as strong as any of them if I would just give in to this thing. Dammit, it's not fair! I shouldn't be penalized for trying not to hurt people!*

He gritted his teeth. *Maybe I should give in and go their way. It sure looks like good guys do finish last.*

The spluttering neon of a sign made him think of what he'd *seen* when Di had been trying to help him. Flashes of white light, flickering shadows, the strain on her face, and through it all he felt nothing. *Good guys finish last—and Di isn't gonna finish at all—*

The cab paused at a stoplight, an angry red eye glaring above the corner. Below it, waiting for the light to change, Dave saw a young girl, clad far too lightly for the cold, in bell-bottoms and a fringed denim jacket. Flurries of snow fell on her granny glasses, and on her long, straight hair, hair bound up hippie-style with a headband; she slouched against the lamppost with her hands shoved deeply into her pockets. Her face was ab-solutely blank; either from dope or despair, he couldn't tell which, and he *didn't* want to "reach" for her to find out. She was probably just another anonymous runaway—*like all the others I've—taken—*

She was certainly too young to be out this late legitimately. Another innocent, or once-innocent; another morsel for some shark in the city to gobble up. *A shark. Like me. Like my "friends."*

Dave turned away from the window, biting his lip to keep the gnawing in his gut at bay.

I've got to do something. I can't just sit there and watch them destroy Di, like all those poor kids I helped destroy.

The light changed, and the cab pulled out with a cough and an explosive backfire. The girl jumped, and stared at the cab with the eyes of a frightened rabbit—started at *him?* Maybe, maybe not. She didn't look much like she was seeing any kind of reality. Her wide, startled eyes were like holes burned into her face.

Then the cab moved across the intersection, and she ran across the street and was swallowed up in the darkness.

Poor kid. If not tonight, then tomorrow, or the next night. Mugged, raped, eaten alive, she's a target, and she'll get hit. The stock situation, the setup, reminded him of a comic book. *But if this was a comic book, she'd be playing target on purpose. And when the bad guys moved in—wham.* Too bad she isn't Hidoro, he thought, sour taste of bile in the back of his throat. *Too bad. What was it Jason said? Trolling for rapists? It almost made me like Hido—*

My God. Trolling for rapists.

I've been holding back, but what if I didn't have *to? What if I made like a comic-book hero? What if I went out looking for other predators?*

Like in—Central Park.

It all fell together.

It might work.

He chewed his lip, thinking hard and furiously. *I'm stronger than any mugger, even if I couldn't take on Doug or Jason.* Now.

I could—go hunting. Now, tonight. Then when I came back, they'd believe *me if I let them think I'd given in, gone over to the wolves. And meanwhile, I'll be getting stronger. Maybe strong enough to be a match for them. One of them, anyway.*

Then when Di shows up—which she will—she's got somebody behind the lines.

He nodded to himself. *It's stupid. It's suicide. And damn if it isn't better than doing nothing.*

The cabby looked at him very oddly when he actually got out on the edge of Central Park, near one of the bridle paths—but a fifty convinced him that he wasn't curious. A second fifty convinced the driver to return in another two hours.

He probably thinks I'm a dealer, Dave thought wryly, turning his back on the cab to face the park. He took a deep breath of icy, exhaust-laden air. Behind him the cab coughed and backfired again as it pulled way; he ignored it and turned his attention to the new senses inside him—and let that strange hunger within him loose for the first time, to go hunting out among the trees.

The trees made a lacework of black, darker than the buildings around them or the sky above them, and seemed to go on forever. The snow, dirty gray by day, was white and pristine in the dim lights of the park, the reflected light from the city itself. It all looked so peaceful, so untouched. And it was all just another kind of trap.

Snow began falling in earnest; fluffy, fat flakes instead of flurries. He raised his head and walked slowly into the park, ignoring the paths, his feet crunching on the granulated snow. He sent that *thing* within him out again, and felt something after a moment. He paused to identify it.

He got feelings first. *Hunger. A clawing in the gut that matched his own. Pain. A man with a monkey on his back, a habit to feed, a habit that was killing him.* He could feel the death waiting inside the man—waiting, biding its time. It wasn't ready yet. It had a while to grow.

Dave's lips curled in something that wasn't exactly a smile, and he moved deeper into the park, slipping between the trees. The cold penetrated his thin boot soles; he hardly noticed it except as a minor annoyance. He was in his element at last. Tonight a predator was about to become prey.

Now he was getting images along with the feelings. *Body shaking, need screaming along his nerves, making him wired to the max. But not so wired that the hands holding his knife weren't rock-steady.*

The feelings, the images strengthened. Dave sensed he was nearing his goal. He peered ahead through the dim light, looking for a particular place . . .

There—that clump of bushes beside the concrete path. Now, how to flush the quarry—

The pain the other was suffering was giving *him* strength and energy. He opened himself to it, and shivered in poisoned pleasure as it poured into him, flooding him, filling his emptiness.

But it wasn't *quite* enough. The hunger within him snarled, and wanted more.

Well, it was going to *get* more.

He slipped silently from shadow to shadow, stalking his prey's hiding place, nearly invisible among the underbrush in his own black clothing.

The other was waiting in ambush—though it was an ambush based more on hope than on planning. Now Dave could *see* the thoughts in his head, just as he'd been able to see the thoughts of the chicks he'd picked up at HeartBeat. *There was a pimp that used this path; so did his girls. So did their tricks. Any of them would do. He was hoping for a john—a john would have more cash than one of the girls, and a john wouldn't be expecting trouble or paying protection—*

Dave smiled hugely, and licked his lips, and the hunger within him purred in anticipation. Of course. The best way to flush *his* quarry—

—would be to look like prey.

He slipped over to the path; paused a moment, then began walking confidently toward the bushes, his boot heels clicking against the concrete. He sauntered along as if he suspected nothing, expected no trouble, hands shoved carelessly down into his pockets.

And all the while he was using his line into the guy to hold him back, just as Jason used *his* line into prey to pull them out into reach. He could *feel* the junkie's eyes on him, burning into him; felt the elation when the guy first saw him, and the junkie realized he was alone, he was dressed expensively, he was unarmed.

It was hard not to look at where the junkie was hiding. Dave knew exactly where he was, how he was crouching in the center of that clump of privet just off to the right; how his legs burned, and his feet were going numb.

Not yet, he whispered into the junkie's mind. *Not yet. Let him get past. Come at him from behind—*

He closed the distance between himself and the bushes. He could feel the junkie's eagerness, straining against his control, a crazed greyhound on a lead of gossamer, with the rabbit in sight.

Five yards.

Not yet—

Two.

Past.

Now—

The bush rattled. It might not have alerted a *real* victim.

But Dave wasn't a real victim. He whirled to meet the attack before the attacker had a chance to realize that something had gone wrong.

The junkie slashed at him, his reactions thrown all to hell by the games Dave was playing with his mind and his balance. Dave danced aside from the clumsy knife stroke, and *reached—*

Touched fear.

Set it aflame.

The junkie froze—

His mouth opened in an utterly silent scream, and he dropped the knife, collapsed to his knees on the concrete. Dave walked toward him, slowly, feeling every step he took echoing in the man's mind, echoing back as the footsteps of everyone he'd ever feared in his life.

The junkie moaned and fell over sideways, quivering mindlessly at Dave's feet. Dave reached down and grabbed his greasy collar; hauled him upright as if he weighed nothing. Transferred his grip to the front of the man's jacket, hauled him up further, and forced the junkie to look right into his eyes.

The junkie wept, unable to look away, and a dark stain spread over the front of his jeans.

Dave smiled.

"Hello, sucker," he said.

And *reached* again.

It was like being reborn.

So much for appetizers. Now what's on the main course?

He left the junkie where the cops would find him the next time they came through. In a pile of greasy rags and limp limbs in the middle of the walkway.

Clearly, most sincerely dead.

And I feel—incredible. No wonder Jason gets into this. It's like—Like sex. Only better.

His mind was clearer than it had been in weeks. The hunger was no longer a factor that drove him—although he was far from being sated. He felt like a god. And the whole world existed for him alone—for his pleasure, to take as he chose, when he chose, *how* he chose.

He froze between one step and the next, and slammed down on that thought.

This's like the first time you did acid. Remember? You thought you were playing so hot—that the lyrics you were coming up with were the best thing since Lennon. So you turned on the tape player.

And the next day he played that crap back. He couldn't understand a word he'd been singing—and he'd written better tunes when he was in kindergarten.

This isn't real; no more real than the acid dreams. It's just a different kind of high. Don't let it fool you the way it's gotten to Jason and Doug.

But the pleasure as the sweet essence of fear had poured into him—*that* had been real. And the new strength, the vitality—that was real enough, too.

Okay, so keep your mind on what's real, why you're doing this, and on business. And business is getting yourself ready. Which you aren't, not yet. You need to hunt again—

He sensed movement, rather than saw it. A car on one of the roads that threaded the park. Running without lights.

Lawful prey.

He sent out his questing senses again; now that he was no longer half-starved, the hunger answered his demands tamely, obediently. He gave himself over to it, confident that it was under his control, and let himself *feel*.

Three. One rigid with fear, two pulsing with lust. One help-lessly weak, two cruelly strong.

He almost laughed. Trolling for rapists—

Pain-fear-pain.

He drank it in. It was wine—but he needed something stronger. And he needed a clearer target.

Frustration-lust-impatience.

He moved in on the impatient one; got a fleeting impression of a steering wheel. He began running surefootedly, through and around the trees, on a course that would bring him out of the trees somewhere ahead of the car. He couldn't even feel the cold anymore, even though his breath was forming clouds in the snow-laden air.

Pull over, he whispered into the burning mind he touched. *This's a good place to stop.*

He could hear the car engine somewhere off to his left; heard it coming nearer, and got a better impression of *where.*

There, he whispered insidiously. *There. The picnic tables. Time for a nice little party.*

He broke through a thin line of bushes and vaulted a snow fence. The snow had melted when it encountered salt-covered pavement and the roadway lay black before him. They weren't too far away—he could *feel* them so clearly—

One—fear so strong she can't move. Two—sense of power and joy in the fear and pain that surges as strongly as the lust. Three— thoughts swirling, blind chaos, nothing clear but the erection that throbs hunger, throbs need, through his body, his brain, in time with his heartbeat.

Dave skirted the edge of the roadway; if he moved out onto the cleared blacktop, they'd see him. He was a match now for both of them in strength—but he wasn't a match for two thou-sands pounds of moving metal.

Ahead, the engine sounds stopped. Car doors slammed twice. He thought he could hear muttered words.

Here—he whispered. *Now.*

Laughter. Tearing cloth. Pain-sounds, shrieks of pure agony filtered through cloth until they were hardly more than whimpers.

He could see the cluster of picnic tables through a thin screen
of young trees. See the dark moving shapes clustered at one end
of the nearest.

Grunts and whimpers in time with each other, with the
rhythmic movements of one—

Here—he called the other, the one who watched and waited
and joyed in the pain. *Here—there is something waiting for you.
Just for you. Better than that—*

It turned, dark amorphous shape, and took the two steps
needed to come into his reach—

Dave took that one quickly—turning lust into pain, pain into
fear, and fear into silent paralysis. Dave held him down with the
strength of his mind alone, drinking in the bliss of pure terror.
But when the fear was everything, when it screamed through
the first one's mind and soul, something snapped deep within
the brain, and brought paroxysm and death.

The last agony of death was ambrosia—but it came too
quickly, it wasn't *entirely* satisfying, and although new strength
swelled his muscles, his hunger sulked and complained—

Not enough. Not enough.

But there was still the other, who, oblivious to the fate of his
companion, was grunting his way to orgasm.

Until Dave interrupted his pleasure with a well-placed punch
to the kidney.

And a knee in his chin as he collapsed.

Followed by a carefully calculated kick to his larynx. And a
lovingly placed boot grinding into his privates.

He opened himself to the agony, standing over the writhing
blot on the ground, letting it flow. *Oh yes—*

The pain was exquisite. The man took a gratifyingly long time
to die, strangling on his own crushed windpipe. His fear and pain

built *much* higher than his partner's had, and Dave was only too happy to enhance it for him. He played with the fear, the anguish, carefully, teasingly, making absolutely certain that the rapist sustained *everything* he was capable of feeling until the very end.

Dave lost all track of time, lost track of anything except the *feeding*, until the last sensation faded away—

A whimper behind him caught his attention—a new source of pain and terror—

And he *almost* reached for it—

Only the girl's eyes, seen clearly, stopped him. The eyes, wide and blank with disorientation and misery, beneath long, lank hair—

Eyes he'd seen just this evening, less than two hours ago—

The child on the corner.

Recognition stopped him cold, and he pulled back before he had *touched* her.

She had been gagged with her own headband; while he'd fed off her rapist she'd stealthily freed herself, huddled her torn clothing back on. Now she stared at him, expecting—more of the same treatment from him. He felt her thoughts pounding their way into his skull.

He's going to kill me. He's going to rape me again and—and—and—

He backed up a step, as his hunger complained mildly at him that he was cheating it of dessert. She stared at him, waiting for him to move on her, stared at the way he was just standing there—motionless, not coming *at* her—

At first she didn't believe. Then—she made the wild jump from seeing him as another attacker, to seeing him as *savior.*

Relief flooded her—she sobbed, and started to throw herself at him—

OhGodohGodohGod—

He couldn't tell if the thought was hers or his.

He backpedaled away from her so fast that she sprawled facedown in the snow at his feet.

"Get out of here—" he snarled at her, holding himself in check by only the thinnest of margins. *If she touches me, I'll kill her too— oh God, somebody, help me—I can't hold it back if she touches me—*

She made some kind of a sound. The hunger coiled to leap.

"*Out!*" he screamed at her, backing up until he ran into a tree trunk. "Go! *Run,* you stupid bitch!"

She stared, she scrambled to her feet—and she ran.

He slid down the tree trunk and huddled on the cold, bare dirt at its roots. Snow fell on him, melting and dampening his hair—fell on the body beyond him, dusting it, then slowly coating it with a shroud of white. He fought with himself with his head on his knees and his arms wrapped around his legs until the hunger subsided, and he stopped shaking.

The cabby arrived as promised. He was a little surprised to actually find Dave waiting there, but the lure of another fifty at this time of night—

Had been more than even Harv could resist.

Oh God, now I'm picking up everything—even passing thoughts. Got to shut down . . . got to.

He smiled stiffly, passed the cabby the promised fifty, and settled into the back seat of the cab. The cabdriver's greed nearly triggered the hunger again.

He shut his eyes and savagely throttled down on it. If he hadn't fed so fully already—

But he had, and it subsided within him with scarcely a struggle.

"Find what you wanted, mack?" the cabby asked conversationally.

"Yes," he replied. "Yes, thanks. I did. Sometimes the only place you can find what you're looking for is in a park at night, I guess."

Let him try and figure that one out.

A fierce cloud of cigar smoke rose to fill the front of the cab as the driver pondered.

Dave sat back and stared out the cab window beside him. The hunger coiled at the base of his spine, a sleeping serpent, no longer pushing him, and no longer opening him to the thoughts of others. He hadn't felt this—good—in years.

I feel fantastic, he thought wonderingly. *Like I could run a mile and never be winded. Like I could do an all-night gig and never need a break.*

And what did it cost? Two rapists and a junkie.

People nobody will ever miss. Scum that the world will be better off without.

The cops would probably thank him. Certainly that girl did.

I could go on like this very easily. How many muggers are there in New York? How many junkies? How many perverts?

What was so bad about exterminating vermin?

I'd be doing the world a favor.

He could do what the law couldn't. Serve the world and save himself.

Like one of my old heroes in the comic books.

It would be easy.

I may not need Di's help after all—

It would make the world a better place.

And what was it Hidoro was talking about? Using my power to get into people's minds, to tilt them one way or another? To—

His conscience supplied the word. The ugly word. *To manipulate them. To use them.*

His conscience supplied something else. The frightened eyes of the rape victim. Her fear. And how *her* fear had tasted just as sweet as that of her abusers.

How close he'd come to taking her, the innocent, after he'd disposed of the guilty.

Bile rose in his throat.

*No. Oh God, no. If she hadn't run, I'd have killed her. I'd prob-
ably have raped her first myself, just to get the most out of her.*

It rang true. It rang with more truth than what he'd *been*
telling himself.

Snow continued to fall; it was coating the street and the side-
walks, lying along the branches of the trees. It made the city
look pure and pristine. Dave bit his lip, and really *looked* at what
he'd done tonight.

*I hurt those people; I made them hurt as much as I possibly
could.*

I enjoyed it.

He swallowed nausea.

*I'm no better than they are. It was just that I picked my victims
a little more carefully.*

And what about the day when there's no mugger, no rapist
around, and the hunger demands to be fed? That day *would*
come, sooner or later.

If I can't get this thing *that's happened to me reversed—one
day I'm* not *going to be able to stop myself in time. I'm going to
take the innocent victim along with the scum. And from there—*

*I'll probably move straight on to taking the innocent. There are
so many more of them. And they're so much easier to hurt, to
frighten.*

He clenched his jaw tightly against the sickness rising inside
him. *No. No. I won't let myself do that. This can't last much
longer. Di will make her move one way or another soon. And after that—*

After that, I'll see this ended—no matter what.

And no matter what it takes.

"Well," Jason drawled lazily from the couch beside the door.
"The prodigal returns. Out helping old ladies across the street,
Davey-boy?"

Dave smiled, and moved into the light from the overhead fixture. "Hardly," he said dryly. He let his eyes meet Jason's, slowly—and gave a little mental *shove*. Not much. Not enough to challenge. But enough so that the blond lead *knew*.

Jason sat straight up, as if he'd been shocked awake. "*What in*—" he began.

Dave's smile widened. Jason's eyes narrowed for a moment, and he looked Dave over appraisingly.

"Well," he said, and began to chuckle. "Well, well. Been busy tonight, have we?"

Dave folded his arms across his chest and sauntered over to the couch. "Could be," he replied enigmatically, examining the fingernails of his right hand with studious care.

"It would appear," said a lightly accented voice behind him, "that the little lamb has developed teeth."

Dave controlled his expression, told the chill walking down his backbone to go away, and turned to face Hidoro. "Shall we say instead that the little lamb has discovered he never was a lamb at all?" He tilted his head to one side, and narrowed his eyes down to slits.

Which makes them harder to read, monster.

"There's a story somebody told me when I was a kid," he continued. "It was about a lion that got raised by sheep. The little guy grew up thinking he *was* a sheep. Then one day the sheep were attacked, and he found out what he really was."

Hidoro nodded, seemingly pleased. "And so you have discovered that you are not, after all, a sheep?"

He yawned; *that*, he didn't have to fake. Dawn was very close, and he was beginning to feel it, to feel how much the night had taken out of him in terms of mental exhaustion, despite all his newfound energy.

"I guess that about sums it up," he replied. *And you obviously never heard that story—or you'd know what the ending really is. How what attacked the flock was a wolf pack. And how the little lion defended his flock and killed the entire pack. I hope my re-membering that story is an omen, you bastard.*

He yawned again. "Now, if you've got no objection—"

"How many did you take, David?" That was Jeffries, coming up from behind like the silent snake he was. Dave avoided start-ing, and turned to face him.

"Three," he said, and shrugged. "I'm afraid I killed them. I don't have as much practice as the rest of you."

Jeffries nodded slowly, and Dave felt *something* brushing at the edges of his mind. He hardened his barriers, and pushed back. Jeffries's eyes widened for a moment before his expression resumed its usual bland cast.

"Finesse will come with practice," he said, his lips twitching a little, something that *might* have been a smile on anyone else flickering briefly across his handsome face. "All male, however. I congratulate you. Your friends cannot seem to realize that the male gives a much stronger and more satisfying reaction than the female. They persist in taking only those men who are al-ready with women." He shook his head. "Homophobic. And foolish. Absolutely foolish. Although the male is harder to frighten, when he *does* become frightened—the male has *such* a store of rage buried within him." He smiled again, this time at Jason, and the smile mocked the blond and dared him to re-spond.

Jason's face twisted in distaste. "I'm not a damn queer."

Jeffries's face hardened, and his voice acquired a coating of ice and steel. "Are you implying that I am?"

This time Jason didn't back down. "How should I know? Are you? You and Doro sure spend a lot of time together. Were you, before you—"

Jeffries strode deliberately across the room, reached down and took Jason by the throat and hauled him to his feet. "Would you like to find out, Jason?" he hissed in the blond's face. "Would you like to find out the hard way? Let me warn you, the *sweetest* prey is another predator—"

Jason wrenched himself out of Jeffries's hands, stumbled backward a few steps, and took a defensive stance.

"You want to try?" he snarled. "I'm ready for you—you just make your—"

"*Enough!*"

Hidoro moved between them, with a leap that told Dave that, no matter what else he was, the creature was no stranger to the martial arts. He drew himself up to his full height and glared at both Jeffries and Jason, and the cold calculation in his face made both of them pause.

"I find our current arrangement much to my satisfaction," he said softly, but with an unmistakable undertone of threat. "But you should be aware that I need *very* little other than a safe haven. I have continued in this alliance because I approve of your plans, Jeffries—"

He stared coldly and dispassionately at Jason. "You, on the other hand, seem to have hardly a thought in your head beyond your next woman and your next feeding."

Jason glowered, but clenched his jaw tightly on whatever it was he might have wanted to retort.

"Until you prove otherwise, Jason-san"—he delivered the honorific with an ironic little bow, his tone so sarcastic that Jason snarled—"I accept and follow Jeffries as the leader of this group—*and I will back him.* I assume you know what that means."

Jason dropped his eyes, and muttered.

"Better." Hidoro stepped from between the two. "Now, if you wish, you may continue your discussion *as* a discussion. I will retire to my resting place. I expect not to hear any further disturbance."

Interesting, Dave thought, watching the *gaki* walk down the hall to disappear into his room. *Very interesting. He's closer to being invulnerable than any of the rest of us, and he's certainly stronger in a lot of ways. He stays with us for convenience—but he could take us over if he wanted. But instead, he lets Jeffries play master. I wonder why?*

He dropped into a chair as Jason muttered an unmeant apology to Jeffries, and the "Master" glared and uttered insincere words of acceptance. Jeffries took over the couch before Jason could resume his seat. Since he obviously didn't want to sit next to Jeffries, and there was nowhere else to sit except the floor, Jason retreated from the living room with the air of someone who had been defeated, but not vanquished.

I figured it was going to come to this sooner or later. Dave pretended to read a magazine, but he was watching every move in this little dance of ascendancy with keen interest. *And we're in Jason's loft, on his turf. Not surprising that he'd challenge. But Doug's no match for Hidoro—assuming Doro stays on Jeffries's side. How smart is Jeffries, I wonder?*

Jeffries might have been reading his mind, for as soon as Jason shut the door of his room behind him, the man asked quietly, "And whose side are *you* on, David?"

Dave tossed the magazine aside; it landed on the coffee table, slid across it, and spilled onto the floor. He looked at Jeffries measuringly for several moments before answering.

"My own," he said, truthfully. *We won't mention that it's also Di's.* "None of you have done anything likely to make a bosom buddy out of me."

"True." Jeffries steepled his fingers together. "I regret the things I said and did to you, but you surely must admit that you were not cooperating. But now—"

"Now is different."

"Obviously. Tell me—just how intelligent is Jason?"

"Smart," Dave replied, seeing no reason to hold back information. *Especially if it's going to help make a schism here.* "Smart, but lazy. I was the group's leader for the last year and a half. Until we all—changed. It wasn't until Jason linked up with you that he took over. He doesn't make a move unless he thinks he's got something to gain by exerting himself. And then—he's damned hard to stop."

"Interesting. That parallels my own observations." Jeffries

stared off into space for a moment. "You do realize that I have larger plans for you all that go far beyond where you are now—"

Dave nodded, keeping his silence.

"I do not think we have even begun to explore the kinds of things we can do. If we can enhance pain—can we not also enhance pleasure? And what would *that* do to your audiences, David? Think about how self-induced hysteria in their young fans carried the Beatles into prominence. And that—could be the opening to a much wider field of endeavor for all of us. The world of entertainment can lead to so many other things . . ." He smiled. "Who would *ever* have dreamed that politicians would listen to actors? Who would *ever* have believed that a half-rate B-movie actor could ride his 'fame' like one of his horses to a governor's mansion?"

Dave snorted. "What makes you think—oh. Yeah. We can play with their heads, can't we?"

Jeffries nodded. "Exactly. I believe Hidoro is cautiously in favor of the plan, so long as we stay discreetly in the background and never actually assume the position of power ourselves."

"Hard to go hunting," Dave pointed out, "when you have a bodyguard or a Secret Service guy in tow."

Jeffries smiled. "Precisely. And I am not entirely certain that Jason has a subtle enough mind to comprehend that."

He does. He's already thought of all this. But I'm not going to tell you that.

"So what do you want out of me?" Dave asked.

"For now—nothing. If Jason should make a move again—" He shrugged. "Well, not *quite* nothing," he amended. "We have some hostages to the vampire's good behavior. I am holding them in the studio. Gypsy children. He seems to set a certain store by them."

Dave carefully schooled his face to betray none of his thoughts.

"I had been leaving them in Jason's charge—but I'm not certain I wish to continue to trust him. He might turn them loose—after all, the man's quarrel is with *me,* not Jason. You see my quandary?"

"Yeah," Dave replied. "Yeah, I can. So you want *me* to keep an eye on them?" *Maybe I can turn them loose when Jeffries goes out. I can at least let Di know they're in here.*

"If you would." Jeffries's tone made it clear that this was an order, not a request.

"How long are you planning on keeping them?" he asked.

"Not more than another week at most. By then the new safe-house will be ready, and we can get rid of them." He lifted an eyebrow. "Already they're more trouble than they're worth. But once we do not need them, for one night, at any rate, we won't have to hunt."

Somehow Dave managed to smile. "Sounds good to me," he replied. "I take it I move into the room next to the studio, then?"

"Indeed." Jeffries tossed him a set of keys. "Hidoro feeds them. All you need to do is make sure no one bothers them."

"Like Jason."

"A hostage is valueless if it's dead," the 'Master' pointed out. "Or gone. I rather think Jason would turn one or two loose to lead the vampire back here, then feed on the rest. I want you to prevent that."

"Oh, I think I can do that." Dave nodded.

And as soon as I'm in the clear, I call Di. Looks like this thing is going to come to a head faster than I thought.

God help us all.

THIRTEEN

Di yawned, and drifted up toward consciousness gradually—rather than being shocked awake by the alarm. There was a warm and silent presence at her back. It was strange, after all these years, to wake up with someone else beside her in bed. Besides Atilla, of course.

It was comforting, and comfortable. And what had gone on between them before they'd drifted off to sleep had been considerably better than that. Considerably. André was certainly living up to the legend of the French as great lovers. Of course, there was the effect of his feeding—and the fact that he'd had plenty of time to practice . . .

I could easily get used to this, Di thought drowsily, and smiled to herself. *And vampires don't snore.*

By turning her head just a little she had a wonderful view of him. Legends aside, he did *not* look like a corpse. He didn't look as wan and ill-used as he had when he was recovering, either. Though he didn't move at all, once he'd actually fallen asleep—

—*"Is this comfortable?"* *he'd asked, words a little blurred with exhaustion, holding her with her head resting on his shoulder.*

"Nice," she'd replied. It had been more than nice, actually, but "nice" seemed like a reasonable thing to say at the time.

"Good . . ." His voice had trailed off sleepily.

"I'll probably wiggle away," she'd warned, watching the gray

outside the window begin to lighten. "I toss a lot. I kick too, some-
times." She'd chuckled. "You may wish yourself back on the couch."

"I won't feel it," he'd replied, with that silent laugh of his. "I as-
sure you, I won't feel it. You could push me onto the floor and I
would not awaken."

"I may try that sometime."

"If you do, chérie," *he'd warned, then yawned, which spoiled*
the effect, "I shall conjure cold frogs onto your pillow."

"Can you do that?" she asked, believing him.

"Well, no—" Yawn. "But it makes . . . a good . . . threat . . ."

He was quite a hormonal experience, just to *look* at. He lay
slightly turned on his side, his hair tumbled in his eyes, the arm
that had been holding her curved as if he still cradled her. He
looked absurdly young, too young, really; she wondered what
his real age had been before he changed. Not that it mattered.

A faint smile still hung about his mouth.

I could get very used to this.

But with that thought came full waking. Reality intruded, the
reality she'd kept at arm's length with lovemaking *Assuming I
have any time to get used to anything.*

Assuming there's anything left of either of us when this is over.

She turned on her back and stared up at the ceiling, at the
pattern of acoustical tiles the Guardian before her had installed.

*All right, let's look at the opposition. They have three full psi-
vamps. Enhanced strength, and if they touch you, or get through
your shields—they've got you. Vulnerabilities are just to sunlight,
and maybe—probably—to physical damage. A gun could probably take them out. If I still had a gun. After mine got melted—no,
I didn't have the cash to replace it. Stupid move, Tregarde. You
should have eaten brown rice and macaroni for a couple of
months, saved your pennies, and gotten another. Now it's too
late.*

She tried *not* to let fear cloud her ability to think, but it was
hard. It had been bad enough *not* knowing what they were going up against. It was worse, now.

Then the gaki. *As far as I can tell, vulnerable only when he's in human form. I've got Len and Keith, Gifted, but not even in Annie's league. One real vampire. Me. Four against four, the numbers say it's even but the abilities sure aren't. So what do I do with what I've got? There has to be a way to use all of us to our best advantage* and *still utilize their weaknesses against them.*

Cold chilled the pit of her stomach as another scenario occurred to her. *What if they put the screws to Dave when he got back to them? What if they know that I know? I'm in the bloody phone book—*

She refused to panic. Not when there was no reason to. *No, wait, think about this. We're safer here than we are anywhere else. The* building *is shielded* and *warded, and my apartment is under shield and ward on top of that. Maybe Guardian's magic wouldn't help me cure Dave, but with all these innocents in this building in the line of fire—*

Staying here is probably better than moving into a hotel. At least I know this place, and it's got generations worth of protections on it.

But what am I going to do about confronting these bastards? I don't know. All the scenarios I can come up with end up with me on toast.

She shivered, pulled the blankets up a little higher, and glanced over at André. *Is that why I went to bed with him? Sort of on the order of the condemned prisoner's last request? Is that why* he *went to bed with* me?

Does it matter?

She reached out hesitantly, and traced the curve of his cheekbone with one finger. *Yeah, it matters. This may not be True Love, but I care for him, I respect him, and he turns me on like nobody's* ever *done before. I can trust him at my back. I want him around. We complement each other. He's a great partner.*

Even if he does need a little nibble every now and then.

She touched a silky lock of his hair, and bit her lip.

This isn't accomplishing anything. I'm just delaying things.

She eased herself out of bed, moving carefully so as not to disturb him, but he showed no sign of being disturbed. The garment she took from the closet was not her usual jeans; it was a simple, black sleeveless robe, calf-length, on the order of a Greek chiton. Her ritual robe. Her fingers tingled a bit when she touched it.

Still plenty of zap left from Samhain. Good; I need it.

She showered and changed—and, with a glance of regret at her typewriter—

I said I'd try, Morrie. I didn't say I'd succeed. Figures, just when it was getting fun. Wonder who else he'll sucker into this? Wonder if they'll use my notes?

—she headed for the Living Room.

For full ritual, every tiny bit of ceremony. No skimping today. She laid out the altar; included the Sword, something she hadn't done for two years. Pulled out every talisman she had. Robed and armed, she cast a full Major Circle and invoked every protective Power she could think of—and *then* got into the serious Magick.

It was late afternoon when she finished. She'd been a little surprised at the amount of energy she'd managed to raise. A lot of it had gone into reinforcing the building protections; a good piece of the rest had gone into passive shields for Lenny and Keith.

The little that was left, she simply formed into a plea and released. Nothing specific—asking for specifics was a lot like wishing on the Monkey's Paw—"Please let me live to be two hundred," and waking up as a Galápagos tortoise.

No, nothing specific. Just—

*Just "Please, I don't want to die—and I don't want anyone I care for to die, either." But if it comes to a choice—screw it, I'll throw myself on the grenade. And hope—*Her thought faltered. *And hope it doesn't hurt too much.*

She changed back into jeans and cleaned up carefully afterward; cleaned the Living Room, then the office/living room, then the kitchen, the bathroom—methodically, thoroughly. Thinking about mundanities kept her from frightening herself into a limp imitation.

And if it comes to that, I don't want to leave my replacement with a mess—she thought bleakly, putting the last of the cleaning supplies away, *if I don't make it*—*I'd rather have a tidy sort of ending. Tie up as many loose ends as I can*—

A knock at the door interrupted her before she could go any further down *that* mental path to the Slough of Despond.

She put her palm against the door and closed her eyes; ran a quick check, recognized *precisely* who she'd expected, and opened it.

Puck, looking not very Puckish. Puck, after the last of his kind had gone over the water. Puck, ready to put on Oberon's armor and defend the elvenlands alone.

"Hi," said Lenny in a fairly subdued voice; he looked at her sharply when she didn't immediately respond, his eyes narrowed.

He motioned to Keith (who was right behind him) to go in, and when his lover had passed, took her face in both hands, and kissed her, very carefully, very gently; forehead, eyes, lips. Then he held her. That was all—but it helped.

"Are you going to be all right?" he asked quietly, no trace of mischief at all in his expression or his voice.

"I think so," she said, looking into his eyes. "I'm just scared to death, that's all."

He let her go. "I'd be worried if you weren't," he told her. "I think we're facing a bad set of odds. But if we're smart—maybe we can beat those odds. I've been thinking about this—Keith and I spent this afternoon talking about it."

He took her by the elbow and steered her in the direction of the living room. "Do you want out?" she asked him as they passed the doorway, not able to guess what his answer would be.

Though I wouldn't blame him if he did—

"Get serious," he said roughly, letting go of her when they reached her chair, taking his preferred seat on the couch next to

Keith. "And leave you to handle it with nobody to help except Count Dracula? Two of you against four of them? No way. Besides, we *still* want a piece of the soul-sucker's hide, or had you forgotten that?"

"Oh," she replied weakly. "I—thanks—Lenny, I didn't expect you to buy in with me on this."

She sat down quickly; no telling when nerves might turn her knees to jelly.

He shrugged. "You didn't get a choice. There are times when the sensible route isn't the right one. Think I'll take right over sensible. Now, the sixty-four-dollar question is—just *what,* exactly, are we going to do?" He took Keith's hand in his, and studied it for a moment. "I'm sort of short on ideas. And all Keith could come up with was to trap them all in a barn and set the barn on fire."

"Barns are a little hard to come by in New York," she pointed out.

"I thought of that," Lenny admitted. "There's the notion of setting their *apartment* on fire, but setting buildings on fire would get us arrested for arson."

"Not to mention all the innocents we could take out that way," she reminded him sternly.

"And besides," said a soft voice behind her, "the *gaki's* other form is a cloud of smoke. I do not think a fire would cause him more than a moment or two of discomfort."

As she turned toward the doorway, André moved out of the shadowed hallway and into the living room. "At the risk of being sacrilegious," he said, flicking on the lamp nearest the end of the couch, "let there be light."

She blinked at the sudden flood of warm, yellow light; glanced out the window, and realized that the sky was a deep gray, slowly turning to black.

"So," André continued, "let us make more reasonable plans, *non?*" He moved around the end of the couch to perch on the overstuffed arm of Di's chair. It felt unbelievably *good* to have him there. "Such as—oh—weaponry. What physical weaponry have we at our disposal?"

"How much money have you guys got?" she asked, recalling her earlier thoughts about guns.

Pockets, purse, and checkbooks were all turned out and the total made. Unfortunately, all *three* of them had just paid bills and the rent. André, of course, had no rent, but neither did he have any money. Among the three of them, they could scrape up a grand total of one hundred and fifty-three dollars and twenty-seven cents.

"Not enough." She sighed, and waved at the two young men to take back their portions.

"Enough for what?" Lenny asked, pocketing his billfold, then putting his arm around Keith.

"For a gun," she replied with vexation, mostly at herself for not thinking of this sooner. "We couldn't have gotten a hand-gun on this short a notice, but I *could* have picked up a shotgun. With all the equipment in that studio, Keith could have found a way to saw the barrel off—"

"But we don't know how to shoot!" Lenny protested—then saw her expression of irony. "Do we?"

"What do you mean *we*, masked man?" she replied with the tag line of an old joke. "I *had* a very nice thirty-eight that used to belong to my granny up until a few months ago."

"What happened to it?" Keith asked quietly.

"The barrel got melted," she answered. "Don't ask. It's not something I'm ready to talk about."

"Oh." He took her at her word, but gave her a very peculiar look. "Why a gun? Aren't we dealing with things that a gun won't hurt?"

"Are we?" she retorted, and sat back in her chair. André put one hand on her shoulder, unobtrusively. "I wouldn't bet on that. The psivamps are just changed humans. I would tend to think that an ounce of lead would make it a major bad day for any of them. And André was handling the *gaki* well enough until it changed—the books say it's vulnerable only in human form. I'd bet a chunk of bullet could at least make it stop and think about what had just happened to it." She shrugged. "It doesn't matter. We don't have the cash."

But if I live through this, I swear, I'm never going to be without mundane arms again.

"So. What are the arms we *do* have?" André asked.

She licked her lips and stared at the ceiling. "Start with me, since I'm probably the best armed of all of you. One two-handed broadsword, sans sheath, which we can't carry out of here without getting arrested, and can't be concealed on anybody's person."

"But—" Lenny interrupted. "We could put it in the car, couldn't we?"

"No 'buts,' sweets. The cops are being real nasty lately. If *anything* happens and they see it, we'll get hauled in. If it's in a sheath, it's 'carrying concealed,' if it's not, it's a blade longer than six inches, which is major bad news. Sir Severale told me a couple of his friends just got their favorite dress blades confiscated last week, and *I* don't even have a Recreation Society card to save me getting my ass locked up."

Lenny sighed. Di did, too. "To continue. Assorted knives, some of which, ditto, but which I'm going to pass out to you guys anyway because they're a bit easier to hide than a broadsword. All of them are blessed in one tradition or another. I don't know if that will make any difference."

"It could not hurt," André said.

"True. I did my level best to transfer most of the whammy from my sorceror's sword into my witch's atheme, but I can't swear it'll take. Assorted clubs, including one cane with a silver-plated handle. Good against werewolves, one would assume, but not against psivamps or *gakis*. We'll all take our choice of those. Except for me, I don't need a club. I have my own hands and feet, being a brown belt in karate." She paused for breath. "That's the physical weaponry. Nonphysical, I have assorted talismans, none of which are going to do us any good because while our enemies may be evil, they aren't creatures of *spiritual* evil. I have psi bolts and levin bolts which *will* probably do us some good. I mentioned the blessings on the knives, the power in my atheme. I have some of the best shields in the business and in a few minutes, Lenny and Keith will, too."

She paused for thought. "I also have a glow-in-the-dark shield aura which apparently radiates at the same frequency as sunlight and gives André fits—so it *might* work on the psi-vamps. All I have to do is get scared enough."

Keith gave her another strange look. "That's the *oddest* form of transference I ever heard of."

"Is that what it is called?" André said, looking interested. "I knew that these psychologists were—"

"Guys," Di interrupted, "can we talk about Freud *after* we survive this little Kaffeeklatsch? Hmm?"

André actually blushed. "Pardon," he said. "Is it me, then?"

She nodded.

"Very well. First, I am very strong. Stronger than any of them alone. Second, I have some knowledge of *savate*. Third, it appears that the *gaki* cannot digest me. Fourth, I see almost as well by night as by day. Fifth, I can be so very silent that I cannot be detected if I choose. Arcanely—I suspect my shielding is as powerful as yours, *chérie,* and I am sensitive to emotions, to thought under some circumstances, and to magic in use. That is all."

"No turning into bats, or fog, or wolves?" Lenny said in disappointment.

He shook his head, his lips twitching. "No, I fear not. Not that anyone I know has ever taught me."

"Rats."

"Nor those," André obviously could not resist saying. Di wondered *how* he was keeping up his spirits, given the odds against them.

"Guys?" Di prompted.

Lenny cleared his throat self-consciously. "No mundane weapons, except one switchblade and the fact that I know how to break just about anybody's knee. Helps, being a dancer. Not much arcane, either."

"Ditto," said Keith. "All I've got is assorted lengths of pipe. I was figuring we'd probably work best as bait and a distraction."

"That is no bad thought," André opined.

"You'll do that better if you're shielded," Di told both of them firmly. "Come, my child." She crooked her finger at Lenny. "Sit at my feet."

"Yes, Great Lady—" He ducked as she cuffed him.

"Hold still, or I'll get distracted, and if I lose this thing, it's gone," she warned, as he settled himself at her feet, back up against the chair.

Something small and light clicked against the windowpane; they all jumped. André was the first to rise and look outside.

"One of my Rom," he said, his voice troubled, although Di could not see his face. "I must go—I will use the back door."

He was into the kitchen before she could protest that that back door only gave out onto the fire escape.

Then she realized that he'd already used that door as an entrance once.

He knows what he's doing. Better concentrate on what I can do.

She held her hands just above Lenny's head, and carefully invoked the passive shield she'd built expressly for him, earlier today.

It came into being just under her hands, Looking like a misty veil. She settled it over him, then released it, and it drifted down and melded with the shields he already had in place. He knew when she was finished, he was more than sensitive enough for that. He opened his eyes, and tilted his head back.

"Want to give it a test?" he asked. She nodded, and probed at the shield; gently at first, then harder, and finally with all her strength, trying to get *through* it to affect him with projective empathy.

"Anything?" she asked after the last probe.

He shook his head. "Not a thing."

"Good. I was trying the same thing on you I think they'll be using, given what Dave Looked like. Keith, your turn."

She repeated the procedure on the young artist, but got something of a surprise. When she probed at him, he went psychically blank. To her Sight, he simply wasn't there.

She opened her eyes, and saw that his eyes were tightly closed and he was frowning in concentration. "Hey," she said, tapping his shoulder. "Leonardo. You, with the mean look. What in hell are you doing?"

"I'm trying to pretend I'm not here," he responded, opening one eye to look at her.

"Well, it's working. You and Lenny had better start having a long, serious talk someday soon. You're Gifted, m'lad. Very. When this is over, I want you to do something about getting your Gifts controlled."

He got to his feet and resumed his seat on the couch. "Okay," he replied, as if not sure what he was agreeing to. "Now what?"

"Now—"

The phone rang, and they all jumped a foot.

Lenny answered it, and handed it wordlessly over to Di. *Dave,* he mouthed, as she took it.

She noticed that her hand was shaking as she took the handset from him. "It's Di," she said.

"Yeah, listen, I haven't got much time." His voice was low, and the noise in the background suggested a kitchen or a nightclub in the process of being set up for opening.

"Go."

"Jeffries and the Jap took hostages to make sure your boyfriend stays quiet. Gypsy kids; around a dozen, I think. So far, they're okay, but they're scared. I thought about trying to get them out; I figured out that I can't. Jeffries figures on using 'em for dinner when he doesn't need 'em anymore, and that'll be in about three days by the plan, but could be sooner if the new place he's putting together gets finished before then. There's also the fact that Jason may make a try for the kids. He's low enough. Got that?"

"Yeah," she said, her stomach sinking. *Gods. He's upped the ante, hasn't he. Now we've got no choice. It'll have to be tonight.*

"They've got me scoped for playing guard tonight, after the gig, so the Master and the Jap can go hunting first. Hot item— Jeffries and Jason are at each other's throats—"

"Dave—I hate to ask you—"

"Ask. But make it quick."

"Can you see to it that the Japanese goes out hunting alone?"

Brief silence, and the sounds of moving furniture. "I think so. Won't take much. Egg Jason on, so the boss figures he'd rather have him under his eye. Maybe hint I've seen Jason scoping out the door to where the kids are stashed. Tell him I'll go out last, with Doug. You're coming in?"

"You know I can't tell you that," she replied.

Dave paused for a long moment. "Listen, baby," he said softly, "I'm on your side. And I—did a little hunting myself; tried to get ones that had it coming. Last night, after I left you. I'm up to strength, like maybe as good as Doug. They figure I've bought into their scene, so they trust me now. I'll see if I can't keep people from hunting until after the gig, like hint to Doug that Doro is keeping an eye on 'em, hint to Doro that Jason may try something; that should get 'em all good and irritated with each other. You've got an ally behind the lines; one who'll do whatever it takes. Okay?"

"Dave—" Her voice broke.

"Do what it takes, baby. I will, too. Dig? There's a point where you gotta commit." A long pause. "I think I found mine. I know you had yours a long time ago."

There was a muffled voice in the distance. "Yeah?" she heard Dave call back. "Okay, I'm on the way." Then, "Do it, baby. You got more people to think about than just us. Ciao."

Click.

She hung the phone up, slowly, feeling as if somebody had just hit her in the back of the head with a board.

"Who?" she heard André say. She hadn't even heard him come back. When she didn't immediately reply, he shook her shoulders impatiently. *"What did he say?"*

She blinked, and focused on his anxious face. "That was Dave. The leader has taken hostages, André—against you. Gypsy children—"

"Sacré merde—"

His face had hardened, chilled—became the face of a practiced killer who knows better than to get angry.

"That is what the *Rom baro*—the leader—told me. What else did he say?"

He could kill with just the look in his eyes, right now.

She swallowed. "Dave said he expects Jeffries to hold them for another three days or so; evidently he's keeping them until their new safe house is ready."

"The *Rom baro* did not know where the children were taken, although he said that those who took them made an effort to ensure he knew *why,*" André muttered. "Bastard, preying upon *children.* His quarrel is with me, not them. My poor Rom. They rightly fear for the children."

"Dave also said that he doesn't trust Jason not to go after the kids if he thinks he can get away with it."

André swore, then bent his head and rested his chin on his fist, face brooding, obviously thinking. "Definitely tonight, then, do you think? *I* would prefer it so."

"Tonight or not at all, love. I don't think we'll have a better chance," she told him, choosing her words with care. *I don't know that we have any chance, but the odds get longer with every hour. They haven't figured out Dave's gone over yet—but they could.* "There seems to be dissension in the ranks, and Dave's going to play on it. He's going to use it to keep them all from hunting until after they're through at the club. Then he thinks he can get the *gaki* to go out alone. He says—" She swallowed hard again. "He says that he'll back us. *He* thinks that we should move tonight. I think that since Jeffries must know that you know about the hostages by now, he won't expect you to make a move."

Oh, Dave—

André raised his head, his eyes hard and unreadable. "Is there any chance, do you think, that this could be a trap?"

"There's always the chance; I don't think it likely."

He brooded again. "The four of us when freshest will face the strongest and most dangerous of them."

"Exactly," she agreed. "If we have any chance at all against them, it will be if we can take out the *gaki* first."

"And we have the ally in the rear," he reminded her, his momentary glance at her sharpening, then remaining, while his expression softened. *"Chérie,"* he said quietly. "I now like the young man very much."

She wiped her burning eyes with the back of her hand. "So do I, love," she replied, thinking of the last words on the phone. "So do I."

They waited in Keith's car, parked by the mouth of the alley behind HeartBeat. André and Di had made brief forays, each in the places they were strongest. The band van was parked in that alley; André had made certain of that. Jeffries was *not* at the club, for Di had gone just inside the door to quick-scan the whole building, and had come up with only three psivamps. Presumably he was guarding the hostages.

The alley dead-ended at the other end. None of the band members were going to get past the car. True to Dave's promise, none of the band members left the club itself. They *might* have taken victims inside the club or the alley, but Di didn't think they would. Not if they were as divided as Dave seemed to think. They wouldn't want to turn their backs on each other.

None of the four in the car entered the club after Di had scouted and reported that the "Master" had not joined his protégés. It seemed safest that way.

Di and André huddled together under a quilt in the back seat, Keith and Lenny in the front. It was cold; well below freezing outside the car, and not that much warmer inside. They were trying to keep their heads down, trying to make the car look empty, so they didn't dare run the engine for the heat.

Di held her watch up to catch the light from the street lamp on the corner, sighed when she saw the time, and tucked her numb hands under her arms. In the front seat, Keith and Lenny were talking, murmurs far too soft to be really heard, but the tone sounded suspiciously like pillow talk.

She closed her eyes for a moment, and put another glaze of protection on them. André's arm tightened around her. "They will have those two only through me," he said softly in her ear.

She twisted a little so that she could whisper to him without the lovebirds in the front seat overhearing. "How did you know what I was thinking?"

He stroked her shoulder. "I told you, I am sensitive to thought under some circumstances. *You* are falling under those circumstances, *chérie.*"

"So you know—"

"How very long our odds are? *Certainement.* I knew it all along. Nevertheless, we shall strive to beat those odds. I am, and always have been, a gambler."

She had to know. Even if it hurt. "Last night—"

"Was *not* because of the long odds." His lips brushed the top of her head. "It—was—is—because I have come, foolishly perhaps, to care very much for you. It is because I wish very much to have the pleasure of repeating last night with you many times in the future. Provided you have no objection."

She let out the breath she had been holding in. "No objections here."

"*Bien.*"

"But those two—" She nodded at the front seat.

"Come first. I have been a man of war, Diana. Civilians, however well intentioned, are to be protected at all costs. As I said, they fall only when I am no longer capable of interposing myself. Or you are. Yes?"

"Yes." She stared at the glare of streetlight on the dirty window, and wriggled her numb toes in her boots. "We think very much alike. I just hope if that happens they have the sense to run instead of playing hero."

"So do I. The time, *chérie?*"

She pulled her arm out from under the quilt and squinted at the watch dial. Her heart began racing, whether from fear or anticipation, she couldn't tell.

Probably a bit of both.

She cleared her throat and raised her voice a bit. "The club just closed. Figure fifteen minutes, max. You hear that, guys?"

Keith answered. "We hear." The seat creaked as they disentangled themselves from blankets and each other. Di and André sat up and did the same. At that moment she felt more alone than she ever had in her life.

"I think my nose is gonna fall off," Lenny mourned. Keith laughed, and said something too low for Di to make out, but Lenny hit him mockingly.

She caught the sound of an engine starting from the alley, and extended a tentative probe—

—void. Hunger. Anger, held barely in check.

"Heads up, people," she warned. "Or down, rather. Here they come—"

Lights flooded the alley; van lights on bright, plus fog lights. The van pulled out of the alley mouth with a blast of horn, and screeched around the corner on two wheels. If there had been anything on the street, it would have been forced over.

"—and they're not happy," she concluded.

"Good for Dave," Keith said quietly. "All right, go for it, Di. I'm on their tail." He pulled quietly out into the street, making no attempt to keep up with the van. That wasn't the plan; they weren't going to have to follow the van itself.

She closed her eyes, and reached for the sense of *Dave*. She found it; she hardly recognized it. Tonight, unlike last night, he had himself under control, no longer torn by the terrible hunger—

For one joyful moment she thought that perhaps she *had* done him some good. Then she remembered what he'd said, that he'd hunted last night. And she Looked more closely, and Saw that the only reason he was in control was that the voracious hunger was still sated.

She felt a tear trickled down her cheek; felt someone wipe it tenderly away.

"Di, I just lost the van," Keith said softly.

She oriented, eyes still closed. "North," she said distantly. "They've turned north. One block, I think."

"Right." The car swayed and André braced her as they made a turn. "Still no luck. They're not in sight."

She located herself; located Dave in relation to that. "A little more west. About two blocks. Then north again."

"Right."

Dave wasn't driving; one of the others, the one not in so much of a rage, was. That wasn't anger driving, it was just recklessness; the one driving had a fine disregard for the safety of anyone or anything else. His carelessness was so much him *that she suspected he'd always been that way. The third seethed with anger, and with hunger; given the feeling of temper, that one must be Jason. Dave must have been baiting him tonight. The fourth—Di couldn't read. It wasn't even remotely human. She caught a touch of smug superiority, and a sense of detachment and a great deal of alienness. She pulled away before it could sense her and scanned it from a comfortable distance.*

It. Definitely it. *This thing had no more sexuality than a snail.
A snail.*

*That thought sent her back, probing delicately, so caught in
concentration that she wasn't even aware of her own body.*

It was a hermaphrodite, the gaki, *both male and female. Capable of reproducing all on its own.*

*And, in this new home, protected on the hunt by its allies, with
a secure base to operate from, and an abundance of prey, it was
contemplating doing just that.*

"Di—"

The shaking of her shoulders brought her back, with-
drawing as carefully as she had probed.

"What?"

"I've lost them again."

She shivered with reaction, now that she was no longer in
contact with the thing. "Two more blocks west," she said absently. *Do I tell them? Would it do any good?*

André spoke into her ear. "*Chérie,* what is amiss? You tremble."

She opened her eyes again, sure of her line to Dave, and
leaned toward him. "The *gaki,*" she said, her teeth chattering,
her heart in her throat. "It likes the setup it's got. As soon as
things get settled, it's going to spawn. It's a hermaphrodite."

"*Merde.*" His lips were compressed into a tight line. "I had a
thought that if the thing was not human, it might not have human motivations. And I wondered if it might be looking to
nest. But I had hoped the damned thing needed male and female."

"No such luck."

She heard him take a deep breath. "We had little choice before, Di, but now we have none. We must destroy that thing."

He finally called me Di. "You took the words right out of my
mouth."

"Whatever it costs."

She closed her eyes. *Even my soul. Lady have mercy on me.*
"Whatever it costs," she repeated sadly.

"Except that." He touched her cheek, and her eyes flew open. "No, *chérie*. Not that. I shall see to it."

A little of the tension inside her eased, though not the fear. *At least I've got somebody who cares enough and is levelheaded enough to give me the shiv if it all goes sour. And probably make sure it's painless. That's something. That's a lot.*

"*Chérie*—" he breathed in her ear. "I am as frightened as you. I truly am. I am frightened *for* you. You may rely upon me—I shall not let that thing have you."

She groped for his hand, found it, and squeezed it.

"Di?" That was Keith, from the front seat.

"What?" she asked, clamping her jaw down to keep her teeth from chattering.

"They're pulling over."

She sat up straighter and craned her neck to see over the back of the seat. They seemed to be in an area of former small industries; lofts, mostly—some of the places still had business signs in their windows, but there were too many cars parked on the street for this time of night, and more than one of the lofts had hanging plants in the windows, and psychedelic posters visible from the street.

A few blocks ahead of them, the band van was pulling over to the side of the street. Just as Di caught sight of it, the lights went out.

"Okay, we know where they're stopping. Don't slow down or speed up, cruise right on by. I'll catch where they're going."

As they passed the van, the last of the musicians was getting out of the back; the rest were nowhere to be seen. Light shone momentarily at a door that opened and closed, giving a brief glimpse of a staircase leading up. Di narrowed her eyes, and briefly brushed Dave's mind.

Third floor. Empty up, empty down. Okay.

She didn't dare stay any longer than that—she had no notion of Jeffries's capabilities, nor the *gaki*'s, and no idea if they were or were not sensitive to psi or magic.

"Down three blocks, then over two," she told Keith. "Then find a place to park."

She felt André take her hand and hold it. She squeezed back, and tried to feel brave.

But she couldn't help but notice that she was beginning to glow, very, very faintly.

FOURTEEN

For once there weren't *enough* shadows.

In fact, there wasn't much cover at all around here.

This was not a good area to be trying anything covert. But if truth were to be known—it was a safer place for a confrontation than a real residential neighborhood would have been.

Safer on the noncombatants, that's for sure.

Di was about half a block behind the boys, plastered into the three inches worth of concealment offered by one of the doorways. *Plenty of time to work into position, too.*

Keith had pulled over into a parking space about six city blocks from their target. André had moved out first—

And once he was five feet from the car, I couldn't spot him. No wonder the legend is that vampires turn into bats or mist. I have no idea where he went.

She could hear the boys' footsteps up ahead of her, echoing through the clear, cold air. She centered, and paused to assess the situation ahead.

And I can't tell where André is now. I can't Feel him at all. Nothing up there but the boys. He was right; his shielding is at least as good as mine, if not better.

Which reminds me; better start thinking like a brick wall.

Behind André were Keith and Lenny, playing bait to the *gaki*. Sooner, rather than later, Hidoro would leave the apartment.

He'd be hungry; she had Felt his hunger as they trailed the van. She hoped that he would be looking for something right on his block, if he could get it; the alliance had no stake in keeping things quiet in *this* neighborhood, not when they intended to leave it in a few days.

Seeing Lenny and Keith strolling toward him—that would be like a kid hearing the bell of the ice-cream truck.

That's what Di and André were counting on, anyway.

Di followed behind the boys, since she figured she was a lot more likely to be detected by the *gaki* than André was. That bracketed the boys with protection. When the *gaki* spotted them and moved in on them, she and André were going to get the boys out of the way and trap the *gaki* between them. Short of flying, it wasn't going to get away from them.

And maybe, just maybe, it had gotten so used to hunting with a partner on watch it would forget about being careful. Maybe it was so used to being invulnerable it would forget that it had a couple of weaknesses.

Di peered cautiously out of her doorway; to her left, silhouetted in the streetlight, the boys, just sauntering along as if they were out for a little midnight stroll. To her right, empty street. Nothing in sight but piles of dirty, granulated snow hiding the curbs. She peered left again, sizing up the territory. One streetlight on the corner; the alley that the boys were just now reaching. A couple of parked cars, and more hummocks of dirty snow. Not much in the way of concealment until she reached that alley.

Now—do I scoot for cover like a commando, or act like somebody who belongs around here?

Act like I belong, I guess . . .

She stepped out of the doorway; paused, as if she had just gotten into her coat, and tugged her jacket sleeves down, then headed in the boys' wake. Her next hiding place was halfway up the block—that alley mouth, a black slash across the middle of the block of industrial brick.

But before she got there, something stepped out of its shadows.

Hell—don't tell me there's a civilian insomniac strolling right out into the middle of—

She reached for it—touched *alien.*

Hidoro.

Oh, shit! Now *where do I—there.* She threw herself to one side and managed to squeeze herself behind the bulk of a parked car before he glanced her way. She peered out from beneath the rear bumper, keeping her head at street level. The *gaki* stared up her side of the street for a long, uneasy moment, before turning to look after the boys.

But once he'd spotted them, he headed purposefully in their direction.

She gave him a few minutes to get past that alley, then scrambled from behind the car, sneakers getting soaked and slipping in the snow. She launched herself at a dead run after him.

And her heart spasmed when she saw the tableau beneath the white glare of the streetlight.

Lord! Too late—no!

The boys clung together; Hidoro faced them. The *gaki* had them pinned somehow; he wasn't more than five feet from them, and they weren't moving, weren't even trying to escape. Their faces were white and blank with fear.

The thing was already turning into its other form—

Gods!

She *reached* and readied a levin bolt, not sure it would do any good, but it would get there before *she* would—

Someone else beat her to it.

Between one blink of an eye and the next, André was *there.*

She didn't see him *anywhere,* but he was there, shouldering the boys aside so hard that they fell to their knees, placing himself between the *gaki* and them, so that they were sheltered behind him.

Relief—

It made her stumble, but she caught herself, and she didn't slow; she still had to bracket the thing herself, still had to take her place on the line. André was counting on her.

"Come, m'sieur," André said clearly; his eyes glittered, and his mouth was a tight, thin line of anger. He was in a half-crouch, balanced on the balls of his feet, like a street fighter. He made a little beckoning motion with his right hand, and smiled, a hard, furious smile. "Come, you want them, you take them through *me.*"

Lenny scrambled farther out of the way, grabbing Keith's sleeve and taking his lover with him. Keith shook his head dazedly; then managed to get to his feet and hauled Lenny up by the back of his coat. They began backing away, step by slow step, eyes still on the *gaki.*

Come on, *you guys—you're supposed to get out of the way and watch for the others while we deal with the soul-sucker!*

They were arguing about that, it seemed—Lenny shaking his head vehemently, and continuing to back away, Keith stalling, pulling at his sleeve, their breath puffing about them in white clouds—

But she had no time to worry about them, because the *gaki* was reaching for something, something under his jacket, stuck in the waistband of his pants—

—pulling out a set of *nunchaku.*

A weapon of wood—

Which, as André had told her, was the *only* thing besides sunlight that could hurt or kill him.

"*No!*"

She launched herself desperately at them, not hoping for anything more than to knock André away from the deadly weapon. She did better than that; she knocked him to the pavement *and* managed to intercept the chuk heading for his temple with her shoulder.

They tumbled together in a heap; she rolled, cursing as she hit her bruised shoulder, and came up on her feet, and at the ready.

Her shoulder throbbed, which did nothing to improve her temper.

"*My* turn, you bastard," she snarled, and put her shields up to full. Predictably enough, she started to glow. Not enough to put André off, but enough to notice.

The *gaki* held the chuks in both hands and smiled—she Felt something battering at the outside of her shields. Behind her, she heard André climbing to *his* feet.

"Nunchaku," she said shortly, never for a microsecond letting her attention slip from the *gaki.* "Wood, André."

She heard a muttered *"merde,"* and his footsteps retreating slowly.

The creature before her seemed puzzled that whatever it was he'd tried to do to her had no effect. "What are you going to do, *gaki?*" she asked in a growl. "If you stay in *that* form, you have to deal with me. If you go to the other, André can take you. You're trapped."

It stared at her, face utterly *blank;* it might as well have been a department-store mannequin. It was wearing black, head to toe; in this light she couldn't tell if it was the band's stage gear or not. "I have to give you a choice," she said to that expression-less face. "I don't like it, but I have to. If you give up, I'll see what I can do about you without killing you. If you choose to fight me—"

It didn't give her a chance to finish, not that she cared, or re-ally *thought* it would give itself up. But the gesture *had* to be made, regardless.

It charged her, chuks blurring in its hands. She danced out of the way, sneakers making a scuffing sound on the salty sidewalk. *Barely* out of the way, and barely in time.

Oh gods—

He whirled around his own center and lashed out at her as he recovered.

Oh gods—he's better than I am.

She ducked out of the way, then had to make a dive and a roll to get out from under a side kick.

I'm in very deep trouble.

She flung out her hand, and hit him with the levin bolt she'd held in readiness. As she'd half expected, it had no effect.

His magic doesn't get through my shields, mine doesn't get through his. I could try a psi bolt instead—

But first she had to get out of the way of the chuks.

She scrambled back and blasted it at him. He shook his head and faltered a little, but a bolt that would have left Lenny blinded and on his knees with a headache only gave the *gaki* a moment's pause.

André could get him, if he didn't have the chuks—

The *gaki* grinned toothily at her, and moved in again. She dodged the chuks, only to run right into a hand-foot combination that knocked her to the pavement. She rolled with it, and came back up—but got to her feet with a muffled cry as pain shot up her left leg from her ankle.

Oh shit. He's better than me, and now I'm handicapped.

I'm not gonna survive this one.

Fear flooded her. Her aura flared; he squinted a little, but it didn't seem to affect him the way it had affected André.

All I can do is buy time and wear him down.

The hilt of her atheme, the little knife she had at the nape of her neck, reminded her of one more option. *And maybe take him with me when I go. Betcha there's enough power in there to make him notice if I do a kamikaze with it in my hands.*

That last thought steadied her, oddly enough. *When you've got nothing left to lose*—The light around her dimmed, and finally died, as she concentrated on surviving the next encounter—taking them one at a time.

She evaded two more attacks with increasingly less success, acquiring two more bone bruises on her forearms. She concentrated with all her might on the *gaki's* eyes, waiting for them to tell her what his next move would be—

:The greatest swordsman in the world fears not the second greatest, but the worst. Why?:

She shook her head and danced back in surprise at hearing a

voice in her mind, and flung a psi bolt at the thing to distract it a little while she recovered. That thought had *not* come from her, not even her own subconscious!

Who then?

André—? Telepathy was *not* one of her strong suits—she got feelings, not thoughts—usually. But André had said something about *that* this evening, too . . .

:Think, woman! Why?:

But she knew; it was exactly like one of sensei's riddles. The greatest fighter fears the worst, because an amateur can't be predicted; he'll make the "mistake" that creates an opening—

So make a mistake—he knows *exactly how good you are. He won't be expecting a dumb move—*

She feinted, working him around into range, luring him closer. This wasn't a trick she'd be able to repeat—so it was going to have to *work*—

He drove the chuks straight down at her. Only this time, instead of diving *away* from the blow, she lunged *into* it—and caught the descending stave in her left hand.

The *crunch* of her own bones breaking was the second-worst sound she'd heard in her life. Before her hand had a chance to start hurting, she closed it as best she could, curled her whole body around it, and pivoted, carrying the chuks out of his hand. They clattered to the ground, and she finished her pivot inside his guard, thrusting upward with all of her momentum behind the heel of her right hand. It impacted with his nose—

A second *crunch,* and a scream like nothing she'd ever heard before. But now her hand was screaming in its own strident voice, and she collapsed to her knees, folding up around it.

No matter. André took the place she'd surrendered—proving that he did, indeed, have "a knowledge of savate."

One kick took out the *gaki's* left knee. A second to his chin snapped his head back as he was falling.

A third pulped his temple, and when he hit the pavement, he did not rise.

André stood over the prone body, his face a mask of cold rage, panting slightly. Di struggled to her feet, her hand protesting every movement. She staggered to André's side; he caught her and held her as she stumbled into him, her hand clutched to her chest.

"Anything?" he asked quietly.

Recklessly she abandoned shielding, opened herself up completely.

Nothing.

Then—

One moment there was a body there.

The next, an evil cloud of black smoke.

"Jesus H. Christ!" she shrieked, scrambling back away from it, expecting it to follow her. Her aura flared, making patterns of light and shadow dance.

André grabbed her elbow and shoved her behind him—

—and the cloud billowed up, rising, coming at them—

—but it was losing color, losing cohesiveness.

Even as they took that in, it faded, thinned, and finally drifted away on an errant little breeze.

She stared at the place it had been, still sensing nothing. André walked forward, slowly, until he was standing where the body had been, where there was now nothing but a pile of black satin. He poked it with his toe, frowning.

"Nothing?" he said, finally.

"It—it's gone," she replied through the throbbing of her hand, around teeth gritted against the pain. She got her jacket open and pulled her left arm out of the sleeve, then zipped the jacket back up with her arm held against her chest by the tight fabric in a kind of improvised sling.

"This one—" Suddenly he looked up, and looked around. "Lenny and Keith—where are they?"

"They were supposed to—"

But there was no sign of them on the street.

Their eyes met in a flash of realization.

"They didn't—" André began.

She scanned, quickly—and found them precisely where she had not wanted them to be.

"They did—oh gods—it's them against *three* psivamps—"

André cursed, and grabbed her good hand; he set off at a run down the street, pulling her after him.

Her heart sank when she didn't see the boys waiting for them at the foot of the staircase. There was no one guarding the door either, not from their side nor the enemy's; they pounded up the splintery wooden stairs without hindrance. Over the racket of their own feet they heard the sounds of a fight above. André kicked at the door on the third landing and it slammed open. The two of them flung themselves without hesitation into the chaos beyond.

Light from overturned lamps spotlighted two knots of struggle, and the shadows of the fighters sprawled huge and inelegantly on the wall. Di identified the combatants in a glance—first and foremost, there was no sign of Jeffries. To the right, between two chairs, one on its side, was Dave, grappling with a slim, dark-haired man. It looked to Di as though they were evenly matched, both of them locked into a stalemate. To the right, on the floor next to the wall, Keith was down, and not moving. At the same moment as they burst through the door, Lenny crashed into the wall beside him, thrown there by a tall blond. Lenny started to struggle to his feet; the blond, his face contorted with fury, vaulted an overturned chair and strode across the wreck of the living room toward him, oblivious to the two newcomers.

"André—the children—" That was all she had time to say before she launched herself at the blond. There was a flicker of motion at her right—and André was gone.

Pain shot up her leg from her maltreated ankle; she ignored it. She knew she had no second chance, and didn't dare miss. So no fancy stuff, no flying sidekicks. Just a rush as primitive as a football tackle, meant to knock him off his feet; one she could control enough to turn into a roll to bring her back *up* on *hers.*

He saw her coming at the last moment, but not in time to get completely out of the way. She hit him sideways, which sent him spinning into an overturned couch. She didn't land quite the way she wanted, and her hand howled at her when she hit the ground with more of a jolt than she'd intended.

It shook her; she was a shade late in getting to her feet, and a shade shaky when she faced him again. She edged sideways, knees bent, in a posture equally suited to attack or defense, until she stood as a defiant wand of protection between him and the boys.

He had already gotten to his feet. He hesitated for a moment, only now *seeing* her—she used his hesitation to study him, look for weaknesses. He was a good foot and a half taller than she was, with an insolently handsome face, and long, wild blond hair. His eyes were narrowed in anger, his jaw clenched. Plainly, he did *not* like being downed. He doubly did not like being downed by a woman the size of the average ballet dancer.

This is Jason, she decided. *And I hurt him in his macho. That's going to make him even madder than he was—which will probably enhance his psi abilities, even if it takes away from his control. He could be more than I can occultly handle now . . . This may have been the wrong thing to do—*

Sure enough, a delicate probe in the long moment they stood staring at one another had to be retracted quickly inside her shields before it got swallowed up.

He's not stronger than my active defenses, but he is stronger than the passive shields I put on the boys. He'll be able to unravel those shields and feed on them before he actually takes the boys. Oh gods, I can't, I don't dare let him get near them or he'll have them—

Somewhere beyond Jason's shoulder, in the darkness that marked an open doorway, there was a muffled pounding. André, presumably, had found the children, and was trying to break down the door to their prison.

Jason didn't seem to hear the noise, didn't seem to notice Dave and the other band member thrashing in a tangle of arms and legs on the other side of the room. He was targeted in on Di, with a single-mindedness that was uncanny and completely inhuman.

She shifted her stance a little, watching his eyes follow everything she did, seeing his very posture shift to match hers. *It's more than that he's mad at me. It's—a lot more than that.* She shifted again, winced at pain from her ankle, and caught a surge of hunger from him.

Oh gods—he's gone into feeding mode. And I'm the chef's special—I've got to break that, if I can. At least for a minute, long enough to distract him.

"Jason," she said aloud, as forcefully as she could.

And reached behind her head, pulling out the atheme.

I'm not about to throw it, and lose my only weapon. But a knife is a knife. But Power is Power.

The blond started, his head jerking a little, his eyes dilating briefly. Then those chill eyes focused again on her. There *seemed* to be a little more sense in them, although he didn't reply.

"Jason, we took out Hidoro, so don't expect the cavalry to come charging over the hill."

—But where the hell is Jeffries? I don't like it that he's not in sight.

He smiled; actually smiled. "Don't expect *me* to shed tears over that," he replied. "Doro was no buddy of mine."

There was a cry of pain from the struggling knot at the side of the room, but the struggle continued. Jason's eyes flickered briefly in that direction, but returned to her before she could take advantage of the distraction.

She gestured with the blade; if he could sense Power—

He could; his eyes widened.

"I'm no flyweight. I've been at this game longer than you have. I'll offer you what I offered him," she said, with a calm that she did not feel. "Give it up now, and I'll see what I can do for you without taking you out. You *have* to see at least some of what I am. If there's a way to help you—"

He interrupted her with a peal of laughter, his expression harsh and sarcastic. "*Help* me? Why in hell would I want *help?* Christ, chickie, you're a bigger fool than Davey is—"

"Or you are," she retorted angrily. "What goes around, comes around, Jason. If you make yourself into a big bad shark, sooner or later a killer whale's gonna come by that figures *you* look tasty."

"I'll take my chances on that, honey." He grinned. "That little toy is cute enough, but you haven't convinced me that *you're* any big threat."

He'd relaxed just the tiniest bit. *Probably figures that if I'm talking instead of attacking it's because I'm not in any great shape.*

Which I'm not—but I'm probably not as badly off as he thinks. Besides, all I have to do is buy time for André to get those kids out—

The pounding ended in a crash. Jason jumped, and his head swung around. It was enough of an opening.

She crossed the space between them in a limping sprint, ending it with a kick with her good foot aimed to take out one knee, and a slash at his face. It would have worked, except that he was faster than she'd thought; he ducked the slash, and the kick went into the couch frame instead.

She bounced back, staggering a little, blinded for a moment with pain and unbalanced with one hand immobilized. When she could see again, Jason's eyes were pits of rage, and she could Feel him battering away at her shields, seeking a weak spot to exploit. "Bitch!" he snarled. "I'm gonna—"

She drew on the stored Power in the blade and gave him no time to elaborate on what he was going to do to her.

Because she heard the sound of many faint footsteps from the dark—and over on the side, Dave was on the *bottom* of the struggle.

She feinted with the knife, then lashed out with an elbow strike and caught Jason in the breastbone with it, gritting her teeth against the screaming of hand and ankle. He grunted and staggered backward. She came on, tiring, and in pain, but this was the only advantage she was likely to get and—

Crack.

In the confined space of the room, the explosion sounded like the impact of a lightning bolt. She jumped back as a bullet struck the floor between herself and Jason, and pivoted on her bad ankle to face the new threat.

Jeffries.

With a gun, and a sadistic smile on his face.

She froze. The fight in the corner had stopped; now the guy she didn't know separated himself carefully from Dave, and backed away. Dave didn't move from where he was sprawled on the floor, in the lee of an overturned armchair.

"I believe it is game and match, hmm?" Jeffries said smoothly. "David, David, I had hoped you had come to your senses—well, apparently not. I do suggest that you, and *you,* young lady, place the witchblade on the floor and surrender. Not that you and your friends won't meet ultimately the same end, but your choice is between painful and excruciatingly painful." He raised his voice. *"And you can take those children back where you found them, young man—"*

Her mind, which had gone into stasis, unstuck. It took a moment to register. First came shock. Then immobility.

Then fear. Overwhelming fear. The kind that used to paralyze her.

And didn't. Not anymore.

Light.

Her shield aura flared, high in the UV and illuminating the room like a floodlight, brighter than a photo flash, and *much* more potent in that moment than the weak winter sunlight.

Jeffries screamed.

There was a clatter as his gun fell to the floor. The man was moaning in pain, and by squinting through her own glare, she could see that he was clawing at his face. He collapsed slowly on his knees, babbling and weeping now, as if the light were cutting right into his brain.

She fed the light with all her strength and the last of the stored Power in the atheme, knowing the brightness to be her only defense. *Maybe it is eating into his brain. I hope so. I hope it burns your neurons to a crisp, you sonuvabitch!*

But she was weakening; running out of energy fast, and maintaining the light was taking a lot more out of her than she had guessed it would. She heard a scuffle of feet behind her, and kicked backward without looking. The impact of her foot in someone's solar plexus told her that her instincts were still working, although the move cost her in red agony from her abused foot. The flare of pain through the black hole of hunger told her she'd gotten Jason.

I can't keep this up much longer—

"André, *the kids*—" She gulped; it was even getting hard to breathe. "Get them out of here."

Running feet; half a dozen shadow shapes flitting across her own glare, one of them leading a taller one by the hand—

Right, he can't take this either, he probably can't see a thing. But the kids are getting him out. Thank the gods.

She sheathed the atheme behind her neck and backed up, feeling her way across the floor, kicking aside lamps and unidentifiable debris. She moved step by slow and uncertain step, until she reached the area where she *thought* Lenny and Keith were, and felt around with her bad foot until she hit something soft. It groaned.

She knelt, carefully, and reached out with her right hand, and shook the leg she encountered. It was too well muscled to be Keith. "Lenny. *Lenny.* Come on, wake up—"

Her light was fading discernibly, and with it, her strength.

"Uhn—" Finally a moan that was a response. "Di?"

"Get up, get Keith, and get out. I can't hold these jokers much longer."

"But—"

"*Move!*" she snarled, nerves ready to snap, and not inclined to take any back talk.

She could make them out now, and that was a bad sign. Lenny pulled himself slowly to his feet, then reached down and helped Keith up. The artist was not in good shape; he leaned heavily on Lenny, and didn't seem more than half conscious. She kept herself interposed between them and the others—

But the light was fading faster, and they were *not* going to make it to the door before it was gone.

Then, like the voice of an angel, Dave spoke out of the shadows cast by his overturned chair.

"Di, baby, I've got the gun. I can't see *now,* but I wasn't looking at you when you flamed on. Get your two buddies out of here, and I'll take care of my *good friends.*"

The last two words were spoken in a snarl of hate.

She hesitated. Lenny and Keith did not. They were almost at the door—

"Davey—" she began. "Davey, I—"

"Don't *worry* about me, just *go!*" She took one step toward him, and saw him shrink away.

"Davey—"

"Go." Then, very softly, "It's okay, babe. It's okay. I know exactly what I'm doing. Listen—be happy, Di. Just—be happy."

One of the others nearest Dave started to move; now she could see perfectly well, her light was no worse than sunlight. She pointed. "Dave!"

He whirled. "*Forget it,* Doug—Di, get the hell *out* of here!"

Seeing that he was looking away from her, toward Doug, she put the last of her failing strength into a final flare, and fell out the door, slamming it behind her and overbalancing, and tumbling down the first flight of stairs—

Dave was waiting for one of them to make a move when Di slammed that door—and sure enough, Doug rushed him, his face an inhuman mask.

Calmly, dispassionately, Dave sighted and pulled the trigger.

The bassist made a choking sound, his eyes wide with surprise as the bullet hit him in the chest. He jerked once and collapsed, his momentum carrying him to Dave's feet.

Silence, and the smell of cordite. Dave kept his eyes on both of the other two. Jason hadn't gotten up yet. Jeffries stared at him out of red, watering eyes, his mouth hanging open in dumbfounded surprise, bloody scratch marks on his cheekbones where he'd clawed at his own face.

"Didn't think I knew how to use one of these, did you?" Dave asked softly. "Funny thing, you know? *She* taught me. Big wheel in the peace movement, and she taught me how to shoot a handgun. I thought she was crazy."

"David—" Jeffries began, his mouth working for a moment before the words came out. "David, there's really no need to be hasty—"

Dave took a deep breath, steadying the fury inside himself. "You asshole. No, I suppose you'd figure that, wouldn't you?"

"David, there is no reason why we can't use our power the way I described to you—"

"Yes there is," he interrupted coldly. "There damn well is. Because I'm going to kill you."

He pulled the trigger a second time; shooting for the head, not willing to take anything from Jeffries, not even the energy his slow death would give—

He heard the noise of unsteady footsteps beyond the door. Someone was limping painfully back up the stairs.

Dammit Di, I told you to get the fuck out of here—

He rounded on Jason, who was just rising from the floor where Di's kick had put him. He kept the gun trained on the blond, making his way slowly over to the door, where he locked it one-handed and shot home the bolt.

Just in time.

Di began pounding on it, crying out his name.

Crying.

No, babe. No.

"Hey look, man," Jason wheezed, spreading his hands wide. "Dave, we been friends a long time, right? Just—get on out of here. I'll—"

The vision of Jack's terrified face rose up between them, and the sound of his screams and Jason's laughter. Abruptly he couldn't take another word. "*Shut up!*" he screamed. "You god-damn dirty son of a bitch! You got us *into* this! Friends? What the hell was Jack, *friend?* You guys *ate* him!"

More than one shoulder was hitting the door now, and he could hear the wood splintering behind him. The doorframe was industrial grade, but it wasn't going to hold much longer.

"I'd like to make you hurt the way *he* hurt, the way those kids you ate hurt, you piece of shit," he said clearly and carefully. "But I don't have the time."

Jason's eyes widened, then narrowed for a moment, as if he were gauging the distance between them for a rush.

Dave didn't give him the chance.

"See you in Hell, you bastard," he said—and pulled the trigger a third time.

Silence filled the room now, a silence that had nothing to do with the clamor outside the door. A silence that said—

You can do it. You have the strength. You can be careful to take only the guilty, only the ones who prey on others. Or maybe Di'll be able to help you. Maybe she'll love you again, maybe not, but—you know she's always been able to pull you out of things before. Why shouldn't she be able to work a miracle this time?

It was such a seductive promise—so sweet—and so easy—

Then the hunger, that thing that coiled at the base of his spine, grumbled and roused from sleep. It raised its head, and looked about—

And felt Di outside the door. Unshielded, unprotected. Who would never know what hit her if he just *reached*—

Just reached. Like it was reaching now.

He pulled it back, even as it was reaching—and knew that he would never have the strength to do so a second time.

"No—" he said aloud. "No. Anything is better than that. Even Hell."

He put the warm barrel to his temple; took a last deep breath, and looked toward the door.

Oh, lady. Still trying to pull my fat out of the fire.

"Not this time, babe," he said. And squeezed.

She heard the first shot when she was still on the landing, and began to crawl back up toward the door. The second came while she was still on the stairs. By the time she reached the door and began pounding on it hysterically, it was locked.

When the third shot came, she redoubled her efforts, not sure why, only having a premonition—she never knew exactly when André arrived to lend his shoulder to hers, but suddenly there he was, and the door was yielding—

When the fourth shot rang out.

She cried out—Dave's name, or André, she didn't know. All she knew was blackness descending to end the pain.

Blackness, shot through with red lightning bolts of pain. Sometimes the sound of her own voice, strangely calm. Then—there was the car, for a moment, and Lenny's voice saying "Saint Francis. I know it sounds strange, but we've got a neopagan on the ER night shift. Ask for Doctor Grame."

Yeah, that's right—she thought, the realization fighting through pain into her conscious, then there was blackness again.

Another interval of darkness.

Then another interval of lucidity—the white lights of a hospital, and a vaguely familiar face. "Does it hurt when I do this?" the face was saying.

Someone did something unpleasant to her hand.

She knew him—from somewhere; the name "Doctor Grame" swam up to stare at her, and another, "Gwalchmai," one and the same person, confusingly enough—so she refrained nobly from kicking his teeth down his throat, or from screaming. "Yes," she whimpered, and felt nebulous shame at the tears pouring down her face.

Why am I crying? she thought. *It doesn't hurt that much—*

Then the doctor did something else, and it *did* hurt that much. She blacked out again, and only came to when someone did something equally rude to her ankle. *That* time she struck out, blindly, not remembering where she was, and only aware of pain and blindingly white light in her eyes. A hand caught her wrist and held it in a way that *should* have evoked a memory, but the memory couldn't get through the pain.

"I advise you," said an accented baritone, "to recall that she is a brown belt, and a bit delirious."

*Baritone? I don't know any—*Errant memory returned. *Oh. André.* She stopped fighting, and the doctor said something she couldn't hear. There was a pinprick in her arm—and the pain went away.

She floated for a while in a sea of haze, keeping her eyes closed, because to open them was too disorienting. They—whoever "they" were—were doing things to her hand and ankle, they were arguing with André about admitting her to the hospital, but she no longer cared. She was trying to recapture the past few hours. Bit by bit, memory came back.

The gaki. *We got it alone, and fought it. I got hurt, we took it out. The apartment. I went into full shield flare. I'm in power-drain shock. Okay, that's why my brain isn't working. We won. Sort of. Davey—*

She began crying again, this time without shame. It was cold by now, and there was a sensation of movement. She opened her burning eyes briefly on darkness, and saw after a bit that she was in the back seat of a car. Being held. By two somebodies.

Her mind, working in slow motion, finally identified them. André. And Lenny. Both holding her, both trying to comfort her. But there was no comfort; Davey was dead, and all his beautiful music dead with him, and she had failed him . . .

Weeping passed into exhaustion and exhaustion into more aimless drifting; after a while, she swam back up to consciousness again, and noticed that someone was carrying her. She opened drug-hazed eyes and saw the steps of her apartment building to her right; Keith, supporting Lenny, just ahead of them. "I can walk—" she protested to whoever was holding her so firmly. "You don't have to carry me."

"I believe the expression is, 'the hell you can,'" André replied dispassionately. "The doctor was most adamant about not putting weight upon that ankle, and even more so about not allowing you to walk where you might slip."

She closed her eyes, because the moving steps were making her dizzy, and when she opened them again, André was putting her carefully down on her own couch.

Her brain was working slowly, but now it *was* finally working. And a hundred consequences of this night's work were flashing across it. She grabbed his arm as he started to move away, and peered up at his sober, worried face, into his expressive eyes.

"I'm beginning to wake up," she said. "André, what happened . . . after? What excuse did you give the hospital?"

"You do not remember?"

She shook her head. "Not a thing."

"When—we heard the last shot, you pushed me down the stairs ahead of you; told me to get Keith while you and Lenny brought up the rear. We ran, but when we were a block away, you told us to stop." He gave her a very strange look. "You truly do not remember?"

"No. Honestly." *Bizarre. My gods. Sounds like somebody took me over for a while. I sure wasn't that copacetic.*

"So, you told us to stop, and—'act casual, man,' is exactly what you said. You began singing, loudly, as if you were very drunk. Something about a 'whiskey bar'; young Lenny joined you. And at *precisely* that moment the police arrived. They passed us by without a second look. We reached Keith's car, and you proceeded to faint dead away." He grimaced. "Unsurprising, since the doctor informs me that you have torn the ligaments upon that ankle."

"I thought it hurt a little bit more than a sprain," she replied vaguely, still trying to figure out what had happened. *She* didn't know any songs about a "whiskey bar."

"We took you to the hospital; we asked for Doctor Grame, but before he could arrive, a most officious young man attempted to deal with you. You nearly"—his mouth twitched—"relocated his private parts to somewhere near his larynx."

"I don't remember that, either." *Her* mouth twitched. "Too bad."

"When Doctor Grame arrived, he wanted to put you into the hospital. I convinced him that this would not be wise; that your friends could care for you adequately. You were kinder to the doctor, although there was a point where I had to restrain you."

"I think I remember that—André, the fight—"

"Is already upon the news; there was a radio in the emergency room." He took her hands, and his eyes grew infinitely sad. "It was a good thing, your David did, that he locked the door against us. The police have no notion that there was anyone in the place except the four they found. They are reporting it as a quarrel over drugs."

"André—" Her throat closed. "All of them?" she whispered. He nodded, and looked down at their linked hands.

"He was very brave, and very wise, at the end. And at the end, he chose rightly. I shall treasure that memory of him. I think I shall always admire what he became." He sighed deeply. "He did what few have the strength of character to do; to overcome the consequences of his mistakes, and to take responsibility for them."

"There was so much he never had a chance to do—" She mourned for that as well as for him. Tears came, slower tears this time, like a quiet rain. André hesitated for a moment, and then took her into his arms, holding her close when she didn't resist him.

"*Chérie*," he said quietly, "I did not guess he meant so much—"

"No." She sobbed into his shoulder. "No, it isn't that—it's that I failed him. I couldn't help him, André—I couldn't save him—"

"Ah," he replied, and held her until she had no more tears left.

She was resting in his arms, completely spent, when it occurred to her that the sky was growing lighter. "André—it's almost dawn," she said into his sweater.

"I know, *chérie*," he replied. "I thought that I might avail myself of your couch once more before I return to my Lowara."

Once more? Then he's going—I never pictured him not being here.

She pulled away, slowly, and sat up.

"I thought you said something about last night not being the equivalent of the condemned man's last meal—"

"I did. But—" He looked away. "I did not intend to make an infernal nuisance of myself. I—I wish to give you time to consider things."

"Things?"

"Consequences, *chérie*." He smoothed her hair behind her ears, and smiled faintly. "There are always consequences. For instance, you know, my Lowara feel that they owe you a great debt. They will not be happy until it is repaid."

She sighed, momentarily distracted. *Just what I need. Another karmic burden.* "I'm sure it'll all even out one of these days. Maybe I can hit them up for a lot of tarot readings."

He quirked an eyebrow at her, and settled back against the arm of the sofa. "You know that they call you the Starchild? For the brightness. They are almost as afraid of you as they were of the captors of their children."

She grimaced. "Lovely. So now I'm a Rom bogeyman."

He touched her cheek, gently, with one of his long, graceful hands. "Oh, not that. Something lower than a saint, but not so low as a 'bogeyman.'" He stood up, and faced the window, looking out at the false dawn. "Well, it is over. We worked well together, I think—"

He began to walk away from her.

"André—"

"I shall take my leave after sunset. Young Lenny said that he and Keith shall look in on you—"

"*André*—"

He stopped in mid-sentence, and looked back over his shoulder at her, expression unreadable.

"Top drawer of the desk. The brass box."

He turned around and walked slowly to the desk and put his hand hesitantly on the drawer pull, opening it as if he expected something to leap out at him. He took out the little brass box and opened it just as gingerly.

And held up the set of keys with an enigmatic frown on his face.

"I don't like the idea of somebody as vulnerable as you spending his daylight hours in public libraries and cheap movie houses," she said, trying to put her thoughts in order. She spoke slowly and carefully to keep the pain that was returning from creeping into her intonation. *I don't want his decisions based on the fact that I'm not exactly in top shape.* "Especially not—somebody I care for. Someday someone who knows what you are is going to feed you a nice thick stake."

Despite her best efforts, some of her pain must have shown in her face, if not her voice. He took a tiny white paper envelope out of his pants pocket and silently handed her a pair of pills, and she swallowed them dry.

"I thought we had agreed that it might be dangerous to become—entangled," he said, standing between her and the light, so that his face was in shadow. Just as it had been the night they met.

Children of the night. All of us. Him, me, Davey . . . the night brought us together. Be damned if I'm going to let it take him away without a fight.

"We did," she admitted. "But we didn't discuss how dangerous it might be *not* to be entangled. You mentioned consequences. There are consequences there, too."

"True." He returned to her side, dangling the keys from his long, sensitive hand. "And would that be dangerous?"

"It might." She waited until he seated himself. "For you, because living the way you do, you're vulnerable. For me—" She faltered. *I hadn't thought about this, not really. But it's happened all the same. What I swore wouldn't. Ever.* "You're tied into me on a lot of levels, André. I like you, and I don't have to hide anything from you."

She took a very deep breath, and made the last confession. "I've been alone too much, and too lonely. You changed that, and I—I don't want to be alone anymore. I'd like you to stay. I'd like you to be with me. Please?"

He looked down at his hands, at the keys held loosely between them. Her heart sank when he didn't immediately reply.

"Well," he said finally, not looking up. "I prefer thinking that I am not a parasite. There is an ugly word for that, *chérie.*"

"I—could use some help—" she said ruefully, raising the plaster-encased bulk of her left hand.

"So I see." He looked a little happier.

She gave him a wry grin. "So tell me what you can do, besides the obvious."

"Well, so this is an interview?" His smile appeared, tentative, but there. "Very well, mademoiselle, I *can* type. And take dictation. I play the violin passably well, so I might entertain you. I fear, however, that I cannot cook."

"You said yourself we work well together. Would you be willing to give me a hand with things like tonight?"

Please say yes—

"Hmm. Indeed, I could help you with other things. I do have certain talents." He tilted his head sideways, and his smile faded as he considered her. "It will not be easy, Diana. I am what I am."

"So am I. No one's ever claimed *I* was easy to live with. Please, let's just try."

He cupped his hand under her chin, and finally gave her that slow, sweet smile she'd been hoping for. "Very well, *petite*," he said softly. "We will try."

The drugs hit her then, and she swayed toward him. He caught her in his arms—and then he caught her up, lifting her easily.

"Wh-what are you doing?" she gasped.

"Putting you to bed, *chérie*. Where you belong. If you will insist on my being here, you must put up with my insistence upon certain conditions." He looked at her sternly out of the corner of his eye as he carried her toward the bedroom. "And one of those is that you must spare your maltreated ankle."

She sighed as they passed the bedroom door and he flicked on the light with his elbow. "I suppose I don't have any choice."

He put her carefully down on the side of the bed, pushing aside the tumbled blankets. "No, you do not."

"But neither do you—"

She still had her arms around his neck, and she pulled him down beside her, cast and bandaged ankle and all.

"Wh-what do you mean?" he asked, eyes going wide.

"I mean," she whispered into his ear, "once I get to feeling a bit better, you're going to *have* to help me finish this blasted romance novel—"

"I am?"

"Uh-huh." She nibbled on *his* neck. "Especially the research—"